Ben.

Hope you enjoy!

Love

Dad —

THE FALL AND RISE OF AMERICA

Joe Hogan

authorHOUSE®

AuthorHouse™
1663 Liberty Drive
Bloomington, IN 47403
www.authorhouse.com
Phone: 1-800-839-8640

First published by AuthorHouse   2/11/2010

ISBN: 978-1-4490-7548-4 (e)
ISBN: 978-1-4490-7547-7 (sc)
ISBN: 978-1-4490-7546-0 (hc)

Library of Congress Control Number: 2010900493

Printed in the United States of America
Bloomington, Indiana

This book is printed on acid-free paper.

PROLOGUE

Our Declaration of Independence states, "That whenever any form of Government becomes destructive of these ends, it is the Right of the People to alter or to abolish it, and to institute a new Government, laying its foundation on such principals and organizing its powers in such a form, as to them shall seem most likely to effect their Safety and Happiness."

The American people have apparently decided that it is time for real political change. Joseph Alexander Winston, after it became apparent that the Democratic and Republican behavior could destroy his beloved country, created an alternative for the American people and formed the Restoration Party. Joe presented a platform and persona that quickly attracted attention and support.

Joe Winston, a handsome man who appears much younger than his sixty one years, was a veteran of the Viet Nam War, a tremendously successful businessman, and more importantly a man of integrity offers the American people something they haven't seen in decades, leadership.

Winston's miraculous rise to prominence is unprecedented in the history of the world. He seems almost too good to be true. He is a brilliant man with an impeccable record of patriotism and business success who is articulate, intelligent, and has the ability to inspire others.

George Patton once said, "Man is made of brains and guts; if he is missing one, he is only half a man." Patton would have admired Joe Winston.

The American people are divided. Most are loyal and patriotic and would willingly die for freedom. Unfortunately, others feel entitled to economic benefits without work, and would die for nothing. We have become a country of givers and takers and Joe Winston must unify all Americans.

The 2010 mid-term elections are destined to become the most historic and significant election ever held in America. Could a political party in existence less than six months possibly have an impact? Will the status quo continue with excessive spending and social programs that will bankrupt our country? Will low and middle income Americans vote for the party that promises them benefits or the party that protects their freedom, fairness, and financial solvency of our country?

During Joe Winston's rise to political prominence he discovers a diabolical and shocking radical Islamist plan designed to economically and socially destroy America. Due to the circumstances surrounding this discovery he is unable to inform the intelligence community. Joe, along with the help of trusted friends, must also quickly find a way to prevent the conspiracy from succeeding.

Our professional politicians recognize that every speech, every comment, and every decision they make is based upon one simple question. How will this impact my re-election? Therein lays the problem with our democracy. When a politician's primary concern is re-election and not what is good for America, our system is compromised. Joe Winston promises his party will fight for a constitutional amendment with a one term limit and to restore *public servants* and eliminate *professional politicians.*

The American people are being decimated economically by a declining and wildly fluctuating stock market, nationalization of banks and financial institutions, excessive taxation, unemployment, and energy dependence. There is an expectation of entitlements and absence of work ethic by over fifty million Americans, a strong trend toward socialism, a housing slump, and the embracing of illegal immigration.

We are being beaten emotionally by a negative press and partisan politics. The inability to see hope in the near future and the underlying fear for the safety and security of our children has taken its toll on hard working Americans. Joe Winston offers practical solutions to restoring economic stability, creating jobs, slashing taxes, and controlling government spending.

The rich are rarely inconvenienced by international or national issues. The poor generally have no desire to become self reliant because they are supported by many social and charitable programs. America's great middle class, the silent majority, is being robbed of its dignity, hope, and opportunity for the future.

They don't stage protest, they don't make demands, they don't lobby, and they don't expect anyone else to pay for their mistakes. This silent majority values the concept of personal responsibility and self reliance. They get up every morning and go to work, with the hope that tomorrow will be better. Joe Winston's message restores the middle class's expectations of greater prosperity and opportunity in the future.

Joe Winston's Restoration Party, is a party that is beholden to no one, except the American people. They are committed to restoring faith and confidence in America. There is a wave of optimism and hope sweeping our country that has been absent for decades.

Will voters remove the politicians whose arrogance, ignorance, and inadequacy have placed our survival in jeopardy? Will capitalism fall to socialism? Will America voluntarily relinquish their freedom and opt for dependency?

As the mid term elections approach the very future of our country is in the hands of the people. They will decide our fate.

THE FALL

CHAPTER 1

CHARLOTTE, N.C.
APRIL 5, 2009

It is 9:30 am in the garage of Bank of America's headquarters at the corner of Trade and Tryon Street in Charlotte, North Carolina. Willie Jackson had his arm around his young nephew's shoulder as they entered the basement entrance and proceeded to their leased storage area. Johnson is carrying a cardboard box that contained supplies needed to prepare and serve lunch and snacks to their customers.

Willie has been operating his two vendor carts for the past eleven years in the building's courtyard. He serves ice cold drinks, coffee, hot chocolate, and variety of sandwiches including his most popular sausage dog with mustard, chili, onions, and slaw. At 75 years young, Willie is a popular local fixture in the area. He knows most of his customers by name and his likeable demeanor encourages people to support his business. His regulars leave generous tips that Willie always humbly acknowledges and clearly appreciates.

"It is going to be a beautiful day and the temperature should be 72 degrees by lunchtime." Willie said to his nephew Johnson.

Johnson smiles at his Uncle and said, "After all that bad weather we can use a little sunshine."

Johnson looked thoughtfully at Willie and is amazed that his Uncle is in remarkably good health for a man who has lived for almost eight decades. Uncle Willie's hair is snow white and his face clean shaven. He was a trim one hundred and thirty pounds and stood five feet and eight inches tall. He always wears a sincere smile on his face and you felt better just being around him. His jovial attitude and polite mannerisms were magnetic and people instantly liked him.

Two of Willie's sons had died in Viet Nam and his wife had died in 2004. Willie did not allow the tragedies of his life to destroy him and has the unique ability to understand God's will. His faith and humility was unshakable.

Johnson had worked with his uncle each summer for the past three years and is now working full time since he graduated from high school. His plan is to make enough money to enroll at Shaw University next year and pursue his college degree. Johnson is Willie's brother's son, but unfortunately, his brother remained addicted to alcohol and provided little direction for his son.

Willie had taken Johnson in when he was eleven years old and the relationship had proven mutually beneficial. Johnson is a good boy and gives much of his money to his "Moms" to help her with his two younger sisters.

The two men are cheerfully preparing their carts and chatting in their storage area. It is a damp room with concrete floors and bare walls that Willie leased from the bank for the modest rate of $300 per month. After all, the area was useless for anything else other than storage, and the bank considered Willie as an asset.

Inside his space there was a small freezer, refrigerator, microwave, sink, stove, oven, and an unenclosed toilet. On one wall is an old tattered brown sofa where they could sit which barely leaves enough room for the two vendor carts. The area is dimly lit by four florescent fixtures and there is no heat, other than a propane heater, or air conditioning. The small space was adequate for Willie's purposes and he enjoyed the daily rituals and anticipation of another day at work.

Willie heard a noise behind him. As he turned toward the unusual sound he was surprised to see two angry looking Middle Eastern men with pistols pointed at them. One was a short man with a heavy beard and ruddy complexion. He was dressed in blue jeans, a blue and white plaid shirt, and a black NY Yankee's baseball cap. The man angrily said, "Move over to that wall and do not make a sound".

The taller man, who was slim, clean shaven, and hatless, walked over to Willie and roughly turned him around and then jabbed his gun in Willie's back. He pushed Willie with the gun to encourage him to move faster; it worked.

Willie assumed they intended to rob him. To expedite their mission and be done with them he preemptively said very politely, "My money is in the top drawer of that cart. It ain't much, but it's all I got, and you are welcome to it."

The bearded man looked unimpressed as he got in Willie's face and gruffly said, "Take off your jackets and lie down on the floor and put your hands behind your back."

Willie thought this to be a strange request for a robbery and his instincts caused a feeling of foreboding. Fear began to creep into his mind.

The gunman's face was dark and foreboding and showed signs of childhood acne. He spoke with a strange accent, unfamiliar to Willie, but his dark eyes and expression projected pure cold evil. "Sir, you don't need to do that, we ain't gonna be no trouble at all."

The man raised his Berretta 9 mm pistol, racked a round into the chamber, and pointed it at Willie and angrily snapped, "Do what I say quickly".

Willie and Johnson had little choice and complied. The intruders duct taped their hands behind their backs, across their mouths, and then taped their legs together. Their faces rested on the cold and damp concrete floor. Willie locked eyes with Johnson and could see a fear in his young nephew's eyes that broke his heart. Willie is a God fearing man and perhaps a bit too trusting but his faith had always given him strength. He tried to reassure Johnson with his eyes to no avail. Hopefully, the men would grab the money and leave quickly.

Johnson could not control his shaking, his terror caused him to wet his pants, and he was hyperventilating. His eyes glistened with huge tears and he could not slow his breathing as he tried desperately to draw upon his Uncle's strength.

Willie felt compelled to close his eyes and pray silently, "Please Lord, comfort my poor nephew Johnson, he is a good boy and….." Willie heard a strange gurgling sound and muffled grunts as he looks over and sees the evil man, who had straddled Johnson and held his head up by his chin. Willie sees the bloody knife in the man's hand and then he saw the terror in Johnson's eyes and the large gaping hole under his chin and watched in horror and disbelief as blood squirted from the wounds to his arteries and he felt nauseated as he saw the life drain from his young nephew's body.

Willie was so shocked and distraught by what he had seen that he never felt his head being pulled up by the other man. He felt little pain, as his sadness was so great. The blood pulsed from his neck with each heart beat and he simply allowed himself to enter a better world.

The two savage men moved the lifeless bodies behind the couch and covered them with a cart tarp. They could not possibly have realized that their actions today would change the entire future of America.

CHAPTER 2

APRIL 2009
WASHINGTON, D.C.

The American voters are predictable. For over 150 years the people have blamed the Administration for their economic hardships. Retribution is simple, throw out the offending party. 2008 is no different, unstable stocks and oil prices, rising unemployment, the mortgage crisis, the failure and bail out of major financial institutions, and a significant increase in deficit spending.

As the first African American commander-in-chief, James Jackson Howard has made history. He stands six feet four inches tall with an athletic build. His short black hair is tinted with gray at the temples and his dark brown eyes suggest sincerity. He carries himself with confidence and every move is deliberate and graceful. His exterior appearance projects the image of a sophisticated and successful person.

Howard is a fifty eight year old Harvard graduate and was formerly a practicing attorney who was elected to the Senate in 2004. With his wife Ann by his side for twenty seven years they enjoyed tremendous success and reared their son, Howard, Jr., who is also a graduate of Harvard law school.

President Howard's campaign benefited significantly by his powerful oratory skills. His philosophy was simple. He promised to cut taxes for 95% of the taxpayers; he tied his opponent to the failed policies of the previous administration, and promised to increase social programs and create an additional two million jobs.

He projects a strong leadership style and his ability to motivate and inspire his audience is impressive as he easily out classes his opponent.

President Howard sits in the Oval Office awaiting his Vice President, Carol Osborne. His expensive black suit is perfectly tailored and he wears a simple white shirt with Presidential seal cufflinks. His attire is complimented by an American flag pin in his lapel and a white silk pocket square. He could easily be a model for a fashion magazine.

Since the Inauguration in January the euphoria he felt over winning a long hard battle had dissipated under the tremendous demands of the Presidency. His external image is far different than the overwhelming and conflicted emotions he now felt. He is well intended but has quickly learned that keeping campaign promises will be difficult if not impossible.

The President relies heavily on his advisors who have supported his efforts for years even though he often disagreed with their methods.

President Howard glances up from his desk as the new Vice President, Carol Osborne, bustled in with a stack of briefings. Her movie star good looks and clear blue green eyes caused her to appear much younger than her fifty seven years.

As the former Governor of New York, her direct and controlled demeanor makes her one of the most popular governors in recent years. She is well respected by friend and foe alike. Her knowledge of international, economic, and social issues would serve this administration well.

She is also about as far left as a person can be and might even be described as a borderline socialist. She puts forth excellent arguments regarding the value of social programs to assist American people who have failed to grasp the concept of self reliance.

Even though she's never been poor, and in fact lived a life of privilege, she is genuinely a compassionate and caring person; her maternal instincts will not allow her to accept the fact that many people simply lack motivation to accept a basic responsible role in society. Howard's advisors insisted that Carol be on the ticket.

She said, "Good morning Mr. President" as she strolled into the office and placed her briefs on the coffee table and settled into the leather wing back chair that sat opposite the couch.

The President stands and walks from his desk to the sitting area and said, "Good morning, Carol. I hope you are well this morning?"

"Thank you Mr. President, I am." Carol replies as she pours herself a cup of coffee.

The Presidents executive assistant taps on the door as she allows Fred Barker, National Economic Advisor, entry.

Fred extends his hand to greet the President and the President grasps Fred's hand firmly and said, "Good morning Fred" as he motions for Fred to sit on the couch across from Carol.

Fred began reviewing his notes for the briefing as Chief of Staff, Harry Belk, strode into the room "Sorry I'm a few minutes late" he mutters as he greets everyone and takes the other wing back chair facing Fred. The President remains standing, as he often does, he is a pacer and likes to stay on the move.

The President's aide enters with fresh coffee on a large silver tray and places the tray on a table by the couch and pours coffee for everyone. When the coffee had been poured and the aide left the room the

President began, "Fred, what can you tell us about the wild stock and oil fluctuations?"

Fred, a slightly overweight and balding man looks the part of an Economic Advisor. He wears glasses low on his nose for reading and his blue eyes are accented by large bushy white eye brows. He sits up straight while shuffling his papers with a somewhat confused look on his face.

He looks at the President while shaking his head back and forth and said "Mr. President we are experiencing unprecedented financial issues. As you know, we have seen oil prices rise and fall dramatically and there appears to be no confidence in the stock market as it continues to bounce from a low of 8,000 to a high of 10,500.

Mostly stock prices are doing well due to the fact we have infused cash into the economy and companies are holding on to the cash which inflates their stock. Oil varies from $40 a barrel to $140. It seems that every time we start talking about energy independence the market gets soft and we forget about it."

President Howard interrupted, "To what would you attribute that phenomenon Fred?"

Fred looked uncomfortable but not unsure of himself as he answered, "Mr. President, I have no explanation. It is true that many Americans decided to use less gasoline, which helps. Now, I am not prone to conspiracy theories but this is not the first time this has happened."

President Howard turned to Harry and said, "Harry, put some people on this and see what you can come up with. I agree with Fred there is something suspicious about this."

Harry jotted down a note on his pad and said, "Yes sir."

Fred continues, "I believe the public has little confidence in our ability to successfully manage money or to provide adequate and effective oversight to the private companies we have bailed out.

The uniqueness of this economy is fourteen trillion dollars of debt and the interest payments. The American people, as a whole, earned 8.6 trillion dollars in 2008 and the federal government's spending exceeded 3.5 Trillion. Earnings this year will be less and our spending will be higher."

The President looks gravely at Fred with his penetrating eyes and said, "What are your suggestions Fred?"

Fred uncomfortably said, "Mr. President, my answer has a lot to do with how you want to be remembered as our President. You have an opportunity to restore sanity to our economy and save our democracy or you could be the President responsible for a major shift toward massive debt that could economically destroy us." Fred paused to allow the President to consider his choice. The President said nothing waiting for Fred to continue.

"If we continue to spend trillions of dollars, bailing out failed companies with bad leadership, investing another trillion to create jobs, and providing additional entitlement programs I believe our economy and our capitalistic democracy will simply fade away." Fred paused again to study Howard's reaction.

He continues, "I also realize that most economist believe that low unemployment and high debt combined with high spending and low savings is best for our economic system. Mr. President there is an old adage that says "figures can lie and liars can figure" it's true that we can make the numbers support whatever you want but I need clear direction from you."

The President glanced at Carol in an effort to solicit involvement and she said, "Mr. President, I just want to remind you that we made promises and commitments to provide health care and to increase our entitlement programs to assist the struggling American people. I believe we must keep our word and deliver what we promised.

If private industry cannot create jobs we must. If we need to print more money, we will simply do it. There is no way we can abandon the people in this country who need our support."

Fred is frustrated by politicians reaction to cost issues and interjects, "Mr. President, I know how difficult this is for you and I want you to know we will do all we possibly can to support you. No President has ever faced more difficult challenges.

You must decide if we are going to put a band aide on our economy for eight years, knowing that in twenty years, democracy as we know it will be dead or will we make the tough decisions now for the long term benefit of our children and grandchildren."

President Howard looked at Fred as he contemplated the question. His thoughts are interrupted as Harry Belk spoke up and said with some authority. "Mr. President, it is essential that we commit ourselves totally to the promises you have made. If you were to succumb to the temptation to postpone initiating your programs I believe you could be a one term President."

Fred emphatically said, "I realize there are political ramifications but when you look at Medicare and Social Security and factor in the baby boomers that will start reaching age 65 next year those two items alone will cost us roughly four trillion a year by 2019.

Sir, we only have revenue of two trillion a year and without a massive tax increase we have no prospects to diminish our debt. Not only that, but deficit spending will continue to increase those numbers and devalue the dollar."

Carol balks at the numbers and said with a hint of superiority "We have a moral and social responsibility to give every American the opportunity for education, health care, housing, a job, and hopes of retirement one day. If that requires higher taxes and deficit spending then that's what we will have to do."

Fred politely looked toward Carol and said, "Carol, we only have 1.9 workers for every retiree and that number could reach one to one in a few more years. We have thirty million Americans who are below poverty and are dependent on entitlement programs, thirty two million on social security, and eleven million drawing unemployment. We also have over fifty two million receiving food stamps.

Somewhere in the area on one hundred million people depend on the government and mathematically there is no way to sustain our social policies."

Harry Belk always sets the tone for meetings and he could either tear you down or build you up said with just a hint of frustration, "Fred, you are way to pessimistic. Sharpen your pencil and figure it out but politically we cannot and will not renege on our commitments."

"I will be happy to do it Harry why don't you tell me where to cut the budget?" Fred said indignantly.

The President's penetrating eyes focused on each one of them and slowly asked, "Does anybody have a reasonable solution? Is our reelection more vital than economic security? Should we be concerned with twenty or thirty years in the future? As for me, I wish to do what is best for the country and Fred, that's the legacy I hope for one day but I need more than sophomoric discussions I need real answers and workable solutions. Do I make myself clear?"

Everyone acknowledged the President's comment as he looked directly at each person and then he said, "Put your heads together. I want solutions in sixty days. That will be all." He stands and walks to his desk as Fred, Harry, and Carol filed out of the room.

President Howard sits heavily in his chair and dejectedly turns to face the window. He notices that it is snowing and then began to mentally review the many challenges he faces.

Terrorists attacks, North Korea and Iran continue to suggest nuclear weapons pursuit, it is increasingly clear that much of the terrorist activity emanated from Pakistan, Pakistan and India are still rattling sabers, and the U.S. has little support worldwide.

American soldiers on the ground in both Iraq and Afghanistan, and intelligence reports indicated radical Muslim training camps growing in South America and our economy is faltering badly.

He puts his face in his hands and rubs his face as if he could wake up and realize it is just a bad dream. As he peers out the window the snow is falling harder and he notices all the people on the streets and has two thoughts. Those people are counting on me; am I the right man for this job?

CHAPTER 3

Imaad and Rajab, both from Syria, arrived in Mexico on March 3ed. Imaad followed his instructions and contacted Jose Ortiz who was to safely move them across the border into the United States.

Crossing the border was surprisingly simple. After Jose delivered them to their pre determined location in the U.S. they curtly thanked Jose, paid him, and were picked up by a ford panel truck. They climbed in back of the battered old white truck and the driver pointed to some food, water and a couple of mattresses they could rest upon. No one spoke as the driver headed north toward their next stop. After some food and water the two men rested on the mattresses and soon feel asleep.

Several hours later the truck arrived at 6641 Belifort Road, in Houston, Texas. Imaad and Rajab were sleeping and were startled when the driver opened the rear door and said, "Welcome to Masjid of Al-Islam my brothers."

Rajab stiffly sat up and rubbed his eyes and realized they had reached their first stop. He stepped out of the truck and into the spacious garage and glanced around as Imaad followed. They stretched and yawned and felt some sense of excitement. Rajab said in Arabic, "Thank you, my brother. Allah Akbar!" He embraced the driver in appreciation.

The driver walked toward the east side of the garage as Rajab and Imaad followed. The driver rolls a large tool chest over to the side and a 4 x 4 trap door is revealed. He opens the door, turns on a light, and the men descended ten steps to a deceptively large basement apartment.

The driver shows them around the modestly decorated area that contains everything they would require and would be their home for the next few days.

The driver said, "Welcome my brothers, please be comfortable and if you require anything you cannot find simply pick up the phone on the kitchen wall and someone will answer. Tomorrow morning Fahid, the Imam, will meet with you to discuss your mission of glory. In the meantime, please relax and get some food and rest.

As the driver is about to leave he turned and said, "The locked door at the end of the hall is forbidden. If you need me simply pick up the phone and I will answer." He repeated.

Their contact is Fahid Mohammed Al-Adel. Fahid is 53 years of age and has lived in America for the past 36 years. He is also a Jihadist and believes that he lives in the country of "the great Satan." Over the years, he had portrayed the role of a passive Muslim and been very careful to never draw attention to himself.

Fahid, reports directly to Aziz Hassan, who directs all operations in the United States, Aziz secretly controlled thirteen terrorists cells and over his thirty four years in America he has implanted thousands of radical Muslims throughout the country. Only Hassan's employer and his thirteen cell leaders know his identity and the thirteen cell leaders do not know their counterparts.

In the forbidden room in the basement he stores weapons, ammunition, explosives, cash, and other instruments of the terrorist trade. He also has the capability to create false documents such as passports, driver's licenses, and social security cards.

Over the next three days, Fahid equips them with passports, driver's licenses, social security cards, employment records, weapons, and a cooler containing 80 pounds of C4 and detonating equipment. He provides them with a six year old car, cash, and miscellaneous supplies for their mission. Prior to their departure the three men prayed for Allah's blessings and the men and headed east for the long drive to Charlotte, N.C.

Imaad and Rajid arrived safely in Charlotte the next afternoon and reported to their new jobs at Watkins Cleaning Company as instructed by Fahid. Their assignment is to work the midnight shift, cleaning floors 35 to 45, in the Bank of America Corporate headquarter. During the following weeks they familiarized themselves with security and carefully put their plan in place.

On April 5th the two men made their final trip down the elevator after cleaning up after the infidels. They had also planted small explosive devices on eight floors which were set to explode at 11:00 am and force the evacuation of the building.

At 9:00 am after killing the two black men, Imaad said, "We are on schedule but we must work quickly."

Rajab is very pleased to have been chosen for this great mission and replied, "Yes, my brother" as he continues to remove the contents of the vendor carts.

Imaad said, "Rajab, once the carts have been emptied place the screws and bolts on top of the explosives."

Rajab continues to work with a sense of purpose as he replied, "I understand."

Imaad prepares four garbage bags that appear to be trash. Each bag contained six pounds of explosives and thirty pounds of bolts and screws.

In less than thirty minutes their work is completed. Imaad said, "Let us give thanks Rajab."

At 10:45 am Imaad and Rajab put on Willie's and Johnson's white server coats, with "Willie's" emblazoned on the pocket. They push their carts out of the garage and up the slight incline, past the fountain, and into the center of the courtyard.

Rajab casually takes one of the heavy brown bags that appears to be trash and places it into the trash container at the north corner of the courtyard. He calmly works his way to each corner of the courtyard, repeating the process three more times. Imaad watched and appeared to busy himself with the vendor carts in the center of the courtyard.

At 10:55 am when Rajab had placed the last bag in the last container he returned to the vendor cart. The two men looked at each other, removed their jackets and placed them in the cart and calmly walked across the street while several arriving customers appeared puzzled as they approached the unattended and empty carts. Imaad removed a cell phone from his pocket and dialed the number programmed to detonate the eight modest explosive charges planted on eight different floors of the building.

The busy noise of automobiles and people on the street quickly succumbed to a series of extremely loud explosions from the middle part of the Bank of America building. As glass, debris, fire, and smoke erupted from the sides of the building a heavy dark black cloud of smoke reached high into the air. The debris began to rain down on Trade and Tryon Streets as fire alarms and screams of fear echoed off the walls of other uptown buildings. Pedestrians on the street below screamed and scrambled to put distance between themselves and the building.

The confusion and chaos that ensued was exactly what Imaad expected. He and Rajab quickly moved another one hundred yards down Trade Street and into the lobby of an office building where the occupants were all running outside to see what had happened.

They could barely contain their excitement as they watched the panic take hold and saw people rushing from the building and seeking refuge in the courtyard where Willie's carts remained.

They stood and watched for thirty minutes as people poured out of the building from all six exits. The uninjured were helping those who were injured. The Fireman and EMS squads arrived and began setting up field operations and treating those who are hurt. There were literally thousands of people on the streets many dazed and confused and others who simply were observing.

Five EMS trucks, eight fire trucks, and hundreds of policemen arrived quickly and more could be heard making their way to the scene. Two of the specially equipped fire trucks had their large ladders reaching high in the sky with its powerful streams of water seeking the fire spurting from the building in at least twelve different locations. In short order the fire coming from the building diminished and it appeared the situation was under control.

The courtyard and the streets are now filled with people and vehicles for several blocks. Dozens and dozens of police cars, rescue vehicles, and fire trucks surrounded the entire area. Many are helping the injured while others excitedly share their horrible stories with whoever would listen but most are stumbling around in a daze gazing at the smoldering building. They were all confused and afraid but relieved to be safely out of danger.

As the flow of people from the building stopped and Rajab saw that the courtyard is packed with people he turned to Imaad and handed him the other cell phone and said reverently, "I would like for you to have the honor?"

Imaad nodded and said, "Thank you Rajab. Praise be to Allah!" as he took the phone, dialed the number, and hit the send button.

Almost immediately the entire courtyard is engulfed in flames that rose hundreds of feet into the air with a tremendous explosion. The thousands of bolts and screws, they had loaded in the carts, tore into flesh, stone, glass, and vehicles as far away as a hundred and fifty yards.

As the flame subsided and the eerie sound of the nuts and bolts ricocheting off objects stopped. The blood and burned body parts that covered the courtyard and filled the fountain combined with the horrible screams and cries for help would be a memory that would never leave the minds of the ones who had the misfortune of seeing this act of cowardice and cold blooded murder.

Two hundred and eighty six hard working and innocent people perished on this day and another three hundred and ninety four were seriously wounded. Fathers and Mothers would not come home again and son's and daughter's were simply gone. Thousands upon thousands of lives were impacted by this atrocious and cruel act.

Imaad and Rajab proudly, but slowly, walked down Trade Street, with the sounds of chaos behind them. They could hear wailing of sirens and cries of anguish in the background and inhaled the smell of objects burning. They were exhilarated by their victory today and looked forward to their next assignment. There is no remorse and no regrets. With all the sadness they inflicted today their hearts are filled with satisfaction and happiness.

CHAPTER 4

At 2:20 pm on the afternoon of the Bank of America attack Robbie Ravenel is sitting in his office reviewing last months financial records for his company. Robbie is of average height and could be considered slightly overweight. He is running the fingers of his left hand through what is left of his sandy reddish hair with a satisfied look.

Robbie has been extremely successful in business and is one of Charleston's most prominent citizens and benefactors. Robbie is a man with a knack for success and is also known as someone who can be highly emotional. He is as straight forward as a man can be and values honesty, integrity, and dedication. Just as he reached the final page and smiled at the results his telephone rang and he reached for the phone and happily said, "Robbie Ravenel."

Pete Brown, the Managing Partner of a law firm, in Charlotte where his favorite nephew, Tommy Dupree, is employed said solemnly, "Hey Robbie this is Pete Brown."

Robbie cheerfully said, "Hey Pete it's been a long time how are you?"

Pete hesitated briefly and said, "Robbie have you seen the news today?"

Robbie said, "No I haven't Pete. What am I missing?"

Pete is not looking forward to telling Robbie and took a deep breath prior to saying, "Robbie I am afraid I have some bad news." Pete hesitated once again before continuing.

"Robbie the Bank of America Corporate Headquarters in Charlotte was hit this morning with a terrorist attack." Pete said.

Robbie is stunned and reached for his television's remote control and turned it on, "That's terrible Pete. How bad is it?" Robbie asked unaware of the impact on his life.

"Robbie it was real bad…..I hate to tell you this but Tommy was killed in the attack."

Robbie finds a channel that is showing footage of the attack and barely hears what Pete is saying. Robbie with a catch in his throat said, "What did you say Pete?"

"I'm terribly sorry Robbie but Tommy is dead and I didn't want you to hear it from a stranger." Pete responded.

There is a long pause as Robbie tries to catch his breath and fight back the emotions that are about to overwhelm him, "Pete. Are you sure?"

"Yes. Unfortunately I saw his body." Pete answered with trepidation and sadness.

There is another long pause and Robbie realizes there is nothing else to say. His hands are trembling and his vocal cords betrayed him as he said, 'Oh my God! Not Tommy….Pete thanks for calling." Robbie slowly lowered the phone to the cradle and put his elbows on the desk and let his head fall into his hands as he wept violently for several minutes before regaining control.

Robbie rose from his desk and headed for the parking garage and headed over to his sister's house to break the news.

By 5:00 pm he is completely drained of emotions and his swollen red eyes could shed no more tears. His heart was breaking and the thought of what he had to do is killing him. He walked into the house and broke the bad news to his family and learned his emotions were not yet exhausted.

Robbie is the CEO of Secureone which is an international security firm. His company holds dozens of major U.S. Government and State contracts, hundreds of private contracts, and numerous accounts internationally. His firm is highly regarded and extremely proficient. Their technology and expertise is far superior to their competitors and exceeds most government agencies.

At 5:15 his cell phone buzzed and he looked at the caller ID and saw that is Bert Braddock, his Vice President of Operations, and a dear friend. He considered not taking the call but pushed the receive button and sadly said, "Hello Bert."

Bert, a retired SEAL is leaning his large muscular body over a security camera in Secureone headquarters and said, "Robbie we heard about Tommy and we want you to know that you and your family are in our thoughts and prayers."

Robbie said, "Thanks Bert. Tell everyone I appreciate it. I will see you later…"

Bert interrupted Robbie and said, "Hold on Robbie I hate to bring this up but I am in the office and we have been reviewing the security cameras at Bank of America. We have discovered some interesting information that I think you might need to review quickly."

Robbie was drained emotionally and growing impatient and said, "What is it Bert."

"Two suspicious men entered the garage level of the Bank of America building this morning and went to a leased storage area in the parking garage. The storage area is leased by a lunch cart vendor named Willie Jackson who works the courtyard at lunch time.

I sent a man over to check it out and he reported the two vendors were dead. Their throats had been cut. The authorities haven't discovered this yet." Bert, no stranger to death or terrorist, paused slightly to organize his thoughts and be as concise as possible and then continues.

"I have good pictures of two men, who appear to be Middle Eastern, exiting that area with the carts and going to the courtyard. They placed four large bags in four trash containers in the corners of the courtyard, removed their coats, and left. Apparently those bags contained the explosive charges that did all the damage. Later I located them on Trade Street with the city cameras about two hundred yards from the courtyard. Apparently they triggered the courtyard explosions with a cell call. No doubt these guys did it."

Robbie's sadness is immediately replaced by anger as he asks, "Have the cops or Feds seen the video?"

Bert said, "Knowing them they want even think about it until tomorrow. They have their hands full with all the injuries and fatalities."

Robbie said, "Bert find these killers and call me back."

Bert said, "We are on it Robbie."

Twenty minutes later Bert called Robbie, "These guys were working for the cleaning contractor for the bank. We have their employment applications and have checked all the information. Their address is non-existent and their driver's license and other identification documents were phonies.

We checked local areas where they may have stayed and learned they stayed at the Doubletree Hotel in South Park. They checked out this morning. We were able to get their automobile license number, make, and model from Doubletree's security cameras."

Robbie interrupted, "Do you have any idea where they are now Bert?"

"I do. We located them on our I-77 cameras headed south and they checked into a Sleep Inn outside of Columbia, S.C. at about 6 pm this afternoon. I have a man on them Boss." Bert said with his square face set and his dark eyes showing anticipation.

Robbie hesitated as he considered his options. He knew what would happen if these two guys were arrested and afforded all the courtesies of this country.

There is also the warrior part of him that whispered in his ear saying this is a real opportunity to put a dent in these bastards. He thought if Bert could capture these terrorist bastards they could retrieve valuable information from these cold blooded killers that law enforcement never would, and more importantly he wanted to avenge Tommy's death.

Bert, a man who spent many years fighting terrorists, held the phone patiently waiting. He knew Robbie was processing his options and he was hoping Robbie would tell him what he desperately wanted to hear. Bert hated Jihadist and had experienced first hand just how ruthless they could be. The death of Tommy made it personal.

Robbie made his decision and issued the orders, "Bert, take Charley and Buck to Columbia and pick those guys up. Take them to our warehouse in North Charleston at the old naval base. Call me when you have them and pick up some secure phones." Robbie hung up without waiting for Bert's response.

Bert could not prevent a big smile from appearing on his face. It was about time that someone, unhindered by the restrictions of laws and civility took action and did what needed to be done. He welcomed this chance and his mindset quickly changed from that of a corporate executive to a SEAL on a hot mission.

Bert had served his country with honor and distinction for nine years. Covert operations were his specialty and assassination is one of his many skills. He had worked undercover in Iraq for three years and was personally responsible for sending at least twenty five terrorist to a tea party with Allah and those virgins. Bert was always amused as he wondered just how many virgins there might be and what happens to them after they service the first guy?

Bert's SEAL career had come to a bittersweet end after he cold cocked a Major who had stupidly and carelessly issued an incorrect order that caused three of his men to be unnecessarily killed. Bert's outstanding service record and the circumstances involved allowed him to resign honorably rather then face a court martial.

As Robbie sat in his study on the third floor of his luxurious home on the Battery, he looked out across Charleston Harbor toward Ft. Sumter at the angry ocean pounding the rocks of tiny historic Fort Sumter and the gathering storm clouds rolling in off the Atlantic. The weather reflected his emotions perfectly. He knew he was doing the right thing and he was mad as hell.

His phone rang and noticed on the called ID it was his best friend Joe Winston. Robbie's wife had called him with the bad news. He picked up the phone and said, "Hey Joe, what's up bubba?"

Joe, with sadness in his voice said, "Just wanted to check on you Robbie. I know how hard this must be for you and your family. Tommy was a great kid and it is just so unfair for us to lose him."

Robbie's eyes felt tired from all the tears and pain and he knew his best friend felt almost as bad as he did, "Thanks. I will be OK.........but I don't think I will ever be the same."

"How do you feel about our still getting together at Volusia National next week?" Joe asked.

"I would never miss an opportunity to be with you guys, I can't wait to be with you guys. I need it."

"I feel the same. See you there." Joe said in an upbeat voice.

"OK bubba. Be careful!" Robbie said as he replaced the phone in its cradle.

Robbie Lee Ravenel was born a "Blueblood" in 1946, in Charleston, S.C. His father was a fifth generation Charlestonian and a prominent attorney. His mother's lineage went back to John C. Calhoun, a former South Carolina Senator and Vice President of the United States.

Robbie was never impressed with himself or felt entitled to any privileges. He had a strong work ethic, excellent values, and a strong motivation to excel. He was always driven to succeed academically and athletically. He stood a couple of inches short of six feet but he weighed two hundred pounds. He isn't fat, he is, as they say in the south, "Big boned". His round face and reddish hair combined with his blue eyes and serious demeanor made him appear to be ominous.

He graduated in the top five of one of the finest private High Schools in the South, Porter- Gaud, and then accepted an appointment to West Point where he graduated with honors. He volunteered to serve in Viet Nam prior to receiving his law degree from the University of South Carolina.

After practicing law in Charleston for six years he acquired a major security company, Secureone. His friend, Joe Winston, provided much of the capital and Robbie provided the leadership. He grew it from a small company to a Billion dollar business. He employed 22,000 people and over 3,000 were former military with a variety of unique skills and abilities, particularly former Seals, Rangers, and intelligence experts.

Robbie sat in his study in deep introspection as he watched storm clouds enter Charleston Harbor and approach the battery as the day suddenly changed to darkness. He knew that his life is changing forever. He knew that his nephew's death was a signal to him that he must embark upon a journey that could jeopardize his life.

He glanced around his office at the pictures of his family, his wife Emily, his son, Brad, and his daughter Sarah and thought of how lucky he is and how much he loved them. He also reflected on how fortunate he had been in his life and how grateful he is to God for instilling such good values in him and blessing him in so many ways. He hoped that his life would make a positive difference in a world where few do.

His office is filled with military memorabilia dating back to the Civil War, old flags, muskets, swords, weapons, clothing, photographs, a bronze star, and many other military medals, books, and other items of historical and personal value.. The walls are covered with old photos and artifacts mixed with family pictures. He is a student of history and is as well informed as most historians.

He is a proud American and recognized that America's greatest asset has always been the American soldier. He never admired or even respected politicians, in fact he loathed them, but his love for the American fighting man was exceptional. He believed that only two defining forces have ever offered to die for us; Jesus Christ and the American soldier, one died for our souls and one died for our freedom.

As the rain storm reached his windows and began to pound on the panes seeking entry he left his office and headed downstairs to enjoy the comfort of his family.

CHAPTER 5

Joseph Alexander Winston is the CEO of Winston's, an upscale department store chain with over a billion dollars in assets and over thirteen hundred stores domestically and internationally, Winston's is a massive operation employing more than one hundred thousand people.

At sixty two years of age he is in outstanding physical condition due to the fact he always worked out at least four days a week. He could easily pass for fifty two with his lean and muscular body, dark complexion, dark brown eyes, and well groomed salt and pepper hair.

He always appears to have a warm smile on his face and is a ruggedly handsome man with a small scar over his right eye compliments of a rifle butt in Viet Nam. He is the kind of person you instantly like. Many people have remarked that he resembles the movie star George Clooney.

He completed his phone call with Robbie, hung up the phone, and looked sadly at his wife, Linda. She walked over to Joe aware of the pain he is feeling for his dear friend's loss and hugged him tenderly. She released him and stared into his eyes with all the love one could show and said, "How is Robbie?

Joe leaned over and kissed her on the forehead. "You know Robbie honey. It will take him a lot of time to get over something this traumatic. Our trip to Volusia National after Easter will really be good for him."

Linda walked over to the bar in their spacious den and asks, "Can I fix you a drink Darling?"

Joe sat down in his overstuffed chair and exhaled loudly, "That sounds good." He replied.

Linda had decorated their home and it was beautiful. The state-of-the-art large colonial style mansion sat on a large hill overlooking the St. James River. A twenty foot wide veranda wrapped around the northeast side of the house and offered a spectacular view at sunset. The den opened out onto the porch offering a beautiful and relaxing setting.

Most of the furnishings on the porch consisted of durable wicker, including chairs, couches, and tables. The large ornamental vases always held fresh flowers and the huge grass lawn between the house and the river is just beginning to change from the winter brown to beautiful green. The large oaks, elms, and weeping willow trees were filling out with leaves and accented the view perfectly.

The center piece of the den was a tremendous fire place that was built with stone from a home once owned by Robert E. Lee. The fireplace is twenty feet wide and the stone went from floor to ceiling. Over the mantle is an oil painting of Joe and Linda on their wedding day.

The seating area around the fireplace consisted of a very large custom-designed L shaped couch. It is oversized and covered with a plush flame stitch fabric of a soft dark brown with beige. The couch is complimented by two plush chairs with soft brown fabric and a large mahogany table.

There is also a large media room with the latest technology and at the far end of the large room is a bar area that consist of a twelve foot bar, complete with six stools and a comfortable seating area with a small black leather sofa and four side chairs surround an antique oak table.

Linda selected original oil paintings featuring Virginia history to adorn the walls. The paintings were selected because of their beauty, color, and significant historical appeal.

Of the many rooms in their home, this room was the most often used for its simple beauty and casual elegance.

Their home also contains a large thousand square foot "safe room" that is impenetrable. They could survive in their safe room for sixty days if necessary. It featured dual ventilation systems that would function on battery or fuel, and a state of the art communication system including computer access, food, water, and weapons.

Linda prepared Joe's drink and poured herself a glass of Silver Oak cabernet. She walked over to Joe and said, "Here you are, darling."

"Thanks honey."

Linda sat on the couch and said, "I love Robbie so much and feel so sorry for him. If it weren't for him I wouldn't have you."

Joe knew what Linda meant and his thoughts raced back to 1968 as Linda felt it would be best to leave Joe alone for awhile. She went to the kitchen to prepare dinner.

He graduated from Harvard Business School in 1968 and immediately volunteered for the Army because he considered it a duty and obligation. It is as clear in his mind today as it was 40 years ago as he recalled the events.

It was hot and sticky in Viet Nam. I was in charge and my mission was to lead my squad of eleven men on a simple reconnaissance mission to an area that intelligence reported as clean.

In spite of the fact there were no VC reported in the area, we still proceeded with caution. As always, we expected the worst but hoped for the best. We were half a click from the river where we were supposed to locate the most likely penetration point if the VC decided to cross the river and approach our base.

Something didn't feel right. My instincts screamed that something was wrong. I halted the squad and they all carefully eyeballed the area around them. We couldn't see anything but my inner alarms were all going off full blast.

I looked at Sgt. Billy Connors and whispered, Billy take two men and check it out and be careful. I don't feel good about this.

Sgt. Connors said, yes sir. Williams you and Jones come with me.

The three men hadn't gone ten yards when all hell broke loose. There must have been thirty guns firing at them and the sand was kicking up all around them from errant shots. Connors was hit in the leg but managed to get back to the limited cover offered by the brush and trees. Jones was down and appeared to be done. Williams was hit three times, once in the right leg and twice in his torso, but he managed to get back to his squad with the help of Eric Rogers as the remainder of the squad was laying down cover fire.

The next two hours were the longest of my life. There were at least 50 VC and we were being barraged with constant heavy fire. We were in no position to return fire as hot rounds whizzed by our heads and cracked the tree branches around us. The noise of the gunfire and the stench of cordite in the air combined with the knowledge that any minute a random round may find you caused intense apprehension along with a feeling of absolute hopelessness.

Five of my men were already down. I tried to radio for reinforcements but the radio was disabled. The shooting suddenly stopped and a VC

Major raised a white flag and stood on a hill with a cigarette dangling from his mouth and said in broken English, Do not fire.

The Major signaled with his arms for his men to stand up and show themselves. It was a show of force and intended to convince us that we had no chance. We could see at least 75 VC and I was confident we had killed many and that there were many more.

The major removed his cigarette and said with a sneer, Surrender or die. We have you surrounded. You have no chance. We will treat you good.

It was clear we had no hope but the very thought of surrender was repulsive. We only had a few rounds of ammo and were greatly outnumbered. Surely the VC had flanked us and cut off our possible retreat. Death was imminent if we continued to fight so we were forced to surrender. It was the most difficult decision I have ever made but I considered that death was a 100% certainty if we fought. If we surrendered there was always some hope. You can't live without hope.

All through the night they beat me unmercifully trying to get information. I gave them nothing. My head was a mass of blood and large knots. My eyes were swollen shut and they had broken my left arm. My men had to watch the terrible beating they gave me and I was committed to die before giving those bastards anything. They had beaten me so badly I couldn't even feel the pain. If that was the way my life was going to end than I was going to die with honor.

The next morning we were bound and loaded on a truck to be sent to prison. I had little recollection of events for four or five hours.

A Marine Captain spotted the truck headed north about 10 miles north of the area where we were captured and knew that some poor G.I.'s were most likely heading to hell and he sure as hell wasn't going to let that happen. He quickly created a plan of attack and his men executed it with precision killing the eight men tasked to transport us.

He strode to the back of the truck and lifted the tarp, not knowing what to expect, when he saw six American men bound and gagged. I can barely remember the marine picking me up and carrying me to a medic who quickly hooked up an IV and began to dress my wounds and set my arm. As I started to regain consciousness and finally managed to see through my swollen eyes I saw a man with a round face, sandy hair, and blue eyes looking at me.

The Captain smiled and extended his hand and said, Welcome back Lieutenant. I'm Captain Robert Ravenel, United States Marine Corp.

As tears filled my eyes, I thought, Hope is a powerful concept.

Linda returned and could see Joe was deep in thought and finally said, "Joe, what are you thinking about?"

Joe returned to the present and looked lovingly at Linda and slowly said, Robbie and Hope.

He took a sip of scotch and thought, Thank you Robbie.

CHAPTER 6

Majid Abdulla Mohammed arrived at the palace of King Abdallah of Jordon feeling confident that the outcome would be beneficial. Majid is a heavy set man of average height and his face is dark and his eyes are unusually humble and kind for a man in his business. He wore glasses with dark rims and smiled easily. Majid, at 68, has been actively involved trying to unite Muslim countries in the Middle East for the past four years but this task is only a stepping stone toward his obsession to destroy the American infidels.

If the true believers are to eventually rule the world it is imperative that the Middle East and all Muslims must be united. Majid was charged with this objective almost fifty years ago and now he is confident that he will see it come to fruition within his lifetime. The entire world must be governed by Islamic Sharia law.

As Majid waited to be summoned by the King he contemplated how close they are to success. The recent election of an African American Democrat in America filled his heart with joy. He is aware that the democrats will seek to understand Muslims and are not prone to aggressive military action. In fact, he is confident that America will continue to pour money into Muslim nations in an attempt to buy their friendship. Majid is always amazed at how naïve and predictable Americans are and how easy they are to manipulate. .

Majid is a patient man and knows that America has only a few years left until his work is complete. He has implemented his ingenious and precise plans for years that are designed to gradually allow the Americans to self destruct.

He continues to fuel the anti-American sympathies with well placed propaganda and all current indicators suggest his efforts are working. However, it is important that Americans continues to realize how vulnerable they are, therefore, it is necessary to remind them once in awhile of how impudent and helpless they are. The mixture of subtle sabotage from within and direct terrorist attacks is a winning combination.

As he waited he recalled the grand plan to destroy America that was created in 1962. He was introduced to a complex plan designed, by his predecessor and mentor, of a fifty year plan to decimate America from within.

Akbar Mullah said to him, America will become a threat to our way of life and Islam one day and we must be prepared for that day. First you will select Muslim's who are faithful to the Islamic faith to send to America for education, work, and integration into their society.

These people will be very special and will be required to become active in their communities, seemingly patriotic, and with the clear understanding that they will play a significant role in the eventual destruction and control of America. These people will be carefully placed in society and must always remain loyal to you and to our cause.

It will be your responsibility to select and train these people and to assure their commitment and loyalty. Do you understand Majid?

Majid's mind was suddenly brought back to the present when the King's aide interrupted and announced that the King is ready to receive him.

As Majid entered the opulent chambers the King stood and walked to greet him, "Majid, so good to see you. Please have a seat."

"Thank you your highness." Majid said as they embraced in the traditional Muslim tradition.

Majid glances around at the magnificent and impressive room. Plush maroon carpet covered the floor with off white marble walls that gleamed with subtle specks of the same maroon shade. Exquisite hand carved chairs with rich blue fabric trimmed in gold made the room both tasteful and comfortable. King Abdallah's large desk consisted of a black marble top trimmed in gold with solid gold legs. A throne took the place of an office chair, completing the majestic design.

The artwork adorning the wall was simply magnificent; all original oil paintings of thoroughbred Arabian horses. Beautiful multi-colored vases contained fresh flowers and their sweet floral scent filled the air.

The King gestures to the seating area in the far corner of the room which consisted of four large plush chairs surrounding a large exquisite coffee table that matched the King's desk.

The King spoke first, "Majid I have been thinking about our old friend Akbar."

Majid replied, "How very strange, I was just thinking of him while I was waiting."

The King said, "How long ago that was! Tell me once again of his plan my old friend."

Majid smiles warmly and said, "I remember it as if it were yesterday. He said to me Americans will become a threat to our way of life and

Islam one day. We must prepare for that day. You will select Muslims who are faithful to Allah and send them to America for education, work, and integration into their society. However, they must always remain true to Allah and our mission. They will pave the way for the destruction of America."

The King was always amazed at the foresight of Akbar as he said, "Please continue."

Majid complied, "He told me that I must send a few hundred of our most talented Muslims each year and spread them throughout American society. We will create Mosques all over America providing a place for our people to pray and the American constitution will allow us to create operational centers under their freedom of religion amendment."

King Abdullah laughed softly and interjected, "Akbar had great wisdom and foresight."

"Yes he did. He told me to support their rise to prominent positions in American society. He wanted to infiltrate educational institutions to influence the thinking of children and to become proficient in business, legal, and political affairs". Majid said as he pauses to sip his rich dark coffee and continued.

"Your Highness, this is the most brilliant part of the plan. He told me that America was facing the integration of the blacks and said this will present us with a great opportunity. He told me that I must support their efforts to achieve parity financially and legally. To support the black leaders who possess influence by providing them with money and guidance through intermediaries and to spread dissent throughout America.

He told me to support all such minority groups' such as anti-war, women's rights, homosexuals, and all others who wished to challenge the status quo. That, as you know, was and is a great success. Furthermore the influx of illegal Mexicans into America presented additional opportunities.

He said that we must create as much internal animosity as possible, to cause chaos and confusion and to keep the media supplied with disruptive material and to gain as much influence as possible in that area. He scoffed at the American's First Amendment and knew this would be a powerful tool and could not be impeded. He emphatically insisted that no one should ever know that we were supporting these activities." Majid paused and once again sipped his strong coffee.

The King listened attentively, smiling often, and said, "I was but a small boy back then but my father often spoke of the greatness of Akbar."

Majid nodded, remembering the King's father and said, "Akbar informed me that in time, the Americans with their freedoms would be forced to capitulate over and over and eventually their great desire to please everyone would please no one and create class war fare within their country. Their economy, society, and political system would fail in time."

"It appears that we are getting close to his plan becoming a reality my friend." The king said.

"True your highness, we are very close. Akbar also told me that we would be no match for their military superiority but we should commit random acts of terrorism to force them to expend large sums of money to defend such acts. The fear of such attacks could paralyze their country. He also instructed me to challenge America's faith and believe in their false God which would further our ultimate objectives." Majid is enjoying the memories and the realities of his progress and found his conversation with the King extremely gratifying as he is the only other person living that understands the great conspiracy.

The King was most attentive and his enjoyment equaled Majids, he said, "Majid tell me of your assets in America?"

Majid was extremely pleased to share this information with the King. As he was a secretive man, it was rare he had the opportunity to discuss his work of the last forty or so years, "We have over three hundred thousand loyal Muslims participating in some way with our plan, we have twelve mosques fully equipped with weapons and explosives ready and able to inflict pain on the United States when called upon.

We have over six thousand entrenched in their education system from grade school to colleges guiding their tender minds and subtly making them aware of the greed and unfairness of their systems. Four thousand work in the investment business, twenty thousand in government service, and over two thousand in law enforcement including the C.I.A, Secret Service, and F.B.I. We have fifteen hundred attorneys who practice constitutional law and adamantly file litigation. We have another two thousand in the media and tens of thousands in practically every industry in America." Majid answered.

King Abdullah said, "How many politicians or powerful people under our influence?"

Majid did not hesitate as he responded, "We have twelve Senators, twenty four Congressmen, twenty judges, and numerous state and local politicians."

King Abdullah is very pleased as he said, "Majid you have exceeded Akbar's expectations and you bring great joy and happiness to all the faithful."

"It is my honor to serve your Highness. Glory to almighty Allah!" Majid replied.

The King stood and walked over toward his desk and said, "Tell me where we stand on our unification efforts."

Majid replied, "I am pleased to report that with the exception of Saudi Arabia, Kuwait, Yemen, and the United Arab Emirates, everyone else is in agreement. As you know, it will be difficult to convince some of these nations to agree since they are tied to American interest. If you could use your influence, it might be helpful."

King Abdullah said, "I will make some calls my friend. Sometimes our Muslim brothers forget where their loyalties lie."

Majid said, "Thank you your Highness. I believe we can complete our efforts in eighteen months. Furthermore, the American economy is in chaos and the citizens have no faith in their leaders."

Abdullah said, "You have done well Majid." He turned and instructed his aide to wire an additional ten million dollars to Majid's account to assist in their efforts.

Chapter 7

Bert Braddock pulls the nondescript van into the Sleep Inn parking lot in Columbia, South Carolina around 9:30 pm. His passenger, Charlie, quietly pointed to a hooded man walking towards their car. "There's Buck," he said to Bert.

Buck slipped into the back seat, "The pricks are in room 206 and I have disabled the security cameras. Now we will wait until the sandman puts them down."

Two hours later the three men silently made their way up the stairs to the darkened room. Bert quickly picked the lock and they carefully entered the drab room. The two men were sleeping soundly in their clothes in their separate queen sized beds. Bert looked at them peacefully sleeping and wondered, "How in the hell could anyone sleep so soundly after the death and destruction they inflicted on the people in Charlotte?"

He pushed back his rage and signaled Charlie and Buck to proceed. They move quickly and quietly as they remove from their pockets a

42

hypodermic needle loaded with Etomidate, a strong and fast acting sedative. In unison, they clamp one hand over the killer's mouths and use the other to quickly jam the needle in their carotid arteries and force the plunger down. The terrorist's eyes blink momentarily but within seconds they are returned to dreamland.

With the two killers disabled for at least the next four hours they carefully check the room and pack up the belongings of their new guests. Within fifteen minutes they have bound and gagged Imaad and Rajab, slipped quietly down the steps, and jammed them in the back of their van. It would take them about an hour and a half on I-26 East to reach their destination in North Charleston. Buck would drive the killer's car.

They are very familiar with the network of interstate security cameras since Secureone had the contract with the state of South Carolina. They know that the Feds will be utilizing these tools and they would not underestimate their abilities. Before hitting the interstate they pull the van off on a desolate side road and Buck followed. They remove a battery operated paint spray gun and they quickly paint the terrorist's white car black and change the license plates. The Feds would be able to trace the murder's car to Columbia but most likely this change would not allow them to trace the car further.

Two hours later they arrive at their destination and roughly pull the terrorists from the rear of the van, dragging them like bags of trash into the desolate building. The Secureone warehouse in North Charleston had been purchased for future expansion several years ago.

The building was solidly built by the Navy about sixty years ago and contained over 90,000 square feet. On the east side is a large dock on the Cooper River with easy access through Charleston harbor to the open Atlantic Ocean.

Bert Braddock, former SEAL, is a large and muscular man with a no nonsense face, cold eyes, and a close cropped military haircut, and a rugged square face. He is wearing jeans, a black turtle neck shirt, and a leather jacket. He is a confident man with an intimidating presence and if you were in a jam you would want him on your side. If you were to form a picture in your mind of a tough SEAL it would be Bert.

He has worked with Robbie for eight years and they are more than co-workers, they are friends and trusted each other completely.

Charlie and Buck were also former SEALS who had worked with Captain Braddock for four years.. They had been on dozens of missions together and had that bond of trust required if you expect to be an effective covert team. They felt safe together and knew their backs were covered and if necessary, each would die for the other.

Charlie and Buck placed the mass murderer's in an isolated area of the warehouse. They roughly secured Immad and Rajab to heavy wooden straight back chairs that they secured to the floor. They covered the floor with plastic normally used by painters, but it wasn't going to be paint that would be spilled tonight.

The small room is windowless and smells of decaying wood and the salty sea. The lighting is provided by four dirty fluorescent light fixtures with at least half of the tubes burned out. The dark and damp room is intimidating.

At 2:00 am Bert makes the short drive to Robbie's home and gently knocks on the side door that enters Robbie's den. Robbie is expecting him and quickly opens the door and said softly, "Come on in Bert. Get some coffee" as he indicates the coffee pot.

Bert pours a cup of badly needed caffeine and said, "All went well and we have them under control. What do you want us to do with these guys?"

The two men settled down into plush leather chairs in the comfortable den as Robbie's pain and determination are obvious and said, "Bert, it is still hard for me to believe that Tommy is dead. A few hours ago he was alive and now he is dead. These bastards are simply pure evil. If we turn them over to the authorities they will never get a shred of information from them and some sleaze ball lawyer will defend them and convince the bleeding hearts that his clients are the victims. We can't allow that Bert. Civility cannot trump evil so we will treat them the way they would treat us."

"Bert shook his head and said, "I agree Robbie. These guys are like martyrs and they are a dime a dozen and they are proud of what they have done. We need to track down their brains."

Robbie stares at Bert with his bloodshot and piercing eyes and said with conviction, "Bert, do what you must to get the information we need. We are going just as far as we have too. Once you have all you can get send them to their fucking virgins."

Bert said, "Whatever they know, we will know. I will teach these bastards that you can't fuck with America."

Bert gulped down his coffee and stands to leave, "Okay boss, time to go back to work."

After Bert leaves, Robbie sits down and sighs loudly. There would be no turning back now, he is committed and he knew it. Unfortunately, it would be necessary to circumvent laws and security checks in order to avenge Tommy's death and turn back the tide of terror. There is simply no other reasonable choice in his mind and he has no second thoughts.

He began to formulate plans for an all out assault on terrorists as he thought, no longer will I sit back and wait for them to attack, I will become the attacker. I have ample resources including the ex-military talent, money, desire, and the most valuable resource of all is my ability to gather military, civilian, and governmental intelligence. My reluctance to get involved has already cost Tommy his life, and I will lose no one else to these evil and sadistic pricks if I can help it. The best defense is a good offense.

Bert arrives back at the warehouse at 2:45 am and walks into the secure room and looks at the two men he detested and then turns to Buck and said, "OK "Buck, let's start with the short ugly one."

Buck Adams is a fireplug of a man with black hair and a powerful persona. He had once been captured by Al Qaeda, in Afghanistan, and tortured for two days. His defiance and courage frustrated his captors and the more frustrated they became the more pain they inflicted. Their determination to break him only strengthened his resolve to stay strong.

During prayer time they made the mistake of leaving Buck, battered and bloody, and semi-conscious with only one guard. Buck managed to lure the guard close enough to him to hit him with a powerful head butt. As the guard crumpled to the floor, Buck crushed his wind pipe with a powerful foot stomp, while still tied to the chair.

He managed to free himself from his bonds with the dead man's knife. Knowing that time was running out, Buck quickly put the man in the chair and placed the all too familiar hood on his head, and then he took the man's AK-47 and positioned himself behind the door.

When his other two captors returned to continue pounding on him, he quickly cracked their heads open with the AK-47 butt and quietly closed the door. He took another rifle, checked the clips, and slung it over his shoulder, and prepared to enter the outer area of his cell. He planned on encountering at least three to five other ass holes.

Buck opened the cell door and silently scanned the area for targets and listened for any sounds. As he worked his way down the corridor he peered around the corner and could see the outer office of this small prison. There were six terrorists talking and laughing. He had no idea what was outside.

He realized he could not do this quietly. He backed down the hall and unbolted one of the cell doors to reveal six Arab men in the cell. He held his finger to his lips and the grateful men understood. He followed suit with the other four cells until twenty men were looking at him with confusion and appreciation. He signaled for them to stay back and be quiet; they obeyed.

His plan was to kill the other six terrorist and then let all the other prisoners rush out the front. His best case scenario is that there were no guards outside and if that were the case, he felt he had a chance. If there were men outside he would just have to shoot his way out.

He stepped in the office and the startled guards turned towards him and saw his bloody face and the AK-47 in his hands as Bert said, "Good bye ass holes."

The panic shows in their eyes as they scramble for their weapons. They were not quick enough as he empties one of his clips into the cowardly bastards.

He quickly signals for the other prisoners to leave. They all rushed out the door and into the sunlight scattering in all directions. He watched and listened. No gun fire. He made his escape and took three days to work his way back to a safety.

Buck Adams courageous actions earned him a new moniker. His initials were B.A. so from that day forward he was referred to as Bad Ass, or B.A. He truly deserved that nick name; he was indeed a real bad ass. Buck "Bad Ass" Adams is a courageous and patriotic American and this country could use more men with his love of country and commitment.

He reluctantly retired from the military because the edicts from politicians compromised the ability of soldiers to effectively do their jobs and placed their lives in grave danger.

CHAPTER 8

Joe pulls out of his driveway in his BMW 760 LI sedan and heads north. It is a chilly morning but he looks forward to the drive through the beautiful Virginia countryside. The brilliant blue sky is dotted with white puffy clouds and the ground is covered with sparkling dew.

Joe is on his way to see his father in law, John Danforth, who invited Joe to his home to discuss "important matters". Joe always enjoys spending time with John and looks forward to the beautiful drive and the visit.

John's farm is approximately twenty miles from Joe's home. There would be little traffic to distract from the beauty of the country side. There are miles and miles of rolling country side with beautiful oak and elm trees. Even though the leaves have not yet fully appeared on trees they are still magnificent. The country side consisted of many large working farms and there are dozens of lakes, behind neat white fences, with cattle and horses grazing in the fields.

Joe turns onto Pecan Lane, the main entrance to John's farm and follows the three mile road which is lined with pecan trees and the tranquility takes hold as you wind your way past grazing cattle and playful horses in large pastures dotted with beautiful reflective lakes.

As Joe rounds the final bend, John Danforth's magnificent colonial home appears on the horizon. Six large columns grace the entrance and a wrap around porch anchored the first floor. Three second floor balconies complete the Georgian feel of the plantation style home.

As the morning sun began its daily climb into the brilliant blue sky, the home is reflected

perfectly in the calm one hundred and twenty acre lake next to the house. At least a dozen ducks are enjoying their morning swim and Joe saw a largemouth bass jump from the mirror lake and watches the perfect ripples on the calm lake make their way to the shore.

As Joe pulls into the parking area, he looks up and notices John waiting for him on the front porch. John is dressed in jeans, a blue and white checked shirt, and gleaming black boots. His well groomed silver hair and pale blue eyes are accented by his still black eyebrows and a warm smile. John's aged and tanned wrinkled face is warm and kindly. His keen mind and vitality belies his eighty years.

As a United States Senator, representing the State of Virginia, he is one of the most respected politicians in Washington. He has served in the Senate for twenty six years and as a congressman for four years before that. John had chosen a life of politics to make a difference. His integrity is unquestioned but his inability to compromise over the years has restricted his opportunities to pass meaningful legislation has been a constant frustration.

Joe steps out of the car and said, "Hey John, so good to see you. You look great."

John walks toward Joe and the two men embrace and slap each other on the back as John said, "Always great to see my favorite son in law."

Joe and John both laughed as Joe said, "You mean your only son in law."

The two men walk toward the front door as John said, "Come on in son and let's get some hot coffee and a couple of Mary's great apple flapjacks." Just then Mary, the Danforth's faithful and long time housekeeper and cook appears.

As they step on the front porch Mary greets Joe with a big hug, "Mr. Joe it is so good to see you. Come on inside and let's put some meat on 'dem bones."

Joe laughs and pats his stomach, "Well I guess I could eat a little Mary."

The men settled in John's library and Mary brought in the flapjacks and coffee.

John always loved the warmth and the lived in feeling of John's home and particularly the library. It is both functional and cozy. On two walls were book shelves that were stuffed with law, history, biographical, and military classics from floor to ceiling.

His desk was handmade for former President Eisenhower and surrounded by three comfortable leather side chairs. The room is filled with family photographs but there are no signs of any ego awards, proclamations, political pictures, or evidence that the man who resided here was anything other than a devoted and humble family man. Large French doors opened onto a wide veranda overlooking the lake, barn, and beautiful countryside.

The two men enjoy some coffee, flapjacks, and small talk as John said, "Joe we have a lot to cover today and I know I can count on you to be open-minded and to give serious consideration to the issues we discuss."

Joe is a little surprised at the serious tone and sensed this visit would not be typical as he said with sincerity, "John you know how much I admire and respect you. Of course, you will have my full attention."

John smiles his knowing grandfatherly smile as he reaches over and picks up his pipe, packs it with tobacco, lights it, and blows a ring of smoke into the air, "Joe, I have been in public service for over forty years. I have seen a lot in my time and a lot of it I didn't like very much. Joe, this country is in grave danger and I believe our very survival is at risk.

There is no doubt whatsoever, that if we continue on our present course our economy will completely collapse and our long and successful experiment with democracy will come to an end"

With concern in his voice Joe asks, "John do you really believe it's that serious?"

John looks directly into Joe's eyes and said emphatically, "Absolutely"

He waits for a reaction but Joe is awaiting further explanation, "Liberals believe it to be their responsibility to provide jobs, food, health care, and housing for everyone. Conservatives believe in personal responsibility and self reliance. Consequently, many people have achieved great success and many depend on the generosity of government and charity. The large majority of Americans fall between the two groups."

Partisan Politics are destroying this country. The time has come for a Revolution!"

CHAPTER 9

Bert is well aware that the apprehension of what is coming is an effective technique in the interrogation process. They were periodically given a little water and some food but no rest room privileges which caused discomfort, degradation, and a strong odor.

Bert had pulled up all the information they could find and has their files. The files are quite extensive and it is clear this is not their maiden voyage into the world of cold blooded murder. Persuading them to give up their contacts would be a long shot simply because jihadist believe their efforts are sanctioned by Allah and do not fear death.

Bert is very familiar with Islamic teachings and understands that women have little value but they loved their sons. Bert discovered his two guests have six sons between them and would dispatch a team to Jordon if necessary.

These zealots have no compunction regarding the killing of innocent women or children and if America is to have a chance it will require our behavior to be equally uncivilized and barbaric. It is the only language they understand and they know it is not within our culture to utilize torture.

Buck, Charlie, and Bert discussed their strategy prior to unlocking the door and entering the room. Bert flips on the lights and Charlie moves a table next to Imaad, the short one, who is clearly the leader of the two.

The killer's hoods are removed and Buck places a satchel on the table and slowly removes the contents; a surgical saw, scalpels, and a variety of curved and straight knives. There gleaming presence causes Imaad and Rajab to feel some concern but they are no stranger to these techniques and do not believe they their captors would actually employ physical harm.

Buck moves the instruments around slowly, with a satisfied grin, apparently organizing his tools while the two murderers anxiously watch..

Bert smiles and looks at the two men and said, "Which of you two gentlemen would like to go first?"

Brad ripped the tape off their mouths as each man cursed and grunted.

As expected, Imaad said, "You cannot hold us here. We wish to have an attorney."

Bert calmly said, "When you were destroying all those lives in Charlotte did you allow those people to have an attorney prior to killing them?"

Imaad smugly said in passable English, "I don't know what you are talking about."

Bert looked at Buck and nodded. Buck stood in front of Imaad and said, "You are a lying cocksucker" and then he hit Imaad with a forearm shiver that spread his bulbous nose all over his face. The snap of his broken nose sounded as if a stick of wood had been broken and blood poured down his face and onto his shirt and pants. Immad shrieked with pain and pulled violently at the bonds that are holding him.

Bert allows time for Imaad to quit his whimpering and turns to Rajab and said, "Rajab, it is important that you know that we know everything about you. The purpose of our visit is to have you tell us exactly what you know. We will ask you simple questions to verify your trustworthiness. We will know when you lie, and when you do, the penalty will be quick and painful. Do you understand?" Bert smiles menacingly at the man.

Rajab looks from Imaad's bloody face to Buck and his instruments of torture and then Bert, as he defiantly said nothing.

"Good." Bert replied as he smiled at he man.

After twenty minutes of asking irrelevant questions to get him accustomed to the process, Bert and his team left the room to prepare a reward of food and water for Rajib's cooperation

The two men, alone at last, began to pray to Allah for strength, salvation, and protection of their families.

The captives had eaten little for the last thirty hours and quickly consume the soup and water they are given. Their physical and mental abilities have diminished significantly during the past day but they did know they would be entitled to the privileges of Americans.

Bert decides to start with the stronger of the two men, Imaad. As Bert stared at him Imaad thought, I will give this infidel dog nothing. Allah will protect me.

Bert pulls a chair over and places it directly in front of Imaad, never losing eye contact as he places his elbows on his knees, holds his head in his hands, and stares directly into Imaad's eyes sending a message of fear and calmly said, "Imaad, I remind you again that the consequences of dishonesty will result in serious repercussions."

Imaad did as he was trained and defiantly said, "I wish to have an attorney."

Bert suddenly slaps him hard on his ear with the clipboard he held in his hand and said, "Did you give those people in Charlotte a chance to call a lawyer before you executed them? Of course not, so you and your shit head buddy will get the same consideration you gave those innocent people."

Imaad musters as much pride as possible under the circumstances and said, "If I die today I will know that my death is for the glory of Allah. He will protect me and welcome me with open arms. I do not fear you infidels. Soon the earth will be purged of you dogs and if I die today my only regret is that I will not see each and every one of you dead."

Bert stares at him again with cold and evil eyes and says, "Imaad I hope you enjoyed you soup. I love pork stew, don't you?"

Imaad's eyes grew wide and he felt a tinge of nausea and wondered if had indeed eaten pig? This would mean he is unclean but he convinces himself it is only a lie. He says nothing.

Bert coldly said to Buck, "Cut off his trousers."

Buck removes a knife and quickly cut off the pant legs at the crouch and removed the material exposing Imaad's legs. When finished he looks at the knife and says, "Hmm! This one is a little dull."

Bert looks at his clipboard and asked, "Who is your contact in the United States?"

Imaad gives his best fake laugh and said, "Mickey Mouse."

Bert, without hesitation, said, "Skin his right thigh Buck." Imaad couldn't believe this and a look of concern and surprise washed across his face.

Buck picks up a shiny scalpel, spits on it, and cuts a quarter inch deep straight line from the top of his thigh to the terrified man's knee. Buck then hesitated, spit on the bloody scalpel again, and cut a horizontal line across the top and bottom of the vertical cut forming something similar to a capital I.

Imaad looks at the precise small cuts in horror and is confused as he feels little pain and there is very little blood. He couldn't believe this is happening. Allah surely is protecting him.

Bert asks, "Who is your contact in the Untied States?"

Imaad grits his teeth as he is now feeling some pain and looks at Bert and said, "Fuck you!"

Bert said in a very controlled voice, "Buck, go ahead and peel him very slowly."

Imaad can't believe what he is hearing. They are going to skin him!

Buck takes his gloved hand and clamped his forceps on the corner at the top of the I and slowly begins to pull the skin back exposing Imaads nerves and muscles.

Imaad screams in agony and struggles with his bonds as the pain attacks him.

Bert calmly waits and stares at Rajib while ignoring the screams for a full two minutes and then calmly asks, "Who is your contact in the United States?"

Once again Imaad said through his clenched teeth and pain, "Fuck you!"

"Do the other side Buck." Bert instructs.

When Buck finishes, Imaad's entire thigh is skinned and the screaming continues for several more minutes as his thigh is now skinless. As tears, snot, and slobber escape from his facial orifices he cannot avoid the horrible sounds of agony escaping from his mouth.

Rajib watches in horror and is having difficulty breathing.

Finally Bert says with a contented and satisfied smile, "Come on Imaad crying like a baby won't help. Who is your contact in the United States?"

This time Imaad could not speak, he simply shook his head back and forth slinging his slobber and snot from side to side.

Bert said, "Okay Buck let's see how he likes salt with his pain."

Buck pulls out a can of Morton's salt and adjusted the top to "pour" as Imaad watches in horror. Buck pours the salt on the exposed nerves which creates an unimaginable pain. Imaad's wrists were bleeding from his convulsions and his agonizing screams struck fear in Rajib.

As barbaric and distasteful as this process is Bert knew that this man is a cold blooded killer and there are thousands more just like him and they must be stopped.

Some people are simply evil and evil people viewed compassionate people as weak. Evil cannot be healed it must be destroyed.

Finally Imaad passes out. Buck douses him with a bucket of cold water and not only awakens him but the drops of water hitting his exposed nerves forces him to violently rock back in forth in his chair trying desperately to escape the pain. There is no escape.

Bert said, "Who was your contact in the United States?"

Imaad yells with spit flying out of his mouth and said, "Never!"

Bert took out his cell phone and pretends to make a call to his team in Jordon and issues orders, "You are going to have to pick up Imaad's sons and bring them to me."

Imaad looks at him as he appears to be listening to whoever is on the phone.

"What is your ETA?" Bert asks and then listens.

He looks over at Imaad and says, "Your three sons are coming to visit you tomorrow. I hope you will enjoy seeing them?"

Bert still holding the phone looks at Imaad as if awaiting a response. Imaad's expression is showing fear but resolve. Bert says, "Imaad I hope it will not be too painful for you when we do the same thing to your sons?

This is a scenario that never occurred to Imaad. He would gladly die for his cause but his sons? They are innocent and they should not be involved. He convinces himself these men will do it. His expression changed to one of compliance as tears of pain and concern cascaded down his cheeks and he says, "Fahid Mohammed Al-Adel."

"Where can we find him?" Bert calmly asked.

"In Houston, Texas at the Masjid of Al-Islam Mosque." Imaad tearfully replies feeling ashamed and defeated.

After extracting a significant amount of additional information from the two murderers they are shot, loaded on a boat, and taken forty miles out in the Atlantic Ocean and dumped. Their car is rolled into sixty feet of deep water in the Cooper River.

CHAPTER 10

Joe Winston personified the image of a sophisticated and intelligent southern gentleman and is one of the most humble men you could ever hope to meet. In addition to his wonderful family he has three inseparable friends in Robbie Ravenel, Adam Fields, and Lee Roth all of whom are extremely successful in business and philanthropic work. Their friendships have been forged over decades and are closer than brothers.

The four men disdained the deception and dishonesty of politicians and never involved themselves in political issues and never granted interviews to the media. Nonetheless, the Wall Street Journal created an amazingly positive feature story of the four men without benefit of a single quote from them. The article, based upon their exhaustive research and hundreds of interview with employees and other business associates, named their story "The Forcesome because the four men were a major force in business.

The four private men never commented on the article and simply continued to pursue their way of life which included the management of four of the largest and most productive businesses in the world. Forbes magazine reports annually on the best hundred companies to work for and for the past eight years their companies held the top four spots.

Joe is sitting in his father in law's library trying to comprehend where John is going with this conversation. Joe looked at John and said, "A revolution! John what are you talking about?"

John laughed and said, "Hold on son, let me finish. Joe our middle class is the strength of our country and they are being basically ignored. Parents are working their tails off, they are paying for child care, they keep chasing the American dream and they keep getting knocked down.

The poor, the lazy, the minorities, the retired, women, gays, and dozens of other special interest groups have activist fighting for their benefits. Joe, the middle class has no lobby or support from any political party or support groups. They just get up every morning and go to work. They pay their bills, work in their churches and communities, pay their taxes without complaint and try very hard to make things better for their families. They are becoming frustrated and they are losing faith in America."

John paused to restrain his anger and to refill his empty coffee cup, "Joe, the truth is that I have been unable to help these people for forty years."

Joe said, "Hold on John, nobody has tried harder than you. No one could be a better advocate for the people."

John ignored Joe's comments and said sternly, "Listen closely, Joe. We have about two hundred and fifteen million adult people in our country and one hundred and twenty million taxpayers. Forty five million are below the poverty level or disabled. Twenty two million are employed by government entities and thirty three million are over age 65 receiving social security and Medicare benefits.

At least one hundred million people in this country depend on the government for total or partial support. Sixty million taxpayers provide 97% of the tax revenue and the other seventy million only pays 3%."

The statistics hit Joe hard as he felt guilty and realized that he had simply been blocking out the reality of the real world. His emotions vacillated between anger and shame.

John, with less passion in his voice, resumed, "Joe I wanted to tell you that next week I will resign from the Senate."

Joe is completely surprised by the serious conversation and now John's revelation really confused him as he stuttered, "You can't be serious John."

John laughed and said, "Yes I am very serious Joe...... There is something else I need to share with you also."

Joe could not believe this conversation could be any more confusing and now John seems to have another bomb shell to drop, "What do you mean something else?"

John said, "Don't over react son, I didn't say I was dying. I intend to remain very much involved. You know how much I love this country, my family, and our way of life. Joe, I intend to form a new political party with the purpose of ridding this country of corrupt politicians and restoring sanity to government."

Joe is becoming frustrated and walked over to the window trying to clear his head and looked out and turned back to John and said, "John, you are talking about trying to achieve the impossible. How the hell could you possibly do this at your age? John, come on, be realistic, you're good but this is too much for you. You have done more than your share."

John looked at Joe with his knowing smile and looked proudly into Joe's eyes and said softly, "I know Joe. I can't do it alone. I will need some help and that's where you come in. Joe let me be the first to congratulate you on becoming the 45th President of the United States of America."

Joe looked at John as if he was crazy and said, "John, have you lost your mind? You know how I feel about politics." Never in Joe Winston's life has he been hit with so many twist and turns in a conversation and he is unaccustomed to feeling so completely surprised and confused.

John realized that he had Joe totally off balance and chuckled as he said, "No, actually I have finally found my mind. Joe democrats and republicans have controlled our government for our entire lifetime. Do you believe they are satisfactorily addressing the needs of America?

Joe, still reeling from all that John has hit him with answered curtly, "No, I don't."

John, pausing for a few more seconds, said, "Do you have any reason to believe things will improve over the next several decades?"

"No." Joe said with some exasperation.

"Are you concerned about the world your children will live in?" John said with the express purpose of inflicting a feeling of guilt.

"Of course I am. What's your point John?" Joe snaps.

John knew he had Joe right where he wanted him as he calmly but forcefully said, "Can you give me any rational reason why you are not utilizing all of your resources, talents, and abilities to protect this country for my grandchildren?"

Joe was extremely intelligent and intuitive and realized that John had led him to a place he is reluctant to go. He finally looked at John and said, "You know I can't give you a rational reason. I despise the manipulation, compromises, empty promises, greed, and disgusting thirst for power that seems to consume most politicians."

John had a satisfied smile on his face as he said, "Well Joe you have a choice. You can keep your head in the sand or you can stand up and try to make a difference. What do you want to do Joe?"

Joe has been completely manipulated by a master and knew it. He looked at John and brusquely said, "I want to get a cup of coffee." They both laughed and walked over to pour some hot coffee as John put his arm around his son in law's shoulders.

In a few minutes they returned to the seating area and John spoke first, "Let me share my theory with you. If you were selling a piece of property would you rather have two interested parties or three?"

Joe answers in a logical business manner, "Three, the more interest the greater value I am likely to get."

John said, "Exactly what I thought. Currently when legislation is presented we have two parties that are interested, democrats and republicans. As you know, they operated on a give and take basis. You vote for mine and I will vote for yours. That results in diluted legislation, ear marks, and excess expenditures. Joe, what if there where three parties?"

"Assuming they are three equal parties I would assume some of the compromises could be stopped. It would be a little like three the branches of government, legislative, judicial, and executive, except one of two parties could gain control of all three and that would be unlikely with three parties."

John said, "Well, well, well, I do have a very bright son in law. Joe we will create a new political party, The Restoration Party, and we will restore America to a country that values freedom, opportunity, self reliance, and compassion. This will only work if we have an outstanding candidate for President that the American people can trust. We need a man who can give Americans hope for the future. Joe I think you are that man."

John's comments are followed by a long silence and finally John said, "Joe I know I should not have hit you so hard with this and I apologize. Before you make a decision I would like for you to give it some serious thought. I have asked Tony to come down here on the 9th so we can do a little strategic planning so why don't you mull it over a few days and meet us here on the 9th. Will you do that?"

Joe admired and respected John Danforth and could never refuse him, "Well John I will tell you this you have given me a lot to think about. I will do that.

CHAPTER 11

Majid Abdulla Mohammed is at his primary home in Palmyra, Syria after three days of travel to Pakistan and Iran promoting the union of the Middle Eastern Muslim nations. His objectives include removal of borders and the creation of a common currency similar to the Eurodollar.

His persuasive communication skills and conviction has resulted in significant progress and he is optimistic that he can achieve his objectives within two years.

Majid's appearance is ordinary and grandfatherly as he approaches eighty. If you were to see him you would think he is a kind and gentle man but things are not always as they appear to be. The wrinkles in his face are covered by his white beard and close set eyes and hawkish nose causes him to appear both cunning and wise.

He always remains behind the scenes, preferring the solitude and absence of attention as he pulls the strings. He is a master of political manipulation and willing to use any method that will work from violence to money.

Majid controls, or enjoys excellent relationships, with all radical Islamic groups and his leadership and support is highly valued. He is equally respected and feared and has no tolerance for failure. He provides financial support and expertise for terrorist operations and orchestrates his plan with methodical confidence and unrelenting determination.

Majid has constituents in every western democracy and in almost every significant country. His long time friend and most important operative is Aziz Hassan who controls all operations in the United States.

Each of Majid's representatives are deeply covered and well respected in their communities and none would be suspected of involvement in terrorist or subversive activities. These are the men he trusts with the future of all radical Muslims. Their cover includes many years of hard work to earn the respect and admiration of their host country.

Through Aziz, Majid controls tens of thousands of loyal radical Muslims in the United States alone. These servants of Allah will execute any assignment with absolute obedience, vigilance, and passionate determination.

His original plan for 9/11 had proven far more successful than he had ever hoped. The United States occupation of Iraq in 2004 was an unexpected bonus that would help with unification and to fuel anti-American sentiment in the United States and abroad.

With the increased cost of oil and the growing financial problems suffered by the U.S., this is a positive indication to him that Allah has indeed blessed him.

Aziz Hassan is more nervous than usual as he travels from America to Syria for debriefing. Upon arrival at Majid's magnificent home he is greeted by his host, "Hello Aziz, thank you so much for coming." They embrace and kiss each other on their cheeks and sit down in comfortable chairs.

Majid's home is enormous and constructed in the style of Arabian royalty. The men are seated on Majid's magnificent terrace constructed of the finest Italian marble that is intricately interwoven and surrounds a beautiful pool. There are dozens of Palms that have been imported from across the world, another dozen date trees, and several citrus trees.

Outside the lush green grass that covers a one hundred yard radius around his home the property is barren and desolate. This is made possible by a complex irrigation system and a meticulous lawn management program. From above his property would appear as an oasis.

The terrace they now occupy is cool and comfortable and the colorful furniture and dozens of original statues sends a message of opulence and announces the importance of the owner.

Aziz says in a warm and considerate voice, "It is always a pleasure to be in your presence Majid."

"That is very kind of you Aziz. Please help yourself to some tea or coffee." Majid politely replies.

The men talk for well over an hour reviewing progress on a number of projects. Majid is a perfectionist and detest incompetence. Clearly he is satisfied with the many wonderful accomplishments of Aziz over the decades and repeatedly expresses his gratitude and appreciation.

Majid is very pleased with the successful operation in Charlotte and saves that topic for last. He looks at Aziz with appreciation and said, "Aziz. I can't tell you how pleased I am with your results in North Carolina. You have done very well my old friend and your efforts will not go unrewarded. You are blessed by the mighty Allah!"

"Thank you but I must confess I am afraid we have a problem" Aziz timidly said with some trepidation.

"Majid's right eyebrow raises which is an indication that he did not like hearing of problems and his expression quickly changed to one of concern, "What problem?" he said with a less congenial tone.

Aziz has difficulty making eye contact and his head is slightly bowed as he apologetically replied, "The men who executed our plan in the United States are missing."

Majid's tries hard to control his anger as he said, "Men just don't disappear, Aziz. I am confused."

"They failed to report back to their contact in Houston. We find no record of arrest or detainment. We did confirm they checked into a hotel about ninety miles south of Charlotte and from there we can find no trace of them." Aziz responds as calmly as possible.

Majid stood and paces back and forth for a full minute, clearly displeased. He stops pacing in front of Aziz and glares down at him and sternly said, "You go back to America and you find these two men. I will not tolerate loose ends. Do you understand?"

Aziz, sensing the meeting is over, stands up and tries to say with confidence, "I will find them."

Majid, clearly unhappy, said, "I will pray to Almighty Allah that you do! Do not fail me!"

Aziz boards his flight back to Chicago. As he settled into his first class seat he is concerned for his life, and the lives of his family, for he knew failure is dealt with harshly.

Aziz had immigrated from Jordon forty three years ago and was educated at Berkley where he earned his undergraduate degree and Masters. All expenses were covered by Majid as well as a handsome stipend each year.

He earned his PHD in Philosophy at Stanford University and at the age of twenty seven and he was employed as a Professor at Loyola in Chicago where he is now a tenured department head. His wife and children are not aware of his clandestine life and he is admired by the university, the community, peers, and students.

He is the last man in the world who would be suspected of controlling all propaganda, legal, economic, educational sabotage, and terrorist activities in the United States. There are currently thirteen cell leaders reporting to Aziz and those cell leaders have over thirty thousand committed radical Muslims dedicated to the destruction of American society.

CHAPTER 12

Joe Winston and John Danforth take a break and head for lunch. After they finished the wonderful chicken salad sandwiches Mary prepared for their lunch and reminisced about family matters. John removes the napkin from his lap and dabs at his lips and chin, finishes his unsweetened ice tea and said, "Joe let's go back to the library and finish our discussion."

They thank Mary for the wonderful lunch and return to the library and as they did so Joe is feeling uncomfortable and a little trapped.

As they settle into their chairs John fixes Joe with hope in his eyes and simply said, "Joe, will you do it?" John knew he had fired his best shots and this is the only question left.

Joe leans back in his chair, closes his eyes, and considers the question before replying. His thoughts are contradictory part of him knows he cannot turn his back on his country and part of him simply detests the idea of such a dramatic change in lifestyle. He replies, "John, first of all I can't even imagine actually becoming a politician. Secondly, starting a new party from scratch would be extremely difficult. I wouldn't even know how to start."

The old Senator is on his game and is following his mental script exactly as he planned it. He looks at Joe and said, "Two good questions. With regard to your image of yourself, that's nothing more than humility. You are the opposite of others who aspire to political office who are consumed by self adulation. That's why you must help.

Your second question requires a lot more consideration, inasmuch as you have been so adept at avoiding publicity in your life. We have been working on this for several months so I would like for you and I to discuss this completely with Tony Papandrea on the ninth. I believe we can provide a good answer for you at that time. Is that okay with you?"

Joe smiles and looks at John with respect and said, "Okay John. I do want to meet Tony and take a little time to organize my thoughts. As you know, you hit me with a lot today and I think I will be in a better position to process this in a few days."

The men chat for another hour and enjoy a short walk down to the lake to enjoy the nice day. John feels as if he accomplished his mission and Joe Winston feels as if his whole world has been turned upside down.

CHAPTER 13

It is mid morning at the warehouse in North Charleston and Charlie, Buck, and Bert are cleaning up the warehouse and destroying any evidence of their recent guests. Bert walks out on the dock and pulls his secure cell phone out and calls Robbie. "What's up Bert?" Robbie asks.

Bert said, "Boss, we finished the assignment and closed the deal."

Robbie smiles and said, "Congratulations Bert, I really appreciate the extra effort you and the boys put into the job."

Bert said, "I have some more good news. We have a hot leads we need to follow up on and I might need your help. When can I see you?"

Robbie replies, "Well, I know you boys have been burning the midnight oil so why don't you get some sleep and meet me tonight at my home around 8:00 pm. Will that work for you?"

"Yes sir, I will see you then." Bert replies with his voice showing some fatigue.

As Bert disconnects he feels more alive than he has in years. Finally fate has returned him to the work he dearly loves and he feels born again. His hatred for those who would harm our country is slightly greater than his contempt of politicians. He welcomes the opportunity to help put America back on the right course.

After a solid four hours of sleep Bert shaves, showers, and puts on some fresh clothes and heads to his meeting. He arrives at Robbie's home on the South Battery at precisely 8:00 pm he climbed the fourteen steps to the large wrap around veranda that offers a beautiful view of the harbor and rings the ornate doorbell. Robbie opens the door and warmly greets Bert, "Hey bubba, how you doing?"

Bert said, "Doing great Robbie, got about four hours of sleep and I feel like a new man."

"Come on in. Can I get you a drink? Robbie said.

"If you are having one, I will join you." Replies Bert.

"I sure am." Robbie said.

"I will have a Bombay and tonic." Bert said.

"Sounds good, think I will have the same thing." Robbie said as he leds Bert through the large home and into the back den.

Robbie's home is straight out of "Gone with the Wind." They walked through the large elaborate foyer with its stunning crystal chandelier and passed by the large library on the left. Ornate double spiral stairs lead to the second and third floor while on their right is a beautiful formal dining room and large living room. Each of the rooms is elegantly decorated and enjoy magnificent views of Charleston Harbor. The highly polished hardwood floors, various rugs, and elaborate drapes accent s the two hundred year old home perfectly.

They reach the end of the hall and Robbie opens the heavy double doors to reveal his spacious and well appointed den. A large leather sofa sat about twenty five feet from the magnificent stone fireplace. Over the handcrafted stone fireplace, which is ten feet wide and goes from floor to ceiling, is a sixty five inch Sony flat screen television. There are two large overstuffed chairs with ottomans one to the left of the sofa and one to the right with a large cocktail in front of the sofa.

The bar, on the opposite side of the room, is made of exquisite old pine beams and is highly polished. A large ornate mirror is mounted behind the bar with several glass shelves holding an assortment of bottles and large wine coolers on both sides.

Robbie walks behind the bar and prepares the Bombay and tonics. He hands one to Bert and said, "Come on bubba, let's sit over here." They settled into the two large chairs and sipped on their cocktails as Robbie continues, "Bert, you know we can talk freely here so tell me what we've got?"

Bert takes another hit of the sweet gin and tonic and said, "First of all we had the right guys. They did the job in Charlotte. Secondly, they gave up two names and I believe that's all they had. One of the guys is the Mexican who brought them across and the other is the imam at a Mosque in Houston. I believe we should make a little visit out west and see what we can find out."

Robbie feels some satisfaction that the men who killed his nephew and many other innocent people are no longer a problem. He also knows these men are nothing more than tools. They need to move up the ladder until they could nail the bastards who are really responsible, "Take whatever you need and enjoy your trip out west."

"We will run an extensive background check on the imam tonight and leave first thing in the morning. The Mexican is just another mule I don't think we need to worry about him at this time." Bert says.

"Good. I will be leaving here on Tuesday to go to Volusia National for a few days. If you need me you, you know how to reach me." Robbie said.

The two men finish their cocktails and have another. Thirty minutes later Robbie says goodnight to Bert. Robbie settles into a front porch rocker to enjoy the view he never tires of.

The moon is full and the harbor is calm. The cool air feels good to Robbie as he thinks about how much of this he should share with Joe, Adam, and Lee. He rocks in his chair and listens to the waves pounding the battery and thinks about the events and emotions of the last few days. He experienced overwhelming sadness, uncontrollable anger, satisfaction, and now a commitment to somehow end the threat of terrorists in America no matter what the cost.

CHAPTER 14

Lee Roth is a member of the Forcesome and owner of the most successful hardware and software computer businesses in the world, Rothsystems. His brilliance is incomparable and he is recognized as the preeminent computer genius. His intellect is complimented by his wonderful sense of humor and natural street smarts.

Lee is a small and wiry man who stands about five feet six inches and weighs one hundred and thirty five pounds soaking wet. His complexion is pale and his hair remains jet black and he usually wears it in a pony tail. His brilliant blue eyes, below black eyebrows, shine with intelligence and his narrow nose and constant smile cause him to look as if he is either high or perpetually happy. He is not handsome but isn't unattractive as his eyes cause people to notice him.

Lee and his partner, Carolyn Garrison return to Lee's home after a fabulous seafood dinner at Wood's in Plymouth. His home is located just off 3A about eight miles south of Manomet. It is a large estate situated on five acres of pristine property overlooking Cape Cod Bay.

As Lee approaches the gate the high tech sensors identify his car and open the security gate. The same process repeats as he approaches his garage. The entire estate is controlled by a very sophisticated computer system designed by Lee and is also voice activated.

Lee and Carolyn exited the car and walked toward the entrance when Lee said, "Open."

They walk into a massive laundry room that includes a mounted flat screen television, a sitting area, and a full bathroom in addition to ample room to actually do laundry.

As they pass through the kitchen and into the great room Lee issues instructions, "Low lights in the great room and music by the Kingston Trio."

The system complied and as the lights illuminated the large room and "Scotch and Soda" begins to spill out into the house.

The great room contains three large televisions with one being designated for video games and interaction with his computer. The seating area features a large ebony table surrounded by a white circular couch and several comfortable chairs. Lee's dining room is magnificent as the custom made table features an ebony top with white legs and could easily seat thirty people. The table is surrounded by throne like white chairs with black trim and a large crystal chandelier. Three sides of the dining room opened into open areas and on the one wall there is a huge built in china cabinet that perfectly matches the décor.

Lee and Carolyn proceed to the large porch overlooking Cape Cod. Lee issues more commands, "open door, open curtains, and low lighting."

Lee escorts Carolyn to a large sofa and asks, "What would you like to drink, diet coke or Ginger Ale?"

Carolyn considers the choices, smiles and says, "Ginger Ale, please."

"Okay, two Ginger Ales coming up." Lee said cheerfully.

He returns with the drinks and said, "Here you go, Sweetie."

She takes the glass and said, "Thanks honey."

Carolyn was married at one time to a man who turned out to be a monster. She was physically and mentally abused for years and turned to alcohol and drugs for relief. Her husband forced her to agree to a no fault divorce and kicked her out in the street without a penny to her name.

Carolyn is a good and decent person who simply became a victim of her circumstances. Ultimately her low self esteem forced her into a world of sex and drugs in order to survive and stop the pain.

Lee only has one real love and that is the world of high technology and therefore refuses to complicate his life with marriage. He considers Joe, Robbie, and Adam his family. He satisfies his sexual urges by utilizing high end prostitutes whom he found convenient and uncomplicated.

Carolyn's relationship with Lee began when she was assigned to him one night and was told that he is very good client who pays exceptionally well. It was the most unusual date of her life. Lee could see that her life was an interesting story and after much persuasion he pulled the whole story out of her. After she unburdened herself of all the pain and humiliation she had kept inside for many years she strangely felt a great burden had been lifted.

The night involved no sex but it was the first step in a remarkable journey for Carolyn Garrison that she couldn't have imagined in her wildest dreams. Lee is a very perceptive individual and a great judge of character. He is also an extremely sensitive and compassionate person who believes in the inherent decency in almost everyone.

Lee employed Carolyn as a low level assistant in his office and required her to take advantage of the drug treatment programs offered by Rothsystems. She was sent to the Betty Ford Clinic for eight weeks and when she returned to work Lee could hardly believe the changes in her.

Her color was much improved and her beautiful blue eyes had lost their sadness and now sparkled. Her confidence and self respect had returned and her appearance would turn the head of any man. Her perfectly proportioned body, confident and beautiful face, and stunning auburn hair combined with her relaxed grace gave Lee tremendous satisfaction.

That was five years ago and since that time she progressed professionally within Rothsystems and remains free of drugs and alcohol. Her relationship with Lee has evolved favorably and Lee purchased her a town house in Boston near Rothsystem's home office.

They were together frequently but there were times when Lee would not see her socially for weeks. He had made it clear that she is never to initiate contact and she understood that Lee's real love is his work. She is content to play any role in his life.

They are comfortable together and as Lee sat down beside her and says, "Windows open." As the windows retract and allow the cold air from the bay inside it causes them to cuddle; the cuddling escalated to passionate kissing, the kissing to touching, and the touching to sex.

When they are spent and freezing from the cold air Lee reaches in the cabinet by the large couch and pulls out a big multi colored quilt and covers Carolyn. He crawls under with his back to her and Carolyn affectionately rubs his neck and hugs him until he falls into a deep sleep.

CHAPTER 15

APRIL 9, 2009
RICHMOND, VIRGINIA

Joe and John stroll down the cobblestone path that leads to the beautiful cottage on the lake. The cottage is a very attractive one story structure painted white with black shutters accenting the windows. There is a large wrap around porch with numerous inviting white rocking chairs and in the back a ninety foot dock extends into the water.

The lake contains large mouth bass and bream and everyone enjoys fishing from the dock because it guarantees you will catch some nice fish.

Inside the cottage there are two comfortable bedrooms, three baths, a great room, a kitchen, and dining area all very tastefully decorated and extremely charming. The tranquil view of the lake and the magnificent trees surrounding the lake would easily inflict someone with immediate relaxation.

Tony Papandrea, had arrived yesterday, and is the current resident of the comfortable little cottage and is busily working on his laptop at a desk in front of a window overlooking the lake. John taps on the door and walks in, "Good morning Tony, you look mighty busy!"

He stands up and walks over to greet the men. "John! Good morning."

John said, "Let me introduce you to Joe Winston." Joe and Tony extend their hands, shake, and exchange greetings.

Tony is slightly overweight and of medium height and his appearance suggests he might be a college professor. His disheveled look and his unkempt thin salt and pepper hair combines with a round jovial face, prominent double chin, and friendly demeanor causing him to be very likeable.

When it comes to political strategy he has no peers. He has managed campaigns for twenty one politicians and nineteen were elected. This situation is quite different, not only would he have to help create a new party; he will be required to help motivate the American People to vote for a Presidential candidate with no political experience who is virtually unknown by 95% of voters and represents a new political party.

Tony looks at Joe and says, "Joe, I sure have heard a lot of nice things about you from John and it certainly is nice to finally meet you."

Joe looks at Tony and said, "Same here Tony, John says you are the best, but more importantly, he trust you."

Tony is very instinctive and as he looked at Joe and observes him he could instantly see and feel his appeal, even though Joe is dressed in simple pleated tan slacks, a dark brown and white checked casual shirt, with a black sport jacket his appearance could be described as elegant.

After his quick evaluation Tony is pleased as he smiles and jokingly says, "I can't tell you how many times I have tried to contact you on behalf of one my clients. Man, you really know how to avoid people."

"Sorry Tony, hope you don't take it personally but I have never had any interest in publicity and the only politician I have ever supported is John." Joe replied with a smile.

John stands up and walks around as he said, "Tony, it took some work but if Joe feels we might have a chance to succeed he has reluctantly agreed to consider the possibility. What we need to do here today is discuss a broad strategy for the mid terms in 2010 as well as the general election in 2012."

Joe listens and watches as Tony nods and asks, "You want me to lead the discussion John?"

"It's all yours." John replies.

Tony leans back in his chair and places his hands behind his neck and gave the impression that he is totally relaxed. After a few seconds he removes his small reading glasses and said, "Joe let me tell you what I can do and what I can't do. First of all, it will be your responsibility to create a workable platform that will not only capture the interest of the people but motivate them to vote for you.

I will build upon the ideas you develop and, of course, help with the promotion which includes television, radio, internet, and the print media.

My primary objective is to do everything in my power to help you, and this party, gain a significant voice in Washington. Joe, you are the center piece, every thing we do will depend upon how well we promote you and how you conduct yourself in the countless interviews and public appearances that will be required.

I am personally sick and tired of the attack and smear campaigns that have been conducted in the past and sincerely hope you will simply state our position as clearly and concisely as possible and let the voters draw their own conclusions." Tony puts his glasses back on and glances at his notes. Any questions so far Joe?" Tony asked with some anticipation.

Joe was carefully observing Tony and in spite of the oversized blue jeans, flip flops, and baggy Harvard sweat shirt he concludes that he likes him. "No, I'm good for now. Please continue."

Tony said, "For the next six months it will be my job to handle your public debut. As you know, you have been very successful protecting your privacy for many years and that will change dramatically in the future.

I will coordinate press releases, interviews with business magazines, newspapers, and television and radio. Joe, initially our objective is to gradually introduce you to America in a non political manner with the sole purpose of increasing your name recognition."

John said with a big smile on his face, "Joe it appears to me that being non political should be easy for you. You have had a lot of years of practice."

Joe laughs and says, "Very funny. Tony, I apologize for that rude interruption. Please continue."

Tony continues, "Joe we want to keep you under the political radar as long as possible but in this business it is hard to keep secrets. Tom and I will be busy organizing state chairmen for the Restoration Party and approaching house members who we feel might be receptive to a new direction.

Our judgment is pretty good in this area and no matter what precautions we take word will leak out. Frankly, I would expect the rumors to begin within two months and you will be asked about it and I am confident you will handle it in a manner that is comfortable to you. The press will become our friend and if my guess is correct it will be the biggest story of the year and perhaps of the century."

John interjected, "Tony will also coordinate media appearance for Lee, Adam, and Robbie if you think that would be okay."

Joe said, "I believe they will support our efforts completely."

Tony takes a sip from his bottle of water and stands up and paces for a few seconds with his flip flops marking each step and continues, "In order to come up with an attractive platform that will unify Americans, I want you to assume that you will be President and you must have solutions to the problems we face.

The public isn't interested in rhetoric; in the past, politicians tell them what they are going to do but never how they will do it. I am hopeful you can do both in a convincing and believable manner. In my opinion, the public deserves the truth and if it turns out that they prefer lies then that's just the way it is. It is their country."

As Joe listens to Tony he finds himself agreeing with most of what he is saying. He also has to fight his natural urge to be resistant. Joe is sitting backwards in one of the dining room chairs with his arms folded across the top on the back rest and glances at John who is relaxing on the couch.

John picks up where Tony leaves off, "I know you detest politics but we will turn that into a positive. The public has lost respect for politicians and they don't trust them. You are an intelligent, articulate, and patriotic businessman who knows how to get things done. In this case the voters are like stock holders attending an annual meeting and you must convince them that their stock is not only valuable but it is about to go through the roof. We want the public to buy stock in Joe Winston and the restoration of America."

Joe considers John's comments and it appears they are waiting for him to speak, "Let me give some insight to my thinking. If we proceed I intend to approach this as if I am going to buy the Federal government and we will do due diligence that will be extremely intense.

If we don't believe we can turn it into a profitable and productive entity I will not continue. I will promise you this, I understand the challenges our country faces and I realize that changes must be made and must be made quickly. I will do my best but I want to be absolutely sure we have a chance."

He pauses and makes eye contact with each man before continuing, "It will be imperative that our party consists of individuals with the highest moral and ethical standards. I will not work with people who can't believe in our objectives. They must be dedicated to our cause. If they cannot be passionate about the survival of our country we simply do not need them. Will you promise me that?"

John and Tony looked at each other and both men smiled. Tony said, "We are in agreement Joe and I hope there are enough honest people left in this country to help us."

The men all stand up as John suggests coffee and they walk to the kitchen. As Joe is pouring a cup Tony said, "Joe I have a pet peeve that I need to share with you. You know how complex our laws have become for business, taxes, environmental issues, or any thing else. Why do you think that is?

Joe is looking thoughtfully at Tony as he sipped his coffee. He placed the cup on the kitchen counter and said, "I have some thoughts in that area but I would like to hear about your pet peeve."

Tony smiles and said, "It is really quite simple. I hate frigging lawyers. We have 435 elected Congressmen and 100 Senators to represent the people. Ideally, these people should come from all walks of life to be truly representative. Well two hundred and twenty eight members currently hold law degrees and another two hundred and fourteen were formerly lawyers. That's 83%......... I would suggest that it benefits their profession to make government and the laws that govern citizens as complex and convoluted as possible and they have definitely succeeded.

If you look back a few decades you will notice that the only profession that thrives no matter what the economy is doing is the legal profession. It isn't by chance that these greedy bastards never have a downturn in business and that is my pet peeve."

Joe notices that Tony's face reddens quite a bit when he spoke of attorneys and it is clear to Joe that Tony does hate lawyers...

Joe said, "Can't argue with there Tony....There is some other conditions. If I do this I will rely heavily on you guys but I will be the one making decisions and once I make a decision it becomes ours. If you are not okay with that tell me now."

John speaks first, "I agree completely. It is your leadership that is needed.

Tony looks at Joe with pride and a new sense of commitment and said, "Joe you are just what this country needs and I am proud to be working for you." He uncharacteristically hugs Joe.

As Joe drives home he knew that this commitment would forever alter the peace and tranquility he has enjoyed for the past 35 years in business. He would miss it, but deep down inside this challenge triggered a new and more meaningful purpose in his life. He has no doubts that he must do this.

CHAPTER 16

Securone's pilot filed his flight plan to Houston, Texas and the G4 lifted off at 7:00 am and three hours later they touched down at Ellington Field in Houston and secured the plane. The three man team picked up their luggage and supplies and loaded them in the white Lincoln Navigator waiting for them.

Charlie climbs behind the wheel and adjusts the seats while Buck takes the back seat. After confirming every thing they need is in the rear storage area he gets in the front passenger seat and motions for Charlie to proceed.

Charlie pulls out the dossier of Fahid Mohammed Al-Adel and reviews it for the fifth time. Charlie punches the address of the Masjid of Al-Islam Mosque on Belfort Road into the GPS and exits the airport.

Bert said, "Man, this is unbelievable. There are over two thousand Mosques in the United States. All these religions are growing like gangbusters and our kids can't even pray in school. What the hell is wrong with that picture?"

Buck replies, "How many Muslims?"

Bert flips the page and says, "Only seven million B.A."

"Holy shit; If most estimates are correct that would suggest that over seventy thousand of them are radical Islamists" Buck exclaims.

Charlie lit up a cigar in the back seat and said, "It would appear that our freedom of religion could result in the end religion. It's ironic that our compelling desire to protect freedom could actually destroy freedom."

Buck angrily says, "Dumb ass fucking politicians. What in the hell happened to righteous leadership?

Bert said, "Jesus Christ! Charlie, are you trying to kill us with that second hand smoke?"

Charlie laughs and blows a thick cloud of smoke toward Bert and said, "Are you shitting me. I have seen people try to kill you with bullets, bombs, and knives so I don't think second hand smoke will be how you meet your Maker...you want a cigar?"

Bert says with mock agitation, "No I don't want a cigar and roll down your frigging window you pain in the ass."

The men ride in silence through some of the seedier areas of Houston following the GPS directions for the next fifteen minutes as each man retreated to his thoughts.

Charlie makes a right turn as directed by the ladies voice and said, "Two blocks on the left."

Bert said, "Charlie, drive slowly by the Mosque and the imam's house and let's get the lay of the land. Let's cover about six blocks every way."

"You got it." Charlie replies.

As they slowly pass by the Mosque and adjoining home Buck takes dozens of pictures with his powerful camera. The grounds and the building are well maintained but fairly non-descript. They familiarize themselves with the low income neighborhood and are preparing to introduce themselves to Fahid later that night.

After two trips around the perimeter Bert said, "Okay Charlie, let's go see Jack."

They drive to the Secureone office in Houston, near the Bush Intercontinental Airport, where they met with another old buddy, Jack Elliot.

Jack is also a former SEAL who was born and raised in Houston. He was once their instructor, in BUD/S school in the Naval Special Warfare Training center located in Coronado, Ca and was partially informed of their requirements. Jack isn't dumb and he knew this was not a company project and smart enough to not ask questions.

They walk into the Securone office where they are greeted by Jack, "Jesus Christ, don't tell me I have you three ass holes back." They all laughed and exchanged greetings.

Bert said, "Hey Sarge, how about taking your old buddies to lunch."

Jack said, "My pleasure."

After the men enjoy a good lunch and told old war stories Bert said, "Jack let's check out the building we discussed."

"Let's go." Jack replies.

They drove east away from Bush Airport and at the intersection of Will Clayton Parkway and Mesa Drive Jack said, "Pull over there Charlie."

The old two story warehouse building owned by Securone is in the advanced stage of disrepair but it is still secure and has a basement that would offer them the privacy they would require. After walking the building and surveying the area, Jack threw Bert the keys and they walked inside.

There are no other buildings within a couple of blocks and there is very little traffic in the area. It is located in a high crime area where people who live there tend to mind their own business and others avoid the neighborhood.

They drove Jack back to his office, "Thanks for your help Jack. We will touch base before we leave."

"How long do you expect to stay in town?" Jack said.

"Two or three days." Bert replied.

Jack said, "Good luck boys and if you need me just give me a call."

Buck said, "Thanks Jack. Take care of yourself."

They checked into a hotel and got some shut eye. At 9:00 pm they left the hotel and ate some chicken fried steak at Harmons. When they finished their generous meals they head back toward the Mosque.

They know that Fahid lives alone in a modest three bedroom home that is next door to the Mosque. At 1:00 am, Bert, Charlie, and Buck enter the home through the kitchen door that Bert picks within thirty seconds.

There is a night light in the kitchen that allows the men clear vision. The could see a small Formica table in the center of the dingy kitchen surrounded by four chairs and the rest of the room is a simple kitchen with refrigerator, stove, sink, and what appears to be about three days of dirty dishes in the sink.

The home smells musky with a hint of curry.

They quietly pass through the kitchen and down a narrow hall and on the right is a dining room and on the left is the great room. Just past the dining room is a small office and the front door faces the stairs leading up to the bedrooms where they expect to find Fahid.

As they carefully walk up the stairs Bert signals for Charlie to ready the syringe loaded with 30 mg. of Etomidate.

The master bedroom is at the end of the small upstairs hall and they could hear Fahid snoring. Buck and Charlie approach the bed and Buck clamps his strong hand over Fahid's mouth as Fahid's eyes grew wide with surprise and terror. Charlie stabbed him in the neck with the needle and Fahid is back to sleep as quickly as he was awakened.

After binding the man's arms and legs and taping his mouth, Charlie threw the man over his shoulder and carries him to the Navigator and roughly threw the man in the back.

Bert and Buck collect his computer, cell phone, and throw all potentially informative files into a trash bag. Once they complete putting the items in the Navigator they leave Charlie as a look out and enter the garage of the Mosque.

Once inside the garage they moved the tool chest that Imaad told them about and proceed down the stairs. They turn on the lights and begin to explore the rooms for more valuable information. There is little to be found in the apartment section but as they proceeded down the hall and opened the door at the end of the hall they are stunned by what they see.

Inside the large room, that is forty by twenty, they see racks of AK-47's, sniper rifles, dozens of hand guns and automatic weapons, one hundred pounds of C4, detonators, and four RPG's with twenty four rounds One of these could bring down a large passenger jet.

Buck said, "God damn Bert this is some serious fire power"

Bert, taking mental inventory, says, "You got that right". He sees five large crates of ammunition, a box of at least fifty pre-paid cell phones, and a safe.

In the corner they also find a file cabinet filled with various shipping invoices and records. They fill two garbage bags with the files and a small Sony laptop computer that sat on a small table.

Bert knew they could not remove all the weaponry and ammunition and had to decide what to do about it. He turns to Buck and said, " Bad Ass, what in the hell are we going to do with this shit?"

"Well buddy, we can't leave it and we sure as hell can't take it?" Buck replies.

Bert paces back and forth for a few minutes as Buck continues to look around. Buck sees a new sub-compact 9mm Beretta Storm that is hard to get, he figures, what the hell and puts it in his pocket.

Bert said, "Hey Buck, our politicians believe in giving these bastards freedom of religion and they don't understand they are using these Mosques to arm terrorist. Why don't we leave the trap door open and start a fire in the garage and call the fire department on one of these cell phones. When they come to put out the fire and investigate they will find this shit and that ought to open their eyes. What do you think?"

Buck looks at Bert and smiles, "I like it. That's why you make the big bucks."

They pick up a cell phone that has a signal, carry the trash bags up the stairs, and put them down in the garage. Buck notices pro Islamist pamphlets and Korans on the other side of the garage and said, "How about let's start the fire over there by the window with that paper shit?"

Bert smiles and says, "Do it. I will call the fire department."

Buck starts the fire and when it reaches the window, Bert dials 911 and reports seeing a fire and gives them the address and hangs up.

They grab the garbage bags and head to the Navigator, throw the bags in the back, and get in the car. Charlie starts the car as he looks around and asked, "What the hell is going on… there's a fire in there?

Bert looks at him and ignores the question and said, "Charlie, move down a couple of blocks and wait a minute."

Charley pulls the Navigator away from the curb, checks the area, drives down three blocks, and parks as he hears the sirens of the approaching fire trucks.

They watched as the firemen enter the Mosque with hoses spurting a powerful flow of water. Bert tells Charlie to head to the safe house.

They fill Charlie in and he said, "No shit. I can't wait to see this hit the papers and the shit storm this will cause."

Bert said, "Don't count on seeing this in the papers. If I know my politicians, this won't make the news. They know the public will react negatively and hold them responsible. That will impact votes and re-elections. They will bury this story if they can."

They drive in silence, mentally preparing for a long night.

CHAPTER 17

Joe Winston calls Adam Fields, as he frequently does. After several minutes of small talk Joe asks, "Adam what are your thoughts on the economy?"

Adam is a brilliant businessman and his success is a direct result of his understanding of the economy and an even keener eye in analyzing and comprehending a company's balance sheet. Joe considers Adam a financial genius and his knowledge of the financial markets has benefited his friends and clients.

Adam thoughtfully responds, "Joe to be perfectly frank I am not optimistic. Pompous politicians drunk with power, incredible government waste, failing economic solutions, energy dependence, unemployment, a ridiculous tax system, and the total absence of trust regarding elected officials. The economy could not be worse and solutions are not forth coming."

Joe laughs as he says, "Good, I feel better now."

Adam laughing along with Joe says, "Sorry Joe did you expect something else?"

Joe says, "No. How in the world did we ever get in such miserable condition?"

Adam said slowly, "Joe I think you know how. We have been heading for a financial disaster for years and we are getting very close to a complete meltdown. The question is can they fix it?"

"Can they?" Joe asks

Adam replies, "There is no evidence to suggest they can fix anything Joe.

Adam Field's and Joe Winston have been friends since college. Adam is the CEO of Fields Financial which is considered the most prominent brokerage firm in America. Twenty five years ago Joe Winston reviewed Adam's business plan for Fields Financial and immediately agreed to finance Adam. Once again, Joe's judgment was excellent as indicated by the business success Adam enjoyed.

Adam is of African-American descent, happily married with two children and two grandchildren. He could easily be mistaken for a professional basketball player at a lean six foot six with short black hair and long arms. His intellect, sense of humor, and commitment to excellence made him easy to like

He resides in a three story mansion that occupies an entire block on the Atlantic Ocean in North Palm Beach, Florida. The home is stucco and the outside is white with pale yellow accents. The windows are all tinted to diminish the heat created by the rising morning sun. The lower level features an elevated and beautiful wrap around porch to maximize enjoyment of the cool evenings, when the sun has passed.

On the second floor there is a large balcony outside the master bedroom with two large French doors that lead from the bedroom to the forty foot balcony that extends fifteen feet to the east. To the north and south of the master bedroom are two other private balconies servicing two other large bedrooms.

Joe said, "Adam, you know we have avoided the press and politicians like the plague. Given the current circumstances do you think we should be more involved and more outspoken?"

Adam is surprised by the question, "No Joe I don't think we were wrong. The press and politicians can't be trusted and I think we have said a lot by not saying a lot."

Joe hesitated, "I agree Adam but if we agree our country is on the brink of disaster don't you sometimes feel a compulsion to become involved and try to help?"

"Joe, I am more than willing to help but to be honest with you no body really wants to listen to solutions. Besides that Joe, we help quite a bit. We provide many jobs, pay a lot of taxes, and provide meaningful services." Adam responds.

Joe said, "Adam I am beginning to have second thoughts about not being involved. We might be able to have an impact."

Adam said, "I know why you feel this way Joe but I don't see any way we can help. Politicians don't want advice they only want money."

"Well, lets talk about it some more at Volusia. See you there Adam." Joe said as the men conclude their conversation.

Adam is in his office/library that occupies a thousand square feet in the south east corner of his home which also affords an unobstructed view of the ocean. His office provides him with access to anything he could want.

The west side wall is lined with book shelves rising fifteen feet to the ceiling. On the south wall there is a fifty inch Sony flat screen television with two 32" monitors on either side to allow him to simultaneously watch five separate channels.

He is sitting in an overstuffed chair in the sitting area opposite his desk and he couldn't get Joe's call out of his mind. It was unusual for Joe to even discuss politics. Adam had the feeling that something is going on.

CHAPTER 18

Fire Chief Emmet Peele arrives at the Masjid of Al-Islam Mosque on Belfort Road as the boys from Firehouse 26 are busy containing the small fire in the garage. He observes there is very little fire damage but the smoke is pretty thick.

Captain Jeff Odom walk over to the Chief and said, "Not much too it Chief. Looks like some books caught fire and it didn't have a chance to do much damage before we got here."

"Who reported the fire?" The Chief asks.

"Don't know Chief. We received an anonymous call at 1:31 am and we were here at 1:37 am."

Odom said, "Looks like the smoke is clearing out, want to go in and take a look around?"

The Chief looks at his watch and says, "What the hell, I'm already up."

The two men walk into the garage and start poking around to see if they could locate the origin of the fire when the Captain looks over at the other side of the garage and notices the trap door.

He points to it and he and the Chief walk over to inspect. The Captain descends the steps lighting the way with his flashlight until he finds the light switch and flips it on. There is some smoke in the apartment area but otherwise it looks undamaged.

The Chief looks down the hall and said with disinterest, "Peele, go check out those rooms down the hall."

"Yes sir." The Captain opens the door at the end of the hall, finds the light switch, turns on the lights, and looks around the room and exclaims, "Holy shit! Chief, you better take a look at this."

The Chief walks down the hall and into the room. His mouth falls open as he stares in disbelieve before saying, "Captain, call Police Chief Roberts and tell him to get his ass down here."

Chief Roberts arrives at 3:20 am with his driver. After they saw the room filled with weapons he notifies the FBI. Prior to sunrise, the mosque is crawling with Feds, local police, and Homeland Security. All present are instructed not to discuss this issue.

CHAPTER 19

Volusia National Golf Club is located in the north east corner of Volusia County in Florida between Flagler Beach and Ormond Beach. The property covers four hundred acres and Six hundred yards of the golf course offers views of the Atlantic Ocean.

When they chose the location for the course they negotiated with the state of Florida to re-route A1A for a substantial monetary incentive.

The club opened for play on May 12, 2002 and there were only four official members, Joe Winston, Robbie Ravenel, Adam Fields, and Lee Roth. Volusia National boasts a Championship golf course designed by Robert Jones and the clubhouse and guest cottages complimented their intentions to protect the natural environment. The four men are equal owners and they enjoyed every minute on the property.

In 2004 they decided to award memberships to outstanding Americans who have demonstrated exceptional courage or risen above tremendous obstacles to benefit and inspire other Americans. They select anywhere from five to ten new members annually and these members, and their families, are entitled to two weeks a year at Volusia National at no cost.

There are now twenty three such honorary members. Six were chosen as a result of uncommon bravery in the military, four are fireman, three are police officers, four are teachers, and seven are citizens who risk their lives to save others. Five more were awarded to individuals who significantly impacted charitable organizations that benefits society.

Each October, they hosted a charity golf event that provides one thousand full college scholarships annually to students who have excelled academically and whose families may be financially handicapped. Only ninety six invitations are extended to the tournament and it is extremely rare for one of the invitees to decline. On the other hand, there are thousands who would pay far more than the $25,000 entry fee for an invitation.

The invitees are mostly wealthy but their genuine concern and contributions to the betterment of America, is the primary reason they are included on the guest list. As far as charity golf tournaments, the Volusia National "Future of America" is by far the most prestigious and exclusive tournament in the world.

The majestic club house sits only a full pitching wedge away from the Atlantic Ocean and offers a breath taking view from the main and upper level of the twenty five thousand square foot facility. The main floor includes the main dining room, four private dining rooms, a large casual bar, locker rooms, pro shop, administrative offices, a huge foyer, billiard room, kitchen, and storage area. There are three French doors that grant entry to a wonderful porch that provides a grand view of the first, the eighteenth hole, and the practice area.

The elevated greens and rolling fairways are perhaps the best in the country and the course is exceptionally well maintained. The 7,150 yard course is much like Augusta National, not a blade of grass out of place.

The fairways are inundated with snow white bunkers and lined with live oaks, oleanders, and six varieties of Palms. If they allowed their course to be rated, it would be among the best in the world.

The entire area is accented with a wide variety of colorful plants and it would be hard to imagine a more beautiful place.

The upper level of the clubhouse consisted of four, two bedroom master suites, one for each of the owners. In addition there is a large great room centrally located where they tend to spend the late evenings.

On the west side of the club house there are four large four bedroom villas with two swimming pools. The Villas are used primarily for guest and beyond the maintenance area is a single story house that provides comfortable accommodations for the staff and for security personnel.

Adam and Joe sit in the upstairs great room watching King Abdallah of Jordon in a televised address to Islamist. The King states, "The Americans wish to teach us how to live in a democracy as they do. I am confused as to how they can possibly suggest our Muslim way of life is inferior to their democracy. Their country currently faces economic crisis and their citizens are revolting in the streets. They steal money from their citizens and legitimize their actions by calling it taxes. Their citizens cannot find jobs and the government attempts to enslave them through benefits.

In spite of the many difficulties they face in their own country they still wish to tell us how to live. If they cannot manage their own country clearly they cannot and should not try to instruct other countries as to how they should manage their government.

My brothers and sisters we shall continue to follow the teachings of Mohammed and to follow the instructions of the Koran. We will resist America's attempts and continue to serve our God. Allah Akbar!"

As the program ends Adam says, "Interesting comments."

Joe is semi prone on the couch and responds, "He does have a point."

Lee and Robbie would arrive later today and they would learn that this visit would be like no other as they would discover that the rest of their lives will be dramatically altered.

CHAPTER 20

Aziz Hassan arrives home after his visit with Majid and is determined to find out what has happened to Imaad and Rajab. He ordered his cell leaders in the Carolinas to find them before he left and impressed upon them the importance of their mission. They were able to confirm that they had checked into a hotel in Columbia, S.C. but from that point they apparently disappeared in the middle of the night. There were no signs of them or their car anywhere.

Aziz called upon all his contacts in law enforcement and no agency had arrested the men and no one knew anything of their whereabouts. Aziz is not used to failing and he intends to find out what happened to them.

His computer signals an incoming e-mail. It is an encrypted message advising him of the fire in Houston and that Fahid is missing. Aziz puts his head in his hands and wonders if the supplies were found and what had happened to Fahid? He leans back in his chair and ran his fingers through his white hair and sensed that something highly unusual is going on and he is convinced it is not the Federal government.

He closes his eyes and tries to think of other likely candidates. Could it be some new black ops strategy? Maybe it is the Israelis? Who else would have any interest in their affairs? Nothing makes any sense and his frustration grows.

Aziz has been in this business for a long time and he knows something is wrong but he could not put the pieces together. Some how these two events are related, Imaad and Rajab had spent three days with Fahid, so that is one commonality. As he thinks about it and deduces that someone identified Imaad and Rajab, captured them, and forced them to give up Fahid. This is a troublesome thought inasmuch as Fahid is one of his cell leaders and there are no more filters between Fahid and himself. The more he wrestles with the problem the more any rational solution avoids him.

He can feel the world collapsing around him and he knows he is in imminent danger. If he couldn't find out what happened to his men, Majid would most likely have him killed. He also knew that if the people who had done this found out about him, they would kill him. He took his prayer rug, fell on his knees, and begins to pray.

When Aziz completes his prayers he feels compelled to risk contacting his cell leaders. He is well aware of the sophisticated technological counter terrorism weapons in control of American intelligence agencies but he has successfully avoided detection for many years and feels relatively safe with his encrypted method of communication.

Aziz and his cell leaders have many pre-paid cell phone they would only use only once. One phone is used exclusively to receive calls from Aziz and if he said "go" they are to access a web site, www.boingboing. net , for a message.

Aziz has a relatively simple but effective encryption method. The web site had four major categories and thirty one sub categories. The first number would refer to the major category and the second number would refer to the sub category. The numbers that followed would indicate the word in the text of the paragraph.

He decides he should warn his leaders to exercise extreme caution until the whereabouts of the missing men has been determined and to relocate all their assets from the other Mosques that had similar storage areas with weapons.

Aziz would never communicate with Majid except in person. However, they did have an emergency procedure. He was to call King Abdallah's aid, Karim Abdul Mohammed, and he would pass the message to Majid. Aziz began to break out in a cold sweat just contemplating Majid's reaction to this new development.

For the first time in his life he felt as if he were the hunted and not the hunter.

CHAPTER 21

Late Tuesday afternoon Lee and Robbie had arrived and settled into their suites. At 5:00 pm their plan was to meet in the bar.

Tom Edwards, a sixty two year old African-American, and trusted employee is the bartender and Betty Hodges is the server. Harvey Kent is their chef and these three employees always handled the wants and needs of their employers.

Lee Roth is the first to arrive and as he walked in the bar he enthusiastically said, "Hello Tom, how have you been?"

"Just fine sir, hope you are doing well and it's good to see you again." Tom replies.

Lee turns to Betty, "Betty, how are you?"

"Just fine Mr. Roth, good to have you back. What can I get for you?" Betty says with a smile on her face as usual.

"Lee scratches his chin and said, "How about an Arnold Palmer Betty."

"Yes Sir Mr. Roth, I know, 2/3's lemonade and 1/3 tea." She replied as she headed to the bar.

Robbie enters five minutes later and he walks up behind Lee who is sitting at the bar and grabs him from behind in a big old bear hug and said, "What's up Geek?"

Lee pokes him in the ribs with his elbow and Robbie releases him, Lee turns around and hugs Robbie and affectionately said, "Good to see you Robbie." Then Lee put his hands on each side of Robbie's face and looks straight in his eyes and said, "I am so sorry about Tommy. I wish I could make the pain go away."

Robbie patted Lee on the shoulder and said, "Thanks Buddy."

Robbie turns to Betty and Tom as he wipes his eyes with the back of his hand and said, "Hey Tom. How are you Betty? I will have a Bombay Safire and tonic with a twist of lime?"

Betty, with her perennial, smile said, "Coming right up Mr. Ravenel!"

Joe and Adam enter the room and they all exchange greetings and hugs and ask about families. After about an hour of small talk they move to the east porch.

The sun has long since passed behind them, so the porch is cool and comfortable. The view of the green golf course, the gentle roll of the waves on the ocean, and a clear blue cloudless sky could make a man forget about his troubles.

If someone didn't know them, and observed their conversation, they would have thought them to be just another group of golfers enjoying cocktails after a round of golf. They would have no way of knowing this really was a "Forcesome" and their conversations over the next few days would shape America's future.

Joe shares with the men his conversation with John and Tony and asks for their support. His friends are stunned by this announcement but as they recover from the initial shock they pledged their enthusiastic support and immense satisfaction.

Betty had just served them two bottles of Silver Oak and filled their glasses. Once she completed her task, she knew to leave them alone.

Robbie gently swirls the liquid around, sniffs the aroma, and takes a sip and holds it in his mouth to savor the flavor. This is a normal ritual for the men and Robbie is their self appointed official taster. Robbie proclaims the wine to be excellent and proposed a toast.

He raised his glass and the others raised their glass, "To our good friend and the 45th President of the United States." Each man taps his glass with the other and they all congratulate Joe.

Lee watched Robbie go through his ritual and lifts his diet coke, swirled it, sniffs the aroma, takes a sip and pauses briefly before pronouncing it an excellent 2009 vintage and everyone laughs. These men thoroughly enjoy each other's company.

They sit around the large round table in four comfortable padded chairs and everyone senses it is time for a little serious conversation. It is their first indication that their trips to Volusia National would never be the same.

Adam said, "Joe, our country is in bad shape and frankly I was resigned to the fact that it would just be a matter of time. I have a little hope now because I know if anybody can do it, you can."

Joe said, "You mean we can do it."

Robbie said, "Joe you have our support and we will work our ass off for you and if it can be fixed it will be fixed."

He pauses and the men could see something is troubling him. Robbie looks up and said, "Boys, I need to share something with you." He hesitates and put his head in his hands and exhaled loudly.

Adam is troubled by Robbie's obvious nervousness and asked, "Robbie, it can't be that bad. What is it?"

Robbie takes a large swallow of the fine wine and looks each one of them in the eye before continuing, he begins slowly and has everyone's attention. "My company provides security for Bank of America. After the tragedy Bert immediately went to the security cameras and located the killers."

Lee said, "That's great Robbie. Have they been arrested yet?"

Robbie looked a little sheepish and said, "No. I decided to handle it myself."

The men look at Robbie with surprise and Joe asks, "Robbie what do you mean you are going to handle it yourself?"

Robbie looks at Joe and said, "If we turned them over to the authorities this shit will drag out forever and we all know our intelligence agencies would never be able to extract information from them that might lead to people who ordered the attack.

I just couldn't sit by and watch these smug bastards become infamous and see them brag about the innocent people they have killed. I'm sorry guys but this shit has got to stop sometime and the politicians have hamstrung our intelligence services. I had no other reasonable option."

Lee is moved by Robbie's comments and finds himself agreeing with his logic, "Robbie how did you handle it?"

Robbie stands up and walks to the rail and looks out toward the ocean before coming back to the table where they are anxiously awaiting his response, "I sent three of my best men, ex SEALS, after them before the Feds could get to them. They were interrogated and after getting as much information as possible we executed the miserable bastards."

Suddenly it seemed as if the birds stopped chirping and the roar of the ocean stopped as they looked at Robbie in shock and disbelief. No one knew what to say. There is a long silence as the men tried to digest what they have just heard.

Robbie understands that his statement would cause this initial shock finally continues, "As unbelievable as it sounds I am convinced I did the right thing. We have good solid information that I believe can lead us to the people who issued the orders and perhaps we can follow the chain all the way to the top. I have a team in Houston, Texas to pick up the man who equipped the terrorist who hit Charlotte. We will interrogate him and see where it leads."

None of the men spoke, as they are still trying to digest this disturbing information.

Robbie pauses and looks down at his wine glass and then raises his eyes to meet his friend's eyes, "I have no regrets and it is my intention to follow the chain of command as high as possible and to do whatever is necessary to rid the world of these cold blooded bastards. I can't keep this from you. You guys are closer to me than anyone and I don't want to do anything to jeopardize your lives but I thought you needed to know."

A slow minute crawled by and finally Adam said, "Robbie, we know you pretty good and I'm sure this wasn't just revenge, was it?"

Robbie looks around the table at his friends and reluctantly, but honestly, says, "Yes, partly it was, Adam. It is also about the changes that have occurred in our country since the terrorists crashed those planes into the World Trade Center. We are losing our country Adam and something has to be done to stop it. I realize this is a big risk on my part but it is chance I must take."

Joe with a thoughtful but neutral look on his face said, "Robbie, how many radical Islamist do we think there are in America?"

Robbie said, "Between twenty and seventy thousand."

Lee said, "You have to be kidding!"

Robbie replies, "Lee, I believe seventy thousand to be conservative but hopefully over the next few months we will find out a lot more."

Robbie spoke, "I don't regret what I have done but with Joe's news I don't want anything to reflect negatively on his campaign. I couldn't live with myself if I didn't tell you and none of you should be involved. This is my fight and I am committed to it."

Joe considers Robbie's words and the relationship that exists among friends for a minute and finally said, "Robbie, the four of us have been through a lot together and thanks to your friendship I have never felt alone. The way I look at it four heads might be better than that one ugly head that sits on your shoulders."

The men laughed and Lee said, "I want to help Robbie. I believe my skills and knowledge of cyber space and technology can be a big help. By the way, I have a little secret since we are sharing. My hobby is penetrating impenetrable computers without leaving a trail and I am pretty damn good at it. You would be surprised at what I have access too."

Adam said, "What a hell of a night. Robbie's killing terrorists, Lee's hacking into top secret computers, and Joe's running for President of the United States. I don't have any confessions boys, but I'm with you."

Robbie looked up at his friends with his glassy eyes and a single tear rolls slowly down his left cheek and his lips quivered slightly. Lee is the first to hug him followed by Adam and Joe.

CHAPTER 22

President Howard is sitting in the Oval office and has just received a debriefing of the Charlotte attack from FBI Director Hansen. Also present are Director of National Intelligence (DNI) Steve Settles, Harry Belk, the Secretary of State, the director of counter terrorist's activities, and another half dozen staffers.

Hansen is concerned with what will be the conclusion of his report and trying to spin it as best he could. After all that is the way it works in Washington, "Mr. President, we were able to identify the two men who perpetrated the attack in Charlotte from various video surveillance cameras. However, they seem to have simply disappeared after they left range of the Bank of America building and the uptown cameras."

President Howard said, "When you said "identify" does that mean you have names and backgrounds?"

Hansen happily answers, "Yes sir. Utilizing our facial recognition system we determined they are Middle Eastern and both are on the "known terrorists" list. They apparently entered the country illegally and all their identification papers were forged. Their names are Rajab Awda and Imaad Yasin who are both Jordanians.

Once we had this information we blocked off a two hundred mile radius and implemented hard coverage for buses, air lines, and trains. Either they slipped out of the area or they are still within the perimeter."

The President asks, "How were you able to identify these men?"

Hansen replied, "First on the Bank of America surveillance cameras."

"How long did it take after the incident?" Howard asks.

It seems as if everyone in the room squirms a little bit and Hansen turned a little pale as he answers, "It was around 6:30 pm."

The President's mouth fell open and he appears to be stunned with Hansen's answer. He composes himself as best he could and asks calmly, "If my math is correct that is approximately six or seven hours after the event. Is that correct?"

"Yes Sir." Hansen replies.

"Could you explain to me why it took that long?" President Howard asks with more than a little bit of sarcasam.

Hansen is not happy with the direction of the questions and his heart rate is a little elevated and his pride is a little diminished as he tries to explain, "Sir we were dealing with a lot of chaos that afternoon and we had to clear the area as best we could in the event other explosive devices existed.

At about 4 pm two vendors who worked the courtyard at lunch time were found in their small rental space and their throats had been cut. We immediately went to the surveillance tapes and picked up the two perpetrators pushing the dead men's cart to the courtyard. By 6:30 pm we had an APB out on them."

The President is angered that his crack intelligence agencies allowed so much time to go by before reviewing the tapes but there is nothing to gain by looking back. He calmly asks, " You are sure they committed this heinous act.".

"Yes sir. There is no doubt." Hansen replied glad to have the time issues behind him.

The President calmly jots some notes on his computer and turns to Bill Craddock and said, "Bill contact King Abdallah and impress upon him that we want these two men."

Bill made a note and replies, "Yes sir."

"Since it has been ten days it appears they are gone. Would you agree? President Howard said as he stares at Hansen with a look that shows his frustration and contempt.

Hansen said, "I would agree Mr. President."

"Alright is there anything else we need to discuss?" President Howard asks with the anticipation that he had heard enough bad news for one day.

Rich squirms in his chair and beads of perspiration appears on his upper lip as he says, "Last night in Houston a fire was reported in a Mosque. The fire department responded quickly and extinguished the fire.

The fire Chief and a Captain were on site and they were checking to be sure the fire was out when they discovered an open trap door that led to a basement. They discovered over one hundred pounds of explosives, some fifty Ak-47 rifles, twelve sniper rifles, four RPG's with twenty four rounds, and dozens of handguns…."

The President bolts out of his chair and angrily said, "In a damned Mosque? For Christ sakes do you suppose this is standard equipment for every Mosque? What the hell is wrong with those people?"

He pauses and sits back down and said, "Go on Hansen."

Hansen said, "Thank you Mr. President, the fire department notified their Chief of Police who notified the FBI. The agent in charge is Andy Johnson and he is handling the investigation with Deputy Director of Homeland Security Elliot Purser.

It also appears that the resident imam, who lived next door, has also disappeared. It seems his computer and many files were also taken. Everyone at the scene was advised to keep their mouths shut until we decide how to handle this."

President Howard enters more notes in his computer and said to both men, "So we have three probable terrorist missing, a supply of weapons in Mosque, and no clues. Is that about it?

All Hansen could do is nod and say, "Yes sir."

The President shook his head with some disgust and said, "OK, what's our next move?

Rick and Harry look at each other and finally Harry said, "Mr. President, I would suggest we expand this meeting to include Secretary Elliot of DOD, Attorney General Robbins, and Rick should invite the best minds available from the intelligence area. This could have serious repercussions domestically, internationally, and politically."

As he typed notes in his computer he said, "Put it together. They can brainstorm this weekend and come up with recommendations and we will all meet next week. This is a high priority; treat it as a national security issue and gentlemen I would like some answers pretty damn quick."

As the intelligence men left the office they are relieved it was over but committed to finding some answers. At this point they had no clue what in the hell was going on. Who could possibly be one step ahead of them?

The President finishes typing, closes his computer, and bangs his fist on his desk. "What next!"

CHAPTER 23

Bert decided to let Fahid cool his heels in the basement for awhile before they started their interrogation. They reviewed all the data they could find regarding Fahid and there is very little useful information. They had downloaded his hard drive to Nick Bernstein, who is Securone's computer genius.

Nick received his masters from MIT in computer science and is simply one of those gifted people in the technology arena. He was booted out of the military for hacking into the CIA's computer system in an attempt to learn what intelligence they possessed that might impact his unit in Iraq. The dishonorable discharge prevented him from gainful employment until Bert Bradford heard about him from an old buddy which eventually led to him being hired by Robbie.

Nick is thirty five years old and looks exactly the way you would expect a computer geek to look. Tall and thin with long black hair. Of course he wears glasses and dresses a little bit south of casual and loves everything about computers and programming. Nick has been with Secureone for five years and is one of their most valuable employees.

At 10:00 pm on Wednesday, April 15th. Bert, Charlie, and Bad Ass unlocked the basement door and enter the damp dark room where Fahid has been strapped to a chair with a hood on his head for about twenty hours.

Fahid heard someone enter and in a panicked voice spoke with fear in his voice as he said "who is there?"

A man walks over to Fahid and pulls off the hood. Fahid squinted as his eyes tried to adjust to the light as the man said, "Hello sunshine, my name is Bert and these guys are Buck and Charlie. How are you doing tonight?"

Fahid looked at the three large men trying to understand what they want and asks, "What do you want?"

Bert turns up his nose as he looks at the puddle in the floor and smells the waste and said, "My goodness, Fahid, do all you radical Muslims shit and piss in your pants?"

Fahid's scared little beady eyes dart back and forth as he whined and tried to sound forceful, "I insist you release me. You have no right to do this to me."

Bert looks at him with contempt and put his face one inch away and yells, "Rights! What gives you the right to murder innocent American people you sack of shit?"

"I don't know what you are talking about." Fahid fearfully lied.

Bert slaps him hard on the left side of his face and backhands him on the right side and snarls at him, "You lying son of a bitch. Imaad and Rajab told me all about your operation."

Fahids eyes widen and he grows more fearful, "I don't know.... any such... men you hav......."

Bert pounds his elbow into the left side of Fahids temple and blood gushes from the four inch gash as Bert says, "I hate a god damned liar. All you smelly rag heads are liars. If you lie to me one more time I am going to start cutting pieces of your body off. Do you understand me?"

Bert knows that this man would break easy he is an inside man, much like a politician, and he never gets his hands dirty. He stares at Fahid who is confused, bleeding, and scared. Just the way Bert wants him.

Bert knows that men like him are very good at convincing young people to become martyrs but they would never consider doing it themselves. Men like Fahid are despicable.

Fahid had never dreamed he would get caught but he is an American citizen and he has rights. He thought who are these men? They can't do this? His fear escalated as he avoids looking at Bert.

Bert turns and looks at Buck. Bad Ass walks up to the chair that Fahid is strapped in and places his medical kit down on the dirty floor at Fahid's feet and opened the satchel. Fahid looked at the shiny scalpels, knives, syringes, and other instruments and his heart is racing as he perspired profusely.

He looks around the room for an exit and saw but the one door. He wonders if he cries for help would anyone hear him. His thoughts are interrupted by Bert who coldly said, "Cut off his right ear."

Fahid looks incredulously at Bert as if he misunderstood what he said. Buck slowly picks up the scalpel and examines it. Fahid trembles as Buck slowly put the scalpel back and pulls out his survival knife. Fahid cries out, "Please, please don't........."

Before he could finish Buck walks behind him and roughly cuts his right ear off.

Fahid screams in agony as blood runs down the right side of his neck and under his shirt. Buck walks back in front of Fahid with the ear in his gloved hand. With a big smile he shows it to him then stuffs it in Fahid's mouth.

Fahid gags and spat out his own ear and vomited. When he finishes throwing up he begs, "No. No. Please no more."

Bert looks at his watch and is pleased to see it isn't even midnight and thought, We are way ahead of schedule, that's good.

For the next two hours Buck and Charlie got as much information as they could. Fahid gave up forty one terrorist that are in his cell but it took his other ear to make him give up Aziz Hassan.

Bert knew that Hassan was big. This could be the mother load. If Fahid is right he is the top guy in the United States.

CHAPTER 24

Bert calls Robbie at 6:00 am and reports that their Houston trip was very successful.

Robbie, Joe, Adam, and Lee are having breakfast when Robbie joins them and informs the group of what he had learned.

Adam said, "what can you do now Robbie to continue up the food chain?'

Robbie looks around and spoke softly, "I am dispatching a three man team to Chicago to set up 24/7 surveillance. We can try to penetrate his computer, bug his home, his phones and see where it goes. If he is the top dog he will be on high alert and I would expect him to have excellent security based on his time in this country."

Lee interjects with his usual enthusiasm, "Robbie, maybe I can help. I have some interesting gizmos that just might be helpful and I have been dying to try them out. I think I can get into this spy shit."

Robbie laughs and replies, "Thanks Lee. I will be most appreciative of any help you can give us. You remember Nick Bernstein in my office, don't you?"

"Yeah, that kid has some serious talent, why?" Lee said.

"I was hoping the two of you could work together and see what you can come up with, if you don't mind." Robbie suggests.

Lee smiles, "That would be great I love showing off to someone who is smart enough to understand it."

Joe is smiling and says, "Sounds like we have a plan. What about the forty one guys under the direction of the Houston guy?"

Robbie says, "My guys are digging up everything they can on those guys and we will eventually get to them. Our primary target will be Aziz and if he isn't the top guy we will keep on climbing."

Adam said, "I know we all have, so called, secure phones but we really need to be careful with our communications, what do you suggest Robbie?"

Robbie said, "My recommendation would be no phone, computer, fax, smoke signals, or any other method be used. Only face to face. We have the best security possible here at Volusia National. If we need to talk we do it here."

There are many serious issues to be discussed but their trip has already been more intense then they could have possibly imagined. They are here to relax and have a little fun. Joe said, "Okay boys, we have had enough serious stuff, let's go play golf and enjoy the rest of our trip?"

Lee decides he would set the teams and said, "Joe and I will play Adam and his chubby friend."

"Hey slim, watch who you call chubby. Adam and I will be more than happy to whip you two turkeys." Robbie said.

As Joe walks to the first tee his mind wanders and he thought, what the hell happened. We are chasing terrorists and I'm going to run for President of the United States.

CHAPTER 25

APRIL 22, 2009
WASHINGTON, D.C.

At precisely 10:00 am, Barker, Belk, and Osborne are meeting in the Oval Office to continue their economic discussions. "Well I hope you have some good news for me Fred, what do you have?" President Howard asked as they settled into their usual spots.

Fred removes his notes from his brief case and answers, "Mr. President, if we implement the tax proposals you have suggested the net result will be about twenty billion dollars in additional total personal income taxes.

We can also increase the payroll tax to two percent and that will generate another two hundred and fifty billion dollars. Earmarks are over fifty billion and we have an opportunity to improve in that area. I believe we can easily cut four hundred billion more from our budget which gets us close to seven hundred billion dollars.

I have discussed this with Harry and Carol and they are unwilling to cut any current Federal programs but concur with the tax increases. Without cuts we can only pick up three or four hundred billion."

Harry interjected with his usual all knowing attitude, "Mr. President the two percent might create some problems with the low income and middle class because any tax saving they would enjoy by a federal tax reduction will be eaten up by the payroll tax. The truth is I doubt they will notice.

Curtailing earmarks are a necessary tool if we are to gain support for our legistion and we have promised many political jobs that we must honor."

Carol chimes in and definitively states, "I agree with Harry. I feel we should consider raising taxes on the wealthy to 50% which could generate another four hundred billion."

The President did not like to hear conflicting opinions. He preferred his staff be in agreement before coming to him. He paces around the room for about twenty seconds and frowns to send a message that he isn't happy.

Fred's opinions are always based upon facts and he realized that figures can lie and liars can figure. He tries to drive home his point and says with a hint of sarcasm, "The taxes imposed upon us by Great Britain that caused the Revolutionary War were mild compared to what we are suggesting here.

The financial facts are pretty simple and that's the area I deal in. The political spin is outside by area of competence. The top 10% of wage earners now pay 70% of all taxes and the bottom 50% only pay 3.3%. The remaining 40% of middle class workers pay the remaining 27%. If we continue to punish the most productive citizens and reward the least productive I cannot imagine a probable positive financial outcome..."

Carol interrupts and challenges his comments, "Fred what would you suggest? Should we allow people to starve and live in the streets?"

Fred hesitates for a moment prior to responding to this tired old emotional bromide and said, "Carol those are not financial questions.

As I said I deal in the reality of financial facts. However, since you asked Carol what is thing we always refer to as the American Dream? Is it freedom and opportunity? Do we provide that? Is it the right to a good education? Do we provide that? Is it providing for the less fortunate? Don't we help them?"

"Of course we provide it but we must also continue to help to raise up our low income and middle class and we must always be willing to help them enjoy a better life. It is the right thing to do." Carol said with righteous indignation.

Fred, barely contains his contempt and says, "Please. Give me a break Carol. Do you think all the wealthy people in this country inherited their money? The top 10% of our wage earners do more than their fair share for America. Eleven million people basically subsidize two hundred and ninety million people and this government. They worked hard, they took advantage of educational opportunities, and they risked their money and created businesses and jobs."

Fred pauses for a moment and realizes that for once he isn't biting his tongue and keeping quiet. He takes a couple of deep breaths and looks at the surprised faces in the room and then continues.

"These people are the leaders of this country and deserve our gratitude. The truth is we have about fifty million people in this country who actually believe they are living the American dream. Living in public housing, Medicaid, food stamps, and simply making no attempt to improve their status in lif…."

Carol could take it no longer and blurts out, "that's the most outrage…."

Fred lost his temper, a rare occurrence for him, and it felt good as he looks at her and cut her off, "Let me finish and remind you of what your hero, Abraham Lincoln said and this is a direct quote. "You cannot help the poor by destroying the rich. You cannot strengthen the weak by weakening the strong. You cannot bring prosperity by discouraging thrift. You cannot lift the wage earner up by pulling the wage payer down. You cannot further the brotherhood of man by inciting class hatred. You cannot build character and courage by taking away peoples initiative and independence. You cannot help people permanently by doing for them, what they could and should do for themselves!"

The President is stunned by this passionate outburst by a number cruncher and Harry Belk looked at Fred with a mixture of awe and disbelief.

Fred's face grew red and as he concludes he glances down at the Presidential Seal at his feet and thought his career in government might be coming to an end. Nevertheless he would no longer sit by and watch politicians destroy his country.

He looks up and glances at the President, Harry, and then Carol as he said, "Carol if we don't learn from the past we are doomed to repeat it. American's simply must take advantage of the wonderful opportunities we provide. If we provide their food, housing, and insurance why in hell would they want to work?"

Carol looks at Fred with contempt and says smugly, "Mr. Barker you are beginning to sound like a conservative."

"Maybe so Carol but I am concerned about this country and pretty soon we have to put the country ahead of politics." Fred said with resignation in his voice.

The room fell silent and the tension is thick. President Howard finally spoke, "Harry, I want you to find and cut four hundred billion from our budget and report back to me in two weeks."

He pauses and looks at his notes and finally continued, "We will also implement the trillion dollar stimulus as we discussed. It is something I have to do. Hopefully, this will buy us some time until we can come with a long term solution."

"Yes Sir" Harry smugly replies.

The President turns to Fred and said, "Fred, I understand what you are saying. My own father fought his way into Harvard with hard work and much sacrifice in times that one would have thought such obstacles insurmountable.

I agree with you that we have too many able bodied and capable citizens who are simply afflicted with laziness. This is a culture that must be changed and a behavior that should be abhorred. It is a huge social and political issue and I am not sure that it is the government's job to motivate the unmotivated or to reward lack of initiative but, unfortunately, it is the world we now live in......"

CHAPTER 26

John Danforth invited twelve of his closest political friends to his home for dinner and informal discussions. Each invitee assumed they alone were invited and they all accepted John's gracious invitation.

Howard Samuel (D) from Illinois arrives at the same time as John Lewis (R) from Colorado. The men exit their cars and greet each other warmly and somewhat quizzically.

Danforth comes down the steps to greet them and invites them into his home. Soon all twelve invitees arrive and are milling around in John's library trying to figure out what in the hell old John is up too.

John taps on his cocktail glass and gets their attention. With a sly smile on his face he makes eye contact with each person prior to saying, "Gentlemen, thank you for coming and I am sorry if you feel I deceived you in any way but you are politicians you should be used to trickery by now."

His guests laugh and await John's comments, "Please find a comfortable seat and indulge an old man for a few minutes. I have some important issues to discuss with you."

When everyone is comfortably seated John stands by the fireplace and rests his right arm on the mantle and resumes, "First of all, of all the representatives of our government, you people, are my most trusted and dearest friends. I know that you are patriotic and as concerned about our country as anyone and I thank you for coming. I will respectfully request that you consider my remarks confidential." John pauses briefly as his audience anxiously awaits his comments.

He glances around the room and could see his colleagues are relaxed and attentive, "Thank you. Gentlemen in August…….. I will resign."

Robert Taylor(R) from New York spoke first, "John you can't give up your seat. This country needs you." His guests look at one another incredulously.

The other men make similar comments as John holds his hands up to hush the men and said, "Come on guys, please listen. I didn't say I was giving up my seat or retiring from the Senate………….. I am retiring from the Republican Party." He calmly said.

Over the years John had mentored most of these men and they all have great respect for him. They recognize and admire him as a man who will not compromise on his beliefs and cannot be swayed by earmarks. He is a man of great character and few men in politics can match is integrity.

Jack Witman (R), California, looks like someone had hit him in the stomach as he said, "John, you can't be serious, can you?

Eric Edwards (D) from Massachusetts kiddingly said, "You are not switching to the Democratic Party?"

John laughs and said, "Hold on, let me explain," he packs his pipe and slowly lit the tobacco with a long wooden match, threw the match in the fireplace, and exhales a large cloud of smoke toward the ceiling.

John sits down in his chair, crosses his legs, places his pipe in an ashtray, and said, "Forget about parties for a moment. Who in this room really and truly believes that this country can economically survive more than thirty more years?"

He looks around the room and there is no disagreement and he continues, "We, the democrats and republicans, have really fouled things up over the last 150 years. Our children and our grandchildren will pay dearly for our mistakes.

It is very clear to me that the vast majority of Senators and Congressmen are quite content to continue driving us straight off the cliff." John pauses, stands up, and walks back to the fireplace for dramatic effect.

"I will not bore you, my friends with the inescapable facts that you know all to well. We have all tried and tried very hard. I know how frustrated each of you is and we all know our parties and our systems have simply become corrupt and those of us in this room cannot gain enough support for common sense solutions.

We have a debt in excess of twelve trillion dollars! We will spend 3.8 trillion dollars this year and collect only two trillion in tax revenue. Total individual earnings will only be 8.5 trillion dollars. Gentlemen we spent over 40% of the total revenue all Americans earned and that scares me to death.

Our trade deficit is averaging seventy Billion dollars a month and our jobs are being exported because we can't find solution's at home. We blame the businessman for exporting jobs when he can save 75% of his labor cost oversees and generate higher profits for their stockholders.

What the hell do we expect him to do? Hire here and pay triple or quadruple wages at the expense of his stockholders?"

John knows that the men in his library are aware of these facts and figures but it is imperative that he try to impact them on the consequences of continuing ridiculous spending programs.

"When I consider our dependence on oil, the war on terror, the dumb ass trillion dollar bail out for Wall Street, and the eminent failure of our Medicare and Social Security programs as well as Freddie and Fannie I become hopelessly depressed and ashamed that I have been a part of this terrible travesty inflicted on American citizens who trusted us." John knew he would soon lose them with the rhetoric but he is hell bent on forcing these issue firmly in their minds.

"I cannot continue to sit by and keep doing things the way we have in the past and expect different results. The time has come for a radical and positive change"

Charles Brady (D) Florida spoke up, "John, as you said, we all share your frustration and I agree with you. Honestly, there are many nights I can't sleep because I am worried about my children and grandchildren. Knowing you as I do, I am looking forward to your punch line."

All the men knew John very well and they chuckled at Brady's remark because they know the hammer is about to fall.

John stood up, picked up his pipe, and relit it giving his guest ample opportunity for more comments.

John Lewis pours himself another drink and humorously said, "Come on John, stop with the drama and tell us what's up!"

The rest of the group encourages John to tell them what the hell he wants to tell them

John smiles and holds his hands up to silence his guests. " Okay!....I have concluded we need a strong third party that will prevent Democrats and Republicans from their horse trading practices that have gotten us into this mess.

I intend to form a new political party that I believe will make a huge impact on America's future. What I want from you, my friends, is your support."

The men look somewhat disappointed and were expecting something a little more dramatic from John Danforth.

Howard Samuels is first to speak, "Come on John, third parties simply can't crack our stranglehold. There are currently over twenty registered parties and a viable third party will just never happen."

John is unperturbed as he replies, "Why can't it happen?"

Jack Whitman replies, "Four things come to mind John. The first is no one has been able to build a national organization that can generate the support and money needed. Second would be that they cannot share in public money. Third is they would be lucky to find a handful of viable and attractive candidates that could seriously challenge democrats and republicans. Fourth is, with all due respect John, you will need a strong party leader."

John took a puff on his pipe and blew out the smoke, "Money, organization, no qualified candidates, and no leadership, is that all?"

"Pretty much", said Edwards as the others nod their heads in agreement.

John said emphatically, "The name of our party will be the Restoration Party. We will restore financial responsibility to Government. We will restore confidence in Government. We will restore integrity domestically and internationally. We will restore jobs in America and we will restore common sense in Government.

I cannot give you the complete platform today because that will not be my responsibility it will be up to our Presidential candidate to lead our party and determine our policies."

Bobby Taylor said with some sarcasm, "Alright John, who do you have in mind that can capture the hearts and minds of the American people?"

John has that satisfied smile on his face that tells his audience he is about to drop something big, "gentlemen,...... our Presidential candidate for the new Restoration Party will be Joseph Alexander Winston."

Immediately there is a buzz of excitement in the room as the powerful politicians look at each other in disbelief.

Brady interrupts and said, "John, has Joe agreed to this?"

"With some reservations and conditions he has." John replied.

Howard said, "Joe is held in high regard in business circles and his record of accomplishment is certainly impressive but he has no political experience. His disdain for politics is well known."

John thoughtfully said, "Political experience got us in this mess. You all know Joe is my son in law so I know him very well. Your objections were money, organization, and a powerful leader. You all know Joe is a Billionaire, as are his three best friends, or as the Wall Street Journal calls them *"The Forcesome."*

Tony Papandrea, whom you all know, will handle the organization and campaign. The public is ready for a real change and now is the time. Gentlemen, I believe we have a winner on our hands and I believe the time has come for us to save America."

After another hour of informally discussion over dinner the men leave and John retires to his library to consider if the meeting had the desired effect.

CHAPTER 27

Volusia National was created with the intent of providing a first class golf course and facility where its members could escape the day to day grind of their complex and demanding careers and simply relax and have a good time. The dramatic revelations of Joe and Robbie's adventures might very well have defeated that purpose. Nevertheless their plan is to play golf and that is exactly what they intend to do.

As they arrive at the first tee Lee, wearing his plaid golf shorts and a bright orange shirt said, "I have never seen a more perfect day to play golf."

Adam is attired in pleated tan trousers and a blue golf shirt, inhales deeply and enjoys the mixture of aromas, fresh cut grass, the pleasing smell of honeysuckles, azaleas, and oleanders, and the ever present salty smell of the Atlantic and replies, "days like this can cause a man to forget his troubles."

Lee takes a deep breath and said humbly to Adam, "I really don't know what we have done to deserve this. I love this place."

134

Joe and Robbie pull up behind Lee and Adam and Adam said, "You guys ready?"

Robbie looks around and says, "I was born ready."

Lee, the ultimate matchmaker and hustler, says, "Ok here's today's game. Adam and I are playing you guys for a $50 Nassau with automatic two down presses. Adam is a six and Joe is a six so Robbie gets 4 shots a side and I get six shots a side."

Robbie said, "Hold on there little buddy. Why in the hell are you getting twelve shots?"

Lee smiles as he looks at Robbie and sarcastically says, "I'm sorry Robbie, I assumed you are bright enough to understand the handicap system. I guess I was mistaken."

Robbie glares at Lee and says, "Are you telling me your handicap is 18?"

"I'm impressed you can add and subtract." Lee smugly replies.

"You little shit you probably rigged the frigging computer." Robbie says with conviction.

Adam and Joe always feel like the straight guys in a comedy act. They just smile at their two buddies and laugh at this ritual that occurs every time they play.

After everyone teed off and headed toward their second shots Robbie said, "Joe, what the hell happened to our country? Do you remember how nice everything was in the fifties, no body locked their doors, people were honorable and respectful of each other, credit was rare and cash was king, and government seemed to unobtrusively do its job.

Now nobody seems to respect anybody, everyone is head over heels in debt, the media constantly stirs shit, crime is ridiculous and we all have safe houses, and our government is going broke in less than two decades."

Robbie pauses as if he was analyzing what he had said and finding it difficult to believe.

Joe said, "It is a different world. It seems that understanding right from wrong has become more difficult over the years."

They arrive at their tee shots and Robbie is about 210 yards away from the par four green. Robbie looks at his partner and says, "Looks like a three wood for me, Joe."

Joe knows Robbie didn't have a chance of hitting the green and supports Robbie's illusion and said, "Give it a ride partner."

Robbie stands over the ball for a little longer than usual and Lee yells across the fairway, "Come on Robbie. Hit the frigging ball!"

Robbie backs away from his shot, looks at Lee, and gives him a smile and the finger.

Lee whispers to Adam, "I will his ass crazy today, he won't break a 100."

Adam knew Lee would do exactly that and laughs

Adam's company, Fields Financial, consumed Adam as it requires all his skills to help navigate his elite clientele through these trying times and unprecedented economic situations. He always manages to find value for his clients even in the most difficult time and these times are no exception. He took little time away from business except for his Volusia National trips and he valued every minute with his friends.

Robbie finally takes a big swing at the ball and tops it about fifty yards into some palmettos. He watches it disappear and bangs his club on the ground and said, "God damn it!"

Lee laughs loudly as he yells, "Good shot Robbie."

Robbie tries to ignore him and got in the cart and said to Joe, "That little shit is going to drive me crazy."

Joe knew the game and knowingly said, "He will if you let him." They drove about sixty yards down the middle of the fairway to Joe's ball.

Joe pulls out his eight iron, waste little time, and strikes it perfectly to the slightly elevated first green and it sat softly on the green about 15 feet from the pin. Robbie yells over to Lee, "Hey Lee how did you like that?"

Lee is a little quieter now since he hit his second shot in the large greenside bunker that is about six feet deep.

Adams second shot is on the green about 30 feet away.

As they drive up to the green Robbie says, "Seems to me like the sixties seemed to start this mess we are in. The war in Viet Nam, the peace movement, drugs became popular, integration, protest, anti establishment groups, special interest groups, and lying politicians trying to buy votes with social programs. It seems like we started trying to be everything to everybody and the more we tried the worse it got.

There are many good things that came out of those times but those times seemed to encourage laziness and entitlement just because you are an American. I don't know what the hell happened. Now we have a bunch of politicians who swore to protect this country and they are destroying it."

Joe locks eyes with Robbie and said quietly, "What ever happened, we're gong to fix it."

"Do you suppose politicians have always been this way?" Robbie wondered out loud.

Joe said, "I remember reading a quote by Harry Truman, he said, my choice early in life was to be a piano player in a whorehouse or a politician. And to tell the truth, there's hardly any difference. I, for one, believe the piano player to be much more honorable than many current politicians."

Robbie laughs, "Man, don't you just wonder what old Harry would say if here were alive today?"

Adam and Joe tied the hole with pars and Robbie and Lee are still giving each other grief. Three and a half hours later they finish the round dead even.

After golf and lunch they sit around drinking beer and hammering out a rough platform for the Restoration Party. They will try to devote the next couple of days to fun and the next few months figuring out a way to prevent a total financial collapse and preparing their plans for the birth of the Restoration Party.

Later that night Joe is visiting with Lee and says, "Lee, we know that information is the most valuable asset one can have. Most reliable information seems to be in cyberspace and that is an arena where you have no peer. We will need your expertise to help us in that area."

Lee said, "Joe, you know you can count on me to whatever I can. What can I do to help?"

Joe stands up and paces around and then returns to face Lee, "Lee, we need to encourage existing politicians who do not have the best interest of our country as their primary objective to resign. In order to do that we need persuasive information to convince them that they might need to consider another career. I need you to do an exhaustive study to determine if any such information might be available."

Lee smiled and put his arm around Joe and said, "It may surprise you but I already have an abundance of such information. What shall I do with it?"

Joe always enters any endeavor with great confidence which results from diligent study and a comprehensive understanding of the issues. He still has a difficult time getting his head around actually being involved in politics and he is encumbered with doubt and uncertainty which is a feeling that has eluded him for most of his life.

In spite of these uncomfortable feelings Joe is confident that in time he will become proficient and he is also convinced that there appear to be no other viable options.

As evidence of how quickly he is adapting he turns to Lee and said, "Find out all you can on every Senator, Congressman, and Governor so we know who we will be dealing with and get the information to me."

Lee thought to himself that Joe Winston is beginning to think like a politician and wondered if that is good or bad?

Joe said, "Lee we don't have to win every race. All we need is fifteen or twenty Senate seats and a hundred or so seats in congress. If we can do that partisan politics will disappear."

CHAPTER 28

President Howard sits with Harry Belk in the Oval Office for a scheduled update on the progress of the Charlotte and Cruise ship attacks.. He is impatient this morning and has difficulty staying still. He paces the floor, he sits down briefly, and just as quickly he stands up and leans on his desk and finally turns toward Harry and says, "Tell me we have some answers Harry."

Belk has spent most of his life in politics and reading people, he knew there would be no way for this update to end on a positive note. He respectfully looks at the President as he replies, "Mr. President, we have spent thousand of man hours and exhausted every conceivable possibility and learned absolutely nothing."

The President is beginning to think that everyone around him is incompetent. The President of the United States of America can't even get good answers. He feels this is totally unacceptable and demonstrates the ineptitude of his administration.

The President angrily say, "How in the hell is it that the most powerful nation in the world can allow our citizens to be murdered in the streets and we can't stop it......nor can we find the people responsible. Harry, are we that god damned incompetent?"

"Mr. President, I don't know what to tell you. What do you want me to do?" Belk stammers timidly.

"I am being crucified by the press. The trillions we have spent on the bail outs and stimulus packages are not producing the desired results, unemployment is increasing, the market will not stabilize, oil prices are increasing dramatically, we can't get a good national health plan together, we are in the automobile business, the sub prime problem was bad enough and now we have another wave of mortgage foreclosures.

Harry, I want you to bring me some fucking solutions to these god damned problems. Do you understand?" The President said angrily.

Belk sensed it is time for him to give the President a reason to calm down a little bit and not to take this so seriously. Harry knew how to spin any issue and this is no exception. "Mr. President may I speak freely?"

Howard gruffly said, "Go ahead."

Belk said, "James we have all worked real hard to put you in that chair. You did a magnificent job on the campaign trail and we need you to exhibit the same strength now. You have only been in the Oval Office for five months and your Cabinet is in the process of reviewing the policies of the prior administration and making the corrections we feel are necessary.

Mr. President the prior Administration's policies failed the American people once again and nobody can expect you to correct eight years of mistakes in five months."

Harry could see that the President is becoming less agitated and senses his wheels are turning. Harry hopes the President will jump in with the obvious answer so it would be his idea and obviously people like their own ideas best.

Finally the President says, "Harry you are right again. It is the prior administrations cluster fuck and we are here to clean up their mess. Make sure that message goes out loud and clear to the Media."

Harry smiles inwardly as he replies, "Yes Sir. I will take care of it immediately."

The President hears the door shut, sits down at his desk, and feels as if he had solved a major problem. His attitude is much improved but he still wants answers and desperately wants to solve this mystery.

He buzzes his Executive Secretary and said, "I want the FBI Director in my office now!"

President Howard is impatient and also somewhat naïve he wants results and if he doesn't get them he is prepared to rip his entire cabinet a new ass hole.

CHAPTER 29

Joe understands the commitment he made to John and the sacrifices he must make. However there is a part of him that wishes he had not involved his friends. He had no right to disrupt their lives but he also knew they would support him no matter what the circumstances.

He thought about Robbie quite often and Robbie had also chosen a path that would be questioned by most rational people and yet Adam and Lee stood behind him just as they would support me. He found some relief in the certain knowledge that he knew he would never abandon one of them.

Joe is hopeful that both he and Robbie can be successful but is well aware that they are walking down a road which is fraught with danger Dangers they are unaccustomed to dealing with.

Joe and Tony arrive at Joe's home for their strategy session and they are seated on Joe's veranda overlooking the James River sipping iced tea and discussing progress. There is a bit of fall in the air and some of the leaves have begun to fall from the trees.

Tony looks at Joe and says "We now have the Restoration Party officially registered in forty one states and I expect to have the remaining states within a few weeks. As you both know, we are getting a lot of questions and generating tremendous curiosity among the media which is good."

John said, "When do Lee, Adam, and Robbie start granting interviews?"

Tony has been around run of the mill politicians for his entire working life and had come to despise the manipulation, lies, and corruption of almost all of them. Working with John and Joe has inspired him and he has never been this enthusiastic about anything.

He looks at John thoughtfully and said, "CBS is devoting an entire one hour program to interview them on September 12th. Following that they are individually booked on eight different programs and doing six interviews each for the print media over the next few months."

"Well, if these boys do as well as we think the demand for Joe should intensify tremendously by the end of September." John remarks.

"October will be a busy month for us with regard to the interviews Joe accepts and how well John and I do recruiting to the Restoration Party" Tony said as he looks at Joe

Joe thought again of how his actions has changed the lives of his friends and said, "I have no concerns with Adam, Robbie, and Lee but the recruiting success is pretty much in your hands. I will help all I can but I wouldn't know where to start."

"If things go as well as I expect it will be a piece of cake. Tony, you have done a great job on your end, which doesn't surprise me, and I can't thank you enough." John said.

"Well I have to be honest with guys. I don't think I have ever been so excited about a job in my life. This needs to happen and we need to win." Tony says with genuine sincerity and some emotion.

John said, "Tony, did you get the results on the name recognition survey?"

Tony picks up his papers and flips through them, "Yes I did John. The name Joseph Alexander Winston was recognized by 8% of the respondents. Don't be concerned by that, Joe you have keep a very low public profile and the results are not surprising. This is just a benchmark for us the important number is the one we will get in November."

Joe feeling the full impact of his changing life said, "I am surprised it's that high Tony. What improvement can we expect over the next year?"

Tony leans back a little in his chair and runs his hand over his head and put his best guess face on and said, "Let me give you a high and a low. I will be shocked if we don't exceed 60% but I believe we can hit 85-90%."

Joe nods and his stomach turns a little as he realizes he would never be able to go anywhere without being recognized. The privacy that he protected for decades will be gone.

John looked over at Joe and could see he seemed to be preoccupied. He quietly asks, "Joe have you cleared your schedule for Tony?"

"I'm clear. Winston's is in capable hands under interim management but I will continue to be available for important issues. This is now my number one priority." Joe said forcing a smile.

"Sounds good, Joe. I think it is imperative that we announce your candidacy by January if we are going to impact the mid terms. Do you think that is possible?" Tony asks.

"Let's just see how things go and then pick the best possible time." Joe says with a smile on his face and a pain in his heart.

"We have almost a full year prior to the mid term elections and Joe can get into the campaign rhythm working with our state candidates." John comments.

Joe rallies a bit, smiles, and pulls out his notes and said, "Let me go over what I believe to be our primary objectives. First I want to emphasize we want dedicated people who's interest will be the country not themselves. I know that limits the pool but on this issue there will be no compromise."

Both men nod their consent.

Joe leans forward in his chair and assumed his CEO position and said, "Gentlemen, I will approach this as a hostile take over because that is essentially what it is. If we are to beat the two parties that have held control for one hundred and fifty years we have to expect they will not only resist, they will unite to try and defeat us."

Tony is intrigued by the business analogy and impressed with the simple power of Joe's voice and delivery said, "Makes sense to me Joe. Please continue."

"We will tell the American people what we are going to do and why we are going to do it but I will not divulge how we will do it until the timing is perfect. It makes no sense for me to tell the company that I am trying to acquire how I will make them profitable. Does that make sense?" Joe asks.

John had suffered under half ass leadership in Washington for decades and is rightfully very proud of his son in law but more importantly he feels that finally right will triumph over wrong said, "We trust your judgment Joe but you need to give us a little guidance."

Joe replies in his usual confident and polite manner, "I can give you a little John just think of five E's; Efficiency, economy, expenses, employment, and energy." He pauses to gage their reaction.

John and Tony seemed confused and unimpressed. It was as if they were awaiting some new revelation that would instantly make everything right, "Relax, I am going to give you more." Joe said.

Joe continues, "Everybody knows our number one problem is efficiency. Government never has been and never will be efficient under democrats and republicans. A hostile take over generally requires practical reorganization and that's what we will do.

As examples, waste and corruptions will be eliminated, ear marks will disappear, bills will be restricted to one issue, federal employees and private employee's compensation packages should be similar. The average government employee earns over $100,000 counting benefits and the average private sector employee earns $50,000 this must be reconciled and balanced, and every purchase we make will give us the best bang for our buck."

I wouldn't be interested in this venture if there is no hope for profits. It is possible to operate the Federal Government within a reasonable annual budget if we become efficient.

The economy simply lacks confidence in our political leadership and the ridiculous methods that have been employed. We will stimulate the economy with the introduction of a new simplified tax system which will increase private industry spending, encourage investment, and will lead to increased employment.

Entitlement programs must be dramatically changed and Americans must realize that it is a privilege to live in America and no healthy person has the right to live off the efforts of others.

A free economy cannot be free with a Federal Government that constantly tries to manipulate the markets. We will stop that."

John interrupts and says, "You will catch a lot of grief over Social engineering it is a major tool of politicians and people tend to vote for the candidate that offers them something for nothing."

"Maybe so John but I am hoping that more Americans are interested in freedom and opportunity in this country than handouts. I will not buy votes with public money and I will make that very clear to anyone. I will do what is right and fair. If the American people reject the concepts we present, we will just have to live with it and so will they." Joe said with finality.

"Our last issue is energy. In ten years we can and will be energy independent in the United States of America. I already know how we will do that and I believe it can be done in five years." Joe said emphatically.

Tony said, "Joe it all sounds good but it also sounds pretty familiar."

"I understand what you are saying Tony. People will have a choice they can believe me or they can keep the people who have gotten them into this mess. I trust the American people and I want to give them someone they can vote for not someone they have to vote against.

Tony I know they have heard this before but a song is only as good as the singer. My job is to convince people they can trust me and I believe I can do the things I promise. Remember the plans we present must support the words we speak." Joe said with conviction.

Tony and John seemed less than convinced simply because they have heard that type of rhetoric for their entire careers. However, their trust and confidence in Joe is not in doubt.

"I have one last issue. "The Restoration Party will fight for a constitutional amendment that limits government service to one six year term." We will rid congress of egotistical, arrogant professional politicians whose only real interest is their power and re-election." Joe leans back in his chair for a few seconds and then continues.

"All Restoration Party candidates must agree to serve only one term if elected until such time as the amendment is passed and ratified by the states." Joe said.

CHAPTER 30

The Secureone national headquarters occupies one of the most unique buildings in Charleston, South Carolina. The space was once a tobacco plant until CEO, Robbie Ravenel, convinced the city to allow him to tear it down and to construct his headquarters in a manner that conforms to Charleston rich historical architecture.

Securone is located on East Bay Street in the shadow of the Cooper River Bridge and the exterior of the building conforms to typical Charleston architecture and is immaculately landscaped. It contains over seventy thousand square feet of interior space and combines old Charleston with modern America.

As you enter the main lobby it will feel as if you just stepped back in time at least a century. The furnishings and the artwork would please even the most skeptical member of the Charleston Preservation Society.

Once you exit the lobby level you will find the rest of the building, that houses over six hundred employees, among the most efficient and modern office building in America. The top four floors consist of administrative and marketing offices that constantly hums with a growing a dynamic business.

The heart of Secureone occupies over twenty thousand square feet of an extremely high tech area which is one floor below the main level. While normal business is conducted on the upper floors the basement is a secure area that houses the most sophisticated technology equipment one could imagine. Access to this area is highly restricted to less than forty highly skilled individuals. This is where most government contracts are monitored.

Since April, Lee Roth and Nick Bernstein have been periodically working together with Bert's team and today they are working in the secure basement area on Aziz Hasan and his contacts that Fahid had given up prior to his untimely demise.

Roth and Bernstein love to play together and thoroughly enjoy each others company. They are kindred spirits and when it comes to the real sophistication of computer programming and capabilities, few understand the complexities of their discussions. If one were to observe them they would appear to be two talented kids playing against each other at the fifteenth level of the most sophisticated video game ever designed.

Aziz employees one of the most sophisticated defense systems available to prevent penetration of his computer and has little concern with someone mining information.

In May, Lee and Nick had a significant break through. Lee smugly asked Nick, "Nick, how would you go about finding a connection to a web site between two or more people?"

Nick appears to be a typical computer gamer he is 32 to years of age and appears to be ten years younger. He looks like a typical gamer, long hair, punk dress, tennis shoes, pale skin, and intense brown eyes that don't miss a thing. He graduated at the top of his MIT class of 1998 and possessed a Mensa IQ.

The man he most admires is Lee Roth and when he had the chance to meet him personally in 2006 it was the highlight of his life. Robbie learned of Nick through a friend and hired him in 1999 and counted him among his best employees and Nick had progressed rapidly within Secureone.

"Well I could easily gain access to the web site and then trace all the hits. From there I could input the names and do a search to see if they visited the site. Depending upon the total hits it could be easy or very time consuming," Nick said.

Lee grinned at Nick and asked, "What if you didn't have two or more names and just wanted to find a pattern of two or more people who visited a site within hours of each other on a regular basis?

Nick looked quizzically at Lee and said, "No way man. You can't do that. Can you?"

Lee had expected that answer and he smiled an all knowing smile at this prodigy and said, "You are right it would be time consuming and you would have to be extremely lucky but what if you could access all the ISP's (internet service providers) and introduce a worm that could tell you in minutes all the hits on any site, the pages they viewed, and when?"

"Lee, you are not going to tell me you can do that are you?" Nick replied with a mixture of excitement and disbelief.

"I can. Nick some times we just over think problems when the solution is really quite simple." Lee replied with pride.

"No shit!" Nick said with awe.

"No shit buddy", he said as he opened his laptop and booted up. They knew Aziz's service provider and Lee quickly pulled up a list of all sites Aziz had visited and concentrated on the dates one week after the Houston situation. Lee hit a few keystrokes and instantly every site Aziz visited appeared.

Nick, like a kid in a toy store, said, "Man this is absolutely amazing."

Lee hit a few more keys and said, "Now this is Fahid's computer and twelve of the forty one other suspects ISP's." He made a couple of more entries and the computer begins processing his request.

Nick said, "What are we doing now?"

Lee said, "I call this worm a "commonality predator". The computer will show all the common sites visited by the twelve computers within specified time frames or with no time frames."

Before Lee finished his comments the computer revealed that there is only one common site, boingboing.com.

Lee smugly says, "This is the site they use to communicate and here is what they viewed. Now I am going to lunch with Robbie at the Yacht club so I want to see how good you are at cracking codes." He stands up and pats Nick on the shoulder and heads towards the door.

Nick is simply blown away by what he has seen and his mind races when he considers the importance and danger of such a tool. He turns around looks at Lee with awe and said, "Man, I have never seen anything more impressive. Enjoy your lunch and I will break the code."

When Lee returns from lunch around 3:00 pm it was Nick's turn to impress Lee. When Lee walked into the room Nick turns to his computer and proudly said, "I've got it!" he hands Lee two messages that had been posted by Aziz.

The first message was immediately after Houston when he instructed them to be on alert and to remove all weapons from the Mosques. The second is in July telling them to resume normal operations.

Lee said, "Great work Nick. Now let's do another search with my little worm predator friend and find out how many others viewed this site from the other twelve computers in our time frame." Lee enters a few commands and hits enter and within seconds a list of three hundred and seventy five names appear.

Lee said, "Looks like we have a few more suspects as he printed two copies. He gave one to Nick and said, "You find out what you can about these guys and I will inform Robbie."

Nick said, "Hey Lee thanks for the lesson."

Lee turns around and walks back to Nick and said with affection, "Man let me tell you something. You have more talent than anyone I know and each year you will learn more and more. Whatever the future brings us in technology I know you will be a big part of it."

He slaps Nick affectionately on the back and then shakes his hand and said, "See you later Nick!"

CHAPTER 31

The Sixty Minutes filming starts at 2:00 pm. Adam is to be interviewed by Steve Craft. Steve has the reputation of being somewhat fair but does tend to favor liberal positions. He is dressed in a blue pin stripe suite, starched light blue shirt, and designer tie. His quaffed hair and pale face would suggest that he spends little time outdoors. He possesses that anchor quality.

Prior to the interview the camera scans the Atlantic Ocean and the beautiful neighborhood inhabited by people of wealth. After slowly completing 180 degrees it focuses on the large and magnificent home of Adam Fields and the announcer voice enters, "We are here tonight to interview one of America's most successful African American men, Adam Fields. Mr. Fields is the CEO of Fields Financial which is one of the most prestigious financial firms in the country."

As the camera probes the inside of Adam's home in an effort to demonstrate how wealthy American's lived. It is actually a subtle effort to encourage the wrath of those viewers who have not earned a privileged lifestyle.

The announcer continues, "Prior to this evening Mr. Fields has never granted an interview to the Media and has steadfastly protected his privacy. He is also a member of the famous Forcesome featured in the Wall Street Journal several years ago which includes Joe Winston of Winston's Department Store, Lee Roth of Rothsystems, and Robbie Ravenel of Secureone; Four men who are definitely a force in American business.

Tonight's program will feature Mr. Roth and Mr. Ravenel in addition to Mr. Fields." The camera slowly shows the viewers Adam's opulent library and finally focuses on Adam Fields sitting behind a beautiful desk and Steve Croft in a side chair facing Adam.

Needless to say this is new experience for Adam and he is somewhat apprehensive but confident. Adam is dressed in dark trousers, secured by an expensive alligator belt, and a white casual linen shirt. Mr. Croft is attired in a tan business suit, blue shirt, and striped blue and tan neck tie.

The interview is scheduled to deal with Adam's business success but Joe Winston's name is bound to come up and Adam, as always, is prepared for anything. The camera zooms in on Kraft as he says, "Mr. Fields, first of all we would like to thank you for inviting us into your home."

The camera moves to Adam who said, "Glad to have you Steve."

Kraft asked his first question, "Mr. Fields, in your opinion, what is the primary problem with our economy?"

As the camera captures a close up of Adam the viewers could see a handsome man with penetrating, but kind, big brown eyes as he looked directly at Kraft and fixed him with a friendly but neutral gaze, "Steve, it really isn't as complex as one would think. In my opinion the major problem, is what I refer to, as "professional politicians."

These politicians have made a conscious decision to make a career out of politics in order to enjoy the power and fame which accompanies their office. If they wish to retain their power it requires that they devote seventy percent of their time to campaigning and raising money.

Their legislative decisions appear to me to be based upon one simple question. How will this impact votes?"

Steve raises one eye brown and asks with a baiting smile, "Are you saying our politicians are not serving the best interest of their constituents?"

Adam looks at him and calmly said, "I am not saying all politicians fit that description but it appears that most do. They delegate the affairs of government to a staff of individuals that were not elected by the people while campaigning and raising money for re-election. I would be stunned if the vast majority of voters do not agree with that assessment."

Steve did not expect such an honest answer but continues, "Mr. Fields I understand your sentiment but how would you suggest this problem be corrected?"

"Steve, it seems pretty simple to me. Holding political office is a privilege and an honor and if someone is interested in something other than serving the public interest they should not run for office. Too many elected officials get carried away with the prestige and power that comes with their responsibilities and lose sight of their real objective. The pressure to hold that office is immense and the ultimate financial and physic rewards are just too hard to resist.

Furthermore, the longer one serves the more likelihood there is that he will become indebted to his fellow legislators and cast a vote he shouldn't in exchange for a vote he has received or may receive.

The solution is one six term limit. This would save billions of dollars in campaign cost and force our public servants to focus on America's future not their future."

As Adam finishes his comments he wonders to himself if he is being too wordy.

Steve hesitates and is once again surprised by Adam's suggestion and tugs at his tie indicating his discomfort. He gives Adam an incredulous look as he said, "Well how do we change it?"

"As long as only two parties are in control, I am afraid our country will suffer continued deterioration and possibly a major economic collapse. There are no solutions when two parties have a one hundred and fifty year history of disagreeing publically but agreeing privately." Adam replies; knowing that the liberal Media would be trying to nail him to the cross tomorrow morning.

"No solutions?" Steve says with a disbelieving look while looking for another answer.

"Not with a two party system Steve." Adam politely replies.

"Are you saying we need a third political party?" Steve continues to push for Adam to bring up the Restoration Party.

"We have dozens of other parties now but the big problem is the absence of wide appeal and the difficulty involved in fund raising for minority parties as well as government support. Men of great wisdom and excellent judgment presented us with a blueprint for success in 1776 and I believe we need to follow their guidance." Adam said while watching the reporter's obvious discomfort.

Steve, in his most penetrating voice raises his right eye brow once again and asks, "In your opinion, what else must be done to return our economy to stability?"

Adam replies, "There isn't one thing that can provide a quick fix. Let's face it our economic situation is a product of decades of mismanagement by our elected officials. The Federal government is out of control and needs to be re-organized by competent leadership. It's too big, too wasteful, too ineffective, and much too costly."

Adam assumes that he is viewed as just another capitalist with no real knowledge of how government works and wishes to dispel the image the journalist will try to create by uncovering his absence of definitive knowledge. His attention is completely focused on Steve as he continues.

"There is entirely too much redundancy. We have over 350 economic development programs, 135 programs serving the disabled, 130 programs for at-risk children, 90 early childhood development programs, 80 homeless assistance programs, and I could go on and on.

The fact is many of these agencies should be consolidated, and better yet, pushed back to the state level where they have a chance of being effectively managed." Adam pauses briefly for effect and takes a sip of water from the glass positioned on his desk.

Steve asks, "Do you believe that a free market economy can actually restore financial stability?"

"Yes. I have no doubt." Adam replies complimenting himself for the short answer.

Steve looks at his notes and asks, "Clearly the disparity of incomes between the rich and the middle class is out of proportion. What are your feelings on taxation in America?"

He pauses and then said indignantly, "If you are asking me if we should authorize the government to steal money from the most productive members of society and give it to who ever they would like for political purposes the answers is a resounding NO. I favor a fair flat tax schedule."

Steve looks at Adam as if he is bewildered and in a condescending voice asks "The administration suggest that it is the patriotic duty of the top 5% of Americans to pay more taxes. How do you respond to that?"

The camera captures a close up of Adam as he answers in a clear forceful voice, "The privilege of living in a free country is dependent upon the will of the people. In any society some people achieve great success through their intellectual pursuits or by hard work. Freedom gives one that opportunity.

I think every American citizen will agree that it is a privilege to live in this country. We have the best schools, the best system of government, the best road and transportations system, the best parks and recreational facilities, museums, the best health care, and I could go on and on expounding on the benefits American citizens enjoy. Unfortunately our country is quickly heading for economic disaster and all Americans need to help us avoid this.

One of the many solutions I would suggest is a temporary increase in federal income taxes with a maximum of 40% and a minimum of 5%. Every American who enjoys the benefits of our country can do their patriotic duty and help save our country.

This would raise an additional four hundred billion a year and I would propose that money can only be used for debt retirement and interest payments. We have a choice to either bury future generations in debt or give them a chance to enjoy freedom."

Steve leans forward to gather his thoughts and stutters a little as he asks, "So you would ask the poor to contribute?"

Adam says, "I will ask every American who loves their country and enjoys the benefits of citizenship to help save our country."

Steve can't believe the interview has come to its conclusion and reluctantly says, "Mr. Field's we thank you for sharing your time with us this evening."

"Thanks for having me." Adam replies with a warm smile.

We will now pause for a brief commercial and ask that you please stay tuned for next segment featuring Mr. Lee Roth, CEO of Rothsystems and perhaps the foremost computer expert in the world.

This is the first time in the last twenty years that Mr. Roth has granted a personal interview. You will not want to miss this segment filmed at Mr. Roth's home in Cape Cod."

Chapter 32

As they had done with Adam the camera crew captured the beauty surrounding Lee's estate and Lee had demonstrated the high tech innovations used throughout his home. The camera manages to focus once again on the opulence of his home and if someone tuned in late they would believe they are about to see a segment from "The lifestyles of the Rich and Famous."

Lee is dressed in blue jeans and a light blue casual shirt tucked neatly into his jeans. He is relaxed as always and is sitting in his high tech safe room, as suggested by the producer. Leslie Stark, the journalist is seated across from him at a table in the center of the room and as the camera captures the room it appears to be similar to a cockpit in a spaceship.

As the camera focuses on Leslie, in a dark blue business suit, white blouse, blue and white scarf, she starts the interview, "Mr. Roth would you mind telling our viewers why you Joe Winston, Adam Fields, and

Robbie Ravenel have avoided the media for so many years and why you have all decided to grant interviews at this time?"

Lee smiles at Leslie as the camera zooms in on his playful and honest face. "That's a fair question Leslie and I will try to give you a fair answer; I have never felt the need to be in the limelight and I value my privacy.

At Rothsystems we offer our employees opportunities to grow intellectually and economically and we try to run our business in a way that reflects what America should be. If you take advantage of your educational opportunities, work hard, and develop good habits you can become extremely successful in America. I think you would discover that our employees appreciate the incentives we offer and feel a sense of ownership in their company. Management and labor work cohesively and the results are self evident.

On the other hand political leaders seem to target voting blocks and if there happens to be twenty million Americans who will endorse a candidate that supports their cause well once that candidate is elected he has a debt to pay. I don't believe government should work that way."

Leslie looked at Lee with a surprised look on her face and said, "Mr. Roth how can you be so cynical about our government?"

Lee chuckles and says, "It's pretty easy Leslie just watch television for about an hour. I deal in logic not emotion in my business. It defies logic to arrive at any other conclusion."

"Let me be clear Mr. Roth. You are saying that Washington believes votes are more important than public good?" Leslie asks.

"Yes that is exactly what I am saying. When you are elected if you want to stay in office you must succumb to special interest groups and large voting blocks. If you fail to reward these groups you will lose their votes. Soon neither hard work or laziness matters and success or failure is unimportant. The only thing that is important to most politicians is votes.

Lee realizes he might be a little too aggressive but the only way he knew how to interact is by being brutally truthful.

Lee continues, "I can only speak for myself. I find most politicians self serving and I simply do not wish to be around them nor do I support or trust them. I apologize in advance if this offends anyone but I feel the same way about the media.

The media can spin any story to suit their own needs and desires. The media stopped reporting news years ago and now they attempt to create news. I realize the media has freedom of the press but I also have the freedom to avoid the media and politicians which I have done until now."

Lee knows that the liberal media will crucify him over the next few days but he is also confident that the logic of his conclusions is irrefutable.

Leslie is almost unable to recover from Lee's remarks and could not process what he had said quickly enough to formulate a provocative question. She asks, "Why have you decided to speak now Mr. Roth."

Lee looks at her with total sincerity and said, "Mrs. Stark, our country is approaching disaster and everybody seems to be trying to ignore the inevitable. I love this country and I am angry. I am angry with myself, for sitting it out, if you will.

Well, no longer will I sit silently. I will do every thing in my power, from this point forward, to help restore America to the great country she is supposed to be."

After ten more minutes of innocuous conversation with Lee; Leslie looks into the camera and says, "We wish to thank Mr. Roth for his candor and interesting comments. Right after this brief commercial you will hear from another member of the famed "Forcesome", Mr. Robbie Ravenel."

CHAPTER 33

The camera pans Charleston Harbor capturing the magnificent view of Ft. Sumter, the battery, rainbow row, the new Cooper River Bridge and finally the corporate headquarters of Secureone.

As they had done with Lee and Adam the camera captures the style and grace of the lobby as well as the rest of the public area before entering Robbie's office where he is seated at his desk with Charlie Ross.

Robbie is wearing the Charleston uniform, which consist of khaki trousers, blue shirt, a blue sports coat, and loafers. Charlie is dressed in an attractive black suit, white shirt, and red tie.

Charlie leans in and asks, "Mr. Ravenel I understand your nephew was killed in the Charlotte terrorist attack. Could you tell us how difficult that day was for you and your family?"

Robbie didn't expect the question and a flood of emotions rushes his consciousness. The camera focuses on a tight shot that picks up the despair in his eyes as he coughed nervously and said, "It was very hard on all of us. A promising bright young man who studied hard in school, worked hard, and cared for others.

It wasn't just a loss to his family it was a loss to the world. It was the most difficult day of my life but like all things you just have to believe that some how that day will strengthen us and better prepare us for the future."

"You are in the security business and understand these issues better than most; do you think anything could have been done to prevent the attack in Charlotte?" Ross asks.

"I don't think so Charlie. The fact is our government has done a pretty good job of protecting us since 9/11. It really isn't possible to prevent people determined to inflict pain from doing so. However, I do feel confident that the people who committed this crime will face the consequences of their evil." Robbie replies with certainty.

"As you know, tonight's program features three of the members of the Forcesome. It is clear that Joe Winston is also an important part of your lives. Tell us a little about Mr. Winston." Charlie said.

Robbie laughs a little and said, "Joe Winston is the finest and most decent human being I have ever known. Lee, Adam, and I have been able to enjoy some success in our lives because Joe Winston supported each of us financially, emotionally, and intellectually. His compassion, friendship, and generosity are unsurpassed and his devotion to family, friends, and God is complete. I wish there were more Joe Winston's in the world."

"Well hopefully we will have the pleasure of meeting him soon?" Charlie said.

"Anything is possible.' Robbie replies with a knowing smile on his face.

"What must be done to rid our country from the threat of terrorism?" Ross asked.

Robbie said, "We are a pretty sophisticated country with some very special technology at our disposal. We need to climb up the food chain and find out who's feeding the monkeys that commit these acts. I believe we have the capability but we too constrained by political correctness and legal implications that significantly impact our ability to win a war on terror."

"Could you pursue that just a little further for our viewers?" Ross asked.

"I will try. Our intelligence community is severely handicapped by political implications and the fact that there are no more secrets. Political agendas result in every action being public and therefore our enemies always know our position and we never know theirs.

We are a civilized and law abiding country but we are required to afford those who would harm us with the same respect and legal rights of an American citizen. I believe we could convince radical Islamist to avoid hostile American contact if we were as committed to protecting our citizens as diligently as we protect our enemies." Robbie firmly said.

CHAPTER 34

Bert Braddock, the ex SEAL, good friend and valued employee sits across from his boss who is casually sitting in his fine leather chair with his feet comfortably placed upon his desk.

Bert places a file on the desk and slides it across to Robbie. He looks at Robbie and said, "Robbie hold on to your ass you will not believe the contents of this file."

Robbie looks at the muscular man with the military haircut and knew that this is a man who has seen things that few could even imagine but his expression suggested that the contents of the folder he had placed on his desk must be beyond comprehension. He removes his feet from the desk and reaches over and picks up the thick file.

As Bert arranges his papers, audio, and video files he adds, "After observing Aziz for almost five months we know him pretty damn well. Among other things, when he is sequestered in his office he has a habit of talking out loud which has been most helpful to us.

He has a large safe in the small storage room just behind his office. We have never attempted to open it because of the possibility of a security system we could not detect. Over the past six weeks, when he opened the safe he has audibly mumbled the numbers. With video and audio enhancement we finally got the complete combination."

Bert nods at Robbie indicating that he should read the file and Robbie flips it open, put on his reading glasses and begins to read as Bert awaited the reaction he knew was coming.

Occasionally Robbie would stop reading and utter a comment. "Unbelievable". "Jesus Christ", "I can't believe this."

Fifteen minutes later Robbie laid the file down. His face seems to have lost color and the incredulous look on his face spoke volumes, "Bert, this is absolutely amazing. If I didn't see it I would never believe it."

Bert stands up, pulls his jeans a little higher, and paces around the desk shaking his head and with a mixture of disgust and respect said slowly, "Robbie the patience, cunning, and ingenuity of these Jihadist is almost incomprehensible. For over fifty fucking years they have been infiltrating our country and sponsoring subversive activities designed to ultimately destroy us from within.

I also have a copy of Aziz's journal that indicates dates, times, amounts, and names to support that report; some big names on that list." He tosses the data to Robbie.

"Damn! In 1961 they were secretly funding the Black Panthers, the NAACP, anti-war protest, civil liberties advocates, pro choice, politicians and political groups and they are still doing it. They not only funded their efforts they coordinated and helped plan their actions. Their plan was absolutely brilliant.

After integration they knew they could capitalize on the guilt of whites and fuel the hatred of blacks against whites. They funded the activist groups and played the liberal politicians knowing they would eventually bring this country to the brink of disaster." Robbie said as his eyes still scanned the documents on his desk." Robbie shakes his head in disbelief.

Bert, with a look of amazement and admiration, said, "Fifty years is a big investment in the destruction of a country but these cunning bastards are smarter and more cunning then any enemy we ever faced.

Their plan was the economic destruction of our country and the creation of class warfare between the haves and have not's. Very much like the Shia and Sunni conflict in their world. Not only have they orchestrated this masterful plan they have basically forced us to subsidize it. According to his records they have spent 1.8 billion on the project."

Robbie, still in a semi state of shock, leans back in his chair, rubbed his eyes with his hands, and stared at the files trying to comprehend the magnitude of this discovery, "Small price to pay for the United States of America. Hell, we spent two trillion in the last two years to try and unravel the damage they have inflicted upon us."

Robbie picks up the copy of Aziz's journal and began to read, "Dozens of named prominent black leaders, political activist, and politicians who have accepted money from these manipulative pricks to do their bidding and it appears that many were completely unaware of their ultimate goal. Hell, I am not even sure they knew who was providing the cash but the cock suckers were willing to take it."

"Aziz is taking orders from someone, do we know who? Robbie asks Bert.

Bert said, "Not yet, but I suspect when we get with Lee and do a significant computer search we can get to the right guy. I think we are real close Robbie."

Robbie leans back in his chair and sighed deeply, "Bert, I can't get over this. This answers questions we have had for years. I will give Lee a heads up and set something up for you guys to brainstorm."

CHAPTER 35

Majid's mood has been excellent for the last few months. As he reads the American papers every day he is delighted to see the constant social and economic turmoil. There is nothing in the world that gives him more pleasure than the suffering of the infidel Americans.

The American economic crisis has dramatically changed his normally reserved and serious demeanor to the point he is almost giddy. His close associates are mystified by his apparent personality change but it is clear the new behavior is far superior to the old. It is almost as if he is a teenager who has fallen in love for the first time.

Majid's efforts to unify the Muslim nations are approaching the first summit meeting to discuss implementation and the unification process. He expects to moderate this historic meeting by March of 2010.

He has been conducting semi-annual meetings with his covert country heads and is especially looking forward to meeting with Aziz Hassan and implementing the final stage of his plan that would lead to the demise of America. He has been consumed by nothing else for the past fifty years and now the end is in sight.

His concern over the missing men lingers in the back of his mind and he is concerned about Aziz. Soon he will have to decide on a replacement for his old friend.

Majid ordered Aziz to come to Palmyra, Syria and he was asked to bring as many comprehensive details as possible concerning the impact of the current health care reform and the reaction of American.

He also requested information on something called "tea parties" which he did not understand. He knew Aziz would compile copious notes and documents and he made it clear to Aziz that he wanted specific details not fluff. Aziz's understanding of American society is also extremely significant inasmuch as he understands the nuances of the American culture and is able to convey the relevance of societal reactions to someone who has not experienced their life style.

He also asked Aziz to implement full time surveillance on President Howard and to carefully monitor his movements, habits, and his security coverage. He was told that this is a very high priority and expectations are high. Majid would expect to receive a comprehensive report.

Few can understand the pursuit of a fifty year goal and the feeling of joy that one feels when he can, at long last, see the finish line. Majid could have chosen a path of hammering America with deadly attacks but opted for the more subtle economic and social attacks.

He could easily have tens of thousands Americans killed tomorrow but to do so would cause other nations to support the Great Satan. The subtle approach is best. Let them destroy themselves.

CHAPTER 36

SEPTEMBER 18, 2009
CHARLESTON, S.C.

Bert Braddock is extremely pleased that events have once again placed him in a position to contribute to the preservation of his country. His past experience and desire for danger is once again being satisfied.

He received notification that Hassan has completed plans to travel to Syria. Bert arranged for a surveillance team to arrive in Syria prior to Hassan in hopes that this trip might lead to Aziz's boss.

He is sending Mike Miller, aka Makin Sharifi, on the same flights. Mike is originally from Jordon and was also a SEAL prior to joining Secureone. He is fully briefed on their objectives and highly motivated as his family had been victims of the Taliban.

After Bert finished putting together all the op plans, arranging for everyone to be properly briefed, and equipped, he calls Robbie.

Robbie picks up the phone and said, "Hello".

Bert said, "Good morning Boss. I have some news for you when can we meet?"

Robbie is impatient for an update and said, "How about lunch at the Yacht Club at 11:45 am?"

Robbie and Lee were leaving Charleston the next morning to meet Joe and Adam at Volusia National and are preparing to discuss the surveillance results and the commonality worm.

Robbie and Bert are meeting in a private room on the second floor of the Charleston Yacht Club overlooking Charleston Harbor. It is a balmy eighty five degrees with winds of fifteen to twenty knots in the harbor. The harbor is filled with sailboats with their white sails catching the brisk wind and a very large freighter entering the harbor by Ft. Sumter.

After lunch is served and they are left alone Bert leans forward and said, "Aziz is leaving for Syria and hopefully he may lead us to his boss. Mike will travel with him and hopefully introduce the transmitters and we have also sent an advance team to Syria to assist."

Robbie looks both ways, as if to make sure no one is there and said with excitement, "Great work Bert. I am sure you have every thing covered."

Bert whispers, "We do and I hope you weren't planning on using our G4 because we are going to need it."

Robbie leans back in his chair and gazes out at the clear blue skies and white puffy clouds over the blue green Atlantic Ocean and watches the boats gliding over the sea. He relaxes and allows himself a satisfied smile and finally returns his eyes to Bert and said, "No problem Bert. You know how big this is Bert. Stay on top of it and do whatever you deem necessary."

Bert reaches across the table and puts his right hand on Robbie's left shoulder and looks straight into Robbie's blue eyes and said with assurance, "Rest easy boss, we have it covered."

Bert's team would be on the ground in Syria fifteen hours prior to Aziz's arrival. They are equipped with the necessary electronic equipment devised by Lee Roth.

The ground team is to locate the "pick up" car for Aziz and place one of Lee's undetectable tracking devices on the vehicle while Mike is responsible for the injection of the microscopic transmitters into Aziz. This experimental transmitter would not only pin point location it would transmit audio within fifteen feet of Aziz.

Mike has lived in the United States since receiving his degree in international politics at the University of South Carolina in 1991. His athletic ability and his 4.0 grade point average attracted the attention of the United States Navy. Mike completed basic training and was recruited to the SEAL program. He excelled in everything he attempted but became disillusioned with the political side of the military and was recruited by Bert Braddock.

Mike's brother and sister were killed by the Taliban in 2002 and his mother was raped and murdered. His father was absent when this occurred and died of despair two years later. Mike was not notified of his death for six months after it occurred.

Mike is more than ready to extract revenge and felt as if divine intervention had placed him in just the right place at just the right time.

CHAPTER 37

Adam and Joe spent the entire morning in the upstairs great room pouring over the Federal Budget, for about the fourth time, and are astounded at the redundancy within each Department and the enormous waste of money.

After five hours of pouring over the Federal budget they easily found expense reductions of six hundred Billion and concluded that massive reorganization and consolidation would be essential. The thousand of bureaucrats in Washington are not going to like the Restoration Administration.

Robbie and Lee joined Joe and Lee around noon and the four men adjourned to have lunch downstairs in the bar. After lunch is prepared the employees were instructed to take two hours off.

When they are alone Robbie said in a conspiratorial voice, "You guys are not going to believe what I am about to share with you."

Twenty minutes later when Robbie had briefed the group of the events that had transpired within the last few days with Hassan and the fifty year plan to destroy America. Each man is speechless and they sit silently for a minute or two with stunned looks on their faces.

Joe finally said, "Unbelievable. Are we so stupid that we could not have foreseen this? What the hell do our intelligence people actually do?"

Adam said reflectively, "At least it seems to explain a lot of events that have occurred in our society over the past few decades. No one would have ever suspected an organized effort from a foreign entity to promote civil disorder. My God, think about it, integration, anti-war, abortion, and all the civil liberties issues they have supported. They have turned freedom into a weapon of mass destruction."

Robbie said, "Well, on the bright side we are hoping that Aziz will lead us to the ingenious son-of-a-bitch who is orchestrating this symphony. Lee, why don't you tell the boys about your gadgets?"

Lee smiles confidently and said, "Well I developed a helpful little, forgive me for the use of a highly technical term, gizmo. This gizmo, or commonality worm, can be inserted into ISP systems and give us instant feedback when two or more parties access a site within specified parameters'." Lee pauses and could see the confusion and decided to simplify.

As an example Joe, if I inject this worm into your computer via a harmless looking email it would be completely undetectable by any virus or spyware system currently known. My worm will tell me who you communicate with, what is said, and what you view. The worm will be spread by the infected computer to other recipients. In a short period of time we have access to all their communications."

Adam said, "Damn Lee, something like that could really be dangerous if it fell in the wrong or right hands."

Lee said, "Yeah, I have thought about all the money I could make selling my little worm but I figured that would make me a prostitute so I decided against it."

Everyone chuckled. They all needed something to break the tension and that weak joke was enough.

Robbie said, "Hell, if you were a prostitute you would be on welfare."

Joe got back on the subject and said, "Tell me about the nano devices that we are going to try with this Aziz character?"

Lee said, "Well I will give this to you in non-technical terms. What Robbie's guys will use is simply a very small tracking and audio transmitter device that has a life span of approximately six years.

The device is implanted in the subject's neck or forearm to be most effective. It is introduced into the subject's body by a modified syringe that employs a needle with a little larger opening. Preferably, the subject would be in non-awake state when injected to avoid a very small sting. The device will be under the skin and will not be visible or detectable. Our tests were very positive and I am confident it will be very helpful in Robbie's efforts."

Robbie asks out of curiosity, "How did you test it Lee."

Lee smiles and said softly, "Well I can tell you what you and Emily talked about last Tuesday night around midnight."

Robbie quickly looks at his forearms and then tries to pretend he didn't. Once again the whole group burst out in laughter.

Robbie couldn't help but laugh also. If someone were watching they would never guess these men were dealing with the very survival of America. Even in the face of grave danger Americans could always retain their sense of humor.

As the laughter subsided, Robbie looks closely at his forearms and said, "You prick, you didn't did you?"

Lee looks at Lee and with his always quick wit and retorted, "I could tell you but then I would have to kill you."

Robbie's cell phone rings and he saw on the caller ID that it was Bert, He signals for the guys to be quiet, "Hey Bert, how is it going?"

Bert said, "Everything is on schedule. All systems are on go."

Robbie said, "Thanks Bert, keep me updated."

CHAPTER 38

SEPTEMBER 25, 2009
RICHMOND, VIRGINIA

Tony arrives at John's home around one o'clock in the afternoon and climbs out of his rental car with his large brief case and walks to the front door. John greets him at the front door and notices that Tony looks more disheveled than usual. As Tony struggles up the last of the entrance stairs he is greeted warmly by John, "Hi Tony it is so good to see you. How are you?

John can see that Tony is a little frustrated as he somberly replies, "I'm fine John. How are you?"

John said, "Come on up here and let's sit down in these old rocking chairs and enjoy this beautiful day." John directed Tony to a rocker and Tony places his briefcase beside the chair and sinks heavily into the rocker.

Mary appears as if by magic carrying a tray with cold lemonade and some home made chocolate chip cookies and said, "Good afternoon Mr. Tony I made these cookies just for you."

Tony pulls his tired body out of the rocker, nods at Mary, and says, "Thank you Mary. I know I will enjoy them."

John let Tony eat a cookie and drink some lemonade before he asks, "Tony it looks like you have got something on your mind; want to talk about it?

Tony glances at John and realizes how happy he is to be in the presence of a real friend and immediately relaxes, "John I have just been doing this shit too long. Dealing with the media and politicians all day is not pleasant and I guess I am just getting old."

John laughs and looks warmly at Tony and said, "Well son if you think its hard now wait till you get to be my age. Getting old isn't for sissies."

Tony could not help but smile as he ran his hand through what is left of his graying hair and said, "I know John it's just been a rough week."

John is rocking vigorously in his chair as he looks thoughtfully at Tony and said, "Well let's talk about it son."

Tony relaxes and said, "Those whore media people beg me all day long for the opportunity to interview Adam, Lee, and Robbie and then they just try their best to tear them down. They completely ignore the excellent points made by the guys and focus in on some innocuous statement and misrepresent what they actually intended."

Tony pauses and grabs another cookie as John looks at Tony with a surprised expression and said, "Tony what did you expect?"

Tony quickly chews the cookie and chases it with the delicious lemonade as he looks at John. A smile begin to appear on his face and soon he is laughing hysterically and so is John.

After a couple of minutes of this Tony slowly gets out of the rocker and walks over to the porch railings and looks out over John's beautiful property where horses are galloping in the fields and cows are grazing.

He turns to John and said, "I don't know what in the hell I expected. Same shit different day. I guess I am just too personally involved in this one and I don't respond well to criticism. Hell John I have been doing this a long time the business just disgust me."

John rocks a little slower and said, "From where I am sitting I would say the boys are a breath of fresh air. They don't hesitate to say what they are thinking or to stand by their beliefs. The public will have to decide if they wish to believe them or the media and I think the American people are smart enough to make the right decision."

Tony knows John is right and he recognizes that for the first time in his life he really believes in what he is doing. It isn't a job anymore it has become a calling. "John it really doesn't make much difference what they say about them as long as they are talking about them the better it will be for us."

John nods his head and said, "Yep. I agree with that."

Tony said, "I have got to tell you John these four men are truly extraordinary. They are completely honest and totally unassuming, they are intelligent and articulate, and more importantly they are very likeable and extremely convincing."

"Good. I'm not surprised at how well they are doing. What's next for them?" John asks.

Tony replied, "I'm getting dozens of calls a day asking about them, the Restoration Party, and Joe Winston. The media is creating their own scenarios and, as you know, some are suggesting that Joe is behind the Restoration Party.

This is all very good for us. I think our boys have about said enough for now so we are going to back off a little until we get closer to Joe making his announcement and mounting our big push for the mid terms."

John flashes a contented smile and said, "Tony, if we can make a good showing at the mid terms we might have a chance to really do some good."

"I understand. How are you doing with converts?" Tony asks as he reaches for his third cookie.

"Currently, I feel confident about six Republican Senators and four Democrats. Looks like a dozen or so congressmen are good to go. I believe after Joe announces we could get fifteen or twenty in the Senate and triple that for the House." John replies.

"I apologize for my grumpy attitude earlier John." Tony said.

"No need. Let's go inside and get some work done." John says as the men walk inside.

CHAPTER 39

Aziz arrives at terminal 5 at Chicago's O'Hare Airport at 9:15 pm. He impatiently waits in line at security and totally detests being treated just like everyone else. He calms himself by taking some pride in the fact that he had something to do with this security. All Americans will be inconvenienced for many, many years due to 9/11and that fact did console him.

He is accustomed to being in control and detests situations over which he has no control and the process of catching a flight is totally out of his control. Finally he clears security and boards Royal Jordanian Flight RJ264 headed to Amman where he will connect with RJ435 to Damascus, Syria.

His flight is called on time. He boards and settles into seat 6B in the first class cabin. He is disappointed to see that someone occupies 6A. He was hoping for a quiet flight. He notices the man in 6A is reading a Syrian magazine as he says, "Please excuse me."

The man in 6A stands to give Aziz plenty of room and said, "Certainly Sir, I apologize I did not see you."

Aziz coolly says, "Thank you!" as he stows his briefcase and takes his seat.

The man sits back down in his aisle seat and politely extends his hand and said, "My name is Mike Miller."

Aziz takes his hand and smiles politely, "Aziz Hassan; Nice to meet you Mr. Miller."

Mike continues reading his magazine until take off paying little attention to his neighbor.

Aziz is extremely apprehensive about his trip and knows that his inability to give Majid some definite answers regarding the missing men will not please him.

This mystery occupies his mind constantly and he detests not being able to solve a problem. He is inclined to believe that it is a covert black ops initiative but has no evidence to confirm his suspicion. There is no other logical explanation.

Flight RJ264 departs on time and within fifteen minutes they are cruising at an altitude of 37,000 feet at 510 knots. The flight attendants start beverage service and Aziz clearly enjoys his tea. Aziz makes no effort to communicate with Mike, as Mike expected, Aziz is a careful man and has survived for decades by being observant and cautious and Mike is no novice. If there is to be any conversation it must be initiated by Aziz otherwise Mike would remain silent for the entire trip. Mike believes Aziz will eventually engage in casual conversation.

After they were in the air for about an hour meals were served, food is eaten, and finally the trays are cleared. The passengers are ready to sleep away as many hours as possible to shorten the long journey.

Aziz orders another cup of tea from the attractive flight attendant and excuses himself to go to the restroom. Prior to his return his tea is left on his arm rest and Mike cautiously empties the contents of a capsule into the tea and stirs it with his pen.

Within three minutes after Aziz finishes his tea he is sleeping soundly and he will not wake up for at least five hours. The cabin is quiet and the flight attendants pulled the curtains and everyone is either watching the movie, reading, or sleeping.

Mike removes his brief case from beneath his seat, quietly opens it and removes the two syringes, and turns off the seat lights. After a glance around the cabin to be sure no one is watching he injects Aziz as he had been instructed and Aziz fails to stir.

After replacing his briefcase Mike lowers his seat and joins the rest of the passengers trying to sleep away the trip.

Buck and his team are already in Damascus and had picked up two rental cars and the remainder of their equipment that had been shipped to their hotel. After checking the arrival time of the connecting flight from Amman RJ435 they determined they had time for a few hours of shut eye and took it.

Flight RJ435 from Amman touchs down in Damascus at 5:04 am. Buck and his team easily found the Mercedes sedan scheduled to transport Aziz Hassan to his ultimate destination and place one of their high tech transmitters under the rear bumper.

Buck and Charley are visually watching the car and his other two men are in a panel truck handling the technology issues. Their checks confirmed the equipment was functioning properly. Billy Jackson is the high tech expert and informs Buck that the audio they were receiving is beyond expectations.

Soon the passengers start exiting the terminal and heading toward the pick up area. Aziz is met by his driver who escorts him to the shiny black Mercedes SL 600 with tinted black windows and clearly bullet proof. The driver opens the rear door for Aziz and he threw his overnight bag inside and slipped into the comfortable seat.

Mike is not far behind and he will ride with Billy Jackson and Andy Johnson in the truck. He will function as interpreter as well as perform other duties assigned from this point forward.

The black Mercedes leaves the terminal and heads toward the Mediterranean before heading north east toward Palmyra which is located in the heart of the Syrian Desert.

CHAPTER 40

Majid finishes his breakfast and is quietly reading American newspapers when his security system notifies him that an automobile is entering his secure perimeter. He stands up and walks over to his security office and looks at the appropriate monitor and saw that it is his driver returning from Damascus with Aziz.

Being the careful man that he is, Majid had chosen to live in Palmyra thirty years ago. Palmyra is located in the heart of the Syrian Desert is often referred to as the "Oasis" because of the abundance of palm-trees and a hot water spring called Afqua.

Palmyra prospered from the second century because of its strategic location and was a regular stop for caravans moving between Iraq, Lebanon, Jordon, and the Holy land and consequently Palmyra thrived.

Majid's magnificent home is the only home for seven miles in any direction and it is impossible for anyone to approach without detection. The area around his home is actually quite lush with many palms and a small lake and it would be hard to comprehend that he is surrounded by hundreds of miles of harsh desert.

In addition to his main home there are two attractive guest cottages. One is used for his staff and the other for his domestic and security teams. He is paranoid about security and makes it a point to have the very best technology and people.

His primary home was constructed in the old Roman style architecture and sat on a hill in the middle of his 127 acres of land. The barn is located about a mile from the residence and houses several thoroughbred Arabian horses that frolic in the equestrian area surrounding the barn.

Within his immaculate 13,000 square foot home are seven bedrooms in addition to Majid's master suite, eleven bathrooms, a very large main room, comfortably furnished and adorned with historic and Islamists artifacts, a dining area that could accommodate thirty guests at the highly polished imported hand carved mahogany table. Over the table there is one of the most ornate chandeliers imaginable. The chandelier had a diameter of fifteen feet and is made of crystal and rubies and is nothing short of stunning. The beautiful chandelier is more than a simple light it is a work of art and Majid paid over three hundred thousand dollars for it in 1989.

His security room is state of the art just as his kitchen, office, and entertainment room. It is indeed a perfect location for this man of mystery. In addition to his eight security men there are another twelve members of his domestic staff.

Majid is waiting in his office as his driver delivers his guest. Majid stands and greets Aziz with a warm, but reserved, embrace, "Aziz, my old friend, I hope your trip was pleasant."

Aziz returns the embrace and replies, "It was very comfortable Majid. For some reason I slept much more than usual, thank you for asking."

Majid said, "I know you would like to refresh yourself and have some breakfast. Your bag has been taken to your usual suite Aziz. Clean up and relax a bit and we will talk this afternoon."

Buck and his crew are tracking the movements of Aziz utilizing the GPS and remain several miles away. All equipment seems to be working properly until Aziz enters Majid's home and immediately the transmissions ceases. Majid, being a very careful man, had installed a jamming device that would prevent anyone from bugging his home.

Buck became concerned when the audio disappears and nervously asks Billy Jackson, "What the hell is going on Billy? I'm getting nothing."

Billy snickers at how dumb non-technology people can be and said, "Buck, they have jammers designed to prevent people from hearing them within the house"

Buck said, "Well what the hell are we going to do?"

Billy replies, "Relax B.A., Mr. Roth is a pretty smart dude. He expected we would encounter something like this so the voice transponder simply marks the time period of interference and records the time period."

Buck said, "So when can we hear it?"

Billy impatiently tells Buck, "We can hear it when the electronic jamming is shut down or when the subject leaves the house."

Buck is frustrated and said, "Shit! Mike, I want you find out who lives in the house and in the meantime we will drill down on satellite imagery and see if we can learn anything."

In less than an hour they learned the palatial home belongs to a man named Majid Abdulla Mohammed. They initiated a comprehensive background check and for now all they could do is wait or visit the old Roman ruins in Palmyra.

Buck's team has no way of knowing exactly what is going on inside the house but within two hours they receive a report on the owner, Majid Abdulla Mohammed. He holds no official status but he is obviously a very powerful man with connections to all the Muslim nations. His passport records indicated a significant amount of travel to the various Middle East nations and his mission apparently is to put together a tighter coalition if not a completely unified Muslim nation.

Since they are well aware of Aziz's role in the United States it is conceivable that Majid Abdulla Mohammed could be the leader of the extremists. Why else would Aziz be here?

His financial records confirmed he is extremely wealthy and his assets are extensive. They suspected what they had found quickly only represented a small percentage of his true wealth. It is assumed that he is nothing more than a very wealthy businessman but this is the first time anyone in the Western world had made the possible connection with terrorism.

At 8:00 am the next morning, Aziz is driven back to the airport. The minute he clears the protected area Billy cues up the tape and they began to listen to the recorded conversations. They heard nothing of significance for the first hour of the playback but soon they heard incredible dialogue between the two men.

Aziz fully and professionally briefed Majid on the economic and political situation in America. When Aziz concluded, Majid spoke, "You have done well my old friend. It appears our plans are working better than we could have expected."

Aziz replied, "thank you."

Majid said, "I want you to prepare to implement "Project Thor" on April 5, 2010. Here are your instructions" (Majid handed Aziz written instructions.)

Majid continued, "Allah has called upon us to be his instrument to destroy the infidels forever. We will bring those arrogant dogs to their knees. This is a mission that will have no excuse, Aziz, you cannot fail Allah. Do you understand?"

"Yes Majid, I understand and I will not fail you or Allah again. I have time to prepare and I will succeed for the glory of Allah." Aziz said.

Majid brusquely said, "Read the instructions carefully. Memorize them and destroy them. Clear?"

"Yes, it will be done." Aziz said.

"Once you have completed your assignment I expect to announce the unification of Muslim nations in the Middle East soon thereafter and the world will be in the hands of Allah." Majid said.

"Congratulations on you success, Majid; It will be a joyous time for our Muslim brothers and sisters when this long journey comes to an end." Aziz said.

Once Aziz left the protected area, it is clear that they have identified the person pulling the strings and Mike is able to translate the playback and conclude there is little other valuable information with the exception of Project Thor and the date.

Mike and his team quietly make preparations to return home and meet with Bert for debriefing and to find out what in the hell is "Project Thor."

CHAPTER 41

OCTOBER 6, 2009
RICHMOND, VIRGINIA

Lee and Carolyn are visiting the Winston's for the weekend and the two men are sitting in Joe's den. It is an unusually cold day for early October and there is a roaring fire in the large Robert E. Lee fireplace. The ladies had gone shopping and Lee and Joe are enjoying some hot chocolate. Lee notices that Joe appears to be troubled and asks, "Joe looks like you have something bothering you. Want to talk about it?"

Joe is sitting in his favorite chair facing the fireplace while Lee is lounging on the couch. Joe did have a few things on his mind and answers, "Lee, I'm accustomed to stress and I am no stranger to problem solving. I consider myself pretty good at my job but the mixture of emotions I am feeling over this is different than anything I have ever experienced. I don't know if I am angry, sad, happy, challenged, bored, disappointed or what!"

Lee listens patiently and does not interrupt as Joe pauses and looks out the large window at the brilliant stars and a crescent moon as he tries to wrap his mind around what he really wants to say. "Let me just ramble for a minute or two Lee and maybe you can help me clear things up."

Lee stretches out on the couch and gives Joe his full attention, "I will do my best."

Joe began, "I am bothered by my sudden loss on anonymity but there is more. Part of me is very disappointed with politicians but my belief in America is strong. Trying to articulate my conflicted thoughts is proving to be difficult. It seems to me that somewhere between the sixties and the eighties things began to drift away from the ideals that made our country great.

Fifty years ago there were no mortgage problems. People did not view their homes as investments and their goal was to burn the mortgage one day. There were few Government subsidy programs and if people were going through hard times they would work harder or get another job, and if that didn't do it, the neighbors or the church would help.

People seemed to have self respect and self determination and they accepted responsibility for their situations.

Schools were basically controlled by the states and local school boards and it seemed to work pretty well. American's were proud and independent. They were generous and kind. If the community had problems they fixed them, together.

Today it appears there is little individual pride or self reliance, we have sixty to eighty million Americans dependent upon the federal government for full or partial support." Joe pauses as he is having difficulty expressing himself as clearly as he would like. He stands up and walks over to the fireplace and pokes the logs and said, "Am I nuts or am I just out of touch with reality? Did people change or did government change people?"

Lee rises from his prone position into a sitting position facing Joe and said, "Now I am a little younger than you Joe and I don't know a whole lot about politics because I have tried to ignore it until now. Joe, you are proudly Patriotic and I mean that with all due respect. You find it difficult to be critical of our country but I am not encumbered by the same restrictions so let me give you a different perspective."

"I'm all ears." Joe said as he relaxes in his chair and looks at Lee.

"After World War II and the Korean conflict America was riding high. We stood up to tyranny and proved to the world that good beats evil every time. Every American was extremely proud of our country and its profound sense of fairness as were the countries we helped to remain free.

We were united, we trusted our leaders and looked up to public officials, and we were damn proud to be Americans.

It seems to me that what happened was freedom. The media, anti-war protest, integration, which was long over due, and we learned that our politicians would gladly sell out freedom for votes.

After Watergate and Viet Nam they became more dishonest, greedy, arrogant, and learned that public service paid well emotionally and economically. Since the sixties it appears to me there has been a continuing decline of integrity among our elected officials which has permeated society" Lee pauses to gage Joe's reaction.

Joe slowly and deliberately asked, "How do we restore confidence in government if the people vote for their own self interest in lieu of what is best for our country?

Something about this remark pissed off Lee, "God-damn it Joe, you are supposed to be a smart man. You can't see it?

Joe is confused by Lee's sharp response and said, "See what?"

Lee looks at him with intellectual superiority and said, "The American people listen to all the political bull shit and don't believe any of it.

The politicians are training them to vote for personal benefits and the public has just lost sight of the importance of individual freedom. Joe I believe most Americans believe this country can't be saved. Politicians are like puppet masters and they are pulling all the strings."

Lee paused and then continued his rant, "Joe, you can't get caught up in all this "political correctness" you are a decent and honorable man and I will kill any son of a bitch that says otherwise. You have to be you. You must speak from your heart. You must stop these bastards from destroying us and you must inspire the voters to place their country first. If America fails we all fail and even the dumbest person can understand that."

Joe with a concerned look on his face said, "Lee, we have poured over budgets for weeks and when you do that you can tend to lose perspective. Politicians have been ripping Americans off for years and it can't continue. The problem is that a luxury once enjoyed becomes a necessity. When we pull the plug on these cash giveaway many people will not be happy and some will be hurt."

Lee said quickly, "Fuck them, and pull the god damn plug. Joe, anyone who lives in this country has the freedom and opportunity to make as much of their life as they possibly can. That's why everybody in the world wants to live here. They are attracted by the greatness of our country and the tremendous opportunity we offer. Look around Joe. What's happening to our culture?

I will tell you what's happening; our culture is being destroyed by the freedoms guaranteed by our country. One of America's great strengths has been the tremendous contributions made by immigrants who wanted to enjoy our culture as it was.

Now many immigrants simply want to take advantage of our benefits and create their own culture within America. Joe, this is a little like wetting the bed. Sooner or later you have to get up and do something about it."

Joe laughs and says quietly, "Lee, the other side of that scenario is insatiable greed of some of our business leaders, politicians, and even religious leaders. It seems as if everybody is trying to screw everybody else and I just can't relate to that thought process. Can it be stopped or is too ingrained in our society?"

"Hell yes it can be stopped and must be stopped. This country is about fairness above anything else. Joe, we have 10% of the population that will always do just fine no matter what government does. We have 10% that just want make the effort. The people you must concern yourself is that 80% in the middle. What's fair to them Joe?" Lee asks emphatically.

Joe considers Lee's comments carefully before responding, "Lee, I find myself starting to think like a politician and that scares me"

"Joe I don't know much, but I do know that all reasonable Americans understand what is happening to our culture but political correctness prevents them from saying it. The question is can you be elected President of the United States of America by telling the truth?"

CHAPTER 42

It is 6:30 am in Belk's office and he has a scheduled briefing with Fred Barker and Billy Hughes who is the Press Secretary. Harry has 30 minutes before meeting with the President and wants feedback from Fred and Billy prior to the meeting.

He leans back in his leather chair and put his feet on the desk and said to Billy, "Give it to me straight Billy what's going on?"

Billy is not shy otherwise he would not allow himself to be pounded by the press almost daily but he did have some concerns, "As you wish Harry. The President is letting his goddamn ego destroy everything we are trying to accomplish. He has got to stop all these news conferences and public appearances he is over exposed and the public isn't buying his bull shit anymore. Harry he talks a lot but never says anything plus he is providing the conservatives with plenty of reasons to criticize his policies and comments.

He is trying to do too much too quick and the result are that we are doing nothing very well. Harry I can find very little to be positive

197

about. I feel like we are still campaigning instead of trying to effectively run the government and serve the needs of the public."

Harry's expression never changes as he listened to Billy and jotted down a few notes in his binder. He turns to Fred and said, "Fred please give some encouraging information?"

Fred said, "It appears to me that the public has had enough of big government, excessive spending, and what they consider to be outright lies. I am told that telephone and email correspondence to the members of Congress is at an all time high which is a clear indication of the public's displeasure. If this trend continues we will not be back for a second term.

I am concerned about the Presidents efforts to influence statistical data to conform to his campaign promises. That is a very dangerous game. The public knows we are in deep debt, they know we can't afford a national health care program; they know that our stimulus program is not working, and they know that we can't keep blaming the prior administration.

They also are sick and tired of the constant media fighting between liberals and conservatives with each trying to prove who has the biggest dick. The public wants to see some positive results and they are running out of patience."

Harry isn't surprised with the information but he is concerned with the attitudes of two top Cabinet members. Harry jots down a few more notes and looks up to give Fred his attention.

"Howard is a terrific pitch man but he doesn't know shit about running the government or a business. Forget the conservatives we have many democrats that are very concerned about his agenda.

Apparently he is incapable of building a working relationship within his own party or building anything that resembles cohesion or unity.

The suggestion of more taxes is offensive to even the middle class. 1.4 million Taxpayers now pay more taxes than the other 138 million taxpayers while 65 million Americans pay no taxes.

We need a minimum of 3.5 trillion a year to run this government and we will only collect about two trillion this year. How in the hell can we run anything with such financial irresponsibility."

Harry interrupts, "Fred you are forgetting that without the stimulus and involvement in the auto and banking industry our country might have gone under......"

Fred stands up and glares at Harry and said, "That's bullshit and there is no evidence to support what might have happened." He quickly sits back down and made no effort to hide his frustration before continuing.

"Harry to be upfront with you I am going to submit my resignation. I don't believe I have anything to contribute to this Administration. We are going in a direction that leads no where."

Harry is frustrated by the negative tone and needs some time to spin it. He let his chair return to its proper position, took his feet off his desk, and leans forward putting his elbows on his desk and calmly said, "Let's talk about that later Fred. I need to go see the boss now and I will talk to him and share your concerns. Thanks for your input."

Harry glances at his watch picks up his papers and heads to the President's working office.

Five minutes later in the Oval Office President Howard turns to Harry Belk and said, "Harry why the hell can't we get anything done?"

"Mr. President I can only tell you that your entire staff is doing their very best to comply with your wishes. It will require some patience and continued hard work.

President Howard dryly replies, "Harry, things are moving way to slow and I am running out of patience. I am getting hammered every day by that god damned Fox network and the right wing talk shows and it appears that our efforts are yielding no results."

Harry looks at the President and firmly said, "Mr. President, we just need to reevaluate our situation and figure a way out of this. Remember we inherited most of this crap."

"Maybe so, Harry. Sooner or later we have to figure out a way to run this government the way it should be run." Howard said.

"We will Mr. President. We will." Harry replies.

"What about the troop dispersal in Iraq and Afghanistan?" The President asks.

"Going as expected. We only have ten thousand soldiers left in Iraq but we have over sixty thousand in Afghanistan and another thirty thousand will be deployed over the next two months. As you know the new deployment did not please everyone in our party.

The Taliban continues to threaten Pakistan and it appears that Pakistan is holding its own with our help. They claim they are pushing them into the tribal areas but the Pakistanis are as corrupt and dishonest as any government I know of." Harry responds.

The President's frustration is apparent as he says, "Harry, do we any positive news?"

Harry figures he might as well give the President a wake up call. "I will be as direct as possible. No we don't have any good news. Hughes thinks you are over exposed and should keep a lower profile and minimize interviews and public appearances."

President Howard frowned as he asked, "What do you think Harry?"

"Given the fact that we need time to actually complete significant legislation I would concur that you should keep a lower profile. After all running the country and being the leader of the free world should be time consuming." Harry advises.

The President did not respond so Harry continues, "Barker is extremely disenchanted and it contemplating resignation."

Howard turns around and glares at Harry and said angrily, "Appointing him was a big mistake and I wouldn't miss him one damn bit. Let him go and find someone who can support our views."

Harry said, "I know you don't want to hear this but I have to report to you that many feel you could do a better job in bringing people together. We need to unify our party and demonstrate that we can build a coalition among those who disagree and work together in a bi partisan way."

"Harry. Have you gone nuts! The republicans do nothing but criticize every thing we try to do." Howard said sharply.

Harry understands politics very well and even the illusion of bi partisanship is better than simply ignoring the minority party. "Mr. President. It's called politics. You need to create healthy bi partisan dialogue."

"That will be all Harry." The President said dismissively.

Harry is a tough political adversary and is largely responsible for the Presidents election and policies. He is not particularly liked on the hill but his ability to bully and intimidate those who oppose him is a powerful and effective weapon.

To Harry it was all about the game. Winning! He is not a particularly patriotic American and he pushes agendas that further his career and his power. He favors big government and his goal is to incrementally cause more Americans to become dependent on the government.

He is disappointed that the President seems to think everyone should simply bow to him because he won an election is fool hardy. He needs to figure a way to reshape the President's thinking.

When he reaches his office he finds Jack Hodges, his closest friend and ally and his chief advisor, waiting on him. Jack hands Harry a cup of coffee and said, "How did it go Harry?"

Harry told his assistant to hold his calls and closed his door, "Jack we have some serious problems. The President is getting weak. He can't keep his ass out the media limelight and he keeps sticking his fucking foot in his mouth. He is losing his confidence and sooner or later that will cost us. He just keeps talking and never says anything. He is losing credibility and his popularity is plummeting and he can't seem to understand he is a President not a fucking King."

Jack said, "Well Harry you did a hell of a job getting that empty suit in the oval office.".

Harry stands up and walks around behind his desk and said, "We need some good wins quick. I am going to kick some ass on the hill and call in every favor I have to get something passed on Health Care. It may be less than we want but it will be a win."

He smiles at Jack and said confidently, "We really need something big and I will find a way to salvage this mess. I will pull this administration out of this shit!"

CHAPTER 43

CHICAGO, ILLINOIS
OCTOBER 25, 2009

Weeks passed without Aziz communicating anything concerning Project Thor. Finally it appears there might be a break. Robbie was notified by Bert that Aziz scheduled a flight to Washington and is hopeful that this trip might shed some light on the mysterious Project Thor.

It is a cold and windy day with rain possibly turning to snow as Aziz finally leaves O'Hare Airport heading to Dulles Airport in Washington, D.C. The entire east coast is blanketed with an unusual early snow that forces a two hour delay.

During the delay he sits in a chair sandwiched between a large lady, who kept accidentally hitting his arm with her elbow and a teenager playing a video game on his laptop complete with the beep, beep, beep sounds. Children are running wild, a couple of black guys seem to think everyone should listen to their boom box, and there were continuous announcements regarding flights.

He closes his eyes in an attempt to escape from his surroundings and for perhaps the hundredth time, mentally reviews the mystery surrounding his missing men. He is an extremely careful man who hates loose ends and these issues are very tough for him to accept and move on.

Logic dictates that a covert Government agency must be involved but his sources have heard nothing. He considers the Mosad but knows they would not dare conduct operations in the U.S. He will not rest until he figures it out.

He hears the gate announcement that his flight is now ready for boarding and reaches in his inside breast pocket, removes his ticket, and checks his seat assignment and proceeds to stand in line once again.

The purpose of his visit is too met with Rashid Rahman, one of his key operatives, and with whom he has worked for the past fifteen years. Aziz has complete confidence in his abilities and has chosen him to participate in Project Thor. He looked forward to implementing the glorious mission given to him by Majid.

Rashid had previously been ordered to implement twenty four hour surveillance of President Howard and to look for specific patterns. He knew it would most likely yield little but nonetheless it is necessary and would give Rashid an opportunity to hone his skills.

Aziz arrives in Washington three hours late, quickly exits the plane, and heads down to the pick up area where he is greeted respectfully by Rashid who is standing at the bottom of the escalator. The two men leave the baggage area and head to the pick up zone and enter a sleek black limousine. Other than greeting each other not another word is spoken.

They are unaware that Buck Adams and his crew are also present. As Aziz and Rashid enter their limo, Buck pulls his overcoat tight and walks toward a waiting non-descript Chrysler mini van.

Mike crawls in the mini van to join Buck and his team. They stay well behind the limo and listen attentively as Aziz's voice transmits clearly to the combination receiver/computer which is instantly translated on the laptop screen.

Aziz speaks, "Rashid, my brother, we have been given the great honor of executing the most important assignment in history against the infidels for the glory of Allah."

Rashid, a short muscular man in his early forties said with a slight accent, "I am deeply honored and with all the strength given to me by Allah, I pledge to you that I will do whatever you ask and I will succeed."

"I have no doubt that you will Rashid. You are my most talented and dedicated friend and I know you will not fail our cause." Aziz responds proudly.

For the next hour they meticulously reviewed the reports of Rashid's surveillance over and over again until Aziz is satisfied. He then turns to Rashid and says, "You have done well and now I will tell you what we wish for you to do."

Rashid looks at him with black penetrating eyes covered by thick black eyebrows. He is the very image of a Jihadist with unruly black hair and full beard. In a logical world he would be arrested simply because of his appearance.

He nods respectfully and says, "I am ready, Aziz."

Aziz focuses his beady eyes on Rashid and his expression becomes deadly serious as he said definitively, "We will destroy the very symbol of these infidels. Within ten weeks we will assassinate the President of the United States."

In the Chrysler van, at least a mile away, the men are stunned and look at each other in disbelief before Buck said, "Jesus Christ!"

Rashid does not hesitate as he replies joyfully, "We will do as you command, Aziz. It will be done."

"I have every confidence in your abilities Rashid; however, we must have contingency plans to cover every possible scenario." Aziz said firmly to emphasize the importance of his comment.

Rashid rubs his chin with a puzzled expression and asks, "What sort of contingencies?"

Aziz instructs the driver to pull over into an isolated section of a Wal-Mart parking lot.

As the car comes to a stop Aziz began to lay out the parameters of his loose plan. It would be Rashid's assignment to bring the general plan to a specific plan.

Aziz has no doubt that Rashid is a capable man of high intellect and physically imposing. In his vast experience he has delivered death to many. He was the mastermind behind the cruise ship disaster among other less notable accomplishments.

Rashid is a loyal and faithful believer who is well connected in the Washington area with contacts in the African-American community as well the white community.

He served three years in prison where he made many valuable contacts that have proven to be useful. He learned that most Americans will do anything for money. He held nothing but contempt for non believers.

Aziz speaks slowly in a conspiratorial tone, "I know you have many contacts, including a member of the Secret Service team, and I will expect you to use only your best men for this mission. Rashid, no matter how carefully we plan this we must prepare for the possibility of failure."

Rashid is some what insulted by the implication and interrupts, "We will not fail for we have Allah with us."

Aziz smiles and replies, "I know Rashid but we are mortal men and it is not for us to know all the ways of the mighty Allah."

"Forgive me Aziz; of course, you are right." Rashid quietly replies.

Aziz continues, "It is important that you not use any black men you must use white Americans. If we succeed or fail a white man must be responsible."

Rashid grins showing his perfect white teeth and said, "I see, this is very clever. If we fail and a white man is accused we can expect a significant amount of civil unrest from our black friends and of course the politicians."

Aziz smiles at his cell leader and said, "Very good my friend. You can see that it will create almost the same result as killing the President. With a well designed plan we can achieve our objective either way."

"When would you like me to do this job?" Rashid asks.

Aziz moves his reading glasses down on his nose and peers over them at his notes and then at Rashid, "The date will be April 5th in Charlotte, N.C. Much will depend on the President accepting an invitation to attend a Memorial Service for those who were killed or wounded in Charlotte.

You will need to get your team to Charlotte by early 2010. Once there you will formulate your plan and present it to me no later than March 20th. This will involve creativity, cunning, and skill; your plan must be perfect."

Rashid nods his head as his mind starts to assemble the plan and his people, "I am familiar with Charlotte. I know the city well. Thank you Aziz for the great honor you have bestowed upon this humble servant of Allah."

He leans over and kisses Aziz on both cheeks and takes Aziz's hand in his clearly excited by his new assignment.

Aziz is pleased and confident with his faithful servant and said, "Now I must return to Chicago and you, my friend, must go to work."

The surveillance team has not uttered a single word as they gave their total attention to the unbelievable conversation they were hearing. Buck speaks first, "Holy shit!"

Buck turns to Mike and said, "Mike, sorry old buddy, but you are going to have to be in Washington for a little while. Keep your eyes on Rashid and if he farts, I want to know how loud and how bad it smells, you got me?"

CHAPTER 44

The far left liberal media concocted a barely comprehensible scenario that concluded that four ultra successful businessmen are so consumed by greed and power that the men are now focused on acquiring control of the United States and then the world. They described it as super capitalism.

The other stories focused on their absence of government experience and that our country cannot be managed by amateurs.

It is crystal clear to the Forcesome why they avoided publicity for so many years and the perpetuation of reckless, dishonest, and totally unsubstantiated information has contributed greatly to the current problems being suffered by Americans. However, it is no surprise.

Joe and Adam are sitting in the main dining room, completely alone, discussing economic solutions. Both men are very efficient businessmen but Adam is much more experienced in the evaluation of companies other than his own.

After a productive afternoon they enjoy an early dinner and are sitting on the large veranda outside the dinning room gazing into black sky filled with brilliant stars. They are smoking Monte Cristo white cigars, sipping Brandy, and simply enjoying the tranquility as a full moon slowly climbs out of the Atlantic Ocean.

Adam draws on his cigar and exhales the smoke without inhaling and said, "Joe, this is what we are fighting for. What a beautiful country we live in."

Joe nods his head and said to Adam, "Well, give me the short version of what we can do to kick start this economy?"

Adam laughs as he looks at Joe, "The best solution would be to close down the Federal Government and let the states fend for themselves."

Both men laugh and Joe said, "That might be a good idea. If we did that there would be no need for a President."

Adam sips his brandy as he walks around the veranda. He is dressed in black trousers and a yellow and black golf shirt that accents his trim athletic body and he is clearly enjoying the quiet evening.

He brings his focus back to Joe and says, "Joe, I don't have to tell you the situation is a dire as it can be. I am not sure we can recover. At the end of October unemployment exceeded 10.2%, spending is down a point in the quarter, there is no confidence in the market, banks have been infused with money and refuse to lend, and the construction industry and affiliated suppliers are dying."

Adam pauses and sips his Brandy as Joe stands near the veranda rail and leans back paying close attention to Adam. Joe has known Adam for a long time and is well aware of his tendencies.

Adam continues and slowly said, "Joe the only business growing is the Federal Government.

Let me hit you with a stat, We are also approaching the point where 30% of all jobs in America will be with some government entity and perhaps another 15% are provide through government contracts. Joe, government does not work for the people anymore the people work for the government."

As Joe considers Adam's comment he suddenly feels a sense of utter hopelessness. Doubt creeps into his mind which is a rare occurrence but he is beginning to grow accustomed to it. He wonders if they are too late!

Adam continues, "America, as we know it, is becoming a multicultural society and we are being diluted and destroyed by the very Constitution that was created to protect this Republic. Joe people do not come to America to become Americans they come here to create their own cultures and take advantage of the rights granted American citizens that do not exist in their countries."

Joe stares at Adam who looks a little despondent as he stops speaking. Adam drew on his cigar and exhales slowly. Adam looks over at Joe and they both began to smile and soon they are laughing hysterically for no apparent reason.

Finally, they stop laughing and Joe said, "Oh man. What the hell have we gotten into Adam?" Joe put his arm on Adam's shoulder at they continue to laugh.

The two men sit back down in their chairs and relit their cigars and finally control their laughter.

Adam said simply, "Bottom line is government is too big, too intrusive, and too inefficient."

Joe said, "Adam the more I look at these crazy numbers the more confused I become. How could this happen? How did we get in this deep? It is almost beyond belief."

Adam said, "By the way you look good on television."

Joe snickers and said, "Thanks buddy. Pretty soon the Forcesome will own this country."

Again the two men laugh.

Adam looks at Joe and said, "I think we are making our points and I hope the public will see through the media lies."

Joe sips his brandy and said, "Well if they give us a chance we will fix it."

Adam said, "Sure we can. I believe that deep inside every red blooded American there is an intense spark of pride and love for our country. It may have been suppressed by events of the past few decades but we can rekindle that little spark and turn it into a huge flame."

The two men sit silently as the night air became chilly and Adam said, "Joe you know I enjoy history. The conduct of government today is far more egregious today than the events that preceded the Revolutionary War.

Deep within all Americans, I believe there is a special gene; this gene will simply not allow them to bend but so far. It would not be unrealistic to expect another Revolutionary type war within the next twenty to thirty years. That keeps me awake at night Joe."

Joe considers Adam's words and knows that class warfare may well be a reality one day. He also knew that would not be a noble fight for freedom it would just be people taking from other people. He thought to himself that he would not allow the situation to worsen and his commitment to restore America grew a little stronger.

CHAPTER 45

They follow Rashid back to his neighborhood and drop off Mike who would have surveillance responsibility. Mike hasn't shaved for the past few days and with his Middle Eastern appearance he effectively blends in with this multicultural neighborhood.

He watches Rashid enter the Masjid Muhammad Mosque on 4th street in Washington, D.C. Two hours later Rashid reappears and under Mike's watchful and professional eyes he goes to an old apartment complex on 7th Street N.W.

Rashid enters the dingy foyer of Gibson Plaza Apartments and checks his mailbox before calling one of the four elevators. A few minutes later Mike sees the lights come on in the corner unit on south east corner of the fourth floor.

After carefully checking in each direction Mike slowly walks to the building and enters the front door as if he lives there and subtlety surveys the area and notices the box Rashid opened is 405.

It has been a long day for Mike as he grabs a cab and instructs the driver to take him to the nearest hotel which is the Marriott Wardman Place. The hotel is only two tenths of a mile from the apartment building which is good for Mike but not so good for the cabbie who was hoping for an airport trip.

The cabbie seems frustrated but his mood changes when Mike gives him a twenty and tells him to keep the change. The snow has picked up a little as Mike moves from the cab to the lobby to check in.

Once he is in his room he contacts Buck and gives him a complete update and a request for the supplies he will need. Buck advises him he will send Charlie to assist and he will bring all necessary equipment and supplies including another implantable tracking device for Rashid.

In apartment 405 at the Gibson Plaza apartment complex Rashid sits at his small and inexpensive kitchen table and sips on a cup of hot tea. He is considering the tremendous honor he received and is jotting down strategic information as it occurs to him. He had served time with a white supremacist, Pete Boykin, and Pete owed him. He would be the perfect candidate for the job.

Pete spent two years in Hagerstown prison as Rashid's cellmate. Rashid recalled meeting Pete in prison. One day Pete was trapped in the shower and being beaten by three members of a Mexican gang who intended to kill him. Rashid walked in and one of the Mexicans said to him, "Get out of here and mind your own fucking business you god damn sand nigger."

Rashid held his hands up as the foul mouthed Mexican walked toward him. He pushed Rashid in the chest, attempting to move him, but Rashid would not be moved. Instead he kicked the angry Mexican in the nuts. The man doubled over in pain and Rashid's knee smashed his helpless face and his body collapsed to the cold tile floor with blood spreading beneath his head.

Pete used the distraction to escape the grip of the big Mexican and rushed to the side of Rashid confronting the remaining two Mexicans. A guard walked in and said, "What the fuck in going on?"

Pete told the white officer, "This clumsy mother fucker slipped on some soap."

The officer told the two Mexicans, "Get this son of a bitch out of my showers."

Thus began the strange friendship between a White Supremacist and a Muslim. The men tolerated each other in spite of their racial and religious differences. Pete didn't like it but he still feels indebted to Rashid.

Rashid decides that Pete would be his white fall guy and would play an integral part in the assassination of President Howard. For money, Pete is like most Americans, except he is more violent, and would do almost anything for money including betrayal of his country. Rashid found Americans to be absent of loyalty, honor, or belief in God. It is his opinion that their actions are based upon the answer to one simple question. What's in it for me?

CHAPTER 46

John and Tony arrive at Volusia National Golf Club at 10:15 am to visit with Joe and prepare for his November public appearances. Joe is notified of their arrival and leaves Adam in the upstairs great room to continue reviewing the Federal budget and indentifying cuts.

He walks downstairs to greet them, "Hey John. How are you Tony?"

John replies, "Good Joe. How are things going with you?"

Tony shakes Joe's hand and said, "Good to see you Joe. Man this is such a beautiful place."

Joe said, "Thanks Tony. Come on guys I will take you to your Villas."

Joe leads them to one of the villas located about one hundred yards behind the clubhouse. On the walk over Tony is impressed with the immaculate landscaping and the surroundings are as gorgeous as any place he had ever seen.

In front of the villa is an inviting swimming pool with comfortable padded lounges and chairs on the deck. There are dozens of tall Palms, an abundance of seasonal flowers, and perfectly manicured grass accenting the pool and villa.

As they enter the ground level of the villa there is a large great room which is tastefully decorated and extremely comfortable, a dining area, and a large functional kitchen fully equipped with whatever they might need. It occurs to Tony that this villa could easily appear as a magazine feature.

Tony said, "Joe this is spectacular. I really appreciate your hospitality."

Joe politely replies, "Thanks Tony the pleasure is mine and we are happy to have you. Come on upstairs and I will show you your suites."

There are two master bedroom suites upstairs complete with king size beds, a large sitting area, and a mounted 52" Flat screen television. The bathrooms are extremely large and include shower, Jacuzzi bath, his and her toilets, and a steam room.

Tony has been to a lot of very nice places in his life but he thought this place is absolutely stunning. He looks at Joe and said, "Joe I might not want to ever leave here. I could learn to live like this."

Joe laughs and said, "You are always welcome Tony. John you know your way around why don't you guys settle in and then meet us in the clubhouse."

John smiles at Joe and said, "We will be over shortly Joe. Thanks."

Fifteen minutes later Tony and John found Joe on the veranda and join him. As the men chat Betty appears on the veranda with a tray of coffee and Danish. She prepares the place settings, pours the coffee, and pleasantly asks, "Can I get anything else for anyone?"

Joe looks at John and Tony and then said, "No thank you Betty." Betty leaves the veranda and the men get right down to business.

Tony starts, "Joe we have you booked for six speeches with major corporations, four major television appearances on ABC, CBS, FOX, and CNN, four major magazine interviews, and four newspaper interviews including the Wall Street Journal and USA Today. You have a busy month my friend."

Joe laughs and said, "Well I can tell you this Tony I am ready to do anything if it gets me out of constantly looking at what our government has been doing with our money."

Tony continues, "We should discuss a few issues that I feel you should avoid and discuss some techniques to escape traps they will set for you."

Joe looks at Tony and sternly but politely said, "Tony, I appreciate that and recognize that you have been in politics for much longer than I but I intend to answer all questions as honestly as I possibly can.

I do not intend to avoid, deflect, or be deceitful in any way. Tony once I start acting like a politician I will lose my advantage and probably my soul. I believe the American people want straight answers and that's what I intend to give them."

Tony looks at John for support and John smiles at Tony and said, "I agree with Joe. After the last election I think the public is sick and tired of hearing direct questions being answered with some irrelevant and unrelated canned comment."

"Well you must excuse me Joe. I have spent two many years teaching politicians how to avoid, deflect, and be deceitful. Honesty is a trait rarely considered. Hell, maybe I am the problem." Tony said as the three men laugh.

Joe said, "Tony I have heard the left's negative comments but it also appears we have a lot of favorable support. I know how they will play and I can only tell you that I want fall for it. I intend to discuss real issues and will avoid being sucked into the usual political bickering. The voters will just have to figure things out for themselves."

Tony is sweating a little in the warm Florida sun and loosens his neck tie before responding, "Joe their wild ass accusations are absolutely incredible but that's just the way they are. I concur with your course of action and I believe as we get more exposure they will look like the idiots they are."

Joe said, "I have a few questions for you. Tony what do you think has happened to our politicians?"

Tony thought for a few seconds and answers, "In my opinion politicians just let government out grow its ability to manage effectively. Politicians are much too busy campaigning and raising money to be bothered by business. The truth is members of the House are simply figure heads. Our country is run by their aides. They have no concept or concern with what they do with our money."

John said, "A politician understands that budget issues are irrelevant."

Joe looks at John and asks, "What do you mean?"

"Joe to become a successful politician you must be able to raise money and lots of it. Budget issues are irrelevant because as long as the government has the ability to tax, why worry about it. This causes them to be cavalier when dealing with significant financial issues. Why be prudent? Why do due diligence? Particularly if a yea vote benefits your re-election or buys you a future vote. Furthermore, once elected politicians are required to reward their supporters." John answered.

Joe looks quizzically at both men and said, "So what mandates prudent and responsible business management?"

"John responds quickly, "Nothing. Joe it is all about re-election, seniority, and ultimate chairmanships. Prudence and responsibility do not enter the equation."

Joe is not totally surprised but still had trouble understanding it, "No wonder our country is in trouble."

John looks at Joe who appears to be pensive and deep in thought and asks, "What is it Joe?"

Joe squints as the sun finds his face and said, "Corruption is always about money or power. Politicians have almost destroyed America in pursuit of money and power."

Tony said, "Joe the only way this can be stopped is by having prudent and responsible people gain control."

Joe acknowledges Tony with a slight nod and continues, "Not only have they failed to protect the people they represent they have betrayed our country."

John said solemnly, "Joe I view the Restoration Party as our last chance to turn this around. We must win."

The three men walk inside to join the others for lunch and a strategy session.

CHAPTER 47

WASHINGTON, D.C.
OCTOBER 28, 2009

Mike had spent yesterday buying some old clothes from Goodwill in order to fit in with the neighborhood. He also purchased personal items and familiarized himself with the entire neighborhood. He learned that the inhabitants are mostly low to middle income with a high concentration of Muslim immigrants and African Americans.

Charlie arrived at the hotel early in the afternoon with two large pull suit cases and met Mike in his room where Mike brought him up to date with Rashid and the neighborhood.

Charlie, Mike, B.A, and everyone working on the project is pumped and excited to once again be involved in significant efforts to protect the country and to do what they were trained to be. He slid the file across the table to Mike and gave him a quick verbal overview, "Rashid was born on August 31, 1961 in Pakistan. Entered America in 1977 on a student visa and graduated from the University of Maryland."

Charlie stands up a removes his sweater as Mike asks, "You want a soft drink or some coffee?"

Charlie throws his sweater on the bed and said, "No thanks. Now where was I?"

Mike said, "University of Maryland."

Charlie continues, "He's an engineer, works for Capital Construction, makes about $80,000 a year. He beat the shit out of a Jewish man about five years ago and ended up serving two years for assault and he is still on parole."

Mike said, "Let's take a look at the goodies."

Charlie smiles and walks over to one of the bags, picks it up, and places it on the table, and then opens it. The bag contains two H&K 45 handguns, clips and ammo, a small laptop computer, a set of flash drives, four cell phones, and all the latest electronic surveillance equipment. Charlie reaches into the side pocket and removes a small case and opens it to reveal two syringes with the injectable transmitters.

Mike grins and says to Charlie, "Well let's go find the son of a bitch and go to work!"

They leave the hotel room separately and meet in the parking lot and climb into the panel truck that Charlie picked up from the local Secureone office.

They drive to 7th street to check out Rashid's apartment. After watching the building for a few minutes Mike said, "I'm going to check and see if he is at home. He reaches behind him and pulls out two communication devices and hands one to Charlie. They place the ear pieces and check the devices.

Mike heads up to the fourth floor with his small back pack while Charlie keeps an eye out for Rashid. Mike is almost sure Rashid isn't home but he knocks lightly on the door. No one responds. Before picking the lock Mike makes sure that Rashid has not placed any tape on his door that would tell him his security had been breeched.

Once inside he is immediately hit with the strong smell of curry. A quick glance around reveals a small living area with a dingy brown couch, a beat up coffee table, two overstuffed side chairs, a small desk with a computer and printer, and a relatively new 40" flat screen sat on a chest of drawers. It appears as if the apartment has not been cleaned for several days.

He walks into the small bedroom and sees a simple single bed which is unmade, a side table with an ashtray filled with butts, a lamp with a banged up beige shade, and several large cardboard boxes filled with clothes. He looks into the small bathroom that is filthy and checks the medicine cabinet to see if he is on anything.

He opens the closet door in the bedroom and after poking around he discovers that Rashid had cut a hole in back of the closet and covered it with a large black suit case. Behind the walls Mike finds four handguns, one AR-15, two sniper rifles with scopes, and ammunition.

Mike returns to the sitting area and plugs the flash drive into Rashid's computer and turns it on. Next he quickly installs his high tech audio and video surveillance equipment and downloads a program to Rashid's computer that will allow Nick to monitor his activity.

When his work has been completed he leaves by way of the stairs and joins Charlie in the truck.

Mike and Charlie carefully observe Rashid for the next two days looking for a way to introduce the anesthesia and inject the transmitter. They noticed that each night when Rashid returns home he would boil some water, make tea, and surf the net before going to bed.

When Rashid left his apartment the next morning Mike took the stairs to the fourth floor and enters the apartment. Mike adds some water to the tea kettle and drops in an appropriate amount of fast acting drugs that would knock him out. Now they just had to wait for Rashid to return.

Since nothing would be happening until late that evening Charlie and Mike knew that they must get rest when they can so they return to the hotel and slept until eight o'clock in the evening. After the good rest they are refreshed and ready to go.

They order room service and enjoy a huge meal before preparing for the evenings work. They dress in the old clothes Mike had purchased to avoid looking out of place in the neighborhood and take the stairs to the parking lot and drive to Rashid's. Mike walks the area and Charlie monitors the computer activity.

Just before midnight Rashid returns to his apartment. Once inside he turns on the television and checks the tea kettle for water. Satisfied it contains sufficient water he turns the burner on high and sits down and boots up his computer.

A few minutes later the kettle signals the water is boiling and Rashid removes a tea bag from the box on the counter and places it in a cup. He pours the boiling water and mixes his tea.

His attention is focused on the Tonight show on television and he is chuckling over something Letterman says as he began to sip his tea. Ten minutes later Rashid rests his head on the table and drifts into a deep sleep.

Charley passes this information to Mike who waits another fifteen minutes prior to climbing the dirty stairs once again. He enters the apartment, as Charley watches on his monitor, and quickly injects the transmitters. One in his right forearm and the other is his left trapezium. Mike looks into the hidden camera and gave Charley a big smile and then gives him the bird.

Chapter 48

The group has been working hard for several days and felt they had made significant progress. They are enjoying their lunch break and everyone is upbeat and pleased.

Robbie informs Joe and the guys earlier that Project Thor is a plot to assassinate President Howard and also tells him about their Washington surveillance operation and plans.

Robbie tells Joe he has additional information they need to discuss so after lunch Joe said, "John if you and Tony will excuse us for a little while we need to take care of some club business."

John said, "No problem Joe. Tony and I will go work on out putting while you guys are working. Let us know when you are ready to get back to work."

Joe, Adam, Robbie, and Lee headed for Joe's suite.

They sit around the dining room table and Robbie said, "I heard from Mike today and he has successfully injected Lee's "Gizmos" into Rashid and from this point forward we will be very well informed.

Mike and Charlie will remain in Washington and will keep us advised as things develop."

Adam, dressed in red golf shirt and blue slacks, spoke first, "Robbie, this whole scenario is simply unbelievable. I really hate the idea that Tommy was killed by these bastards, but if it were not for that catastrophe, you would not be involved, and our entire country would be facing some tragic times."

Robbie nods and Joe said, "I agree Robbie. What can we do to help? I know this is costing you a fortune."

Robbie emotionally said, "I'm fine guys. I am willing to go broke if necessary to stop these sadistic bastards."

Lee said, "You can't go broke Robbie. I count on my winnings down here to help me live my lavish lifestyle."

The men enjoy a laugh and Joe turns to Robbie and hands him a check and says, "Lee is worried about losing his annuity on the golf course and insisted that we all contribute to your project."

Robbie takes the check and looks at it and then he looks at his friend with moist eyes and says, "Guys you don't have to do this...... but I know I couldn't stop you..."

As he places the three million dollar check in his pocket the men embrace.

They walk out to the putting green where Tony and John are honing their skills and Joe asks, "Who's winning?"

John smiles at Joe and says, "I think Tony has played this game before." Tony said, "Joe I can't wait to play this course. When are you going to let me?"

Joe said, "If you can stay another day you can play tomorrow."

Tony looks disappointed and said, "Shit I was afraid of that. I have six interviews tomorrow. I have to be in Washington."

Joe said, "You let me know what works for you and we will arrange it."

The men went back to meeting room and took their seats as John said, "Tony is going to go first and discuss the impact of the interviews over the past month."

Tony rocks back in his chair and said, "You guys have done a great job. All your interviews have been very well received and, as you know, the requests for more are pouring in. Based upon your comments, the media is going absolutely nuts to interview Joe, which is exactly what we wanted. The negative side is that you evil capitalist are trying to take over the whole world"

Everyone laughs and it was indeed a laughable theory.

John said, "There is also quite a buzz on Capitol Hill. As expected, they suspect something is up but they don't know what and that drives them crazy. I am getting dozens of questions from my colleagues and from the media regarding the intent of the Restoration Party.

Some are not so nice and others are very positive. I believe that once Joe gets a round of coverage most astute politicians will figure it out."

Tony said, "You can call me stupid if you want too but I have never seen the media or the public so ready for a dramatic change. They may not know what they want but they want leadership they can believe in."

Joe said, "Sounds like things are going pretty well and the next ninety days should help us make an impact."

Tony replies, "You are right about that Joe. We want Lee, Adam, and Robbie to become more selective and only do about one or two interviews a week. November will be the month we focus on you Joe. We are starting you with a one hour interview on ABC's Primetime on November 2ed. The topic will center on business and the economy"

"Sounds good Tony, I look forward to it." Joe replied.

CHAPTER 49

Joe Winston is relaxing in the guest waiting area after the make up artist prepares him for the glare of the lights. In ten minutes, the heavily promoted interview will begin. Joe is dressed in a beautiful black suit, white shirt, and a silver and black tie. As usual, Joe is completely relaxed, confident, and his only preparation is his knowledge of the facts and his complete honesty.

If someone were to imagine exactly how the President of the United States of America should look their image would be very close to Joe Winston.

Bill Harris, the ABC anchor, is considered one the most aggressive interviewers on television. His dark blue suit, pale blue shirt, and regimental tie are, of course, coordinated perfectly by one of his sponsors.

He is known to be professional and fair but he will not shy away from asking hard or even impolite questions. Bill has carefully reviewed all the interviews with the *Forcesome* and his staff has researched Winston's business operation in preparation for the interview.

Journalists are always looking for a smoking gun but Bill found no guns and no smoke. The more they investigated the more he became convinced that Joe Winston is the real deal and he is looking forward to the interview.

The interview opens with a three minute video presentation highlighting Joe's background including military service, business success, and his relationship to Robbie, Adam, and Lee. It is a very generous and accurate portrayal of Joe. The outstanding introduction for Joe is convincing evidence that Joe Winston is a charismatic, compassionate, and dynamic leader.

Bill and Joe are seated at a table in two identical chairs at forty five degree angles. The camera zeros in on Bill as the producer points his finger indicating they are on the air.

Bill smoothly picks up his notes, looks at Joe, and begins the interview, "Mr. Winston, first of all we wish to thank you for agreeing to visit with us the evening."

Joe responds with a warm smile and a slight nod of his head, "It is my pleasure. Thanks for having me."

Bill asks several questions related to Joe's business and the *Forcesome* over the next ten minutes. After the first commercial break the serious questions begin, "Joe, you have avoided the media and political involvement for well over twenty years, why have you decided to speak now?"

Joe maintains friendly eye contact with Bill and smiles as he replies, "My reluctance to become a public figure is primarily a matter of choice. I failed to see any benefit to being in the public eye. I am not much different than most of your viewers who seem to be convinced that all business leaders and politicians are dishonest and unethical. I have never felt the need to defend my actions or to seek attention or adulation."

Joe's remarks are natural, sincere, and well delivered. One would think he has spent countless hours on television and there are not signs of him being the least bit nervous.

"In recent years I have become disturbed with the message our politicians are sending to our citizens. I have made the decision to speak now to try and convince the American public that integrity, honor, and hard work are virtues that do exist and should be encouraged.

I believe that our country, as we know it, will soon face a financial crisis of such magnitude that recovery will be almost impossible. Therefore, I realize that my failure to be involved in government affairs was a mistake and it is now my intention to do everything within my power to correct that error in judgment."

Bill leans forward with a baffled expression and softy asks, "When you say crisis Mr. Winston what are you referring too?"

Joe's legs are crossed and he is the picture of a confident and relaxed man as he replies, "Bill I refer to a multitude of issues so let me try to break them down for your viewers.

Let's start with a financial crisis. Our government is responsible for protecting our citizens and our government, and our elected representatives, should be role models for the rest of us.

Bill our country now has over one hundred trillion dollars of unfunded liabilities, a fourteen trillion dollar national debt, and this year they will spend two trillion more than they collected in taxes" Joe pauses for a few seconds to allow the figures time to float around in the viewers heads.

"Most Americans can't relate to numbers of that size and the truth is they really don't seem to think it impacts them personally so let me put it into perspective. If your family makes one hundred thousand dollars a year and you owed FIVE MILLION dollars would you sleep well at night?

Bill asks, "How do we fix it?"

The first step in my opinion would be to dramatically reduce the size of government. The second step would be a fair tax system. The third step would be to discontinue government interference in our free market. The fourth step would be to stop social engineering in our country. The fifth step would be to find creative ways to provide goods and services to other countries.

Bill even if start seriously pursuing the elimination of our liabilities today it most likely will take twenty to forty years to have a significant impact. If we do nothing we could lose our freedom in America."

"It appears you are not happy with our political leaders?" Bill asks with a smile on his face and still trying to formulate questions in his head.

Joe returns the smile and said, "Bill I would say that is accurate. I believe there is a lot of room for improvement."

"What do you feel is the most important improvement opportunity?" Bill weakly asks.

The camera embraces Joe's remarkably sincere, confident, and believable face as he replies," I don't mean to cover all politicians with the same blanket but their direction and rhetoric concerns me greatly.

Our most important improvement opportunity is to win back the trust and confidence of the American people. I believe many of our economic problems are rooted in a basic lack of trust. The people no longer trust their public officials, business leaders, religious leaders, the media, police, and the list goes on. Trust must be restored before our economy can once again prosper.

A recent survey among high school students concluded that 77% of all students feel you could not become successful in America without compromising your integrity. The young people of America form these opinions by watching politicians on television, reading magazines and newspapers, and getting way too much disinformation on the internet. It is no surprise they feel that lying, misrepresenting, and back stabbing are preferable to honesty.

Politicians should be an inspirational role model and, in my opinion, their behavior has contributed to the demise of strong moral values that our country was founded upon as well as our respect for elected officials"

Bill changes directions and digressed, "What are some of the other factors that could lead to a major crisis in our country?"

Joe replies, "What separates America from most other countries is our freedom. The government's primary responsibility is to protect our freedom. When they assume control of automobile companies, financial institutions and banks, mortgage companies, and now they try are trying to gain control of health care and force private companies out of business that is a significant blow to freedom.

Bill they promise no new taxes on the middle class but they are deceptively placing excess fees and taxes on such things as soft drinks, alcohol, tobacco, products that contain sugar, guns, ammunition, hunting equipment, and numerous other items that they deem harmful.

They are deciding what we can and can't do and that isn't freedom. These things may be harmful but shouldn't the decision to use or not use these products be the individuals?

Bill asks, "So it is your belief that government is becoming a threat to private industry?"

Joe leans forward and emphatically said, "Not only are they threatening private business they are threatening our very freedom. There is no question about it Bill. Private business cannot compete with a government entity because the government has no concern with profit or loss.

They have the ability to tax. Private business is a little different because they most make a profit to pay their employees and encourage investors.

Bill realizes he only has time for one more question, "Mr. Winston one year from today we will have our mid term elections. We understand you support a new political party, The Restoration Party, what will be your involvement?

Joe replies, "I fully support the Restoration Party and will do everything in my power to assist the party in the mid terms. All members of the party must agree to only serve one term and also must agree to demand a constitutional amendment to limit all elected officials to one term. This will do much to correct the problem we now face with professional politicians and a two party system.

Over the next year we will invite all Americans to learn more about our platform and hopefully for the first time in 150 years perhaps the democrats and republicans will no longer be able to dictate policy in America."

CHAPTER 50

Robbie, John and Tony had been working all day reviewing the information that Lee provided after extensive computer hacking on all members of the House. It never ceases to amaze Lee that most people perceive their computers as safe. When someone as gifted as Lee Roth initiates a computer search he will find everything worth finding.

Lee had forwarded to John a large box containing files on 62 members of the House and the Senate. Each file contains irrefutable evidence of their transgressions which included everything from illegally accepting money, excessive gambling debts, sexual misconduct, and numerous other violations that these men would not want the public to see.

After Mary prepared a delicious dinner of fried chicken, butter beans, mashed potatoes, and macaroni and cheese the men are stuffed and ready for a nap. Since a nap is out of the question they adjourn to John's library to watch the Joe Winston interview.

They watched the first fifty minutes of the program in complete silence, except for commercial breaks, and they are all in agreement that Joe is doing very well. They have no illusions that tomorrow on the "talking heads" shows the liberals would pick him a part with a viciousness that would be comparable to a grizzly bear protecting her cubs"

Tony is a realist and knows it will be several more months and hundreds of more speeches before the public would definitively signal that they are willing to help restore the values, traditions, and common sense that have been absent for decades.

CHAPTER 51

During the commercial Joe takes a careful look at the studio and realizes the set they are using is one, of perhaps a dozen, spread around the well lighted and massive studio floor. It occurs to Joe that the viewers see an attractive and impressive set but in reality the hidden area is nothing more than a dingy warehouse floor. He thought of how government works; they only let you see what they want you to see.

Bill Harris, in his strong announcer's voice said, "Welcome back to the conclusion of our very special interview with Joe Winston, Mr. Winston you have been quite critical of politicians this evening….do you believe that serves any useful purpose?"

Joe could not be more relaxed as the camera focused on his confident and believable face, "Bill I have simply responded to the questions you have asked as best I can. It is my belief that I have not unjustly mischaracterized the situation. America needs honest, ethical, and caring men to restore her to greatness and I see little evidence of those qualities in Washington today."

Bill asks, "It is highly unlikely that a new political party could possibly impact next years mid terms. If your party fails would you describe how you see the future?"

Joe sits up in his chair and reassumes a comfortable position and said, "First I do think we will have an impact. In the unlikely event we don't, history is a great predictor of the future, and if this trend continues we will face incomprehensible inflation, excessive unemployment, loss of individual freedom, and the collapse of our economy.

As you know the solutions being employed in our country now have failed in Europe and South America and the American people will not allow government to rob them of their freedom.

When government official are sworn in they take an oath to protect this country from foreign and domestic threats. Well I don't worry nearly as much about foreign threats as I do about domestic threats. The inability of professional politicians to work together has divided this country and has the potential to destroy our country." Joe answers forcefully.

Bill is mesmerized by Joe's honest and forthright response but calmly asks, "What can we do about it?"

Joe smiles and said, "I would ask the American people to carefully observe the Restoration Party over the next twelve months. If they do they will see real leadership, viable solutions, and hope for our future. It will take every American's support to restore our country.

Bill looks at Joe and said, "Mr. Winston we are almost out of time but if you would like to make a closing comment please feel free to do so."

Joe thanks Bill for the opportunity and welcomes the opportunity to hit a couple of points that he feels are important, "Bill as we know Americans are competitive. The history of competition among sports team, individuals, and even corporations is replete with great stories.

I have been asked how having three viable political parties will benefit the people and I would like to answer that question.

"Republicans and Democrats are also competitors and some times competition can simply go too far. They have become preoccupied with beating each other and as a result legislation today is reflective of the majority party. We are a Republic and all American viewpoints should be considered but partisanship is the norm.

If the Restoration party achieves a significant number of seats in congress ALL Americans will be represented and the best interest of our country will be served and bi partisan legislation is practically guaranteed.

Tomorrow morning the Media will find much to criticize about my comments but I don't think most Americans who are working hard and trying to take care of their families will find my comments objectionable. I was recently asked a question and the question was, can someone be elected to public office by telling the truth? My answer is we will find out at the mid terms. Thank you for having me."

CHAPTER 52

Rashid's time is primarily spent at the Mosque or Capital Construction but he appears to have no particular schedule and complete freedom of movement. In his trips between locations it is apparent he is well known by the people in the community.

It is seven o'clock in the evening when Rashid removes his cell phone and dials a number. He says, "Pete. How are you my old friend?"

Pete Boykin says in mock contempt, "Rashid how's my favorite sand nigger?"

Rashid smiles, not offended, and quietly said, "If it were not for this sand nigger, you would already have been rejected by Allah and feeding worms …ha-ha-ha."

The neo Nazi skin head knows this is true and contrary to his core beliefs he likes Rashid, "What's up Rashid?"

"I need to see you Pete. Can you meet me at Obrien's Pub tonight around eight?" Rashid asks.

Obrien's Pub is a large tavern that appeals to a wide variety of ethnic groups which is perfect for a community that consisted of mostly upper low income to middle class workers.

Pete answers, "No problem. I will see you tonight."

Charley and Mike decide that Charley will be the inside man and Mike would monitor the transmissions from the truck. Charley's dress is suitable for the community; he wore old blue jeans that are a little too big, a blue and white flannel plaid shirt over a black tee shirt, and a dirty brown heavy down jacket with a hood. Charley is a couple of inches over six feet and like most ex SEALS has kept his body in peak condition. His hair is short, black, and kinky and his black face is covered in a five day growth of graying beard.

Charley assumes the role of a humble working class man and enters Obrien's at 7:30 and does a quick inventory of his surroundings. To his left he sees a large bar roughly twenty five feet long with a few patrons drinking and watching the mounted television that is surrounded by bottles of whiskey.

To his left there is a row of ten booths with only a few occupied. Between the bar and the booths there are about a dozen tables that seat four to eight people.

As he walks toward a small table he notices there are six televisions spread around on the walls and Irish memorabilia cluttered the remainder of the walls. He takes a chair and notices the smell of beer, whiskey, and smoke. He could also smell the slight odor of floor cleaner along with the pungent odor of sweat and cheap perfume.

The pub is dimly lit and about half full with workers eating dinner and having a few pops. Loud laughter and the sounds of dozens of voices filled the air along with the sounds of Z.Z. Topp's hit record "Legs" blasting from the juke box.

The waitress strolls over and he orders a beer and takes his jacket off.

One would assume that a bar named Obrien's would attract Irish Americans. This bar had been purchased from Obrien by a man named Sal who is from Iran. Sal simply wants to make money and enjoy the freedom of America. Unfortunately the bar became a haven for neo Nazi skin heads. Sal despised these people but he took their money and kept his mouth shut.

At 7:45 pm a bald headed man struts into the tavern and speaks to a few other men who also share the skin head look. The man is medium sized but very broad and muscular from years of pumping iron. He carries himself as if he is important and many of the patrons acknowledge him either out of respect or fear.

As he walks down the left side of the pub between the bar and the tables there are two middle aged black construction workers drinking beer and having a few laughs after a hard days work. The bald man passes behind them as one of the men steps back from the bar and accidentally bumps into him.

The black man is embarrassed by his clumsiness and apologizes to the bald man and politely offers to buy him a drink. The bald man looks at him with cold eyes and backhands him hard across his right jaw. The old man is stunned and falls back toward the bar as the bald man grabs him by his shirt, just below his chin, and forces him to the floor and screams, "Get your fucking black ass out of here and don't come back!"

The other man tries to help his friend up and the bald man hits him hard in the stomach and he doubles over and goes down. The bald man stares at Sal behind the counter and said, "Sal you need to keep these fucking niggers out of here."

Charley had seen enough and is smart enough to know he should stay out of it but he couldn't. He walks over to the fracas and helps the two men onto their feet. The bald man looks at him as if he is stupid and grabs him from behind and roughly turns him around and said, "Mind your own god damn business and get your black ass over there and sit down."

He notices that three of the bald headed man's friends are close by to back up there friend. Charley glares into the shorter mans eyes and says very quietly but firmly, "I think you might want to walk on away."

Charley already knew how the man would react and isn't disappointed as the bald man unleashes a hard kick at his groin. Charley quickly thrust his hips back and caught the man's foot with his hands and flips the man hard onto the ground. Behind him he sees another man coming at him with a knife and quickly rotates his body and parries the knife while grabbing the man's wrist and breaking it on his knee.

As the knife fell to the ground and the man screams Charley sees another man reach behind his back to draw a handgun. He took two quick steps toward the man and executed a spinning back fist that catches the man hard on his jaw and drops him instantly. The small 9mm Keltech hand gun drops on the floor and in a flash it is in Charlie's hand.

The bald man is on his feet again and witnessed his boys being whipped by this black man and now the black man has a gun. Several more of Pete's friends came to his side but the small pistol held by Charley keeps them back.

Charley helps the two other black men up to their feet and points them toward the door. The bald man is leaning against the bar picking his teeth with a tooth pick says calmly, "You better get your black ass out of here and never come back. If you do you will be one dead nigger."

Charley backs slowly toward the door with the gun by his side and said in a menacing voice, "If I do come back you will need a lot more help than you had tonight. Go fuck yourself!"

With that Charley leaves the tavern and knew he was finished in Washington.

The bald man pats his buddies on the back, shakes his head, and then walks to the end of the bar where Rashid is smiling as if he is a drunken monkey.

Pete says, "What's so fucking funny"

Rashid still laughing said, "Same old crazy Pete."

Pete tells Sal to bring him a whiskey with a beer back and said, "What the fuck do you want Rashid?"

"I have a job for you that I think you will like. This job pays a lot of money and will provide you with much pleasure." Rashid teasingly said.

Pete throws back his whiskey and chases it with his beer, "How much fucking money and what kind of job?"

Rashid hesitates and then slowly said, "One million dollars."

The surprise on Pete's face was obvious and it is clear that Rashid has his attention.

Pete finally manages to ask, "A million dollars? What the fuck for?"

"That's right, "one hundred thousand up front and the other nine hundred when you complete the mission." Rashid says without a hint of a smile.

Pete leans forward with extreme interest and stares at Rashid and asks, "What's the job Rashid?"

Rashid leans forward until their noses were almost touching and whispers, "We want you to kill your nigger President. America should not be controlled by a nigger and everyone knows this country was made by the European Americans and no nigger should be telling them what they can or can't do. How about you Pete? Do you like your nigger President?"

"Fuck you Rashid. We would kill the cocksucker for nothing but I am going to take your money." Pete said as if he just scored the winning point.

Rashid knows that Pete Boykin is a man of pure evil. He has no conscience, no remorse, and no respect for anyone. He knows how far to push and he knew when to back off.

"A million dollars and we will help you plan it and provide you with necessary equipment and plans. Can you handle this job?" Rashid said tauntingly.

Pete thinks about the money and the fact that he would be happy to be the President's assassin and replies, "Hell yes I want the job but it will be two hundred thousand up front."

Rashid said, "done; I am delighted my old friend. I am glad I saved your sorry ass in prison."

"Bullshit. I could have whipped those three wet backs."

CHAPTER 54

President Howard has managed to remain arrogant in spite of the absence of any notable achievements. He is somewhat delusional and feels eloquent words will make problems disappear.

He has not proven to be adept at creating coalitions within his own party and he completely ignores the opposition. His feels no remorse when he addresses the American people and feeds them half truths and misrepresentations. He has no compunction in denying the truth and embracing a lie and justifies this behavior by convincing himself it is simply politics.

The truth is he was in the right place at the right time otherwise he would never have had a chance of being President of the United States.

His frustration, which is basically at his own inadequacies, is being blamed on his Cabinet and his staff. Their frustrations force more misrepresentations, more blame of the prior administration, and more programs that create the illusion of help for the middle class. His approval ratings have plunged to under 45% and he attributes the decline to talk radio and right wing radicals. He is fast becoming the most manipulative and vindictive president in our history.

The bail outs, bank and auto takeovers, health care, unemployment, constant apologizing for America's arrogance and the terrible economy hangs around his neck like an anchor. The realization that being President is much more difficult than running for President has not occurred to him.

In a short period of time he has managed to offend business leaders, religious leaders, and every American who works hard to build a comfortable life for their families. His list of constituents is down to his left wing liberal democrats, the down trodden, the lazy, and radical activist groups.

President Howard is in his limousine with Harry Belk driving down sacred streets among the thousands of white crosses and well manicured grass at Arlington Cemetery. He is scheduled to honor our Veterans on this Veterans Day in accordance with tradition.

He is deep in thought and not very talkative as his mind wanders back to the day he learned his older brother was killed in Viet Nam. His brother's death had been devastating and he always felt it was unnecessary as Viet Nam was simply a political war and for years he harbored tremendous resentment.

He wonders how many other brothers, sisters, fathers, and mothers had felt the same pain as he but as a politician he can't always express his true feelings. As a politician he must always be on guard against any comments that could cost votes. It isn't about truth it is about being elected to office and staying there. Always saying the right thing no matter what you actually do.

Harry interrupts the President's thoughts and says, "Sir, it's time and here is a copy of your remarks" as he hands the folder to the President.

President Howard abruptly turns to Belk and takes the folder and quickly glances at it, "Thanks Harry."

He is unaware of the damage he has inflicted on the military by requiring criminal trials to known terrorists, reducing the defense budget, severely restricting troop's action on the battlefield, diminishing the effectiveness of intelligence agencies, and being indecisive regarding strategy.

The military functions on absolute obedience to the chain of command and he is the Commander in Chief but he is nonetheless viewed as a weak liberal with no clue of how the military works. He has no more empathy for a man in a fox hole than he does for the man in the moon.

At the tomb of the Unknown Soldier, surrounded by crosses as far as the eye can see, marking those who died for the cause of freedom the President awaited his turn to make a few comments to honor those who made the ultimate sacrifice. He is having difficulty focusing and memories of his brother fill his mind.

In attendance are the families who have lost loved ones, veterans who are paying homage to their fallen heroes and friends, patriotic Americans, top military officers, and enlisted men.

He watches the moving ceremony honoring our fallen heroes and remains preoccupied with the death of his brother. Finally, he is called upon for his remarks.

He steps forward to the microphone and tries to show his most compassionate and authoritative face as he said, "Our country is extremely grateful to all of our military men and women who have sacrificed tremendously for the cause of freedom. We honor their service and will always admire and respect them."

He pauses as the audience applauds and his mind cannot dispel thoughts of his brother. He loses his place in his notes so he decides to wing it, "As President, I will continue to do everything in my power to protect each and every military person from the fate suffered by our brave veterans who have previously given their lives for freedom…even in places we did not belong."

He pauses in anticipation of applause, while looking for his place in his notes, and there is none. The uncomfortable silence and whispering that follow is unprecedented as the thousands in attendance and watching on live television are shocked at the insinuation that the men who lay in Arlington Cemetery died in a place they did not belong.

The President failed to realize what he said and found his place again and continues with his prepared remarks for another ten minutes finally concluding with, "God bless America and God bless our soldiers."

There is a small smattering of polite applause while others simply look at each other with stunned expressions on their faces and a few actually booed. There is a feeling of betrayal, anger, and sadness that simply penetrates the hearts of the patriotic men and women.

As the President leaves the stage he is confused and surprised at the reaction, Harry Belk walks up beside him and says, "Mr. President we really fucked up today."

President Howard says with a confused look on his face, "What in the hell are you talking about Harry?"

Harry realizes the President did not realize what he said and with respectful sarcasm he said, "soldiers died in places we did not belong… you might as well have said they died for nothing Mr. President."

President Howard quietly said, "Oh shit!"

CHAPTER 54

The Winston's always enjoy their annual Christmas party and tonight is no exception. In addition to family they are happily entertaining over one hundred and fifty guests. The past few weeks were difficult for Joe and the time and energy he had invested in the Restoration Party had robbed him of what used to be his normal life.

Tonight he is being rejuvenated by the presence of so many people he truly enjoys during his favorite time of the year.

They are blessed with a beautiful snowfall for their Christmas party, their home is filled with happy people, the decorations are beautiful and the fifteen foot Christmas tree is perfect.

Seasonal music plays softly in the background. Santa Clause is entertaining the children and grandchildren and just seeing all the joy around him gives Joe great pleasure.

The evening could not have been better and Joe hated to see it end. Around eleven o'clock most of the guests had left and Joe is engaged in conversation with one of his oldest friends Jake Hall.

Joe enjoys Jake's company and had spent little time with him in years. They attended elementary and high school together and Jake had worked part time at Winston's with Joe in high school. At one time the two boys were inseparable.

Jake's parents separated when he was ten years old. His father was an alcoholic and his mother was forced to move in with Jake's grandparents. Jake became a wild child and ran with the wrong crowd and headed for serious trouble. He didn't care. He seemed to live for drinking, chasing women, and irresponsible behavior. Joe lost touch with Jake and they drifted apart toward totally different worlds.

Joe saw little of Jake until he went to Viet Nam. He was on R&R and bumped into Jake in Hawaii. They had a few drinks together and relived old times and Joe was pleased to learn that Jake had turned his life around.

He had served two tours in Nam. He received a battlefield promotion to Lieutenant during his first tour and made Captain prior to the completion of his second tour. He had also been awarded the Silver Star and a Purple Heart. Jake was a different person and Joe was both delighted with and impressed with how he had changed his life.

Joe and Jake stayed in touch and saw each other several times a year. Jake became a very successful businessman in the insurance business and devoted much time, money, and energy into making the community better. Joe had heard that Jake was a popular speaker in the business world and within local High Schools and Colleges.

Joe and Jake had never really discussed what changed Jake's life and how he made the transition from a fast drinking, irresponsible woman chasing, lazy person to a hard working successful and respected person.

Jakes wife and family had been unable to attend because his father in law had been hospitalized and they went to North Carolina to be with him. Joe is not the least bit tired and really wanted to catch up with Jake so he convinces Jake to stay awhile a catch up.

They went to Joe's den and settled into chairs in front of the fireplace after Joe poured drinks, "Jake, I have always wondered how you turned your life around. I expected you to have killed yourself before you were twenty." Joe said.

They laughed and Jake replies, "I tried Joe. I really did." Jake pauses before continuing. "After so many years why do you ask?"

Joe said, "Fair question. First I can't tell you how happy I am that you did. Second, I believe you are one of the most honest people I know. We were once very good friends and I miss seeing you."

Jake took a sip of his scotch while maintaining eye contact with Joe and said, "Yeah, we used to have some good times...I have missed you too Joe....... Looks like you are getting involved in politics?"

Joe said, "Yes I am Jake but I don't intend to become a politician. I don't have much choice Jake I have to do what I can. Jake a lot of people in this country need to change. You did so I am curious how and why you changed?

Jake said, "Fair enough. Now do you really want to know what changed me?"

Joe looks at him with great sincerity and says, "Jake, I need to know."

"O.K. Buddy, you asked for it so buckle up your chin strap" Jake said with a smile.

"Joe, I made a lot of mistakes in my life and I guess I can blame a lot of people but the reality is that I make the choices. More importantly, I had the right to make those choices.

I was given a choice when I was nineteen years old; go to jail or join the military and I chose the military. The military gave me something I could never have gotten in civilian life. I really learned about teamwork, personal responsibility, hard work, and pride in my performance.

As a teenager I made a lot of bad choices. My mother did her best but I was determined to get attention and I did so by reckless driving, drinking, fighting, and chasing skirts. Those years I spent fucking up were my formative years and I learned what didn't work."

Joe smiles but remains silent as he absorbs his friend's story.

"After my first tour of duty I was on a thirty day leave and met Olivia and feel in love. We were married and I had a son. I was determined that he would have a loving and caring father and that Olivia would be proud of her husband. That was another choice I made and it was a good choice. I choose to go in the military and I choose to marry Olivia. Joe I learned to make good choices not bad choices. It is just that simple."

Joe walks over to the fire and tosses in two more logs and turns to Jake and says, "You are right our lives are determined by the choices we make."

"I was fortunate enough to survive my bad choices and learn that lesson." Jake says.

Joe looks warmly at Jake, who he truly likes, with admiration and says "Jake you were always a great friend and it really is good to see you again."

Jake glances at his watch and says, "Joe it's really good to visit with you but I need to get out of here. I'm driving to North Carolina in the morning and I need to be on the road by 0600."

Jake stands up and Joe walks him to the front door. He notices it has stopped snowing and isn't all that cold as he says, "Jake do you have any time the next few days. I really do need to discuss a few things with you?"

Jake says, "I will be back on the 20th; how about breakfast on the 21st?"

Joe says, "Sounds good to me; how about Karol's Kitchen downtown, o700?"

"I will see you there. You know Joe I have never told anyone that story before." Jake said.

CHAPTER 55

Aziz Hasan sits quietly in his study meticulously planning for several major protests he would launch in January. The lawyers under his influence are busy filing complaints with the Federal Government regarding the treatment of detainees in Guantanamo Bay and demanding the facts regarding the apparent American policy to torture.

He applied great pressure to force the administration to bring the 9/11 terrorist to New York for trial and the more controversy he could generate the more Americans will turn against each other.

Additionally, his minions are demanding stimulus money for the organizations they control. He indirectly controls unions, mortgage companies, finance companies, brokerage firms, medical facilities, media outlets, and many charitable and social organizations. He is confident that they will receive somewhere between thirty and fifty million dollars that will ironically be used to assist in the destruction of America.

Aziz is almost giddy as he prepares for the extraction of money from the United States and the onslaught of negative publicity. After all these years in the United States he is still mystified as to how such a gullible country could become the most powerful country on earth.

With his many influential contacts in the media his attempts to destroy the Republican Party is almost complete. It is now unpopular to be a Christian, the concept of self reliance is all but dead, businesses are now being controlled more and more by an incompetent government, class war fare was closer, those Americans who achieve success are being punished, and personal liberty and real freedom would soon be a thing of the past.

Aziz is without question the most powerful man in the United States that no one ever heard of.

After living in America for many decades it is difficult not to be impacted by their lifestyle and it is a constant battle for him to lead this double life. Often he actually feels as if he is a loyal American. He is both offended and fascinated by the American culture.

The prominence of greed, self indulgence, and a total lack of appreciation for their country is repulsive. However, the concept of freedom is extremely powerful and he understood he had never enjoyed true freedom and that most American's have no idea of the power of freedom.

There are times when he feels his accomplishments have not been adequately rewarded or acknowledged. He wonders if years from now when the demise of the United States is documented by historians would he even be mentioned? It troubled him that his service to Allah would be no greater than a nitwit suicide bomber.

He lives a simple and humble life as a college professor and has never tasted the riches that Majid enjoys. He is tired and his journey has been long and grueling and his "American" alter ego screams at him that he is entitled to more. He often turns to Allah and asks that the thoughts be removed from his head, but yet, they persist.

He has not yet received confirmation of the Presidents schedule for the Memorial service in North Carolina but he isn't concerned. He knew the President would be there to pay tribute to a group of dead infidels and pledge to protect everyone else. Yes, he would lie, as it is easy and natural for American leaders.

After seeing Joe Winston on television he decides that he needs to keep Joe and his friends on his radar. He was provided with a complete dossier on each of the men and after carefully reviewing the files his concern intensified.

CHAPTER 56

Jake Hall is a man who is very decisive and extremely determined. He is not the kind of man who would function well on a committee when others wished to debate a subject to death. Jake abhorred those types of people and learned long ago that his impatience and desire to excel are much preferred to indecisive twits who simply wish to find something wrong with every suggestion.

He is extremely results oriented and politics is not his forte. Jake believes there is either a right way to do things or a wrong way. There is no compromising right.

Karol's Kitchen is a popular place for breakfast because the food is great, the service is outstanding, and it is a very cozy restaurant. This morning is like every other morning the smell of frying bacon and coffee, the buzz of dozens of people talking all at once, businessmen working on deals and families enjoying breakfast together.

After breakfast and small talk Jake asks, "Joe why in the hell would a nice guy like you want to be involved with a bunch of Washington ass holes?"

Joe replies, "I don't see where I have a choice. I can do nothing and watch the "ass holes" destroy our country or I can do what I can to stop them."

Jake looks at Joe with respect and says, "Joe you are a good person and I admire your leadership and business skills as well as your values. Why in the world would you jump on a sinking ship?"

Joe looks at Jake with understanding and says, "So what should we do Jake? Do we stand by and wait for the end? Or do we do everything in our power to save our country?"

Jake smiles as if Joe is a well intentioned child who doesn't understand and says, "Joe the American people don't want freedom or opportunity. They want security and if they can get that without any effort that's even better.

Politicians believe that all Americans have a RIGHT to own a home, a RIGHT to have health care, a RIGHT to be well feed, a RIGHT to an income, and a RIGHT to have a cell phone, internet access, cable converter boxes or anything else they may want.

Joe there is no advantage to getting a good education, working hard, and becoming successful because our government will take our money and give it to the lazy sons of bitches that bleed this country dry."

Joe listens to the passion in Jake's voice and knows he has a point t but he also believes that no challenge is too great if one is totally committed. He allows Jake's words to sink in as he considers Jake's comments. There are no easy answers.

Joe says, "We have both worked hard and been rewarded for our efforts. We both agree that our country is in serious trouble. There are many questions and few answers. I agree with what you have said but that isn't the point. The point is that we have a choice and we can do nothing or do something. Those are the only two possible decisions to be made.

Jake looks at Joe with resignation in his eyes and says, "I love this country Joe. I have seen men die for freedom, I have seen people live without it, and I see people in America that don't appreciate it.

I understand the meaning of sacrifice and so do you. I will do anything in my power to return America back to what she should be. Based upon my comments it should be pretty clear to you that I am not very optimistic. I need you to give me something to hang on to, some glimmer of hope, I need to be inspired Joe. Can you do that?"

Joe understands Jakes reluctance and while Jake was speaking Joe's mind was creating a scenario that he believes will work, "I understand where you are coming from Jake. I was there six months ago. As you know we will announce a new political party soon and we have everything in place to be competitive in the 2010 mid term elections.

Jake the most serious problem is the American people's total and complete lack of confidence and trust in our leadership. Remember how high patriotism was after 9/11? How everyone rallied to support World War II? Korea? Americans need a cause to rally around Jake. They need a reason to work together and they need to be proud of their country's leaders. If they are convinced that America is facing economic destruction I believe they will respond.

Jake I can't give you specifics now but I can tell you this. I will provide them with a powerful cause to rally around which hopefully will unify our country. Jake I need you to trust me as I trust you and I need you to help me. Can I count on you?"

CHAPTER 55

President Howard and his family spent the Holiday period at Camp David. Ann knew her husband was burdened with tremendous responsibility but she has never seen him so utterly despondent.

When they finished another political dinner and their guest's are gone she takes him by the arm and kisses his cheek as she leads him to their suite. They sit on the couch in front of the fireplace. It is cold and windy outside and the warmth and beauty of the fire is therapeutic. Ann cuddles close and took the President's hand in hers and says, "What is it James?"

He smiles, kisses her hand, and says with an almost reassuring smile, "nothing for you to worry about Honey."

"James I have known you too long. Please talk to me." She says with pleading eyes and great love.

The President turns to Ann and says thoughtfully, "Ann I need something good to happen. Perhaps I was a bit too optimistic and took on too many projects to quickly. Nothing seems to be going right. I never dreamed it would be so difficult. I feel as if I am failing."

"You are one the smartest and most caring people I know. It just takes time. Be patient and keep pushing Darling. You are doing what you believe is right and you have never failed and you never will fail." She said as she holds his face with both hands and kisses him.

The President could always talk to Ann and feel safe, "Ann all these grand plans seemed much easier when we were campaigning. Actually getting them done is a different story. Perhaps I am trying to do too much too quickly. It just feels like everything is slipping away."

Ann calmly said, "You can always slow down some of the projects. Just deal with the major problems for now. You are ambitious and want the best for our country but nobody expects you do it all in your first year."

The President listens to his wife as he stares in the fire, "Perhaps you are right. I do have a lot on my plate."

Ann sometimes needs to lead her husband and she softly said, "James if you can get the economy back on track and create jobs that's all you need to be re-elected in a landslide." She kisses him on the cheek and seductively says, "Come on Honey. Let's go to bed."

The President is deep in thought and replies, "I will be along in a few minutes."

Ann blew him a kiss and said, "Don't be too long. I will be waiting."

As his gaze returns to the fire he knew Ann was right. The economy must be turned around. He had promised three million more jobs and here he is a year later and two million more jobs have been lost. He mulled Ann's comments over in his head and concluded she is right.

The facts suggest he has lost credibility with most Americans by showing tremendous favoritism to the United Automobile Workers union, trying to create a health care program that the country can't afford, creating Czars, and by asserting control and authority over private business. The repayment of political favors could come at a higher price than he is willing to pay.

As he gazes into the dancing fire he considers how hard he worked in life and how so many others thought he was crazy. There are too many Americans who feel entitled to free pass.

He remembered what his father once said to him, "Son, you can't make chicken salad out of chicken shit." He smiles as thought of his Dad.

He put his elbows on his knees and rests his head in his hands and wonders if he would be strong enough to deal with all the issues that he faced.

All great leaders are capable of publically displaying great strength, immense confidence, and to instill those attributes in others. However, in those private moments when they are alone they have the same self doubts, concerns, and emotions that most people feel. He is feeling insecurity and weakness for the first time in his life.

Ten minutes later James climbs into the warm and inviting bed to find Ann's naked body waiting for him. She snuggles close and kisses him passionately on his ear as her hand strokes the inside of his thigh. He becomes fully aroused and feels the passion and desire take control of his body. He rolls her over on her back and enters her and for a few minutes he is focused on his own pleasure and thinks of nothing else.

After Ann and James are spent he walks by the window on the way to the bathroom and Ann starts giggling. She is trying to stop but instead she is cannot stop her self from laughing.

James looks at her wondering what is wrong with her and couldn't help but smile as he says, "What is it?"

He is standing directly between the bed and the window and doesn't realize his naked body is silhouetted against the window as Ann laughs so hard she can't answer. She finally controls her laughter long enough to tell her concerned husband that the vision of him walking naked by the window with a semi erection leading the way would be a great magazine picture.

The image occurs to James and they both began to laugh hysterically. He can't remember the last time he laughed.

CHAPTER 58

NEW YORK, N.Y
JANUARY 11. 2010

Christmas rolls by with no improvement in the economy and the mood of the country is dark once again after the all too brief holiday season.

One could not drive through a neighborhood without seeing real estate signs indicating "For Sale" or "For Rent". You couldn't walk through a mall or down a street without seeing once thriving businesses closed. America is experiencing some very dark days.

Joe Winston's much anticipated interview with Fox News is being aired live today. The interview had been exuberantly hyped by Fox and is expected to draw a huge audience. The numerous interviews with Lee, Adam, and Robbie had the public thirsting for more Joe Winston.

Joe's name recognition poll has climbed from 8% to 61% in less than six months. The public's dissatisfaction with government diminishes more and more each month and they are looking for alternatives. The promised changes were expected to be positive but the public only sees more of the same.

Tonight three journalists will ask unrestricted and unknown questions of their choice. No politicians would ever agree to a format such as this. Joe did not object and readily agreed to the format. The interviewers would be Bill Myers, Megan Lee, and Charlie Hardin.

The opening video included shots of Winston, Fields, Ravenel, and Roth in former interviews as the introductory music concluded and the camera zeros in on Bill Myers who said, "Welcome to a very special program; we are pleased to have as our guest tonight one of America's most influential business leaders, Joe Winston. Welcome Mr. Winston we are delighted to have you here this evening."

The three journalists and Joe are seated in comfortable chairs with Joe on one side and the reporters on the other. Joe is dressed in dark brown slacks, a black and brown sports coat, with a colorful tie of brown, yellow, and black.

As the camera pans to Joe he appreciatively says, "Thanks for having me Bill."

Bill said to viewers, "Let me introduce my fellow journalist Megan Lee and Charlie Hardin." The camera pans to each of them as they smile and nod as talking heads do.

Bill announces, "Mr. Winston insists on not having prior knowledge of the questions we will ask tonight which is a rare occurrence and demonstrates his desire to have honest and forthright communication with our viewers. Megan you have the first question."

Megan nods and says, "Mr. Winston our economy is decimated, unemployment continues to grow, and the public is extremely apprehensive about the future. Do you believe the current administration is wrong in their approach and what do you think needs to be done to restore our Nation to financial soundness?

As the camera focuses on Joe he replies, "Thank you Megan. It would be a mistake to place blame on this administration. The situation we find ourselves in is a result of many decades of a failing system of Government.

Our Declaration of Independence and our Constitution are perhaps the most brilliant documents ever conceived to guide a country. When we consider the fact a relatively small group of men created and agreed on these documents over two hundred years ago it is even more remarkable.

In my opinion, the problem's we face today are a direct result of attempts by both Republicans and Democrats to politically interpret these documents and to modify them in a manner conducive to their own ideology with out regard for the best interest of the people.

Clearly the intent was for the Federal Government to serve the States but in the last few decades these roles have become reversed and the States are clearly subservient to the Federal Government. It is my opinion that the Federal Government has engaged in social and fiscal engineering, micro management, and excessive ineffective regulation that has all but destroyed our free economy."

Can this situation be reversed? Of course it can but it will take years and some significant changes. I am optimistic that when you take politics out of the equation and put the welfare of our country first we can rebuild our economy.

The failures of Freddie Mac, Fannie Mae, AIG, Chrysler, General Motors, and our banks and other institutions were inevitable and predictable. The Federal interference in monetary policy and ineffective regulation has been detrimental to a free market economy.

Simply put the aforementioned companies were encouraged to grow and expand excessively utilizing leveraged buy outs, fiat money, and naïve accounting principals. They became too big to manage and practiced unsound financial management principals. In short, those companies were guilty of the same mistakes our Federal Government has made. They outgrew their ability to effectively manage.

This has resulted in our politicians trying to make political points by condemning these entities from behaving exactly like the Federal Government. The Federal Government has never worried about financial responsibility simply because they always have the ability to tax the people or simply print money. Megan, the Federal Government has been the role model for business and individual irresponsibility.

I will say this unless dramatic changes are made quickly the damage that has already been done may be irreversible."

Charlie who is wearing a blue suit, white shirt, and conservative tie asks, "Mr. Winston I am sure you have seen the stories that suggest that you and your friends are conspiring to gain control of the government for reasons of pure greed. Would you care to comment?"

Joe laughs and shakes his head in disbelief and answers, "It has always been one of my objectives to own one hundred trillion dollars of unfunded liabilities with no hope of recovery Charlie."

Everyone laughs at just how ridiculous the stories being circulated are for a few seconds and then Joe continues, "I will have to plead guilty to your point that we are trying to gain control of government.

As everyone knows we are now experiencing the birth of a new political party, The Restoration Party, and by the end of this month we should be officially registered in all fifty states and hopefully our candidates will have a big impact on the mid term elections in November."

Charlie follows up with, "Mr. Winston what exactly will be your role with the Restoration Party?"

Joe flashes his usual pleasant smile and replies, "As you know Senator John Danforth is organizing the party and I will support his efforts in any way that John sees fit."

Bill asks, "No third party has had any influence in over one hundred and fifty years what will be unique about the Restoration Party?"

"Clearly many of our solutions will resemble conservative monetary philosophies however we do not intend to be politically motivated. Members of our party will be restricted to one term only and we will fight for a constitutional amendment to require one term limits. Public servants should devote one hundred percent of their time improving this country and no time running for re election.

You will find the leadership offered by members of our party to be extraordinary. If candidates are seeking money or power they will not be welcome in the Restoration Party. We have but one purpose and that is to improve the quality of life for all Americans.

We will attempt to unify Americans not divide them. We are all fortunate to live in this and every citizen will be expected to contribute to the success of our country.

We will downsize government significantly, give more power to the states, and protect our country for our children and grandchildren."

Megan asks, "Mr. Winston, specifically what role will you play?"

Joe answers, "Megan once the party has been completely organized and our platform is hammered out the executive committee will make the decisions regarding individual roles." part

Megan asks quickly before Bill calls on Charley, "Will you run for President?"

Joe quickly answers, "Megan our country is facing serious problems and I, like every other American, should be willing to do everything in their power to resolve those problems. Our party's executive committee will make those decisions, not me. I will support whatever decision they make."

Bill announces, "We will return shortly with more from Joe Winston."

CHAPTER 59

During the commercial break the studio is buzzing and people are moving all over the massive studio. Make up artists are touching up the journalists and they are reviewing their notes. Joe stretches his legs and awaits the producers signal for the next segment.

Bill said to Charlie Johnson, "Charlie you're up!"

"Thank you Bill. Mr. Winston you have been very frank and we appreciate your comments. What advice would you give the President?" Charlie asks.

Joe smiles and replies, "first of all I would not give the President any unsolicited advice he is the CEO of the United States and he is the one who will dictate the direction of the country."

Charlie chuckles and said, "Well let me rephrase the question. If you were the President what would you do to correct our problems?"

For the next five minutes Joe repeats the same concepts he has advocated previously as if this is the first time he shared the information. He concluded with a few fresh ideas,

"We need congress to be representative of the people. Today the halls of congress are filled with lawyers. 65% of our elected representatives are either lawyers or have graduated from law school.

Lawyers are about the only professional group that remains unaffected by the economic difficulties faced by business and individuals and I don't believe that is simply a product of good fortune. Our country must have Tort reform.

We need barbers, salesman, construction workers, and people who simply wish to be of service to our country. Public service is a privilege and those who serve should not receive better health care and pension benefits than working people.

I challenge anyone watching this program to try and speak directly to his representative in Washington. Unless that person has given a substantial amount of money to his campaign he will never speak to his Senator or Congressman. I will ask our citizens to make the effort and confirm my observation.

Americans must stop fighting each other. The media must stop trying to create news that serves its agenda. Employers and employees must work together for their mutual benefit. The American people feel hopeless and politicians prey upon their weaknesses. They will promise anything to get elected and spend billions to keep their jobs. This must stop." Joe concludes.

Bill said, "Mr. Winston. President Howard promised no new taxes for 95% of the taxpayers and many people feel that was the reason he was elected. Do you agree?"

Joe replies, "The President is very good politician and an excellent speaker. I believe he would have been elected anyway simply because his opponent offered nothing new and the public was ready for a change.

However, I do believe that "no new taxes for 95% of the people" is a perfect example of how our political system works today and it is also an unfair representation that many Americans simply misunderstand. All one needs to do is look at the use taxes they have added in the past year and the numerous other taxes they call fees and the middle class and low income workers have been unjustifiably slammed.

It is very popular to attack the top 5% of wage earners, and some deserve to be attacked, but you must remember that these people who worked hard, risked capital, created jobs, and pay 90% of the taxes in this country are not the enemy. We must remember the facts; 1.4 million taxpayers pay more taxes than the remaining 138 million. I see no possible way that you can burden 1.4 million taxpayers with the obligation to pay almost another trillion in taxes.

They are the people that make a free economy work. Individuals in a free society who are fortunate enough to earn a substantial income earned that privilege through education, hard work, and ingenuity.

I understand how people who do not earn large incomes can resent those people but the essence of freedom is that every single person is free to learn and earn as much as they can. It is the obligation of a citizen to reach his full potential and every American must contribute fairly to society."

CHAPTER 60

Pete Boykin and his two partners in crime, Roy and Ron, are sitting in a small long term hotel room in Pineville, N.C, just outside of Charlotte, discussing their preliminary plans to assassinate the President.

The room contains two queen size beds with a beige flowered cover, two chairs with matching fabric, and a cheap fake pecan table, in the small area called a kitchen there is a sink, refrigerator, microwave, and small stove.

The rooms smells of tobacco smoke, beer, disinfectant, and staleness. There is one large single window, next to the door, that looks over a parking lot and the dirty brown carpet almost matches the ugly beige curtains and flowered bed spreads.

They arrived in the area two days earlier, with a full set of fake credentials, and each of the three men were placed in jobs in and around the Bank of America Corporate center in uptown Charlotte.

The three men are extremely careful not to be seen together and each night they would gather in Pete's room for briefing. Pete chose Roy and Ron because they are smart, loyal, and ruthless. Nevertheless, he decided it would be less risky if he did not inform them of their target until the time arrives. It is of little consequence to Roy and Ron since they are going to make $25,000 each and kill a black man.

At this time their primary objective is to become completely familiar with uptown Charlotte. They need to know each street, alley, walkover, and building exit in a three block area. Tonight Pete is reviewing their progress and he intends to drill it in their heads until they could not forget.

The Winston interview is playing on television and his comments disrupt their discussion and they became enthralled by Winston's interview. They had simply involuntarily stopped talking and started watching just like millions of Americans are doing.

At the commercial break Pete said, "This man seems to have the right idea and a good grasp of what America is all about."

His buddy Roy said, "He don't seem like all them other political assholes."

Ron said, "Who the hell is he?"

The three men look at each other and neither of them has a clue.

The commercial break ends and the man said, "Welcome back to our program and our guest, Joe Winston."

Pete informs his friends, "Joe Winston." As if they could not hear or he had suddenly remembered.

Pete returns to the map of uptown Charlotte and said, "You did okay tonight but I want you to keep at it. You need to know uptown better than the assholes that were born and raised here."

The men nod as Jack walks over to the refrigerator and removes three beers and hands one to each of his co-conspirators.

Roy drains half of his can and said, "Pete, when are you going to tell us who we are going to pop?"

Pete glares at him and says. "When I am good and fucking ready; you just keep doing what I pay you to do."

Ron says, "Don't be such a prick Pete. For twenty five g's we know it ain't no regular nigger."

Pete replies, "If you fucking guys can't keep your yaps shut and follow orders just give be back the money and haul your sorry asses back to D.C.!"

Ron and Roy nod as if they understand and Pete stands, up glaring at them, indicating the meeting was over and the two men leave.

Pete opens his suitcase and peels off the bottom to reveal a stack of papers. He stretches out on the bed and began to read the papers on blow guns and various poisons. He figures low tech might be able to counter high tech.

CHAPTER 61

Harry Belk, like millions of other Americans, tuned in to see the much touted Joe Winston interview. He also thought that his father in law, John Danforth, was a self righteous man who is incapable of reason. He considers John to be naïve and lacking a realistic understanding of how the real political system actually works. Harry is alone in his office sipping on a beer as he casually keeps one eye on the interview.

When the interview concluded he calls Jack Morgan, his second in command, and asks, "Did you watch that Winston interview?"

Jack said, "I did. What do you think?"

Harry said contemptuously "I think he scored a few points with the public tonight and I think he will be our opposition in the next Presidential election representing The Restoration Party."

Jack said, "Pretty impressive guy!"

"He's just the latest hack of the day. Check him out from top to bottom. Also check out his buddies and see what we can learn." Harry instructed as he sits at his desk thinking of strategies to be employed.

Harry says, "Notify our press connections to see to it he gets hammered tomorrow and every day for the next two years."

Jack compliantly said, "I will get right on it."

Harry hangs up the phone and leans back in his chair and realizes he hasn't taken one sip of his beer during the entire hour. That concerns him....

CHAPTER 62

Richmond, Virginia
January 23, 2010

John and Tony have been busily preparing for the first Restoration Party Convention to be held in about two weeks. Their tasks have been made much easier by the news Medias constant infatuation with Joe Winston as well as the critical and ridiculously biased reports by radical media organizations. The refreshing and honest interviews on television and in print every day is clearly having an impact on mainstream America.

Adam, Lee, and Robbie are also equally impressive in expressing their honest and heart felt respect for Joe and the United States of America in their many interviews.

The momentum that has been created combined with the frustration of the American people would serve the Restoration Party well.

The President's State of the Union message, though eloquently delivered, was cordially received and quickly discounted as the empty rhetoric of a politician. His comments are only briefly mentioned by the talking heads as they are falling in love with a new mistress.

John and Tony, with the help of over 600 volunteers, in Virginia, Washington, and Texas completed the tedious planning for the executive meeting and for the general session and have confirmations for over four thousand prominent special guests. They have also issued press credentials for over three thousand media representatives.

John looks up from his desk and his eyes survey his once beautiful library. Stacks of papers are everywhere, four desks for assistants are spread around the room, computer terminals and telephones are everywhere, and wires are running all over the house. "What a mess." John said.

Tony looks at John and said, "Let's take a break John. I need a drink."

John laughs and looks at his watch, "Well we have been going pretty hard and four o'clock is close enough for me."

The two men stand up, work out the kinks, and walk over to the bar where John pours two scotches. "Here you go old friend." He hands the drink to Tony and taps his glass on his friends and says, "Tony you have done one hell of a job."

"I have a good role model." Tony replies.

The two men sink into the overstuffed leather chairs and lean all the way back while stretching out their legs. They are dog tired and sit silently for a moment, glance at the television bank, and sip their scotch. John looks at Tony and said, "You know what old buddy, we are going to pull this off."

Tony laughs and takes a big swallow of the 18 year old scotch and said, "We sure as hell are John. We sure as hell are."

CHAPTER 63

Harry Belk travelled to Chicago with the President who is scheduled to address the American Medical Association at a formal function. They arrive at the Conrad Chicago and settle into their suites by 3:00 pm.

The President has several brief meetings with some of his contributors, local dignitaries, and advisors who happened to live in the Chicago area which allows Harry to have a couple of free hours.

Harry has plans to meet with an old friend who has been very helpful to him for the past thirty years. His friend has always come through for Harry no matter what he needed; money, advice, or influence.

The last couple of months have been a bit more positive for Harry and his spirits are a little higher than normal. He twisted a lot of arms, called in all favors, promised over two billion in earmarks, and the Senate passed a partial Government health program by a vote of 60 to 35.

It was far from what he had hoped for but it was a step in the right direction even if it was a partisan bill. Medicare X was his idea and it obviously satisfied a lot of opponents and gave the administration a badly needed win.

It is rather basic, those who lacked insurance or are uninsurable can enroll in Medicare X with individual cost based upon income much like Medicare. In order to get it passed he had to exclude non citizens but the point was they had passed a National Health Care program and won. He had no doubt that over the next few years he would make the program incrementally more comprehensive.

The normally intense negativity between conservatives and liberals has almost disappeared from television as both parties are now attacking the inexperience and frivolity of a viable third party.

There also appears to be a groundswell of opposition from hard working Americans with growing concerns about our annual deficit and National debt. Nevertheless, Harry views this as a minor inconvenience and knows that it makes no difference what Joe Citizen thinks he is in charge and he intends to be in control for a long time.

It is only a short walk to Loyola University and he decides to enjoy a brisk walk in spite of the strong winds and chilly twenty five degrees. He makes the half mile walk in about twenty minutes and made his way to the office of Professor Aziz Hasan, his old friend and mentor.

As he walks into the outer office the professor's administrative assistant, Kathy greets him, "Mr. Belk so good to see you again. The Professor is waiting, please go in."

Harry smiles warmly at Kathy and walks over and gives her a formal embrace and says, "Good to see you too Kathy. Hope your family is well."

"They are Mr. Belk and thanks for asking." Kathy says with genuine appreciation.

Harry opens the door to Aziz's office and walks in where he is immediately embraced by his old friend. "Harry, you look very well. Come in and have a seat."

Harry slapped Aziz on the back and warmly said, "So good to see you my friend. How is your family?"

"Everyone is fine Harry and they all said to tell you hello." Aziz replies.

The office is a typical professor's office, messy. Aziz's old desk with his worn out chair, a large library table covered with books and papers, book cases from floor to ceiling on two walls, and a large window overlooking the campus.

Aziz is wearing an old grey suit that appears to be a little to large on his slight body, a white dress shirt, and the usual bow tie. The two men engage in congenial small talk for a few minutes while Aziz serves coffee and sweet rolls to his guest.

As the two men take their seats Aziz begins the conversation, "Harry I want to congratulate you and the President for passing the National Health Care Program. It is a fine step in the right direction and I know how hard you have all worked."

"Thank you Aziz. It was difficult and far short of where we want to be but we are confident we will get the rest over the next few years." Harry responds.

Aziz fixes Harry with his beady eyes and asks, "Tell me about the economy Harry; there is a lot of concern from the public."

Harry sips his coffee and said, "Well the market rebounded nicely at the end of last year and as soon as we spend the remainder of the stimulus money employment will improve which will drive the GDP. If we can get money into the hands of the people their complaints will diminish quickly enough."

Aziz, as if challenging one of his students, politely asks, "Harry what about the deficit and the growing national debt? Any plans to reduce this debt which will encourage our foreign friend to continue buying government securities?"

Harry laughs and squirms a little in his chair, "Well Aziz we need to increase taxes and perhaps have a national sales tax but the major burden will fall on the minority of voters. We will trim the budget a little and once we get out of the Middle East that will save us four or five hundred billion a year and put the public sentiment back with us and reassure foreign investors."

Aziz knows that Harry is being optimistic and insincere for that is his nature. Aziz is not surprised with Harry's answers and is more certain than ever that the end is near for America.

Aziz asks, "What about all the anti government sentiment. Does it concern you?"

"Aziz you know as well as I its just politics as usual. The conservatives continue to sing the same song, reduce taxes, free economy, downsize government but the truth is they have no candidates that could possibly challenge us." Harry replies.

Once again Aziz looks at Harry thoughtfully and asks, "What about this Joe Winston guy and this new Restoration Party?"

Harry laughs and says, "There isn't much chance of a third party having any impact. If anything they will hurt the Republicans. Winston is a very charismatic guy with absolutely no experience in government and there is no way he can garner much real support.

He has an impressive background and he's squeaky clean but even with John Danforth and Tony Papandrea pushing him they won't be able to sell it."

"Don't underestimate him Harry he is not a man who is unaccustomed to failure and the public seems to be very frustrated with politics as usual. They often vote for change and if they would elect an African-American President they just might vote for a squeaky clean, articulate, and charismatic non-politician. The man appears to be very smart, passionate, and determined." Aziz said with caution in his voice.

Harry listens respectfully and responds with a smirk on his face, "We will keep a close eye on him my friend but don't worry about him he has no chance."

"Would you like some more coffee?" Aziz asks.

"Thank you Aziz that sounds good. It is a bit cold outside." Harry responds while enjoying his reunion with the man who has had such a positive impact on his career. He always wondered how a college professor could possibly have so much influence but he is glad he does.

Aziz pours Harry a fresh cup and walks over to the other side of his desk and sits the cup

in front of Harry. He takes the seat next to Harry and puts his hand on Harry's shoulder and says, "Harry you are a wonderful public servant and we appreciate your many sacrifices and contributions to our country." He hands Harry a piece of paper with a series of numbers on it.

Harry looks at the numbers and reads them out loud, "234HB764521. What's this?"

"A gift my friend for your service to America." He hands him another piece of paper with a receipt from a Swiss bank for a one million dollar deposit and a telephone number.

Harry looks at the paper with mock surprise and says "Aziz, please, I can't accept this."

Aziz stands up and kisses Harry on each cheek and said, "Your supporters are very grateful Harry and they insist that you use this money wisely. Now you must go to work and save America."

He walks Harry to the door, as always in control, and said, "It was really good to see you Harry. Thank you so much for taking time to visit a grateful old man."

Harry put the papers in his coat pocket and reaches to shake Aziz's hand, "Thank you Aziz I value your counsel and appreciate your friendship more than you will ever know. Generous Patriots, such as you, are what makes this country great."

As Harry left the third floor office in the Crown Center, his spirits are greatly lifted by his visit...... and the money as he heads back to the hotel. He hardly noticed the temperature has dropped into the teens as he briskly starts his trek back to the hotel and buttons his over coat nor did he notice the student with a computer sitting in the cold on a bench outside of the Crown Center.

CHAPTER 64

Rashid had received confirmation that President Howard would attend a Memorial Service for the victims of the April 5, 2009 terrorist attack on the Bank of America Corporate headquarters in Charlotte and booked a flight to Charlotte.

Rashid arrives in Charlotte at 10:05 am on a direct flight from Washington. He takes a bus to the Hertz rental car agency and picks up a Ford Explorer he had reserved. He is familiar with Charlotte and heads to Pineville, N.C. to meet Pete Boykin at the International House of Pancakes on the Pineville-Matthews Road.

Rashid, wearing blue jeans, a dark blue wool shirt, and a leathers jacket, enters the restaurant and pauses briefly searching for Pete. His keen eye, sharpened by combat and covert activity, locates him quickly and he walks toward the booth to join Pete. As he takes a seat across from Pete the waitress approaches and asks, "May I help you?"

Rashid politely replies, "coffee please."

Rashid shakes Pete's hand and smiles, "How have you been doing?

Pete, wearing jeans and a white tee shirt in order to show off his muscles and tattoos, curtly replies, "We are doing fine Rashid."

The waitress returns quickly with the coffee as the restaurant is not very busy and ask Rashid what he would like.

Rashid smiles at her and said, "Coffee and blueberry pancakes."

She turns to Pete and asks, "More coffee sir?"

Pete doesn't even look at her as he simply points at his cup.

The waitress leaves and Rashid puts his elbows on the table, leans forward, and says in his conspiratorial voice, "We have confirmation that he will here."

Pete is tiring of all the waiting and is pleased to hear the news as he leans forward and asks, "When?"

Rashid looks around and said softly, "He will arrive on the day we discussed around ten in the morning. They will meet at the same place at 1:00 pm and depart by 4:00 pm."

Pete is smiling as he glances around before speaking, "Good, we will be ready."

Rashid said with skepticism, "Have you put together any tentative plans?"

"We have." Pete said.

Rashid looks frustrated as he asks, "Well are you going to tell me about it?"

"I will tell you when I'm ready." Pete says with some impatience.

Rashid starts to speak when he notices the waitress returning with the coffee which she places on the table. "Thank you."

When the waitress walks away he looks at Pete and controls his temper. He never liked the prick but he did need him, "When can I expect to have your complete plan?"

Pete smiles and in his best smart ass says, "When I am good and fucking ready."

Rashid grins and speaks through clenched teeth, "Just so we are clear my friend. I must notify my superior, the man who pays you, by March 15th of the complete plan. If you can't manage to get me your plan by March 5th I can find someone else who would welcome the opportunity to make a million bucks and I will expect you to return what you have received."

Pete believes Rashid's bluff and smirks as he says, "Rashid, you are full of shit. You can't find anyone crazy enough to do this but me."

"That's where you are wrong my friend, there are plenty of crazy people in this country who will do the job for free and I am getting a little tired of your fucking shit. This is a business arrangement and I need your plan by March 5th. Now will I have it or won't I?" Rashid spoke without a hint of humor and it is clear to Pete that he is deadly serious.

Pete slowly picks up his coffee while staring at Rashid. It is a matter of pride that no one controls him and sips his coffee and concludes that he would play the game, "Relax Rashid. I will give you a list of supplies today and a detailed plan by March 5th."

Rashid slowly smiles and is satisfied that he has Pete's attention and says," Good. I knew I had the right man for the job. I will come back down here on the 5th and we will review your plan. Will that be satisfactory?" Rashid said.

"That works for me Rashid." Pete said nonchalantly.

Rashid feels relieved as he sips his coffee, "I don't wish to interfere in your plans Pete but are you feeling pretty comfortable with your plans so far?"

Pete smiles proudly, "I think you will be very pleased."

"I can't wait Pete. It is a very difficult task and the security will be extremely tight. We also have a brief window to make this happen. You know you don't have a chance with firearms or explosives and getting close to the President will be almost impossible. This will require superior tactical planning." Rashid said with skepticism and the suggestion that Pete is incapable of superior plan.

Pete has a cocky look on his face as he smugly replies, "Rashid it will be surprisingly simple. Don't worry your little sand nigger ass one bit; just have my money ready...... There is one thing I will need quickly."

Rashid ignores the insult and said, "Name it and I will do my best."

Pete glances around to be assured no one is within ear shot. Once satisfied he said, "I will need a complete list of all the victims families with pictures, addresses, phone numbers, and as much background as possible. It occurs to me that most of this could be obtained through the DMV computers and other methods you may know about."

Rashid listens carefully trying to determine what Pete is thinking, "Why do you need that?"

Pete checks his quick temper but could not completely hide it and curtly asks, "Can you do it or can't you?"

Rashid thought carefully before answering, "I think I can do that Pete."

Pete said, "The sooner the better. I figure that the families of the victims will receive special invitations and perhaps be seated fairly close to the President. Hopefully, we can manage to get our hands on a couple of invitations."

"I knew you would come up with a good idea and that sounds like it could work. Check the encrypted web site tomorrow and I will tell you how quickly I can get this to you." Rashid enthusiastically replies.

Rashid catches the waitress's eye and signals for the check, "Pete we are counting on you. I will see you right here on the 5th of March."

The waitress drops the check on the table, apparently not expecting much of a tip, and leaves. Rashid left thirty dollars on the table and shakes Pete's hand. Pete said, "See you on March 5th."

The two men walk out to the parking lot climb into their cars. Pete went east on the Pineville-Matthews road and Rashid heads west towards the airport.

Mike, dressed in a business suit and wearing clear eye glasses, folds his computer and heads east about three minutes behind Rashid. The men are both booked on the 2:05 U.S. Air flight back to Washington.

CHAPTER 65

It is a pleasant but chilly day on Sullivan's Island and the view from Robbie Ravenel's magnificent beach home is spectacular. To the east is the Atlantic Ocean and to the south is Charleston Harbor and historic Fort Sumter.

Robbie's home contains eight bedrooms, ten bathrooms, a gourmet kitchen, a wonderful library, and a huge great room. The simple elegance of design and complimentary furnishings presents a very relaxing and livable environment.

There is a strong north east wind, which keeps the normally busy beach almost deserted and provides Robbie and his guest with even more privacy than normal. His guests arrived the previous night and include Joe, Lee, Adam, John, and Tony and their intent is to review final preparations for the convention.

Robbie is an early riser and finds himself in the kitchen pouring his first cup of coffee before daylight appears. He sits at the kitchen table and enjoys watching the darkness surrender to the inevitable light.

His thoughts are focused on his recent covert activities and until his nephew had been killed he never considered the considerable resources available to him. His security business evolved into a company that has access to substantial secretive and confidential data.

He thought of how his business combined with Lee's exceptional technology skills creates a pretty formidable covert operation under the experienced leadership of Bert Braddock.

His thoughts were interrupted by Joe, "Good morning Robbie. Is that coffee any good?"

Robbie pours Joe a cup of coffee and they turn toward to the ocean to watch the total demise of darkness as Robbie replies, "Of course it is."

He had given the staff a couple of days off and starts preparing breakfast for his guests. The aroma of bacon frying, coffee, and blueberry muffins combines with the sweet fragrance of the salty ocean air causes one to become abnormally hungry. As the aroma drifts into the bedrooms the men are drawn to the kitchen like ants to sugar.

After they spent the morning discussing the Restoration Party's first Convention and are confident that they are well prepared Robbie said, "John will you and Tony excuse us for a little while."

John replies, "Go right ahead Robbie Tony and I have about a hundred phone calls to make."

Robbie, Joe, Adam, and Lee left the kitchen and go downstairs to Robbie's exceptionally large safe room and after they are seated around the large table Robbie says, "I know you have each been updated on the plans to assassinate the President so we need to decide on our next course of action."

Joe speaks first, "I realize there are several options but one thing is for sure it isn't going to happen."

The other three men nod in agreement and then Adam said, "The big question is how we prevent this in a manner that won't compromise our actions?"

Lee chimes up and said, "We have taken some pretty aggressive steps that could bury us but I don't regret anything we have done but we do need to be extremely careful."

Joe leans back in his chair and looks at Robbie, "Robbie what are your thoughts?"

Robbie said, "We can just have Bert handle it and be done with it but that will virtually destroy our progress to date. Aziz will be history."

The men discuss the pros and cons of their options for the next hour and finally Joe said, "If we turn this information over to the FBI and they arrest the white guys that could trigger a lot of racial distress.

Hasan and Majid are already concerned about the loss of their operatives in Charlotte and Houston. If we stop the assassination they will know they have been completely compromised and they will shut down this group and create a new operational plan with new players and we will lose the advantage we now have.

The decision as to what to do weighs heavy on each of them. There are pros and cons and much is at stake and it appears there is no reasonable option. They exchange glances as each man searches for the appropriate response.

Joe has a thought and continues, "Robbie could you put together a file which includes all the information we currently have?"

Robbie answers, "Sure."

Joe sits silent for a few minutes tapping his fingers on the table and each man is waiting for him to speak. "I think we should let the government stop this attempt on the Presidents life and shut down the terrorists operations in the United States."

The men look at each other with confusion.

Robbie responds, "What's your plan Joe"

Adam interrupts and says, "To whom and how would we provide this information?"

The men look at Joe and then at Robbie. Joe asks, "What do you think Robbie?"

"I guess the director of the FBI or the Secret Service?" he replies.

Joe continues pacing as his friends watch and they could see the wheels turning and then he says, "Tell you what. Let's package the information, check and double check to be absolutely sure we are protected and I will let you know who will receive the file."

"Joe you know I trust you but this confuses me; can you give us a little more insight?" Robbie asks.

"I will Robbie but give me a couple of weeks to work it out to my satisfaction. I also want three exact copies and I mean exact enough that no one could question the legitimacy of one over the other. Same paper, same printer, same everything." Joe emphatically said.

Robbie looks at Joe with some confusion and said, "Why three copies Joe?"

Joe gives Robbie a smile and said, "I will tell you guys a little later when I work it out, okay?"

As the men stand up and prepare to walk upstairs and join Tony and John, Joe says, "Boys this is getting a little scary I am beginning to think like a politicians."

They find them in the kitchen and Adam asks, "You guys finish all your phone calls?" Tony smiles and walks behind John and puts his hands on John's shoulders and says, "This old man is working me to death but we are doing fine."

John looks at the group and said with a wry smile, "We do have a little information that I think might please you."

"Well don't keep us in suspense." Lee said.

"Dallas is running out of hotel rooms for our convention. We now have over 56,000 confirmed to attend with no signs of registrations slowing down. We have issued press credentials for 5,300. Boys this is exceeding our wildest expectations." John says with a huge smile on his face.

Everyone expected to do well but this news is exceptionally gratifying and the positive feedback inspires them even more.

Robbie looks at his watch and notices it was one o'clock, "Tell you what guys let's go to Shem Creek Bar and Grill and get some lunch."

Joe said, "I need to talk to John so why don't we take a car and you guys take one."

As they left the beach house Joe turns to John and said, "John you know politics much better than I so what if the Chief of Staff receives some information that involves a serious issue such as National security; what would he most likely do with that information?"

John looks at Joe and knows not to ask any questions and answers, "Well the first thing Harry Belk would consider is how this information can strengthen the Administration and his party. He will try to find a way to gain political capital and he doesn't much give a damn about America his only interest is maintaining power.

Hell, if he felt the information would not benefit him he probably wouldn't say anything."

As Joe begins to cross the bridge he asks, "Would that go for all politicians?"

John looks at Joe and then glances out at the intercoastal waterway below them and sadly replies, "I am afraid so Joe. You can't imagine how devious and corrupt politicians can be."

Joe thinks about John's comment and said, "John I will never understand a politicians mentality. How did you live with it for all these years?"

"It hasn't been easy son. I actually thought I could eventually make a difference but I learned that men are very weak and once they enter the Washington inner circle they discover that power is a mistress that few can resist." John said.

Joe is slowly learning to understand the mind of politicians and at that moment he feels certain that he can beat them at their own game and knows how he would handle the valuable information they have compiled.

Later that evening the men are relaxing on Robbie's wrap around porch after a fine seafood dinner. It is chilly evening and all the men are wearing jackets. High in the black sky the stars appear to more abundant than usual. The soft northeast breeze and the rhythmic roar of the surf combine with the wonderful salty smell of the ocean to virtually compel one to be calm and introspective.

Their conversation covers a wide variety of subjects and foremost among their topics is the arrogance and deceptive nature of the current administration as well as past administrations.

Adam says, "It appears that mainstream America has finally decided to pay more attention. Every since the break last August we have been hearing from ordinary American citizens who are tired of politics as usual and the internet is giving everyone a voice."

John, bundled in one of Robbie's old jackets, said, "I can tell you that my office has had to add four lines and hire additional staff to handle the growing number of contacts. I am sure that others are receiving far more inquiries also but they are reluctant to share such information."

Lee, pours his third diet Coke and says, "I just can't believe how cunning and unprincipled these guys can be. They do everything in their power to divert the public's attention from the only serious issue we face, the economy.

They manage to make health care, torture that may have occurred years ago, cash for clunkers, the war, trials for terrorists, and any other issue more public and important then our massive debt and failing economy. How in the hell does the media allow him to skate on these issues?"

Adam rocks in his chair and turns toward Lee and said, "Lee he is just keeping his campaign promise to create a new America."

Robbie laughs and said, "I kind of liked the old America. The concept of a Republic is more appealing to me than living under a fascist system of government. This administration is really scary. Our President is clearly an empty suit or intentionally trying to destroy our country."

John said, "Personally, I am more optimistic than I have been in thirty years. Boys I am telling you we are going to send some talent to Washington and seat a lot of new Governors in November. The rise of America has begun."

CHAPTER 66

For weeks the media has been hyping the First Restoration Party convention and could talk of little else. Of course the "talking heads" continue to scoff at the idea that a third party could have any chance. The "heads" were also adamant that the Restoration Party is a conglomeration of inexperienced conservatives who could not possibly grasp the complexity of government and the voters would never turn the country over to amateurs.

The more existing politicians tried to discredit Joe the more foolish they seemed to look. Clearly the Restoration Party is now being taken seriously by millions of voters and some politicians.

It is hardly necessary for the Restoration Party to waste much money for advertising because they are getting 24/7 coverage on the news networks, Joe Winston's popularity is growing rapidly and the American people seem to be drifting away from the status quo of current political parties.

The executive committee for the Restoration Party reserved most of the Four Seasons Resort at Las Colinas for their convention and it is their responsibility to hammer out their platform and to fine tune the convention to be held in Cowboy Stadium.

Over the last two weeks Joe has either personally or by telephone visited with 241 new Restoration Party candidates and twelve existing members of Congress who are disenchanted with their party.

It is almost midnight when John and Joe finally stop for the day and are sitting in the living room of a two bedroom suite. It was a very long day and John wearily said, "Well son, how did it go? As he plops down hard in an inviting overstuffed chair.

"I am impressed with the quality and commitment of the people I have had the pleasure of meeting. Visiting with these people inspires me." Joe said as he pours two glasses of wine.

John sips on his Merlot and said, "As they say, you have to kiss a lot of frogs to find a prince, and buddy, we have kissed a lot of frogs."

John clicks on the television to a local station and the flat screen comes to life with a live report from Cowboy Stadium. A helicopter circling overhead is sending feed to the studio with the bright city lights, the stadium, and the parking lot.

The reporter yells, over the whoop-whoop-whoop of the helicopter blades aggressively moving the air, as his blonde hair flies in different directions, "This is truly unbelievable…The parking lot and surrounding areas are completely filled with people hoping to be present for this extraordinary moment in history.

No one would have dreamed that so many people would be drawn to a third party convention. We have estimated a minimum of eighty five thousand people are here ten hours prior to the commencement of the Convention." He concludes his report and the studio anchorman appears.

"Tune in tomorrow morning at eight am when our live coverage of the Restoration Party convention officially begins their historic journey. We will be there from the opening gavel to conclusion. This is Jerry Ellison and this breaking news is presented by Ford Motors."

John and Joe are suddenly wide awake and their fatigue is gone as they look at each other in disbelieve and are clearly overwhelmed by the out pouring of support.

John's entire life now seems to be validated as he wearily stands up and walks toward Joe with moist disbelieving eyes, his lower lips trembling and making little effort to fight back tears of shear happiness.

Joe sees the joy on John's face and stands to share an emotional embrace with his father in law.

CHAPTER 67

As the sun rises on the brand new magnificent Cowboy Stadium the crowds are large, enthusiastic, and looking forward to this historic and life changing day. There is no concern about the economy, unemployment, debt, National Health care, immigration, terrorists, or the difficulties that are impacting millions of Americans. There is only hope and optimism.

Reporters are trying desperately to capture those feelings in words but adequate eloquence eludes them.

Thousands, who are unable to gain entrance, are simply trying to remain in close proximity to this dramatic event surround the eight giant screens outside the stadium quickly installed on the outside of the stadium. Millions of more Americans utilize their televisions, computers, and radios to participate in what promises to be a significant historical change in politics.

The joy and excitement being experienced by many is not shared by all. Inside the belt way in Washington the existing leaders of the free world are experiencing something akin to being tied to the railroad tracks and seeing the train speeding toward you.

Inside Cowboy Stadium the patriotic decorations are impressive, thousands of American flags, state flags, and the new red, white, and blue Restoration Party banners surround the field. The attendees are extremely well behaved as they enjoy the first day's speakers.

Around four o'clock the convention is adjourned until seven o'clock and the attendee's enthusiasm remains high as does their anticipation for the prime time program. In the meantime, the vendors in and around the stadium would have ample opportunity to exercise their entrepreneurial talents.

The Stadium is filled with patriotic music during the three hour break and the delegates are more than ready when the evening's program begins. John Danforth approaches the podium while happily waving to everyone and anyone.

For those not close enough to personally see him the giant screens allowed full vision of the stage. He receives a thunderous ovation that continues for four minutes. When the delegates are finally encouraged to take their seats Senator Danforth said, "Please join me in honoring America by singing our National Anthem."

The Navy band began to play as the words appeared on the giant screen behind the Senator and each of the eighty or ninety thousand inside Cowboy Stadium sang with every ounce of emotion and patriotism they could muster as did the thousands outside the stadium. When the song reaches its conclusion many in the audience are filled with emotions they had not felt in years and they openly weep with pride.

Senator Danforth is comfortable behind the podium and large Restoration Party banners are prominent, "As you know I have submitted my resignation to the Republican Party and pledged my allegiance to America and the Restoration Party."

John continues, "For many years I have felt as if I were alone… as I did my best for the American people and for my fellow citizens of Virginia. Today I no longer feel alone. I feel that I have the support of the most dynamic and patriotic leaders in this great land of ours. Please allow me to introduce the Restoration Party's gubernatorial candidates for 2010."

Over the next twenty seven minutes John introduces the twenty one new gubernatorial aspirants. When all had been properly introduced and are standing on stage John continues, "I am also very proud to announce twelve current Governors who have today resigned from their former party and joined the Restoration Party."

As John introduces four former Democrats and eight former Republicans they assume their position on stage and John said, "Ladies and gentlemen please welcome these thirty three talented and exceptional people who are willing to give their all to restore America to the country it is destined to become and to help us restore State's rights."

The delegates once again come to their feet and offer tremendous applause as the candidates bow and waive gratefully to the audience.

Clearly the quality of impressive new candidates and the defection of former Democrats and Republicans send the media, and their former party, into an uncontrollable frenzy.

When the delegates and spectators finally settle into their seats and the gubernatorial candidates have left the stage John resumes, "Great leaders are what America needs. Men who have strong moral character and understand they work for the people. The Restoration party has vetted hundreds of prospective candidates seeking only the best and I am confident we have succeeded. However, that isn't for me to decide it is for you to decide when you cast your vote on November 2, 2010."

John pauses to receive the gracious cheering and applause from the attendees and then continues, "It is now my pleasure to introduce our candidates for the Senate. There are 36 seats to be decided in November and it is my hope that the Restoration Party will fill the majority of those seats."

Once again he is interrupted by an audience that is extremely enthusiastic. When the exuberance subsides John introduces twenty one new candidates who take their place on stage.

He continues, "I am now pleased to introduce twelve of America's most dynamic and caring public servants." He introduces five former Democrats and seven former Republican Senators who have submitted their letters of allegiance to the Restoration Party.

These well know Senators take the stage and four of the candidates make dynamic short speeches that fill the audience with inspiration, enthusiasm, hope, and love for their country.

The convention and world wide audience is still buzzing over the excitement when John Danforth introduces Robbie Ravenel who had also developed quite a following based upon his many public appearances and common sense direct approach.

Robbie is assigned the task of introducing the Restoration Party's Vice Presidential nominee, Betty Parker, who is the Governor of Wyoming and the Presidential candidate Joe Winston. Robbie discharges his responsibilities professionally and as Joe and Betty take the stage with their families they are joined by all the Restoration Party's candidates.

The joyful cheers from the delegates expressed approval of the candidates, satisfaction with the announced platform, and tremendous hope for the future. It is obvious to any observer that this day will mark a positive change in American politics and hopefully lead to changes that would restore common sense, create opportunity, and begin a new era of responsible government.

Twenty five minutes later all the candidates, with the exception of Joe and Betty, drifted off the stage and Betty happily approaches the podium and acknowledges the warm reception and requests silence.

Betty Parker, a plain speaking lady with strong traditional values and a popular advocate for less government, eloquently accepted her party's nomination and delivers a dynamic twenty minute presentation that is extremely well received.

Joe Winston warmly congratulates Betty and steps to the podium as complete silence fell upon the stadium. Everyone in the live audience and the millions at home are anxious to hear every word.

Joe is dressed in a conservative black suit, exceptionally white shirt, and a beautifully designed elegant black and white tie with crossing diagonal stripes. His posture is ramrod straight and his tanned and warm face surveys the crowd with genuine appreciation, gratitude, and confidence.

In a strong but humble voice he simply says, "I proudly and humbly accept the Restoration Party's nomination."

With those words the audience once again clamors to their feet while cheering loudly and chanting Joe, Joe, Joe, Joe.........

Betty Parker, dressed in a grey suit, joins Joe along with all the Restoration Party's candidates as the Navy band plays "America", thousands of red, white, and blue balloons are released. The audience waves the American flag and the Restoration Party flag. The celebration continued for twenty minutes and nobody wanted it to end.

In the history of journalism never have so many journalists had so much to write about and none seemed to be qualified to adequately articulate or capture this historic moment.

CHAPTER 68

Newspapers across the country hit porches, cable networks are humming, and radio talk shows could only talk about one event, The Restoration Party convention and the nomination of the popular and competent Joe Winston for President. Whatever else happens in the world would not be known to the general public for days.

Washington is stunned. Nobody seriously believed that a third party could muster such overwhelming support in such a short period of time and to say they are surprised would not come close to adequately describing the shock waves that penetrated every corner of our nations capitol.

The number of defections to the Restoration Party deeply disturbed each party. They never saw it coming; most likely due to their arrogance and self adulation which has suffered significant damage overnight.

Harry Belk is pissed off and is making no attempt to hide his displeasure. He feels betrayed, as he usually does when things don't go his way, and his predominant thoughts are revenge. That's just the way he's wired.

Belk is not a man who wears well for long. He lost his wife when she realized his one true love is politics and there is no room for family in his world. His world is one of manipulation, deceit, and win at all cost.

He detest losing and demands loyalty. He could not believe the defections nor could he believe the coverage being heaped upon this ridiculous new party of amateurs. He considers anyone who supports the Restoration Party ungrateful traitors

He thought of Aziz who had cautioned him not to underestimate Joe Winston and the Restoration Party and that's exactly what he had done.

He will be watching the convention tonight with the President and his key advisors. It really pissed him off to see the President suggesting it is that important. He had advised him to simply ignore them but he would not listen.

He goes to the restroom and washes his face and tries to calm down before being forced to watch the concluding night of the convention and he dreads having to endure this humiliation in the presence of those who will most likely blame him.

As he enters the Situation room he sees that everyone is there and as he enters it appears to him as if everyone stops talking and looks at him. The attitudes in the room ranged from anger and frustration to fear and concern. Most are playing it by ear and the reality is their emotions would be determined by the President's reactions and he feels as if he had been run over by a train.

The second day of the convention starts sharply at 10:00 am with short but powerful speeches from more candidates and concludes that evening with another powerful acceptance speech by Joe Winston.

It was the longest day of Harry Belk's life and there is a dark cloud of despair and disappointment permeating the room in direct contradiction of what they have just witnessed on television.

When the President turns the television off the room falls silent. President Howard stands up and looks at the people gathered around the table and his gaze fixes upon Harry, "Harry could you tell us how in the hell this can happen while we are sitting on our asses fat, dumb, and happy?"

Harry's face reddens and he feels complete embarrassment as he responds, "Mr. President we have been carefully monitoring their activities for the past six months and I have simply reported to you what I have been told. It appears to me that the confidence I placed in the teams responsible for the information was unjustified. I can assure that tomorrow morning some fucking heads will roll."

The President's anger does not subside. Belk is perhaps his closest ally and he knows he can not rip him a new ass hole in public as he said, "Harry being caught like this is unacceptable and unprofessional and I do expect you to hammer the incompetent idiots in whom you misplaced your trust."

Belk says, "Yes sir."

Howard is still pacing the room and is trying desperately to maintain control as he intentionally slows his speech, "Harry these ungrateful defectors deserve to feel the full wrath of this office, do you understand me?"

Harry feels as if his bull shit has once more saved him says firmly, "Yes sir. I understand completely and I will see to it."

The President goes to his working office to be alone. He put his feet on his desk and is leaning back in his high back leather executive chair with the POTUS emblem. He closes his eyes and thinks of all the issues he is dealing with and now this shit.

Howard rarely curses but he abruptly jumps up from his chair and walks to the window and bangs his fist on the wall and said, God damn it…..another fucking problem to deal with!

CHAPTER 69

VOLUSIA NATIONAL, FL
MARCH 6, 2010

Joe, Lee, Robbie, and Adam are taking a well deserved break from the grind of the past few months. It might well be their last time to relax prior to the mid terms which will keep them all very busy.

The day is overcast but still comfortable at sixty eight degrees. They had completed their round of golf around noon and are seated on the veranda at Volusia National having lunch. As usual, no other guests are on the premises. Lee, after taking a big bite of his egg salad sandwich, asks Joe, "How are all the campaigns going?"

Joe finishes his glass of tea and replies, "John says they are going very well and millions of people are becoming members of the Restoration Party and in spite of little effort to raise money the web site is bringing in an average of one hundred and twenty thousand dollars per day. It appears to me everything is going very well."

Robbie chews on his hamburger and talks with his mouth half full, says, "Can you guys believe all that has transpired in the last year?"

"Has it only been a year? Adam asks incredulously. "Seems like ten."

Joe asks, "Robbie anything we need to know about our friends under surveillance?"

Robbie takes a big swallow of his root beer and replies, "Boykin met with Rashid in Charlotte and requested all the data on the survivors and family members of the Bank of America attack.

It appears they want to assume the identity of one or more of them with the hopes of being able to get close to the President. Rashid gave him the information he requested about two weeks ago and also shipped him a box with twelve professional blow guns complete with various tips and poisons.

Apparently they feel the wooden blow guns and darts will not be picked up by any metal detectors and can be easily concealed. It is my understanding that one can become pretty accurate with these weapons and hit their target from as far away as forty yards."

Lee appreciates the simplicity of the plan and said, "That might actually work."

Robbie said, "It might but they will never get the chance."

Lee laughs and said, "Well maybe those rednecks will get drunk and shoot each other and save us all a lot of trouble."

The men all chuckled at the thought of it and Joe said, "How about the packages Robbie? Have you got them all ready?"

"We do. Each piece of paper will have the same water mark and will be completely untraceable. What do you want me to do with them?" Robbie asks.

"I understand that Belk lives alone. Is that right?" Joe said.

"That is correct. His wife and family have been gone for years. That prick only cares about his power and politics." Robbie said.

"I would like for you put one of the packages in his mail box and be sure we get pictures of him removing the package and if possible pictures of him reading or giving them to anyone. Lee is it possible to imbed one of your little devices somewhere in the package?" Joe asks.

Lee said, "I know the package will have papers but will any memory sticks be included?"

Robbie said, "Mostly paper and one memory stick?"

Lee said, "I can put one in a memory stick."

Robbie said, "No shit! I never even thought about that."

"When can you do it Lee?" Joe asks.

"Anytime you want." I have several of the prototypes in my office.

Robbie said, "You ain't gonna ask me to fly to Boston in the middle of the winter are you old buddy?"

Lee laughs and said, "Nope. It will give me an excuse to visit your holy and historic city of Charleston."

Joe said, "We need to give them at least two weeks this will be a major operation and will involve every agency in Washington I would imagine. I'm not sure they can even get in done in two weeks."

Lee said, "When we leave here I will swing by Charleston and Robbie and I can leave there and drop the package off in Washington to whoever will deliver it if that's ok with Robbie."

Robbie said, "We have a man in Washington keeping an eye on Rashid and I'm sure he will look forward to a different assignment. Today he is in Charlotte eyeballing Rashid as Boykin delivers his plan. We will work it out."

"Can you get the package to him by March 15th?" Joe asks.

"No problem Joe," Lee said.

Robbie said, "What about the other two sets?"

Joe said, "If you have them with you I will take them now."

"I will get them to you before we leave." Robbie said.

Adam said, "Man this is a beautiful day. Who wants to play an emergency nine?"

The men left the veranda arguing about who would be partners and what the game would be as they headed to the first tee.

CHAPTER 70

Since the news event of the year and perhaps the decade had concluded in Dallas with the Restoration Party's first convention the Washington in crowd, on both sides of the aisle, have been trying desperately to discredit this upstart party without success.

The President, on advice from Belk, decides to let Carol Osborne accept a prime time interview with NBC to attack the simplistic and ridiculous reforms suggested by Joe Winston and his party.

Vice President Osborne is dressed in black business suit complimented by a beautiful white blouse and scarf and is seated in her White House office. As always, she looks confident and professional. Dick Wolf is seated in the side chair beside her with the fireplace burning in the background and there are several light trees illuminating the room and as many as six technicians performing their duties behind the scenes.

The Vice President spent almost an hour in make up as she is very meticulous and desires to make the most favorable impression on the viewers.

Dick Wolf asks his first question, "Mrs. Vice President as you know the Restoration Party exploded on the scene over the past few months and it would appear they might become a formidable opponent. Would you please comment on the immense popularity and support they have gained?"

The Vice President smiles cordially and replies calmly, "It would be my pleasure Dick. It is apparent that our citizens are distressed with what they perceive is the pursuit of reckless policies that could destroy our great country and we understand their frustrations.

Apparently we are not communicating effectively with the American people and we must do a better job helping them to understand the reasoning supporting our decisions.

With that being said it would appear to me that the new Restoration Party is basically a reformation of conservatives who disagree with the Republican Party. While the leaders of this new party have effectively articulated their objectives and have temporarily caused people to become infatuated with their rhetoric I can assure you that these inexperienced, but charismatic businessmen have but one objective. That is to promote the same old Republican ideas of deregulation, big business, and reduced taxes.

Furthermore Dick, as you know the voters overwhelming elected our party in 2008 and has previously rejected those ideas that actually caused the current economic difficulties faced by our Administration. We continue to make great strides in correcting their mistakes but unfortunately it takes time. I can assure your viewers we are on the right path.

Dick said, "Mrs. Vice President Joe Winston said that the Federal Government has too much redundancy and does not function effectively. He has indicated his desire to reduce the size of Federal Government and to place more responsibility on the States. I haven't heard Republicans suggest this?"

The Vice President smiles at Dick and replies, "Well I really don't know where Mr. Winston got the idea that States are not receiving the benefits promised to them by our Constitution. If the Federal Government were not here to offer aid to individual states for education, health care, creation of jobs, welfare for the underprivileged, and many other programs we would be failing to meet our Constitutional requirements."

Dick said, "Mr. Winston used the analogy of the huge heath care argument put forth by the Democrats that competition is necessary in order for consumers to get the best value and thus a Government health care option should be required. He says the same competition should exist between States and the best regulated and best managed States would prosper and this would cause the other States to become more competitive. Therefore, this benefits the residents of the well managed States. Do you disagree?"

The Vice President forces a small condescending laugh and said, "I certainly do Dick. He is referring apples to oranges. The Federal government works closely with the Governors of each state and we make every effort to assist them. If the Federal Government suddenly withdrew financial support for education in States there would be an immediate crisis in schools across America."

"Mr. Winston has said that each State has the responsibility to educate their citizens not the Federal Government. I take it you do not agree?" Dick asked.

"Of course the State has an obligation to its citizenry and our role is to assist them in any way possible. I think most reasonable people would agree that we must have some uniformity in education across the country." She responds.

Dick said, "Let's hit another topic. Mr. Winston says one of the primary problems in this country is "Professional Politicians" and that he would fight for a constitutional amendment that would limit members of the House and the Senate to one six year term. Would you care to comment of this?"

"The comments we hear from this new party are designed to appeal to voters who do not quite grasp the complexities of the Constitution and the management of Government. For Government to function effectively it takes time for members of the House and Senate to acclimate themselves to the difficulties they will face.

To deny the American people of experienced members of the House and Senate would devastate our country." She smugly replies.

Dick checks his note pad and asks his next question, "The Restoration Party claims they would cut the Federal budget down to two trillion dollars a year, prohibit deficit spending, reduce the current cost of Government by six to eight hundred billion dollars a year, and create a fair tax code that will result in millions of new jobs. Is it possible?"

"Dick the first thing the public must keep in mind is that Mr. Winston and his three wealthy friends are capitalist. Granted their businesses have been very successful but the disparity between management and labor has grown dramatically. There is a huge difference in making money and running the United States of America and I don't believe the public would be very happy with capitalist amateurs determining their future.

Dick had we not stepped in with our massive stimulus package, to offset damage inflicted on this country by capitalist, our country could have well experienced times worse than the great depression; most economists agree that our actions averted a major financial catastrophe.

As I said earlier this is simply a new conservative initiative with the same old ideologies. Dick you can't simply change your name and become a different person." She laughs.

"Mrs. Vice President, in conclusion Mr. Winston claims that Americans are disillusioned with politician's unethical behavior and constant bi partisan bickering. With out regard to party he has said they have been dishonest, irresponsible, arrogant, disrespectful, and consistently fail to listen to their constituency. How do you respond?" Dick asks.

"It is unfortunate that the American people have been lead to believe this by a few biased media outlets that seem intent on ratings not factual reporting. Those of us in this Administration are running a transparent government and we feel that much of the misconduct of the prior Administration has rubbed off on us.

We intend to support all Americans and assure every American that they will have national health care, a good education, jobs opportunities, the ability to own a home, and to pursue the American dream." She says with the smile of a mother talking to her child."

CHAPTER 71

Harry Belk arrives at his home around nine o'clock, parks his car in his garage and closes the door, loosens his tie, and then walks down the driveway to his mailbox as is his custom. He looks inside and sees thick brown envelop about five inches thick.

His curiosity causes him to tear the envelop open and reveal the five inches of papers with a memory stick tapped to the top page. He glances at the papers and his heart beat accelerates as he reads the attached note.

The enclosed documentation provides specific proof of a conspiracy designed to destroy the United States of America. Circumstances prevent us from providing you how this information was obtained but we have confidence that you will initiate the appropriate steps to prevent the economic destruction of our nation.

He is completely unaware that behind a house across the street a man is quickly taking photographs with a high speed, high powered, and high resolution telephoto lens.

He turns and quickly walks up the driveway to his front door, inserts the key, and quickly walks inside and slams the door shut. He heads to kitchen, opens the refrigerator, and removes a Miller Light. He places the papers on the kitchen bar, opens a drawer, removes a bottle opener pops the top, and drains half of the beer.

Belk finishes off the beer and opens another and then picks up the papers and walks to his office and takes a seat at his desk and boots up his computer.

He sips the beer and began to peruse the papers and two hours later he put the file down and leans back in his chair not believing what he is reading.

He downloads the memory stick and finds that payments to him were documented with times, dates, reasons, and amounts. He also notices that Aziz Hasan is the major conspirator along with four of his closest democratic senators. This causes him immediate concern and he feels fear grip him.

He sits motionless for a long time processing the information and his options and none of them seem very good. The big question is who provided him with this information and why?

Finally he decided to take a long hot shower and just try to think clearly. His stomach is churning and he realizes he is hungry so he quickly prepares a peanut butter sandwich prior to his shower.

Thirty minutes later he returns to his desk with wet hair and a bath robe covering his body. He erases all incriminating information relating to him and the four senators and then considers erasing Aziz's information but it simply isn't feasible. Aziz would never know he is involved and if he erased Aziz it would be obvious that vital information had been tampered with.

He walks around the empty house with a nagging feeling that something isn't right. He continues trying to figure out why this was delivered to him and more importantly how he could use the information positively. He flopped down in a chair in his living room, in the dark and considers his political and personal options. He realizes his actions could make or break this administration and his personal career.

It isn't that he doesn't grasp the great danger the United States faces, after all, he is a politician and all he really cares about is political wins and staying in power. This administration badly needed some wins; something good must happen and it occurred to him that the information he received could be just what he needed to regain the Administration's popularity and destroy the opposition. He decides that he can turn this into a huge win!

He glances at his watch and is surprised to see that it is 3:30 am. He reaches for his cell phone and calls Charlie Settles the Director of National Intelligence and a strong supporter of the administration and a man he recommended for the job. The phone rings three times before Charlie picks it up and sleepily says, "Settles."

Harry said, "Charlie its Harry. Sorry to wake you up but it's important."

"What is it Harry?" Charlie asks with concern in his voice not annoyance.

Harry pulls out his schedule for tomorrow and said, "Charlie I am clearing my schedule for tomorrow morning and I want you to do the same. We need at least four hours."

Charlie is now sitting on the side of his bed and said, "I have a busy day tomorrow Harry and I don't think I can clear my schedule. What's so god damned important?"

Harry smiles and said, "Charlie I don't give a shit what you have tomorrow this is the most important issue you will ever deal with in your fucking life. Be in my conference room at seven, OK?"

Charlie can tell by Belk's voice that this must be something big and reluctantly said, "Okay I'll be there."

Belk's wheels are turning as he read and re-read the documents and his instincts told him this would be the most important political decision he would ever make. His head is literally spinning with the upside but he also realizes there could be a huge downside. The source of the information and why he is the recipient is his greatest concern.

CHAPTER 72

Harry Belk falls asleep around 4:00 am and is jolted out of his less than restful night at 5:00 am when his alarm clock did its job. He reaches over quickly to silence the dreadful noise and papers fly off the side of the bed. He had fallen asleep reading the files and taking notes.

Charlie Settles is waiting for him when he arrives and Harry takes him to the conference room and said, "Charlie this room is secure. Phones, computers, faxes, and there are no bugs. What you are about to see will blow your mind!

I have to see the President and you will need a couple of hours for a quick perusal. I will be back about ten but I would suggest you clear the whole day. Charlie, don't utter a single word of this to anyone until we agree on a course of action. Got it?"

Charlie's curiosity is high as Harry's unusual hyperactivity served to heighten his interest even more. He has no idea of the significance of what he would soon learn as he said, "I got it Harry! It better be damn good."

As Harry leaves the room he flashes a big smile and said, "It will be. I will send in some coffee."

Harry walks directly to the President's office for a 6:00 am meeting with his economic advisor and his committee he opens the door and said, "Excuse me. I am very sorry to interrupt but it is imperative that I have a few minutes with the President."

As they left the room Harry said, "Thank you very much. If this wasn't of the utmost urgency I would not have interrupted."

The President looks at Harry and senses there is something important on his mind. He rolls his eyes and said, "Thanks Harry those guys can bore the crap out of me."

Harry pulls up a chair and said, "Mr. President I need to inform you that our intelligence investigation of the terrorists attacks has yielded documents that a radical Islamist conspiracy has been in place for fifty years and is about to reach its culmination."

The President is dumbfounded as he listens to Harry and suddenly he becomes much more attentive and sits up in his chair and put his arms on his desk and leans forward, "You have my attention Harry."

For the next thirty minutes Harry gives him a brief synopsis and informs him that he would be meeting with the Director of National Intelligence, Defense Secretary, and necessary personnel they feel should be involved. He also requested that the President schedule an emergency meeting in the Situation room this afternoon at 5:00 pm with everyone he felt should be included.

While Harry gives his report the President is beginning to see the political implications and the opportunity to finally demonstrate to the republicans that democrats are clearly superior in every aspect of government.

He said, "Harry this is incomprehensible. We are talking about hundreds of prominent politicians, attorneys, businessmen, educators, judges, and maybe thousands of others. Good God Almighty! How in the hell could this happen?"

"Mr. President I believe we can lay it all out for you by this afternoon. Now if you will excuse me I must get to work." Harry said.

"OK Harry you go ahead and if you need me interrupt." The President commands.

Harry got up and left the room and is pleased the President didn't ask where the information came from. As he got to the door the President said, "Good work Harry."

Harry walks into the conference room and finds Charlie with his jacket off fully engrossed with the computer. When Harry walks in Charlie looks up and said, "This is unfucking believable Harry. To think these bastards have been at it this long and we didn't have a god damned clue. This is going to make the whole intelligence community look like a bunch of dumb asses."

Harry pours a cup of coffee and pulls a chair up to the conference table and said, "I think we can avoid that Charlie."

"What do you mean? How can it be avoided?" Charlie said with a quizzical look.

Harry has a sly smile on his face as he said, "Charlie I'm going to make you a frigging hero. You will go down in history and become more famous than fucking J. Edgar himself."

Charlie stands up from the computer station, pours a fresh cup of coffee, notices that his hands are trembling, and pulls a chair up to the desk, "Tell me how we are going to do that Harry."

Harry looks at Charlie and his face is hard as he says, "Charlie nobody knows how we acquired this information."

He pauses until he could see that Charlie knew where this is going and continues. "Picture this. After the tragedy in Charlotte last April Charlie Settles, with the support and dedicated help of thousands of intelligence professionals launched an investigation to track down the evil perpetrators of this horrible and vile act In the course of this investigation he discovered a conspiracy that was initiated fifty years ago with the intention of destroying America."

Charlie said with a smile now on his face, "Well don't stop now Harry. I can't wait to hear the end of this story."

"As a result of the most important intelligence initiative ever undertaken in this country this dangerous conspiracy which included the assassination of President Howard and the economic destruction of our country has been thwarted.

Today, with the help of thousands of intelligence professionals, working harmoniously together, almost sixteen hundred arrests have been made........we can fill in those blanks later." Harry has a look of satisfaction on his face.

"You think we can pull that off Harry?" Charlie said with some apprehension.

Harry looks quizzically at Charlie and said, "Why not?"

"Well one problem is that nobody else knows a damn thing about a project of this magnitude." Charlie said.

Harry looks condescendingly at Charlie and said, "First of all you are investigating terrorist incidents and as everyone knows they all don't share information. Until such time as your **covert** team completed the investigation absolutely secrecy was required.

 Furthermore the identities of these men will remain classified due to the possibility of retaliation. The operation was as Top Secret as any investigation every conducted in the history of the intelligence community."

Charlie listens attentively as Harry weaves his version of events and found it plausible. When Harry finishes Charlie said, "Harry you are one devious son of a bitch."

Harry smiles and said, "Thanks Charlie."

Harry continues, "Charlie you need to get your people on board today. Brief everyone, start getting warrants and putting agents and swat teams in place to arrest everyone. That's your area not mine.

We meet with the President at five and he will invite his key advisors and the usual ass holes. Start formulating your action plan. Hopefully, we can nail everyone down in one day.

Remember this Hassan character is the key so use your top team with him." Harry feels a little bad about his old friend but consoles himself the old concept business is business.

Charlie is jotting down notes and said, "I'll get started right away and I will see you at five o'clock if not sooner."

Harry enthusiastically says, "See you later J. Edgar Settles."

CHAPTER 75

Pete Boykin and his fellow co-conspirators had received the "go ahead" for their plan and have been devoting their time to blow gun practice in the woods near Ft. Mill. Pete has also been reviewing the most likely relatives of the victims of the Charlotte Bank of America attack who have received VIP invitations to the President's speech.

They have also received information that the President would meet privately with this group of individuals one hour prior to the scheduled speech. There are 749 invitees, including dignitaries, who would meet with the President in the Blumenthal Performing Arts Theater. This would greatly enhance their opportunity to kill the President but would complicate their escape from the building.

After spending days and days reviewing the invitees he identified the three people whose place they would take. They picked three men who had lost their wives, had no children, and lived alone who are approximately the same height and weight as Pete and his friends. Their plan is to enter the homes of these three men the night before the event and eliminate them and assume their identities.

After hours and hours of practice with the two-piece three foot long blow guns Roy had emerged as the best shot and would be the primary shooter. Pete would be the back up shooter and Ron would try to create a diversion from the left side of Theater prior to Roy and Pete taking their shots.

They rehearsed dozens of times and devoted an equal amount of time with their primary and alternate kill plan and escape routes. They are confident.

The men were meeting in Pete's room and relaxing with a few beers watching the Fox News Network discussing the phenomenal rise of the Restoration Party and Joe Winston. Bill O'Reilly is reviewing recent polls, "The Gallup Poll released the results of a survey today indicating voter preferences if the election were held today and here are the results. If the election were held today 53% of voters would vote for Joe Winston, 21% would vote for President Howard, and 15% would vote for Republican Jerry Haywood.

It also appears that if the election were held today the Restoration Party would win fifteen gubernatorial elections, seventy two Congressional Seats, and place eighteen of their candidates in the Senate." Bill smiled and shook his head and then continued.

"Politics in America will never again be controlled by a two party system. It appears there is a new party to be reckoned with. Please stay tuned we will be back in ninety seconds with more on Joe Winston." Bill said.

Pete said, "Man that Joe Winston guy is knocking them dead. He looks he will be the kind of leader this country needs."

Roy took a big slug of his Miller Lite and said, "That report is total bull shit."

"What the fuck are you talking about?" Pete said.

Roy laughed and finished his beer and slammed the empty can on the cheap coffee table and said, "President Howard ain't going to get any votes."

The three men laughed hysterically and Pete raised his beer can and said, "I'll drink to that!"

CHAPTER 73

WASHINGTON, D.C.
MARCH 30, 2010

Today is the day that the United States intelligence and law enforcement agencies will make history and restore faith in American intelligence. President Howard, Harry Belk, and most of the top advisors will gather in the White House Situation Room at 2:00 pm to receive the results of a coordinated effort, code named "Roundup."

Over six thousand intelligence and law enforcement professionals from every agency imaginable and covering almost every state will participate in the arrests of all known conspirators. Charlie Settles sits in front of his communication center, surrounded by monitors and support people, as he initiates Operation Roundup.

Fearful of leaks Charlie limits his total plan to less than a dozen key people. As law enforcement is provided warrants and specific arrest instructions they would assume it is simply business as usual. Most of the teams executing warrants are also advised to wear small clip on video cameras with audio capabilities as a part of an experimental program. They would not realize until much later the significance of today.

The brilliance of the plan is that Charlie control actions between various law enforcement agencies and only Charlie would have access to everything. His team in the control room understands this is just a massive coordinated arrest of conspirators. No one has a need to know how the conspirators were indentified nor do they care. Everyone is focused on results.

Ten minutes later the control room is filled with the sound of phones ringing, dozens of conversations and Charlie's laptop is rapidly recording incoming information.

Charlie is particularly relieved when he receives confirmation that Hasan and Boykin are in custody. At 1:00 pm Charlie leaves Langley and heads for the White House Situation room where he will notify President Howard of the results. Belk makes sure that Howard be personally involved just in case things got side ways. Then it would appear there may have actually been a black operation under his direction which no one would question.

In the Situation Room Charlie began his report, "Mr. President as of this moment 80% of our targets are in custody. The assassin, Pete Boykin, and his two side kicks have been arrested and the person we think is leader of terrorist's activity in the United States, Aziz Hasan, is also under arrest."

Charlie pauses to see if the President hasa comment as he hit key strokes on his computer to pull up a summary page.

The President, who is happier than he has been since being elected, said, "Good work Charlie, please continue."

Charlie proudly announces, "Mr. President this operation will go down in history as one of the most successful intelligence operations in the history of our country and I am proud to have been able to contribute to your Administration. The information I am about to share with you is quite remarkable."

Here are the hard results at this time; we have confiscated forty two RPG's and four hundred rockets. Three hundred and fifty six AK-47's and ninety thousand rounds of ammunition." The people gathered around the table gasped and buzzed like a Hornet's nest as Charlie paused before slowly continuing.

"We have also captured over six hundred handguns, sniper rifles, and over one hundred pounds of Semtex. We have also confiscated over three million in cash, equipment used to forge documents, and dozens of vehicles."

The FBI director said, "This is incomprehensible. Charlie were did you find all these weapons?"

Charlie looks at his computer screen and replies, "Mosques. We have only completed four of nine mosques targeted."

The room continues to buzz for several minutes before the President said, "unbelievable they have been using freedom of religion as a weapon against us. Please continue Charlie."

Charlie said, "Mr. President it will take several days to complete our inventory, review of documents and computer hard drives, but early indications are that this information will literally shake the world. We have already arrested over eleven hundred of the known conspirators and have warrants on another nineteen hundred and we suspect that barely scratches the surface.

Most of the unknown people are on the muscle end of the operation and this afternoon our units are rounding up the brains."

Bill Craddock, Secretary of State asks, "I understand we have many so called prominent people implicated Charlie can you tell us a little about them?"

"Yes sir." Charlie responds as his fingers deftly tickle the keyboard and he glances at the President to see if there are any objections. There are none, "I will start at the top. We have hard evidence involving nine senators, twenty two congressmen, forty one judges, sixty two Wall Street executives, two hundred and sixty one educators, one hundred and ninety one attorneys, seven hundred and twenty four from the Mass Media, and perhaps three hundred other businessmen. It is also important to note that forty two states are involved.

Once again the room erupts as the shock of what they are hearing seems incomprehensible. Feelings are mixed as they are grateful they have uncovered the information and embarrassed this on going plan thrived, unnoticed, for five decades.

President Howard said, "This situation must be leaking out to the press by now and I am instructing each of you to say absolutely nothing about this until such time as I personally authorize it. Am I clear?"

CHAPTER 74

Harry Belk continues his sleep deprivation as he works until almost 3:00 am. He is concocting his spin of yesterday's events. He is jacked up but the hard truth is the absence of sleep will eventually overtake him and his reasoning process will deteriorate.

He had continued to give serious thought to the conspiracy information he received and finally concluded that the only possible organization that would have sufficient resources and reason would be the Israeli's intelligence agency the Mosad. He assumed they were conducting illegal activities in the United States and this was their only option and his good fortune. He could live with that…

He arrives in his office at 5:30 am feeling somewhat sluggish and quickly pours a cup of strong hot coffee. The major newspapers are on his desk and he turns on the multiple televisions in his office to get a feel for how "Roundup" is being reported.

As he views the news reports and scans the papers it is apparent everyone is simply guessing and most guesses are ridiculous. He smiles as he considers the impact of the President's remarks scheduled for 1:00 pm in the East Room.

At 9:00 am the Oval Office is crowded with key advisors who are in a celebratory mood. After months and months of bad news everyone is pleased with yesterday's arrests of thousands of conspirators who were hell bent on destroying our county.

This administration will bask in the glory of a huge success. The meeting lasts for two hours and everyone is in agreement with regard to the press briefing.

The President's speech is in the process of being fine tuned and his remarks will cover the basic facts of "Roundup" and congratulatory remarks for the outstanding investigative work by his intelligence agencies.

After the President's announcement the Media will be clamoring for detail which the President will refer to Charlie Settles.

Due to all the news reports everyone is confident that most Americans have made arrangements to be near a television so they might discover what happened yesterday. This would be the biggest news story of the year and possibly of the decade.

At precisely 1:00 pm the President walks confidently to the podium in the East Room and faces the crowded room and said, "Good afternoon. Since the terrorists attacks on a cruise ship in the Caribbean and the heinous act of mass murder in Charlotte, N.C., one year ago next week, our intelligence community has been conducting a massive investigation to locate and capture the individuals who ordered and executed these despicable acts.

Yesterday, the investigation concluded and a massive conspiracy was uncovered resulting in the arrests of thousands of individuals attempting to undermine our economy and to kill our citizens.

The information gathered by our dedicated and hard working intelligence community learned of a plan that has been active for decades that was designed and implemented by Islamic radicals determined to destroy our country by manipulation of our economic, political, legal, educational, and business systems.

Additionally this investigation determined that the infiltration of these radicals also included the Media as well as a planned assassination attempt on my life scheduled to be executed next week.

I am most grateful for the heroic efforts of our intelligence community and the cooperation of law enforcement agencies across the country.

The mastermind of this conspiracy for over forty years is currently in custody as are the men who plotted to assassinate the President of the United States. The evidence is conclusive and our Justice department will send a strong message to those who might attempt to harm us in the future.

Steve Settles, Intelligence Director, orchestrated the investigation and the arrests and he will be available to answer your questions at the conclusion of my remarks.

However I would like to say that the Islamic radicals violated the very core of our religious beliefs and our constitution by utilizing nine Mosques across our country to store weapons intended to be used against innocent citizens.

The weapons recovered and the people we have arrested will minimize the impact of extremist in the future. However we are certain their remains thousands of other like minded individuals in our country and we will relentlessly hunt them down and punish them.

Tremendous damage has been inflicted upon our country and today we begin to repair the damage and to become more diligent of such activity in the future.

In closing, I wish to thank Charlie and the thousands of people who participated in "Roundup" their tireless and dedicated efforts most likely saved my life and the United States of America. Thank you for your time and now Director of Intelligence, Charlie Settles, will answer your questions."

CHAPTER 75

The President's comments and subsequent remarks by Charlie Settles sparked National and International outrage as well as injecting a new sense of confidence and pride in the American people. After months of the administration taking a back seat to the Restoration Party operation "Roundup" combined with the recent eloquent remarks by Vice President Osborne it now appeared they are once again gaining momentum.

Late that afternoon Charlie Settles and Harry Belk celebrated their victory with the President in the Oval Office. President Howard smiles broadly and pats Charlie on the back and said, "Charlie I owe you big time. We really needed something good to happen and by God you made it happen."

Charlie smiles nonchalantly and humbly said, "Just doing the job you hired me to do Mr. President. The FBI did all the real work with the help of every intelligence and law enforcement agency in the country. It was a real team effort Mr. President."

Harry quickly interjects, "This has been a great day for us and now the Justice Department and the Secretary of Defense needs to do their job and put all these criminals away."

The President frowns as he asks, "We don't expect any problem in that area do we?"

Harry stands up and walks to the fireplace and then turns back toward the President and said with caution in his voice, "You never know Mr. President. You have seen the great influence they have exerted in our country for many years and I am confident they will continue to do everything in their power to discredit our country."

The President let Belk's remarks sink in for a few seconds and said, "We will stay in close contact with the Justice Department and we will also make every effort to have those conspirators overseas brought to justice. We will not lose this victory and they will not steal it from us."

Harry said with a big smile, "Well all I know is that we are back on top of the world once again and we have just kicked our new competition, The Restoration Party, right in the ass."

The three men laugh and enjoy a few minutes of happiness in what has been a mostly unhappy first year in office.

CHAPTER 76

ORMOND BEACH, FL
APRIL 14, 2010

Joe, Robbie, Adam, and Lee are enjoying a long week end at Volusia National. It is 8:00 am on a cool day that requires a jacket and they are finishing their breakfast on the Veranda. Lee is reading the Boston Globe and says, "It would appear that President Howard is enjoying a tremendous resurgence in the polls."

Adam laughs and said sarcastically, "It is amazing how their extensive and penetrating investigation saved our country. I don't know about you boys but I sure sleep better at night knowing that we have all these professional intelligence agencies protecting us."

Robbie picks up the tone of the conversation and said, "Well let's just let them enjoy themselves while they can. Joe, I understand many of our candidates are losing their enthusiasm as well as a lot of ground in the polls."

Joe sips his coffee and puts the cup back on the saucer and nonchalantly replies, "We need to keep an eye on those who lack commitment. Anybody can deal with easy we need people who can deal with hard."

Adam said, "Looks like the charges against these conspirators are going to be vigorously contested. Eventually, they may discover that they have nothing but hearsay as evidence and I believe the Attorney General is going to have a hard time finding actual witnesses for the Government. It looks to me like this could drag on for years."

Robbie says with a grin, "What in the hell do you know about law?"

Adam looks at Robbie and said, "Everybody knows any idiot can become a lawyer."

The men all laugh and Robbie finally said, "Adam is right. In spite of everything the actual prosecution in criminal courts might be difficult."

Lee speaks up, "It appears to me they picked up enough evidence to convict all the big players."

Robbie said, "You are right about that Lee but they will have difficulty with most of the lower level grunts."

Lee grins and said, "It really makes very little difference the conspiracy is dead and we know there are many different ways to fight wars and we will be more diligent in the future."

Robbie stands up and stretches as he said, "Let the Democrats enjoy their fifteen minutes of fame but I hope they will remember the sun don't shine on the same dog's ass all the time."

Again, the men laugh and Joe stands up and said, "Looks like a good day to play golf;. Let's go."

At that exact minute in Washington, D.C. a Federal Express package is delivered to the office of Republican Senator Alex Hawkins of Maryland who is one of the most vocal critics of the Administration.

CHAPTER 77

Senator Hawkins and the Republican Party are taking a real beating in the polls and are currently running a distant third in all polls. Their Party is dying and Senator Hawkins is desperately trying to rally the troops but fighting an uphill battle. He is serving his third term in the Senate and is well thought of by his fellow Senators.

He is a large man with piercing blue eyes and exceptional confidence and he carries two hundred and twenty pounds on his six foot three inch frame and has a tendency to intimidate his opponents. He is a man of strong principals and integrity who has a good grasp of right from wrong.

He is perhaps the strongest voice in opposition to President Howard and personally the two men don't like each other. The President would not give Senator Hawkins the time of day and would rarely be in the same room with him if he could avoid it.

The Senator is sitting in his office sipping whiskey from a tumbler with the United States Senate emblem embossed on each side. His feet are on his desk, his tie is loosened, and his jacket is thrown casually on the couch.

It had been a difficult day and the distraction of the conspiracy has just about over shadowed all of the important issues that need attention. The truth is he is a little depressed with the kind of frustration that comes from fighting an uphill battle for a long period of time. In spite of all his hard work having to watch the democrat's crow over "Roundup" is just more than he can bear.

Over time it simply wears you down and there are no signs of improvement in sight and he is seriously considering retirement.

It is about 6:00 pm and he hears a knock on his door and Jeff Johnson, his Chief of Staff, opens the door and walks in with a big smile on his face and a opened Federal Express box in his arms.

The Senator looks at Jeff and gruffly said, "What in the hell are you smiling about?"

Jeff has known the Senator for twenty years and said, "Why the hell aren't you smiling?"

The Senator isn't in the mood for this and said, "Jeff this shit is getting old. I am getting tired of running like hell and getting nowhere. I'm trying to get drunk so what in the hell do you want?"

Jeff pulls up a chair, loosens his tie, and put his feet on the Senators desk. The Senator looks at him as if he is crazy and Jeff said, "Alex I am about to put a big old smile on that ugly mug of yours."

The Senator takes his feet off the desk, pulls his chair closer, put his elbows on the desk and rests his head in his hands as he looks at Jeff, "Okay. Make me smile or get the hell out of here!"

Jeff places the box on the desk and removes the contents without speaking. The Senator said, "What have you got?"

Jeff answers with a smirk, "The answer to your prayers Senator." He pauses briefly enjoying tantalizing his boss and then hands the Senator a piece of paper. The Senator takes the paper and notices it is unsigned. He reads the letter.

"Senator Hawkins, this is an exact duplicate of the papers sent to Chief of Staff, Harry Belk, on March 15ᵗʰ. This information was compiled by private citizens and given to this Administration to prevent the President's assassination and the complete destruction of our Country.

I was concerned that the information provided would be used for political gain or in fact altered. Based upon the arrests and news accounts my suspicions have been confirmed. After you carefully review the enclosed documentation you will see that information was removed from the original documents that implicated other important people.

Furthermore, they have suggested that this information was acquired as a result of their exhaustive investigation. As you will see they have discovered nothing; all relevant information leading to these arrests was simply given to them and that is supported by the attached photographs, documents, and memory stick. I trust you will know what needs to be done with this information."

The Senator is suddenly interested and as he rises from his desk he asks Jeff, "Have you reviewed any of this information?"

"No sir." Jeff replies.

Hawkins smiles, rolls up his sleeve, grabs the papers, and sits down at his conference table and said, "Well let's see what we have."

CHAPTER 78

WASHINGTON, D.C.
APRIL 14, 2010

It is almost midnight before Senator Hawkins and Jeff finish reviewing the information. Senator Hawkins looks at Jeff and says, "I wish I could say this is unbelievable but I can't. Now we need to decide how to handle this information."

Jeff looks at the Senator with astonishment, "Alex you have just received a Silver bullet that can be used to completely discredit the Democratic Party and Howard's Administration. This is a no brainer we call a press conference and humiliate the bastards."

Hawkins leans back in his chair and rubbed his eyes, "Jeff, it isn't that simple."

"Sure it is." Jeff said.

The Senator said in a patronizing voice, "I know you are looking at this strictly from a political perspective but we do have an obligation to do what is best for our country. There is a right way to do things and a wrong way."

Jeff is somewhat outraged and indignantly said, "What the hell are you talking about Alex? These lying bastards deserve to be drummed from office.

The President and his Administration certainly didn't have any qualms about politicizing this situation. You have to be kidding me; they told the American people this was the result of a long investigation and led the people to believe that our dumb ass intelligence agencies actually did some good work.

They intentionally protected four Senators and Harry Belk and burned our guys. Come on Alex what other options do you have?"

The Senator listens attentively to Jeff and understands his frustration, "Jeff we ain't them! The American people already think we are a bunch of arrogant, self serving, lying assholes if we spring this on them without first trying to find a more subtle way to resolve this we are just going to contribute to that belief."

Jeff stands up and walks around the room, not hiding his frustration, and said, "What the fuck other options are there?"

Alex calmly says, "I believe I should share this with the President and hear what he has to say. It could be he doesn't know about the deletions."

Jeff is extremely loyal and is also tired of suffering. He wants blood. He laughs out loud and said, "Are you kidding me? You can't even get an appointment with him. He would rather eat shit than see you."

Alex laughs and good naturedly said, "Maybe so, but I need to try."

He walks over to Jeff and puts one of his big hands on each of Jeff's shoulders and looks at him as if to say he understands.

"What do you want me to do?" Jeff said with resignation.

Alex said, "Get on the phone right now and get our leadership in my office at 7:00 am. Call the President's office and tell him it is urgent that I see him after 2:00 pm tomorrow. Tell him it is concerning the Conspiracy bust and additional information we have uncovered."

Jeff is taking notes and said, "I will give you four to one he won't see you."

CHAPTER 79

Senator Hawkins and Jeff arrive at the office at 6:00 am to prepare for their meeting with the Senior Republican Senators. Jeff said, "Thanks a lot for having me wake up ten United States Senators. They were not very happy."

"Well it's a tough job Jeff but somebody has to do it." Alex laughs.

Alex continues, "Did you reach the President's office?"

"I was told he has a very busy schedule but he would try to find some time and they will get back to me." Jeff said.

As the other Senators arrive Alex greets each one of them warmly and reassures them that the topic of conversation would be well worth time.

When everyone had arrived and been served coffee and Danish Alex said, "Gentlemen thank you for coming on such short notice. I will tell you that the information I am about to share with you will destroy the Democratic Party for years to come. With your permission I am going to have one of my staff members notify your office that you will be unavailable until after lunch. Is that Okay with everyone."

Several of the Senators grumbled but Alex reassures them that nothing they had scheduled could be more important.

Over in the Oval Office Harry Belk is having his morning meeting with President Howard and the President said, "Got a message early this morning that Senator Hawkins has requested an urgent meeting with me concerning the Conspiracy arrests. What do you think?

Harry said, "I would guess that he is upset that some of his fellow Republicans got nailed and wants to try and work a deal. I see no reason why you would want to waste your time with him. All he ever does is hammer you every chance he gets. I have never seen a more arrogant and unreasonable man. We have tried to work with him but he is simply unable to compromise."

"He is an obstinate and unpleasant man and I would rather be nailed to the cross than to spend time with him." The President said.

"Mr. President, if you like, I will handle it. I will inform him that your schedule is jammed due to your trip to Europe in a few days. He can call us after that." Harry suggested to the President.

"Do it!" The President said.

Senator Hawkins concludes his presentation of the information he had received with his leadership and they are simply giddy over their apparent good fortune. After being advised the President has no time for him the group decides to schedule a press conference for 5:00 pm.

CHAPTER 80

WASHINGTON, D.C.
APRIL 14, 2010

The Media was notified of the Republican Press Conference, to be headed by Senator Hawkins, and given a teaser that would assure the Mass Media's attendance.

When the White House Press Secretary notified Belk he is confident it is much ado about nothing but nevertheless he informs the President. The President feels some anxiety as he asks Belk, "Maybe I should have spoken with him. At least we would know what is on his mind."

Harry Belk gave the President a confident look and said, "Mr. President I am sure it is yet another Partisan political ploy. The Republicans are desperate since "Roundup." Sir, they are just getting tired of us pounding them."

President Howard hears Belk and wants to believe him but he has that sinking feeling in his gut that something bad is about to happen and there is nothing he can do to stop it.

The press conference is extremely well attended and at precisely 5:00 pm Senator Alex Hawkins steps to the podium and gains the journalists attention, "Yesterday afternoon a package was delivered to my office with the following message. The Senator reads the message and pauses for a reaction. You could have heard a pin drop.

In the White House Harry Belk is watching the news conference, alone in his office, and when Hawkins finishes reading the message he knows the shit is about to hit the fan. He realizes he is now sweating profusely, his hands are shaking, and it seems as if there is less oxygen is available.

Senator Hawkins continues, "After reviewing the contents of the package I felt the most prudent course of action would be to notify the President. We requested an appointment and informed his office it is an urgent matter concerning the Conspiracy and assassination. We informed his office we had additional information and we were advised the President is unavailable.

Due to the highly sensitive nature of this information and our National Security we feel we have no other option except to give full and fair disclosure to the public. As you heard in the message I have already read, the package I received is an exact duplicate of the original package that was delivered to Harry Belk, President Howard's Chief of Staff, on March 15, 2010.

Enclosed in this package are photographs taken of Mr. Belk as he removed the package from his mailbox." Senator Hawkins pauses as a loud murmur fills the room.

Hawkins continues, "After a quick review of the documents which includes audio conversations, transcripts, and other significant documentation it is a simple process to match up this information to the arrest records of the Conspirators.

President Howard, in his comments of March 31, 2010 indicated that these arrests were as a result of his intelligence agencies diligent and thorough investigation. If the Administration did receive an exact copy of the documents I have in my possession they failed to acknowledge the arrests resulted from a tip from some unknown persons. There is a huge difference between finding gold and making gold.

I respectfully request that the President of the United States of America confirm or deny if they did receive the same documentation I received."

He pauses for a sip of water and every reporter in attendance tries to ask him a question and it takes several minutes for him to calm them down and allow him to continue.

"Furthermore we discovered that there appears to be other powerful individuals whose names appear in my package, complete with information including times, dates, and monies they received for services. These conspirators within the President's Administration and among the democratic members of the Senate were not named in the indictments." Hawkins said forcefully and with some indignation.

Once again he is required to wait for the journalist to stop shouting questions prior to continuing. He finally manages to be heard over their questions and informs them if they can't control themselves the press conference will be concluded. They quickly became silent and focus intently on the Senator.

"The credibility of this information must be verified and I am today calling on the President to appoint a bipartisan committee along with independent counsel to completely investigate this information to determine the facts and authenticity of the information."

Standing behind Senator Hawkins are nine Senior Senators and he turns to them and introduces each Senator and said, "At this point we are the only individuals to review the anonymous information I received. Now I will take any questions you may have."

Senator Hawkins declines to answer most questions and refuses to give the names of the people who were omitted. He feels it is best to stand by his statement and would leave the reporting of this information to the imagination of the journalist.

In the White House Harry Belk's worst nightmare has just begun. He sits in his office completely disarmed with no clue of how he could get out of this situation. He tries to weigh his options; should I turn over the papers and accept the consequences? Can I spin my way out of this? Should I deny, deny, deny? Hell, should I just shoot myself!

He knows he has little time. Any minute now the phone will ring and it will be President Howard. How could he explain this? He feels like a trapped animal and has a compulsion to run.

The way Hawkins presented this information even the President could be implicated. Jesus Christ! What the hell am I going to do?

His door is shut as he paced around the room saying, God damn it! God damn it! God damn it! It is as if he is on death row waiting for the guards to march him to the electric chair.

His phone rings and he is startled. He turns and looks at it but he couldn't pick it up. All four lines are blinking as he stands facing a wall and lightly banging his head against it.

There is a firm knock at his door and a strong and authoritative voice says, "Mr. Belk, this is Agent Johnson of the Secret Service. The President would like to see you immediately."

CHAPTER 81

Jake Hall and Senator Danforth are seated in John's library watching Senator Hawkins's press conference. John and Jake are mesmerized by this demonstration of American politics and stunned by the information Senator Hawkins shares with the world.

At the conclusion of the press conference Jake turns to John and asks, "It seems to me that Senator Hawkins acted as professionally as he could and was simply rebuffed by the President. Am I right?"

John smiles at the newest member of the Restoration Party's Executive committee and calmly replies, "I would say that is a fair observation Jake."

John looks at Jake and in a conspiratorial voice and asks, "Anything else strike you as unusual about the conspiracy and Hawkins?"

Jake looks at John for a moment and it occurs to him, "Yes there is. Who is providing the information and why?"

John had picked up his pipe and is packing it as he asks, "What do you think?"

Jake watches as John performs his pipe ritual and answers, "Normally I guess you would just follow the money. In politics it might be to look for who benefits."

John is as comfortable in his old chair smoking his pipe as if he were born in that position. He is enjoying his visit with Jake and finds him to be very principles and very perceptive, "Who seems to benefit by all this "Roundup" fiasco?"

Jake feels as if he is at the master's feet and is trying not to embarrass him self, "Well after the arrests the democrats and after Hawkins press conference neither one of them seems to benefit. They are both damaged."

John simply maintains eye contact with Jake and says nothing. Soon Jake's eyes grow wide and he turns to John with a look of astonishment on his face and blurts out, "The Restoration Party benefits!"

John simply nods his head with a blank look on his face. Jake waited for him to speak but he says nothing. Jake's mind considered the complexity of the situation and realizes that there is no way that these events could have been orchestrated by his party. He walks around the room and alternatively looks at John and scratches his head. John continues to enjoy his pipe and watching Jake's agony.

Jake walks over to the large window and looks out at the lake and thought of Joe and his friends and began to think that maybe........no impossible!

CHAPTER 82

The large Secret Service Agent has a serious look on his face as he quickly escorts Harry Belk to the Oval Office and opened the door for him. Harry feels like a child being taken to the principal's office. Harry walks in and sees the President looking out the window with his hands clasped behind his back.

When the President hears the door shut he waits for a minute, trying to control his anger, and then turns around to face Harry, "Harry what the fuck is going on?"

Harry knows his career is over and trying to spin his way out of this is useless so he decides to fall on his sword and try to salvage something.

For the next thirty minutes he fills the President in on everything and admits erasing the information for the good of the party and the administration.

When he finishes the President looks at him with disdain and said, "What in the hell is wrong with you. You have placed me in jeopardy and may have just single handedly destroyed the Democratic Party and all we have worked for. Where are the files now?"

"Charlie Settles has them." Belk sadly mumbles.

The President pushes a button on his desk and Agent Johnson walks in and said, "Yes Sir."

Howard says sternly, "Find Settles and bring him to my office and tell him to bring the files that Belk gave him. If he tries to resist arrest him."

"Yes Sir." Agent Johnson replies.

President Howard sent for the Attorney General, The Vice President, the Director of Homeland Security, the FBI, and the CIA Director's and instructed them all to be in his office within one hour.

Two hours later all present have a clear picture of what happened and it is clear to the President that he needs to take swift action to minimize the damage and to assure the American people that he was unaware of how they had come about the information. There must be some way he could extricate himself from this disaster.

Attorney General Robbins said, "Mr. President, in the interest of National Security, I would advise you to recover the documents now in the possession of Senator Hawkins."

The President looks at Robbins thoughtfully and responds, "That might be a good idea. If we control all the documentation it could minimize our damage."

Osborne is truly outraged by the discovery of the conspiracy and is particularly distressed by the criminal actions of elected officials, "Mr. President, you are going to have Belk, Ames, Desimini, Rogers, and Allison arrested aren't you?"

The President leans back in his chair and gave the impression he is much more relaxed than he really is, "Yes Carol they will be arrested if any documentation confirms their misconduct."

Carol knows she has to ask the tough question, "Mr. President how in the world will you convince the American people that you were completely unaware of this plan concocted by Belk and Settles?"

The President stands up and paces back and forth giving careful consideration to the question and angrily asks, "Carol do you think I knew about it?"

Carol is surprised by the tone of the question and glances around the room, knowing that many believe he knew, and replies, "No Sir. I am sure you would never be a party to this type of behavior."

"Thank you. All I can do is tell the truth and hope the people believe me. Even if they don't I am still the man who hired Belk and Settles and what does that say about my judgment?" Howard asks.

President Howard gives careful consideration to the feedback given him and could see no good choices. If we classify the documents our case against the conspirators could crumble and if we don't the political repercussions will be disastrous.

AG Robbins reiterates, "Mr. President, clearly the documents that Senator Hawkins has in his possession should be confiscated inasmuch as the contents are a matter of National Security. That is the correct course of action for now."

Jack Morgan, as of two hours ago, is appointed as temporary Chief of Staff, asks, "From a political perspective would that not suggest a cover up?"

Robbins fires back, "The fact is, it is a matter of National Security and these documents need to be classified."

The President watches his other advisors in the room and they seem to be in agreement, "Robbins, how in the hell will you possibly prosecute these criminal without releasing the documents to their attorneys?"

"Mr. President you are correct that our case against them might be jeopardized. However, it appears to me that for the time being, while we carefully review both sets of documents, this is the best course of action. From a political perspective I believe it would be better to release the documents in a couple of months when things cool down." Robbins replies.

Morgan asks, "Mr. President. Will you want to address this issue publically?"

Vice President Osborne offers, "Mr. President if you don't address the comments and insinuations made by Hawkins it will look as if you are involved."

President Howard, now pacing the room, always welcomed the opportunity to address the nation but acts as if he is unsure that would be the prudent course of action said, "I don't know Carol. I hate to get sucked into a public disagreement with Hawkins."

Osborne knows Howard very well and takes the bait and offers him the encouragement he is looking for, "Mr. President if you fail to address the issue the Media will crucify you."

He thinks for a minute or two and finally said, "Okay Jack get to work on it and set it up for tomorrow afternoon."

Robbins said, "Mr. President what do we do with the Senators, Settles, and Belk?"

Howard considers the question and replies, "At this point, we have no direct evidence that suggest they are involved. Until we have something I don't see how we can take any action. We need to see how the documents that Hawkins has compares with the documents Belk received. Mr. Robbins you advise them of their rights for now."

Forensics will need to check the documents very carefully before we can determine a course of action. If the evidence is there we will take the appropriate action."

He pauses before continuing and with a puzzled look on his face asks rhetorically, "Where in the hell is this information coming from?

Is there a group of private citizens with more power than the Federal Government?

No one had an answer for the President but the knowledge that some entity could gather this much intelligence in a relatively short period of time is troubling. President Howard instructs Robbins to confiscate Hawkins set of papers and classify both sets until a proper review and analysis could be conducted. He also issues a gag order for all parties who might have seen either document.

CHAPTER 83

WASHINGTON, D.C.
APRIL 16, 2009

The incredible ebb and flow of the tides of politics is not for the timid. It is a brutal business and becoming more cut throat each day. For years the two current parties have just tried to destroy each other and that is their sole intent at this time. They have failed to accept the fact that the Restoration Party could actually become a threat.

Senator Hawkins arrives at his office at 6:00 am finds a team of FBI agents in the process of searching his office. Agent Williams approaches Senator Hawkins with a cold but courteous "Good Morning. Sir, I am agent Williams with the FBI and I have a warrant for the search and seizure of any documentation in your possession that relates to the recent conspiracy arrests." He hands the paper to Hawkins.

Senator Hawkins isn't totally surprised but he is angry that the President did not handle this in a more professional manner. He did not intend to take out his anger of Agent Williams but his voice could not hide it. He said, "Well Agent Williams can I be of any assistance in your efforts?"

Williams is a professional and understands the political implication but he is just doing his job. He said, "Yes Sir. Have you made any copies of the documents?"

"No Agent Williams. I have not" Hawkins snapped.

Williams removes another piece of paper from his breast pocket and hands it to Senator Hawkins, "Sir these documents have been classified TOP SECRET as they relate to our National Security and the order I have just given you states that you are not to discuss any information relating to these documents without the express written consent of the President of the Untied States of America. Sir, do you understand the President's order."

Hawkins quickly reads the document and replies, "I do."

Agent Williams pulls a form from his pocket and said, "Sir I need you sign this document stating that you understand that this is a matter of National Security and that you are not to disclose any information contained in said documents."

He hands the form to Hawkins with one hand and removes a pen from his other and hands it to Senator Hawkins.

Other teams were completing the same procedure with the other Senators and Staff members who were aware of the contents of the documents.

CHAPTER 84

Joe and Lee arrive back in Richmond in time for the President's scheduled remarks and John and Tony join them to watch the broadcast and discuss the next six weeks agenda.

It has been less than ten hours since the documents were proclaimed classified but the news Media has already been fully informed. In spite of the Presidential Order instructing those with knowledge of the documents of its TOP SECRET and National Security implications this is simply another indication that there are no secrets in Washington.

John laughs and said, "In Washington a kept secret is almost as rare as the truth."

Lee laughs and said, "In my opinion all this partisan bickering continues to make the democrats and republicans look like a bunch of jack asses."

Tony smiles and says, "They are simply natural adversaries trying to destroy each other."

Lee looks at Tony and said, "Cats and dogs. It really is too bad."

Joe isn't particularly amused that politicians of national prominence are being ridiculed but he understands the reasons why. Nevertheless, he finds it disturbing that so many Americans have so little respect.

"It occurs to me that the President's talk today will not end this it will simply elevate it to a new level of disappointment for the American people ; More suspicion and more confirmation of their childish behavior." Joe remarks.

John said reflectively, "Joe the truth is that most politicians have the unique ability to believe their own lies and deceptions. The arrogance of a politician is under rated by the most cynical American."

Lee said, "Okay boys we are about to start. I can't wait to hear this bull shit."

The Presidential Seal appears and then disappears revealing the President of the United States of America. He is seated at his desk in the Oval Office and he looks like a man trying to act like he is upbeat but disappointed. From the serious look on his face one would think he is about to declare war on the rest of the world.

As always, he looks impressive in his fine black suit, tailored white shirt with a crisp collar, and an elegant black and white tie. His eyes reflect his absence of sleep.

Before the President began to speak John said, "I will guarantee you one thing he will admit to no wrong doing by himself or any member of his staff."

President Howard struggles more with this speech than any other. The more advice he receives the less confident and more confused he became. Finally he is forced to make a decision and is prepared to convince the American people of his convictions.

The camera captures and close up he says, "Good Afternoon my fellow Americans.

The last few weeks have been more demanding than any period in the history of our great Nation. The discovery of a massive conspiracy to destroy our country and to assassinate its President, over three thousand arrests, the great joy experienced by the American people as they learned of our termination of the conspiracy, and then the partisan announcement by a United States Senator that attempted to undermine our great accomplishment.

Let me assure each and every American that information asserted by Senator Hawkins will be fully investigated within the framework of our Judicial and Administrative guidelines. This matter involves our National Security and I can assure you that this Administration takes your security very seriously.

I realize that many rumors have been disseminated throughout the Media and most of the reports are untrue. If this investigation implicates any individuals that have not yet been arrested I can assure you that all guilty parties will be arrested and they will be prosecuted to the full extent of the law.

Our country continues to face difficult obstacles such as our economy, unemployment, our Afghanistan initiative and many other significant issues. We will be diligently doing everything within our power to put Americans back to work and to create a thriving economy that will benefit all. I ask for your continued support and prayers. God Bless America!"

The announcer recapped the President's comments and announces they would return after commercial break with comments from Senator Alex Hawkins.

Lee is first to speak, "John you called that right. He said absolutely nothing."

Tony said, "He did what he is expected to do. The son of a bitch has classified the documents and put a gag order on Hawkins."

Joe said, "Well I guess we will never know what is really in those documents."

John looks at Joe suspiciously, "Probably not Joe. If Hawkins mentions anything he read or learned in those documents he could be placed in jail." He makes eye contact with Joe and thought he saw a little mischief.

Hawkins is standing in the rotunda of the Senate building as the camera zooms in on the Senator.

The announcer asks, "Senator Hawkins thank you for joining us today. What are your impressions of the President's remarks?"

Hawkins is clearly angry even though he tries to appear composed. He removes his glasses and puts them in his pocket and stares straight into the camera.

"Thank you for having me." He pauses and looks directly into the camera with his sharp blue eyes and said, "My fellow Americans. No one is more pleased than I that this conspiracy and the Presidents assassination was discovered and prevented.

When I arrived in my office at 6:00 am this morning I was greeted by a team of FBI agents who were instructed to confiscate the documents I spoke about and to inform me that the documents are now classified TOP SECRET as they impact our National Security.

Furthermore I was required to sign a Confidentiality Agreement that precludes me from discussing the contents of that information without the express written permission of the President.

As a member of the United States Senate I will comply will all lawful orders and I have no choice except to obey"

He pauses for dramatic effect and angrily says, "I don't like it one bit but I am bound to silence…….."

He continues, "I would like to comment on the unprofessional manner in which this has been handled. Once I received the documents my first action was to notify the President of the United States. I made every effort to do so in an attempt to work together to resolve this situation professionally and quietly.

My request was designated urgent but I was informed by the President that he could not possibly see me for at least a week. I find it interesting that he has now found some free time to address the matter.

The public will simply have to determine how they feel about the President's conduct and pray that the day will come when politicians will put the public interest before any political party's interest."

Tony comments, "Alex did about all he could do. I think he won this round and his comments certainly do impact the President negatively."

Lee gets up and pours himself a diet coke and said, "Man, politics is a dirty business."

CHAPTER 85

VOLUSIA NATIONAL
MAY 2, 2010

Once again The Restoration Party's organizers are gathered to discuss strategy. The group includes Joe, Lee, Robbie, Adam, John, Tony, Betty Parker, and Jake Hall. They spent the morning playing golf and after golf they had lunch. They are now deeply involved in strategy discussion on the veranda.

John asks, "Tony why don't you give us a broad overview of relevant information."

Tony stands up and said, "My pleasure John. Well as we all know the last month or so the Restoration Party has been pushed from the headlines by the conspiracy arrests and subsequent disagreements between President Howard and Senator Hawkins.

The public perceives this as more of the same and according to polls have now placed elected officials just beneath rattlesnakes in popularity.

It is clear, that even though the Media is now all over this story, that the Restoration Party and our candidates continue to do exceptionally well in the polls. I think our limited but targeted speaking engagements are doing well. You guys are keeping the message powerful and positive and the public continues to respond well."

Joe said, "Tony I agree with you that our message continues to be consistently effective but I have seen some of our candidate's interviews and they are having a hard time breaking old habits.

I want you to get the word out that we are about solutions not blame. We gain nothing by being critical of what happened in the past. Have them stop the finger pointing and focus on our platform. If we don't we become just like them."

Tony jots down a note, "I agree Joe and I will make damn sure everyone understands to keep it positive."

John said, "Last night I received a call from a friend of mine in the Attorney General's office who said the Government might have a hard time convicting all the people that were arrested."

Lee asks, "Why is that John how much more evidence do they need?"

"The Attorney's representing these people is demanding copies of the documents sent to Harry Belk and Senator Hawkins that have been classified. Furthermore, they will be filing a motion to exclude all evidence found due to the lack of any direct testimony or probable cause.

In discovery the accused have a right to see all evidence the prosecution has. If they can't see the documents they have no case. This could develop into a pretty big legal controversy even though the Patriot Act gives such authority but no matter what this will turn into a mess.

If the documents remain classified every one of those bastards might walk. The President will have to release the documents or thousands of people who conspired to destroy our country will go free."

Robbie asks, "Is there any chance the President will declassify the documents?"

John leans back in his chair and answers, "I don't know Robbie. The public impression is that President Howard is involved in a cover up of some sort and the only way he can change public opinion is to do just that.

I don't know how damaging that will be to him personally or his administration but if he doesn't he will definitely have no chance at a second term."

Joe asks, "John it looks to me like they are pretty much in a no win situation, is that right?"

"I think so. However, I can't believe the President would fail to release the documents under the circumstances. How do you turn thousands of people loose who conspired to destroy our country and assassinate our President? John asked.

Tony said, "The other big question is how this will impact the Republicans. Senator Hawkins comments and popularity is improving and he has kept his mouth shut even though rumors continue to be published by the press crediting "high ranking officials". It looks to me like they will get a little bump at the Democrats expense."

Adam listens carefully to everyone's comments and now asked, "It would appear to me that their behavior benefits us significantly."

Tony reaches in his brief case and pulls out a thick blue file and opens it, "We are leading handily in one hundred and ninety races and are gaining ground on another seventy races for the House. We have the lead in nineteen Senate races and twenty one gubernatorial seats.

These don't include our transfers from the Republicans, Democrats, and Independents. I would say we have a good chance to eliminate partisan politics in America."

When Tony finishes the men look at one another with nods of satisfaction.

Later that evening in Joe's suite he and Robbie are having a nightcap. Robbie said, "Joe we still have a little bit of a problem. Majid Abdulla Mohammed. It is pretty clear that he is the mastermind of this grand conspiracy and he's still in play. What do you think we should do?"

Joe thought about the problems that Majid could still cause and knew that this man is passionate if not obsessed with the destruction of America and finally responded to Robbie's question, "Well I don't think for a minute that a man as dedicated as Majid would not have a back up plan. It stands to reason that he has alternatives that Aziz is not aware of. He could cause a lot of trouble."

"The problem is we don't have a clue as to what those back up plans might be." Robbie said.

Joe said, "For now I think all we can do is watch him as close as possible and try to find out what he may have up his sleeve. For the time being we'll just keep an eye on him and try to find out what else he may have."

CHAPTER 86

CHICAGO, ILL
JUNE 15, 2009

Aziz Hasan is confined to the Cook County jail after being denied bail and is becoming increasingly depressed and humiliated. He is well aware that after many years of tremendous success he has ultimately failed. He is not doing well behind bars and has frail body is becoming more and more frail each day. Much of his time is devoted to prayer and asking forgiveness.

He knows he is perceived as the mastermind of this conspiracy and he will gladly give his life before implicating anyone else and death is not something he fears.

Aziz is sitting in his cell when his door clanks open and a gruff guard said, "Alright get your ass up. It's time for you shower."

Aziz looks forward to his showers and obediently stands up from his bunk and picks up his toiletries and follows the guard. Aziz tries hard not to ignore the walk as everything he will see is depressing. He locks his eyes on the guards back and follows obediently. After passing through two security gates they arrive at the shower room and the guard said, "You have ten minutes." The guard then left the area.

He removes his jump suit and walks slowly to the empty showers and turns on the water and adjusts the force and temperature until it is as hot as he can bear. He looks forward to washing and cleansing his body just as he tries to cleanse his soul with prayer.

He steps under the strong spray with his arms and hands against the wall bracing his body and feels his body instantly relax under the powerful stream of hot water and for a moment it seems as if he is not in this horrible place. He is just a man taking a refreshing shower and for a short time his troubles are washed away.

As he stands there, enjoying this brief respite from confinement, his mind wanders back to the Bank of America bombing and to the Mosque in Houston. He is still trying to put the pieces together. He could not shake the feeling that he had missed something. He has been over the facts thousands of times and remains mystified. Still every day of his life he will go over it again.

Suddenly his relaxation is interrupted by a hard and sharp pain in his upper right back and he finds himself confused and wondering what is wrong. What just happened? He sees blood on the shower floor making its way to the drain. He is having trouble breathing as he slowly turns around to see a man wearing a skullcap standing in front of him with a bloody shank in his hand and an evil grin on his face. The man said, "You failed Allah and now you must pay. Allah Akbar."

Aziz raises his hand and tries to speak but there is no air in his lungs and no words come out as the man drives the shank deep into his heart and turns and walks calmly out of the shower room.

CHAPTER 87

RICHMOND, VIRGINIA
JULY 4, 2010

Joe Winston's hometown of Richmond, Virginia planned a massive Fourth of July Parade and fireworks display to honor their hometown hero.

The entire Capitol District has been cordoned off from N. 5th St. to N. 18th St. and from E. Main St to W. Broad St. to accommodate the anticipated crowd. The City set up large projection televisions in the numerous parks along the James River so everyone could hear and see Joe Winston's comments and enjoy our nation's birthday.

The parade includes hundreds of well known dignitaries and started promptly at 3:00 pm in the afternoon and terminated at 5:00 pm in the Capitol District. The entire parade route was jammed with loyal Americans who are enjoying the festivities and the promise of a new future with native son Joe Winston.

Joe will address the crowd at 8:30 pm and in the meantime over one hundred and fifty thousand people will enjoy picnics by the river, the sounds of four different banks spread throughout downtown, and participate in numerous activities for children and adults. Spirits are high and hope is in the air.

Earlier that morning John informs Joe that the President announced that the forensics study of the two sets of conspiracy documents is complete and that he and Alex Hawkins are in agreement with the contents and all implicated individuals are currently incarcerated.

He also announced that the documents were now declassified which would aide in the conviction of the treacherous conspirators.

As the sun slowly slips toward the horizon John Danforth steps to the podium and welcomes everyone and introduces Joe Winston.

Never before in the hallowed history of Virginia have so many people assembled for any event and their generous applause and cheers continue for over ten minutes as Joe and his family along with another three dozen dignitaries and many veterans are standing on the large stage decorated tastefully with a large American flag being the prominent focal point.

Joe finally manages to encourage the crowd to allow him to speak, "My fellow Virginians thank you so much for your warm welcome."

Once again he is interrupted by the exuberant crowd.

Joe continues, "two hundred and thirty five years ago, in St. John's Church, Patrick Henry said "give me liberty or give me death". Today I say that liberty will prevail in America as we all work together to rebuild our Nation into the most fair and prosperous Republic in the history of mankind."

Once again Joe is the recipient of thunderous applause and chants of "Joe, Joe, Joe, Joe."

As Joe continues in a forceful voice that is uncharacteristic of his usual calm and deliberate speech pattern the entire crowd falls completely silent and respectful, "America is great because of the American people. Not Government.

America is great because of the ingenuity and hard work of the American people. Not because of our government.

America is great because of the generosity and compassion of the American people. Not because of the government.

America is great because when our backs are against the wall no nation can compare with our indomitable spirit and ability to work together for the good of our country.

America is great because we are a country ruled by the people. Not by government."

As Joe pauses the familiar chants began again, "Joe, Joe, Joe, Joe, Joe."

With a forceful and confident voice Joe continued, "The Restoration Party will restore meaningful education to our children, we will restore jobs and opportunity for every American, we will restore financial responsibility and reduce the impact of government intrusion into our lives, we will restore morality and freely acknowledge God in our lives, and America will remain the land of the free and the home of the brave."

"Joe, Joe, Joe, Joe, Joe, Joe, Joe" the chants continue for several minutes.

"My fellow Virginians this cannot be done without the support of each and every American. For too long our politicians have sought to win your vote by promising something for nothing. The American people are people of pride and honor and we are not built that way.

The American people want opportunity and they desire to accept responsibility for their own welfare. The American people do not want hand outs they want a chance to care for themselves and their families.

I will not stand here and tell you that you need to make no sacrifices because you must. Your children must sacrifice time to study and to become productive adults. We all must avoid the temptation of self indulgence until we have satisfied our responsibility. When we see less fortunate people struggle and unable to stand on their own; we must lift them up.

Ladies and gentlemen the role of government is to promote the general welfare of its people not to provide welfare.

We the people will work together to solve the problems we face.

We the people understand that each of us has the responsibility to provide for our families.

We the people understand that without sacrifices progress is impossible.

We the people understand that for our Republic to work each and every one of us must ask the question that President Kennedy asked, ask not what your country can do for you ask what you can do for your country."

As Joe pauses the night if filled with signs of life; babies are crying, children are playing, people coughing or laughing, and the sound of distant fireworks signifying others celebrating America's birth day.

"Employers have a responsibility to adequately compensate their employees and employees have a responsibility to become productive and valuable assets. By doing so employers will enjoy low turnover and employees will enjoy greater income and additional security."

Let us all remember that citizenship includes duties, rights, and privileges. We hear much about rights and privileges and little about duties. Duties include self reliance, responsibility, hard work, compassion, self improvement, and service to your country.

If citizens contribute nothing toward the betterment of society, performs no duties, and only desire the rights and privileges of citizenship. Those citizens endanger the brotherhood built by our ancestors who worked hard and fought hard for our freedom, rights, and privileges.

Each of us must strive to do our duty and to be a good citizen if America's republic is to survive.

Joe pauses once again and the chants and applause continue for several minutes before Joe resumes his passionate presentation, "As I see the sun quickly sinking in the West let this day and the ways of the past disappear. When the sun rises tomorrow morning let each of us pledge to work a little harder, care a little more, face each new rising sun with hope and optimism for the future, and strive to be a good citizen. Thank you and Happy Birthday America!"

As Joe concludes his comments the last remnants of the sun falls below the horizon and the Richmond Orchestra present an emotional rendition of God Bless America as the lights and sounds of the spectacular fireworks display fills the sky.

CHAPTER 88

WASHINGTON, D.C.
AUGUST 21, 2010

The failures of President Howard's Administration have been a huge disappointment for the American people who had such high hopes when they elected him. In two years they have accumulated trillions of dollars of debt and accomplished little or nothing. .

Howard continues his history of bad decisions by bringing four terrorists, who proudly admitted their guilt in the 9/11 attacks, back to New York for criminal trial.

Their inability to understand that radical Muslims consider these men heroes and those who lost loved ones were incensed at this decision resulted in massive demonstrations and a jihadist suicide bombing that killed eight and wounded sixteen Americans and the trial hasn't even started.

After the historic election of a black president America had high hopes for meaningful change. The reality is that history will report that his presidency did more damage to America than any of his predecessors.

He has no chance for a second term and the public appears to be poised to send a strong message at the mid term elections.

He crawled in bed with labor unions whose only interest is their own welfare and manipulative politicians whose only interest is power. Howard is basically not a bad man he just surrounded himself with idiots and allowed himself to be molded into a compliant President who became a victim of horrendous advice.

His approval ratings after the conspiracy arrests hit 61%. After Hawkins's press conference the ratings plummeted to 33%. When it became necessary to arrest Belk and the four Senators his approval rating dropped to 26%.

Nevertheless Howard is a politician and continues to look for ways to recover from his disastrous first two years as President. Politicians are cursed with the inability to accept how badly they are doing and always believe it is simply something else, not them.

He decided to meet with John Danforth and see if he could find some common areas that they might agree on and proceed from there. He could see no down side and he just might be able to use the old Senator.

His executive assistant raps on the door, opens it, and says, "Mr. President. Senator Danforth is here."

Howard stood up and walked toward the door and said, "Please show him in."

By the time John clears the door he is startled to find the President almost directly in front of him. "Good morning Mr. President." John said as he extends his hand.

President Howard smiles warmly and shakes John's hand, "Good morning Senator. Thank you for agreeing to see me."

"The honor is mine Mr. President." John said.

The President motions to the sitting area just as the Steward knocks on the door and enters with a tray of coffee. The Steward sits the coffee on the table and fills two beautiful china coffee cups, embossed with the Presidential Seal. The Steward asks the Senator, "Would you care for cream or sugar Senator?"

"No thanks." John cordially answers.

The President said, "Thank you Charlie."

As Charlie leaves the room he said, "Yes Sir."

President Howard is relaxed as always as he sips his coffee and said, "Senator I must say that the rise of the Restoration Party has been remarkable."

John is well experienced in dealing with politicians and simply said, "Thank you Sir. Many people have worked very hard."

Howard said, "Mr. Winston is quite a remarkable man."

John smiles and said, "Well Sir he is the best son and law a man could have."

The two men chuckle and the President ask, "With his talent and leadership I am surprised he has taken no interest in politics until recently."

John sips his coffee and leans back in his chair and crosses his legs, "Joe never cared much for politicians as you may have heard him say. He simply realized that he has been a bit selfish with his time and talent and finally realized that perhaps he could be of some help to his country."

The President's face became more serious as he leans forward and said, "John our country is in serious trouble and we all need to work together to get out of this mess."

John is thinking, now we need to work together? You have buried yourself and all of a sudden you want to build a coalition...Does he think I am senile? What arrogance! John studies the President as he drinks his coffee and does not reply.

The President continues, "As you know my party has been pretty much destroyed for years to come thanks to Harry Belk and his treacherous behavior. However, I am still committed to do the best I can for our country. It occurred to me that if we can some how work together over the next two years perhaps we could resolve some of our problems."

John listens in disbelief to the President and curtly said, "What did you have in mind Mr. President?"

Howard stands up and walks around the room, disappointed that John is now in control by virtue of his questions. He looks at John as if he is considering what to do, talk with him or throw him out. He presses on, "We must find a solution to unemployment, health care, our debt, and our involvement in the Middle East. I was hoping that you and I might work a little closer together to find some answers."

John put his coffee cup on the table and with a thoughtful look on his face said, "Mr. President I have always been willing to work with you to resolve those problems. In the past neither you nor your party has indicated a willingness to work with us."

The President knows John is right and he deserved that shot. He changes his position in his chair and says, "Senator I will be the first to tell you that I received some very bad advice over the last couple of years. I am embarrassed by the fact that people I thought I could trust turned out to be less than forthright with me. I made a bad mistake and will freely admit it."

John is surprised to hear a politician admit he made a mistake but nevertheless he understand that a good relationship with the President is never bad. He said, "Mr. President if there is to be any possibility of a cooperative relationship you must be willing to dramatically reduce the size of government and consider short term tax relief to encourage investment."

The President doesn't wish to cave in too quickly and say, "Senator I am more than willing to visit those issue or any other issues that will benefit our country."

He pauses and knows he has made a concession and now needs a concession if they were to have a chance of moving forward. He says, "Would you agree that corporate greed must also be a high priority?"

John quickly responds, "Mr. President I am glad to hear that you have an open minded but I don't believe corporate greed is responsible for our economic woes. I do believe that as a result of inadequate regulation some companies were allowed to improperly expand and that needs to be addressed."

The President smiles coyly and says, "Senator I understand your view point and you could be right. I am glad to hear we agree on better regulation."

John says, "Well maybe we do and maybe we don't Mr. President. We can both agree that a small minority of business leaders have been abusive but we can't say that corporate America is the cause of our dilemma. We can't condemn all business because of the transgressions of a few.

That would be like saying that eighty million people who are completely dependent on the government are worthless and lazy. Great political rhetoric Mr. President but the truth lies somewhere in the middle."

The President is resigned to being conciliatory asks, "What other issues should be pursued?"

The Senator is tiring of this political game and says with disinterest, "More effective regulation, restrictions on the Feds manipulation of our free markets, one term limits, and a simplified tax code would be good for starters. I believe you are familiar with our platform."

The President's phone buzzed and he walks over and picks it up and listens for a few minutes before hanging up, "Senator I want to thank you for your time today but I have to go. I would like to talk later if you are agreeable?"

John stands up and walks toward the door with the President and Howard said, "We will get together again real soon."

John stops about three steps from the door and turns to face the President. He had a seed to plant, "Mr. President before I go I would like to make a comment for your consideration if you will allow me."

Howard looked at the Senator with a hint of curiosity and replies, "Certainly."

Senator Danforth, in his usual and slow manner, maintains eye contact with Howard, "You know as well as that politics has become a dirty business. The American people are tired of it. I would simply like to say that I believe you to be a man who loves his country. Your presidency will not be judged by the first two years......but the next two years....

The President is a little taken back by John's comments but simply says, "Thank you very much for your time Senator and I will keep that in mind."

John said, "Thank you Mr. President." His seed has been planted.

CHAPTER 89

The definition of a team would generally be a group of individuals working together to achieve a common goal. These men are not just a team they are perhaps the very best team ever assembled. They are all extremely talented and committed to each other and there is not the slightest bit of jealousy.

They differ from a conventional team inasmuch as they do not necessarily pursue common objectives other than the success of their respective businesses. In spite of the fact they all work in completely different fields each man has been instrumental in the others success. They are connected not only by a strong personal bond but by a similar business management style.

Their history spans several decades and in that entire period of time they have never had a serious disagreement or even spoken a harsh word. They are indeed a major force in American business as reported by the Wall Street Journal and a terrific example of true friendship.

Lee is unquestionably the most intelligent of the four men and perhaps one of the brightest minds in the entire country. In spite of his intelligence he also enjoys another attribute that few intellectuals possess which is common sense.

Lee has a wonderful sense of humor and is one of the most compassionate and caring people in the world. Lee is the little brother of the group.

Adam is more serious than the other three men and never makes a move without careful analysis. Impromptu is not a concept he is familiar with. No one is better with numbers, logic, and understanding complicated financial situations than Adam.

He is gifted with a photographic memory and he can scan a company's balance sheet and immediately pick up on the company's weaknesses and strengths.

Adam is fiercely loyal to his family and friends and his stability and counsel have proved valuable to his friends many times.

Robbie is the emotional member of the "Forcesome" and often acts impulsively. He has the innate ability to read people extremely well and combines his book sense and street sense as well as anyone. Tradition, honor, and loyalty are the attributes he embodies.

He is intensely competitive and a shoot from the hip risk taker in business. Rarely in his life has he experienced failure and he has never broken a commitment.

It is said there are three kinds of men; those who watch things happen, those who don't know what is happening, and those who make things happen. Robbie Ravenel is definitely a man who makes things happen.

Joe Winston is the lynchpin of the group, the big brother, and each of his friends owe him more than they could ever repay but Joe's payoff is their friendship. He is a loving husband, a wonderful father, a great boss, and a deeply religious and patriotic man.

To Joe it has never been about what he could get it had always been about what he could give. His genuine passion for others and the joy he receives from helping them achieve their objectives is the only currency he ever needed. He personifies the statement that if you help others get what they want you will get what you want.

Their morning round of golf was rained out and they are in the bar relaxing. Lee commented, "Looks like we are going to do well in the mid terms. John is very optimistic."

Robbie. Who is always confident, said, "We sure are getting plenty of help from the ineptitude of this Administration."

He takes a pull on his scotch and continues. "Can you believe the legal bullshit surrounding those conspiracy bastards?"

Adam, with his usual control, said, "The good news is no matter how it ends Hasan is dead."

Robbie looks at Adam and asks, "What if they let the bastards off?"

Adam shrugs and replies, "They may end up getting off Robbie, and if they do, it will just be another nail in the liberals coffin."

"It seems to me they have already exceeded their quota of nails." Lee said.

Robbie looked at Joe and asks, "Joe. Do you really think we can pull this off?"

Joe smiles and confidently replies, "All I can tell you is that we have been working hard and have workable solutions for every problem. We have done the best we can and that's all we can do."

Adam said, "The more I study the government's fiscal policies I am absolutely amazed that we are not in worse condition. If you look at the financials as a prudent business person considering a business acquisition you would not believe the numbers. You could buy the government for about ten cents on the dollar and sell it for a dollar fifty in a few years."

Lee asks, "How in the hell will we ever pay off the debt?"

Adam looks at Lee and smiles, "On the installment plan. The American way......That's the most difficult problem we face even if the debt doesn't grow more in the next couple of years. It appears we will have at least a fifteen trillion dollar debt by the end of 2012. When we consider the annual interest we pay on that debt it could take twenty our more years to get back in the black."

Robbie listens intently as Adam spoke and said, "Adam that's pretty damn scary! Are there any other ways to pay that money off more quickly?"

Adam said, "We are looking at a few items that will help. The Federal Government consumes 25% of the oil in this country. We could enter into a partnership with the oil companies that hold rights to the Bakken reserves in the Dakotas and Montana, pipe the oil into Dugway Proving Ground, which is a U.S. Army base in Utah, and create a refinery just for the Federal government.

This would take six or eight years to complete but the end result would be to provide Government oil at a greatly reduced price as well as bring down the cost of gas in this country."

"What other options do we have Adam?" Lee asked.

"Mostly small stuff Lee but the removal of eighty thousands troops from the Middle East would save us three to five hundred billion a year. If we concentrate on rebuilding America not the rest of the world we can get back to a smooth economy fairly quickly." Adam replies.

Joe is sitting in a chair by the railing with his feet propped on the rail listening to his friends. He said, "I don't know what we would do without Adam. He is devoting most of his time drilling down in these budgets and looking for solutions. Adam you are amazing my friend."

Adam said, "Actually Joe I am having fun. This is like a giant puzzle and I am determined to solve it. I guess I am like Lee and his hacking hobby."

Joe said, "I will drink to that my friend." The men laugh and finish their drinks as Robbie orders another round.

Robbie said, "I will tell you one thing I sure do miss the days when nobody knew who the hell I was. With all our television and media exposure I can't go any where without being recognized."

Lee said, "Man I can't believe how bad it is. I can't go anywhere without people wanting to talk to me. They even ask for my autograph."

Robbie laughs and said, "Now that is unbelievable. Who in the hell would want the autograph of a computer geek?"

The men laugh as the round of drinks Robbie ordered arrives. Robbie said, "On a serious note. Joe you are getting most of the attention and we can't kid ourselves there are a lot of people in this world that do not want to see you in the White House. You need to do something about security."

Lee speaks up and said, "Who would want to harm good old Joe?"

Robbie said, "Lee you can't be that naïve. There is a long list starting with Democrats and Republicans and ending with about two dozen countries. Not to mention people who are simply crazy."

Adam said with a serious tone, "Joe I believe Robbie is right. The days are gone when you can just walk around like a regular guy. The hopes of our country are embodied in you."

Joe, thinking this is a little bit silly, said, "I appreciate your concern and I will think about it."

Robbie disagreed with Joe's answer and as usual did not hold back his opinion, "Bull shit! Joe this isn't just about you anymore and that "aw shucks" caviler attitude want stop a bullet. You don't need to think about it you need to act now."

Adam and Lee look at Joe and nod their heads in agreement with Robbie.

Joe looks at them and said, "You guys are just worried that I might screw up our golf game."

"Come on Joe. This is serious. We need to do this and I am just the man to do it. I'm going to make Bert Braddock your chief security man along with two other guys. Their job will be to stay out of your way but to cover your back. Joe they are very good and you are too important to us and this country not to do it. Okay?"

Joe thought about it for a few seconds and knew Robbie is right, "Okay Robbie. I like Bert and I feel comfortable with him."

"Consider it done Joe and by the way the tomorrow you are going to be my partner." Robbie said as the men laughed.

CHAPTER 90

Election Day is finally here and it promises to be another historic event. Joe Winston would be very pleased if his party could gain thirty or forty seats in congress and a few governorships. That would be enough to disrupt the stranglehold politicians currently had on the country and maybe enough to force bipartisan negotiations.

The day turns out to be a complete disaster for the Democrats and it is clear by 7:00 pm that the Restoration Party is exceeding expectations and the voters are sending a strong message to Washington.

The historic and popular election of President Howard was perceived as the maturation of America and his "star power" status and great hopes of the people have now melted like snow on a ninety degree day. He sees no hope for the future and dreads the embarrassment of being a President with no influence or power for two more years.

He is lying on his bed in the residence area of the White House wallowing in self pity when Ann walks in and cheerfully said, "Hi Honey. How are you doing?"

"I'm just peachy." The President replies as he wonders why she was so damn upbeat.

Ann knows her husband very well and understands the impact of the mid-terms. She lay down beside him and strokes his head and said, "Well, no matter what I love you."

Howard didn't respond so Ann grabs his hand and pulls him off the bed and said, "Come on Honey I have some hot chocolate in the living room."

She drags him toward the living room and he reluctantly follows her. She gently pushes him down in the comfortable easy chair that he loves and pulls his feet up on the ottoman and said, "Now you sit right here and relax for a few minutes."

She pours the hot chocolate and places the cup by his chair and pours her self a cup and sits down on the ottoman and drops two marshmallows in each cup and said, "James I know how hard this has been for you but we need to find a way to salvage your Presidency and get re-elected."

He sarcastically laughs and said, "Re-elected. Are you kidding?"

"No I am not kidding James and I know you are not a quitter. You are an intelligent and creative man who can solve any problem and it is time for you to stop this pity party and figure out what our options are." Ann said sternly.

"Ann don't you get it! It's over. We don't control the House and we don't control the Senate. What the hell can I do?" he said with frustration and a slight hint of anger.

Ann patiently listens and got down on her knees in front of him and took his hand in hers and caressed it as she said, "What you can do is to figure out how you can overcome this disaster and rise to the top like you always do. You have options but you are not focused on solutions you are dwelling on the past."

James always valued Ann's advice and support and somewhere within him he knows she is right. He finally said, "Ann not only have I lost Congress my own party is even deserting me."

Ann, still holding his hand, said, "That's a start James if the Democrats have abandoned you than perhaps you need to consider new alliances."

James looks at her with some confusion and said, "What do you mean new alliances?"

Ann stands up and walks over the fireplace and then returns to her chair and sits down and fixes James with her brown eyes and said, "James your job as President is to the very best job you can possibly do for the American people. Clearly your party has left you and you can never work with Republicans." She pauses for effect and then continues, "But you could work with the Restoration Party."

James abruptly stands up and walks over to the window and looks out at the cold rain falling and thinks about what Ann said. After a few minutes of deep thought he said with a small smile on his face for the first time in a long time, "Perhaps I can. John Danforth is a real gentleman and one of the most principled men I have ever known. Joe Winston appears to be a decent man and he certainly has some interesting and innovative ideas. Yes. Perhaps I can."

CHAPTER 91

Joe Winston arrived home at 4:00 pm and is completely exhausted. He has been traveling all over the country for the past two months stumping for the Restoration Party. The votes had been counted and the results were extremely satisfying.

The Restoration Party picked up a total of 22 Senate seats and 202 Congressional seats. .

In the Gubernatorial races the Restoration Party won a total of twenty three states.

It was truly a dramatic election day and history had been made and no party controls the House. The American voters turned out in record numbers and their message was loud and clear. They are sick and tired of business as usual and this time they really voted for change.

Joe enters the back door with his overnight bag and the look of a man who had just won a Marathon in record time but is completely spent. Linda hears him coming in and rushes to greet him. She wraps her arms around him and hugs him very hard with great affection.

Joe drops his bag and holds on to her very tightly as she cries softly on his shoulder. Finally she releases him and places her hands on his shoulders looks proudly into his eyes and kisses him softly and says, "Joe I am so proud of you."

Once again they embrace and she said, "Come on in and sit down Honey. You look tired."

He said, "Thanks Baby. I am dog tired but very, very happy. What a great day."

Joe plops down in his chair in the den and immediately relaxed and feels the tension leave his body. It feels wonderful to be home with Linda.

Linda pours his drink and brings it to him. She leans over and loosens his tie and said, "I love you."

He kisses her and said, "I love you too Baby."

She sits down on the floor in front of his chair and asks with a hopeful smile, "I sure hope we can spend a little time together now?"

Joe takes a deep pull on his Scotch and sits his glass on the side table and said, "Yes we can. How does a week in Aspen the week after Thanksgiving sound?"

Linda loves cold weather, snow, and Colorado and responds by putting her arms in the air and exuberantly exclaiming "Yes!"

Her excitement pleases Joe as she stands up and sits in his lap and gives him a big old loving kiss and said, "Joe I can't wait." She kisses him a dozen times all over his face until Joe laughs.

She calms down a little and refreshes Joe's drink and asks, "Will it just be us?"

"Whatever you want Honey?" Joe responds.

She thought for a minute or so and said, "Well I know you won't go shopping with me and I do miss Emily, Kathleen, and Carolyn we haven't seen much of each other since this all started and I do miss Robbie, Lee, and Adam. Can we all go?"

Joe said, "Well I need to check with them but it would be fun for us all to be together again."

Linda asks, "How about Mom and Dad, can they come too?"

Joe looks lovingly at Linda and said, "I don't think so Honey. You know that after all these years of John being unable to get cooperation from the Senate leaders he will most likely become the Senate Leader."

"Are you serious?" Linda asks with surprise on her face. "I didn't even think of that."

"I am. John will be very busy after Thanksgiving and I know he can't go. Why don't you ask your Mom if she wants to go?" Joe said.

Linda said, "Can I call the girls and ask them?"

"Sure you can." Joe said.

With that Linda leaves the room and heads for her office off the kitchen and Joe settles back into his chair and closes his eyes. He had never felt more contented and more alive in his life.

Three hours later he awakens to Linda gently shaking his shoulder and quietly saying, "Joe. Come on Honey it's time for dinner."

CHAPTER 92

PALMYRA, SYRIA
DECEMBER 4, 2010

Majid is still despondent as he sits in his office sipping hot tea and brooding about the great losses his plan suffered in America and the change in America's political situation. After so many years of careful planning and extreme patience his perfect plans are destroyed in a single day.

He could easily be considered the King of all Jihadists and now, throughout the world, his brothers would know that he had failed and the shame he is feeling is almost unbearable. He must redeem himself and accomplish the task Allah bestowed upon him decades ago.

The only way he can regain his dignity and respect would be to strike a mighty blow against America and he is prepared to do exactly that.

His excitement at the election of President Howard and control of Congress by Democrats was the best case scenario for his plan. He knew they would pursue Socialist ideas, punish their most productive, grow government, and pursue a more Global philosophy.

All of this suited his purposes perfectly plus he knew the Democrats would minimize the importance of National Defense. Joe Winston's party will not be as easy.

Majid didn't survive this long without having options and he is still capable of inflicting great damage to the Americans. He has emergency assets still in place that were kept from Aziz.

On the East Coast near Norfolk, Virginia in a warehouse on the waterfront he has two Electro Magnetic Pulse bombs and a delivery system in place. Washington is hardened against EMP but New York and the New England states are not. He has the capability to cripple the northeast United States for years.

The EMP would completely disable all electronic devices, cars, and almost anything that has any electronic dependency. Basically the bomb explodes ten the thirty thousand feet in the air and fries all electronic components.

His opposition to WMD's included his fear that America would retaliate with tremendous force, most likely Nuclear if that were to occur. At this point he didn't care about repercussions he only knew that he must complete his mission and inflict as much damage as possible on the infidels. He still has cards to play and he intends to play them when the time comes.

Majid looks at his watch and walks to the south east corner of his estate. He enters a code to open the door and enters a large sitting area with all the conveniences. He continues past the sitting area and opens another door that opens into some type of medical treatment room. There is a tall thin man sitting in a chair with an IV in his arm circulating his blood through a dialysis machine.

The man's face is covered by a long gray beard and his eyes show the weariness of a long hard life. He speaks to Majid, "How are you today Majid?"

Majid pulls up a chair and sits in front of them man and says, "Osama, we need to talk."

CHAPTER 93

WASHINGTON, D.C.
JANUARY 21, 2011

The spirit of cooperation and civility among politicians is clearly evident as the House and Senate complete their first couple of weeks. The constant partisan bickering is dead much to the dismay of the Mass Media.

John Danforth is elected Majority leader in the Senate by a vote of 95 to 5 and quickly fills the prestigious Chairs with a mixture from each Party demonstrating his willingness to share power not flaunt it.

Senator Danforth makes it abundantly clear that their first and primary objective is to reduce Government spending, begin to reduce the massive debt, and to allow our free economy to function freely but with more effective regulation.

Naturally, there is some resistance and many Democrats still clung to the ideas of redistribution of wealth and excessive taxation and fees on taxpayers.

No one felt the disagreements were harmful and in fact all parties should be heard and contribute to the formation of policy. All opinions were respectfully considered prior to decisions being made. The way it is supposed to work.

In early January Senator Danforth appointed Adam Fields as a Special independent advisor to the Congressional Budget Office. Nothing could have prepared him for the absolute frivolity and absence of accuracy that existed within the Budget office.

After two weeks of observation and listening it is clear to him that their mission was to make the numbers justify the intent of the Bill being considered and the concept of accuracy was non-existent.

Senator Danforth and President Howard enjoyed several casual meetings at the Presidents behest. The President is certainly not in agreement simply based upon ideology but he is also bright enough to know that he didn't have a lot of bullets in his gun. His interaction with Senator Danforth convinced him that John is a man he can work with.

Today they are enjoying a working lunch and Senator Danforth, between bites of his salad, said, "Mr. President I know you are familiar with two significant changes our Party pledged to implement and I wanted you to be aware that the Bill will be on your desk within the next two weeks.

The first bill will be an Amendment to the Constitution limiting our elected officials to one six year term maintaining the replacement of 1/3 every two years in Senate and doing the same for Congress."

The President knew this would be his first test and he knew what he had to do. He still has mixed emotions, which is natural for someone who has spent years in Chicago politics, but he also knew that his only chance for saving his Presidency would be what he called "resistant compliance". Meaning he would not simply roll over he wanted to be given the courtesy of being convinced this would be in the best interest of everyone.

"John to be honest with everything going on I haven't given it a lot of thought. Do you feel as if you have sufficient votes to pass this amendment?" Howard asks.

"Yes Sir. It appears that more than 70% will support the amendment." John answers nonchalantly. "Once you sign it the approval of 66 2/3 of the States will be required.

The President deftly speared a piece of Salmon and lifted the fork to his mouth and chewed very slowly while looking at John, with what he hoped, passed for respect.

The President leans back with a satisfied look on his face and said, "John you know our Constitution is truly amazing when you think about it. I am always impressed with the composers of that document. What wisdom those men had."

John replies, "I agree Mr. President. They were extremely wise men with a clarity and foresight few posses today. Unfortunately life got a lot more complicated didn't it Mr. President?"

The two men laugh and the President replies, "Wouldn't it be amazing if we could bring them back to 2010 and get their reaction?"

They laugh again and felt more comfortable with each other. John said, "I don't know Mr. President they might not be very happy with us."

The steward brought them both a small piece of apple pie for dessert and John said, "Mr. President I don't normally eat sweets but apple pie is my weakness?"

The men finish their meal and John said, "Mr. President the other Bill will involve political campaigning regulations that will basically restrict paid campaigning until sixty days prior to election. I think we can all agree that the public is tired of two year political commercials and the money wasted on this could be better used elsewhere. The question is will you sign them?"

CHAPTER 94

CHARLESTON, S.C.
MARCH 3, 2011

Joe and Robbie are driving from the airport to Robbie's house after brief conversations about their families Robbie asks, "So Joe what's going on. You appear to have something on your mind?"

Joe looks at Robbie with a smile and said, "I sure am glad I don't play a lot of poker with you. Am I that easy to read?"

Robbie said, "Only when you want to be. Now tell me what's on your mind."

Joe sighed and said, "Majid is a ruthless, intelligent, and patient man and I am more convinced than ever that he hasn't used violence more frequently because that would distract from their primary mission and maybe inspire massive repercussions.

My concern is that the primary plan has been destroyed and he might resort to violence in an effort to salvage his pride. I don't think there is any doubt that he has weapons of mass destruction and I know he will not hesitate to use them."

Robbie glances over at Joe as he turns east on I-26 heading toward down town Charleston, "I agree. What do you want to do?"

The question made Joe very uncomfortable and he knew his answer would violate his ethical standards but the truth is if he fails to act and a tragedy occurred he could never forgive himself. He looks at Robbie and asks, "Can Mike take him down?"

Robbie said, "Yes. We are prepared for that contingency."

Joe, with a pained expression on his face, said, "Robbie we just don't have another option."

Robbie said, "Joe none of us likes doing things this way but if we just sit back and wait it could cost thousands of lives. I will notify Mike."

The men didn't speak for the next five minutes each dealing with their personal morality and justifying their actions. Finally Robbie changes the subject and said, "It looks like John is doing a great job in Washington."

Joe's immediately changed his attitude from modest despair to optimism and replies, "I can't believe the progress he is making in the last couple of months. Finally we are making decisions based upon the welfare of the country not politics.

President Howard signed the changes regarding election guidelines and term limits without Federal benefits and he and John are getting along great."

Robbie laughs a little and said, "What choice does he have? The only way he can avoid being the worst President in the history of our country is to play ball with John."

"You are right Robbie but according to John there is more to it than that. He thinks President Howard is basically a solid man with excellent values. The problem seems to be that he was misguided by the Chicago politicians as he was groomed to become President and fell victim to bad advice.

John says that it is almost as if he were brain washed. I can see where the opportunity to become President can blind a man to reality." Joe replies.

Robbie looked skeptical and said, "Okay. How are they doing with trimming the Federal Budget?"

"John says that thanks to Adam's hard work they are about to complete legislation that will reduce Federal spending by six hundred billion a year. He says most of the cuts will not cause any meaningful disruption in services but it will necessitate the elimination of a million Federal jobs.

He really thinks we can cut another million within two years which will bring the number of Federal employees down to a mere nine million." Joe responds

Joe picks up his brief case and pulls out a binder and opens it, "As you know they are basically shutting down 80% of the IRS with the simplified tax code and the new one page 1099.

Adam feels that the tax relief and employment incentives we give to private industry will immediately encourage businesses to expand and expects three to four million jobs to become available within a year.

The new regulations regarding mergers and acquisitions will force a drastic reduction in a company's ability to drive up their stock for short term massive gains and long term disasters. It will become extremely difficult for companies with over ten thousand employees to expand.

The concept is relatively simple we don't want to interfere in free trade but we never again want to have a company that is too big to fail.

As Robbie pulls his black Navigator into the Yacht Club parking lot he said, "Sounds like Adam is having a lot of fun."

Joe said, "He is a genius and he will be the one responsible for turning this economy around."

Joe's purpose for visiting Charleston is to address the Charleston Chamber of Commerce and as they enter the Club he is immediately engulfed by dozens of reporters.

CHAPTER 95

Majid Abdulla Mohammed has seen enough and is convinced that this new Restoration Party is leaving him with no alternatives. Prior to unleashing the most destructive terrorist attack in history he knew that he must advise King Abdallah.

He summons his automobile and leaves his comfortable estate at 9:00 am for the long desolate drive on the only road to the airport where his plane awaits. His house guest insisted on riding with him today as he often did. Majid and Osama Bin Laden have been allies and friends for several decades.

After he completes that task he will notify his operatives in the United States to implement Operation Silence. Once he sets the plan in motion it will be implemented within 48 hours and hundreds of thousands of Americans would suffer.

Mike Miller had been dispatched to Syria on February 27th and has been carefully observing Majid's secure estate for over a week.

Three miles from Majid's estate, along the flat and dusty dirt road, Mike sits high on a hill concealed by some large rocks to the east of the road. His location is perfect and if anyone looks in his direction they would also be looking directly into the sun.

Mike is very familiar with the surrounding area and the security measures employed by Majid. He heard the hum of motors in the distance and knew that in a few minutes three bullet proof and armored Mercedes Benz 600's would round the bend and come into his view.

He removes his high powered binoculars and looks down the road to see how many cars are coming. As they round the curve a mile from his location he replaces his binoculars and watches the dust being kicked up by the three cars as they come closer. Mike reaches into his pocket and removes an object that appears to be a cell phone.

As the first black Mercedes passes Mike's marker he calmly presses the first button on his electronic detonator and immediately pressed four more in succession.

Each of the three cars are thrust at least twenty feet in the air as they are engulfed by a powerful fireball that rips the bullet proof vehicles into thousands of pieces. The noise is deafening and the smoke and flames from the explosion extend over a thousand feet in the air. The ground where Mike stands shook so violently that Mike almost lost his balance.

As Mike calmly watches the destruction he gathers his belongings and began walking to his vehicle. He could still hear the noise of the explosion ringing in his ears and the clouds of dust and debris is still falling around him. The pungent odor of explosives, gasoline, burning rubber, and death filled the air.

He couldn't help but smile as he thought about all the technical security precautions Majid had taken. It never occurred to him that he would become a victim of the terrorist's favorite weapon, the IED.

Instincts should never be ignored. If Joe Winston waited a few more days America would have suffered a devastating attack that could ultimately have destroyed the entire country.

No one will ever know how close we came and no one would ever know what became of Osama Bin Laden.

CHAPTER 96

RICHMOND, VIRGINIA
APRIL 13, 2011

Joe Winston is sitting in his modest but very nice office at Winston's corporate headquarters enjoying the normalcy of simply running a billion dollar plus business. His schedule is fairly devoid of personal appearances but he is in constant communication with John regarding legislation and issues of importance.

It seems to Joe that America has already undergone a remarkable transition. Unemployment if improving substantially, politicians are working together, and the economy is beginning to return to normal. Americans are optimistic and to future has never looked brighter.

As Joe pours a cup of coffee the buzzer on his desk phone announces a call from his executive assistant, "Joe you have a call from Mr. Jack Morgan in the White House."

Joe walks back to his desk and pushes the transmit button and said, "Put him through."

Joe knows that Jack Morgan is the new Chief of Staff for President Howard and is curious as to why he would be calling. He picks up the phone and said politely, "This is Joe Winston."

Jack Morgan in a very cordial tone said, "Mr. Winston my name is Jack Morgan, Chief of Staff for the President of the United States. How are you this morning?'

"Very well Mr. Morgan. What can I do for you?" Joe responds with curiosity.

Jack said, "President Howard asked that I give you a call to see if you and Mrs. Winston could arrange to be in Washington on April 20th to have dinner with the President and his wife?"

Joe is surprised by the invitation and hesitates briefly before saying, "Mr. Morgan I am very flattered by the Presidents invitation and we would be most honored to have dinner with the President and his wife."

Morgan sounds relieved with Joe's response, "That's terrific Mr. Winston and I am confident the President will be pleased. With your permission I will arrange transportation for you and Mrs. Winston and provide you with all the pertinent details in the morning."

Joe said, "That will be fine Mr. Morgan. May I ask who else will be in attendance?"

Morgan replies, "It will be just the four of you"

Joe, now even more curious, said, "We look forward to it Mr. Morgan."

"Thank you Mr. Winston. Good bye." Morgan said.

Joe hangs up the phone and paces around the room for a few minutes. This invitation just came from the blue and is totally unexpected. His mind is now working in overdrive trying to understand the reason for this invitation but he could come up with no logical explanation.

Joe picks up the phone and dials his home number and Linda answers on the second ring, "Hello."

"Hey Honey how are you doing this morning?" Joe asked.

Linda laughs and said, "Well sweetie I am doing just as well as I was two hours ago when you left. What's up?

Joe laughs nervously and said, "Do you have any plans for the 20th?"

Linda said, "Let me look at my schedule.......Not a thing. What would you like to do?"

Joe said, "I thought we would go to the White House for dinner."

Linda didn't miss a beat and said, "Honey I didn't know you were proclaimed King."

They both laughed and he said, "Very funny. I got a call from Howard's Chief of Staff and he invited us to the White House to have dinner with the Howards."

Linda said with disappointment in her voice, "Is this one of those grand dinners where every slimy diplomat, social climber, and politicians attend. If it is I am busy."

Joe chuckles and always appreciates Linda's humor, "Actually it will just be us and the Howards."

Linda is surprised and confused by this information, "Joe, this is very confusing. What's this all about?"

Joe said, "I don't know Honey but I guess the only way we will find out is to go. That okay with you?"

"It's fine with me Joe. This should be very interesting." Linda replies.

CHAPTER 97

RICHMOND, VIRGINIA
APRIL 17, 2011

Joe and Linda are having dinner with John and Kathleen at the Senators home. Mary prepared a Shrimp Boil for dinner which consists of corn, hot sausage, onions and spices, and shrimp all cooked in a large pot filled with a combination of beer and water.

It is one of their favorite meals and Mary serves it with her wonderful hush puppies, cole slaw, and her own special cocktail sauce that will make your eyes water.

Everyone is dressed in jeans and old clothes as this is a messy meal to be eaten with enthusiasm and they will basically eat with their fingers. They are all hungry as Mary place the food on the table and John gives the blessing.

They quickly busy themselves peeling shrimp and stuffing the delicious food in their mouths as they talked about their grandchildren and other mundane topics. Their primary concern is eating.

After dinner Kathleen and her daughter adjourn to Kathleen's combination sewing room and office while Joe and John moved to John's library.

Joe said, "Well John I got an interesting invitation this week."

"Tell me about it son." John replies.

"President Howard's Chief of Staff called me and said the President and First Lady would like to have dinner with Linda and me in the White House."

John immediately stops tinkering with the television remote control and said, "Now that is surprising. Are you going to go?"

Joe sits down in the plush leather easy chair and put his feet on the ottoman and replies, "Yes we are going to go."

"Who else will be attending this dinner party?" John asked curiously.

"I asked that question and was told it would just be the four of us." Joe said.

John let the information bounce around in his head for about thirty seconds and finally said, "That is very unusual and very interesting."

Joe asks, "What do you think this is really about?"

John looked pensively at Joe and said, "Joe I must tell you that this is very surprising. The President has been unusually cooperative and he and I have developed a very cordial relationship. I find him to be a much more likeable fellow in recent months. I have no idea why he invited you.

John pauses to collect his thoughts and takes a seat opposite Joe and said, "The truth is that Congress is beginning to become a very cohesive group and we have been very effective in our bi-partisan efforts. It is almost shocking how well things are going. Perhaps this has something to do with the Presidents improved cooperation."

Joe listened attentively to John and said, "I think it has more to do with your leadership and the Restoration Party. The country is beginning to move in the right direction now and Congress appears to be regaining trust. Maybe the President doesn't have any other options except to simply comply with the wishes of Congress?"

John said, "That's probably true. You know as bad as his first two years were his name will appear on some of the most important legislation every passed in this country. By the end of his term his stock could rise considerably.

I can't wait to hear about your dinner with him. By the way when is it?"

Joe said, "It will be on the 20th. His Chief of Staff indicated they wish to keep this quiet, which is probably a good idea, so they will pick us up in a helicopter and fly us directly to the White House.

John rested his head on the back of his chair and looks at the ceiling for almost a full minute and finally said, "I guess all I can say is that I hope you and Linda have a good time and be careful."

CHAPTER 98

Secret Service Agent Bill Dale greets the Winston's at the private aviation area of Richmond's airport and made every effort to see that they were comfortable on the short flight to the White House.

When the helicopter landed at the White House Agent Dale escorted the Winston's to the White House and through security directly to the Presidents quarters. He tapped on the door and it is promptly opened by President Howard.

The President, dressed in slacks and a long sleeve shirt, reaches out and shakes Joe's hand warmly and kisses Linda on her cheek as he said, "Mr. and Mrs. Winston thank you so much for coming. Please come in."

Joe said, "Thank you very much Mr. President the pleasure is ours,"

As the President lead them to a comfortable sitting area Ann appears and walks toward them with a genuine smile on her face. The President said, "Permit me to introduce my wife Ann. Ann this is Mr. and Mrs. Winston."

Ann warmly embraces Joe and said, "Mr. Winston it is a real pleasure to finally meet you." Then she turns to Linda and said, "Mrs. Winston thank you so much for coming."

Linda instantly likes Ann and it seems clear they will get along wonderfully. Ann said, "It is our pleasure Mrs. Howard."

Ann said, "Okay. Let's set some ground rules. Please call me Ann and with your permission I will call you Linda. These guys can do what they want. Is that alright with you Linda?"

Everyone laughs as Ann completely put everyone at ease and Linda said, "Well Ann that sounds like a grand idea to me." The two ladies reached their arms out and held hands as if they were old dear friends.

President Howard said, "Tell you what if you will allow me to call you Joe you may call me James."

Joe and the President laughed and Joe said, "We have a deal Mr. Pres....I mean James."

For the next hour and half the four spoke of their children and their backgrounds and if someone didn't know better they would have thought they were life long friends. After desert was served Ann asks, "Linda have you ever been to the White House?"

Linda answers, "No Ann this is my first time."

"Good. I always welcome the opportunity to show guests the White House. The truth is I am much better than the tour guides." Ann laughs.

Linda said, "You are in charge Ann. I can't wait to see it all." With that the ladies stand to begin their tour and the men stand as they leave the table and walk out of the room giggling and whispering to each other.

Joe said, "Looks like those two hit it off pretty well James."

The President said, "Ann always amazes me. She has the unique ability to make people feel welcome and it appears to me that Linda possesses those same qualities."

Joe says, "I agree."

Howard said, "Joe why don't we go over hear and relax with an after dinner drink

As they are seated in an area surrounded by history Joe could not help but think of all the prior residents who occupied this residence. The steward serves the men Amaretto coffee and leaves the room.

The President speaks first and said, "Joe I want you to know that our conversations are not being taped and I would like our meeting to remain confidential."

"That's fine with me James." Joe replies.

The President, of course, has reviewed the dossiers on Adam, Robbie, and Lee as well as Joe. Nevertheless, over the next fifteen minutes, the President asks Joe to describe his relationship with each man and Joe does so.

President Howard said, "Joe I must tell you that I am envious. You are a fortunate man to have three wonderful friends."

Joe smiles and responds, "I have been truly blessed and consider myself a fortunate man. I couldn't ask for three better friends."

Howard says, "I looked at Mr. Ravenel's background and his contributions to this country are extraordinary. As you know he has more government security contracts than anyone and General Elliot informs me that his bids are always among the lowest and his work is always exceptional."

Joe says, "Robbie is an incredibly loyal person and very successful businessman as well as a wonderful human being. To him it has never been about money. His satisfaction comes from being of service."

The President says with some sadness, "I know the death of his nephew in Charlotte must have been devastating to him."

Joe is a little surprised by this comment and wonders if the President actually has some indication that Robbie might be involved. However, his face reveals nothing as he said, "Yes it was very hard on Robbie."

The President changes directions and says, "Joe I must tell you that I have watched you carefully over the past couple of years and the impact your presence has had on the country is nothing short of miraculous. Your leadership and the creation of the Restoration Party and its positive approach and civil conduct are genius."

Again Joe's expression reveals nothing even though he somewhat offended at the President's implication. "Thank you Mr. President but the Restoration Party was created by the republicans and democrats inability to adequately satisfy the needs of our citizens, not by us. I think most Americans believe that we should be positive and civil."

The President observes Joe very carefully as he is speaking and gets a glimpse of Joe's candor and honesty. Like Joe his expression remains passive as he says, "I never thought of it quite that way Joe but in retrospect you could be right. It is amazing how much more congenial Congress is now. It appears the nastiness and border line hatred is gone."

Joe said, "I agree Mr. President and it is my opinion that Senator Danforth and you have achieved some significant objectives over the past few months. It is amazing how much more supportive Americans become when they don't see their leaders fighting each other every day."

Howard reflects on Joe's comments and finally says, "Joe I want you to know that I really looked forward to meeting you tonight. You are one of those rare individuals who still believes that integrity, honor, service, fairness, and hard work are the way to success."

"Thank you James I have been influenced greatly in my life by those values as well as a strong belief in God. James you sit in a chair that few men in history will ever occupy. Would you be kind enough to share with me your thoughts at this juncture of your life?"

James laughs and says, "I'm sorry Joe. It does appear that I have been asking all the questions and you have been kind enough to answer them. Well let me see. What are my thoughts?"

The President hesitates trying to decide how much he could trust this man and how much he is willing to share. He has lost most of his mentors and close advisors and has spent a great deal of time trying to answer the question that Joe is now asking.

The truth is he needed a confidant and for some reason he feels Joe is a man who would not break a confidence.

Finally he said, "Joe I am in a quandary. I have only known you for a few hours but I trust you and I would welcome your guidance. You have asked me a question that I have been asking myself for months and perhaps, with your help, I can finally answer it."

Joe is sensing that the President is about to confide in him.

President Howard pauses, looks at Joe as if he is trying to decide if he should trust him, and continues "For twenty years I knew that I would be the President of the United States. I know that may sound arrogant but it isn't.

Many of my past mentors and advisors let it be known that I was going to be groomed for the job and they impacted upon me that if we are to succeed we must constantly discredit the Republicans and resort to any tactics necessary to reach our goal. I was convinced the opposition pursued the same policies and that's just the way it is in politics.

It occurs to me now that perhaps I was simply indoctrinated to believe in the liberal ideology and to despise capitalism. Joe this is hard to admit but perhaps I was blinded by ambition. Somewhere along the way it became a game and the only way you can win is to destroy your opponents.

I think that down deep inside I knew that this type of political behavior did not serve the best interest of America but I convinced myself that we had to win first and then perhaps we could really do some good.

Once your party became prominent I began to listen to your solutions and watched your methods and could not help but admire your altruistic approach and sincere desire to serve the best interest of our country.

Then the conduct and advice of my close advisors caused me to become a conflicted man and as I look back now I am somewhat ashamed of my past behavior and unsure of what I should do now."

Joe is surprised by the President's revelations. His respect for the President increases dramatically but he senses the President had not finished and remains silent.

The President stands up and walks over to the fireplace feeling a bit confused. He has never been this open and honest concerning his feelings with anyone other than Ann.

He turns to Joe and said, "Joe I have never been this frank with anyone in my life and I want you to know I am a little uncomfortable but I do appreciate you listening. Maybe that answers both our questions."

The door opens and Ann and Linda burst into the room laughing and clearly enjoying each others company. Ann said, "We had a wonderful tour and a terrific time. Joe I just love your wife."

Joe stands up and smiles, "Thank you Ann I love her too."

Ann looks at James and says, "Well I hope you boys had a good time?"

James walks over and put his arm around Ann and kisses her on the cheek and said, "We had a wonderful time Honey and I think we need to spend more time with these two."

CHAPTER 99

John Danforth is the only guest to appear on Meet the Press today and the first question is asked by the host, Jim Harold, "Senator Danforth it appears that Congress has been extremely productive since the mid term elections. To what would you attribute this unprecedented era of bi partisan politics in Washington?"

John answers, "Jim it isn't very complicated. Congress simply recognizes that constantly attacking political opponents, particularly in a public forum, is counter productive. It is also very clear that if we continue trying to destroy each other we are only destroying our country.

The public was feed up with that type of behavior and demands that we conduct the business of government professional and responsibly."

Guest journalist, Ed Johnson, asks. "Senator Danforth in the last six months Congress has passed more meaningful legislation than anyone can remember. Would you share with our audience some of the major legislation completed as well as what is pending?"

John said, "One term limits and campaign reform will assure Americans that the people they elect will now devote their full time to the improvement of our country not re-election.

Our decision to withdraw the majority of troops from Afghanistan and Iraq resulted in six hundred billion in savings. If we fail as a country we can be of no service to other countries.

Our decision to put more emphasis on clandestine and high tech operations in Pakistan and Afghanistan to rid the world of extremist will not hinder our national security and we believe will cause us to be more productive in hunting and destroying those radicals who seek to do us harm.

The National Intelligence Committee will consist of one senator from each party, The Senate majority leader, and the President will dictate the actions of highly trained and specialized intelligence operations. We have implemented sever penalties for any public official leaking information.

The simplification of the tax code will result in at least an additional two hundred billion in savings and when the code is combined with incentives for private business to create jobs the impact on our citizens will be dramatic. We expect to put two to three million people back to work by the end of the year.

Our decision to break up large banks and to focus attention on state, regional, and local banks will continue to free up money for business expansion and normal credit requirements and the creation of a Mergers and Acquisitions regulatory committee will no longer allow large companies to expand without sufficient equity.

With regard to energy independence the refinery being built on Government property in Utah will be complete within four years and the oil reserves from the Bakken site will provide enough oil to support our entire government. This will drive down the price of oil and save the government twenty billion a year. We continue to move toward more Nuclear and other alternative options. Our goal is to be energy independent within eight years.

The dissolution of Freddie and Fannie and the removal of Government from private mortgage transactions will benefit our economy and home buyers.

It cost the taxpayers over four hundred billion to do this but the short term loss was necessary for the long term benefits.

The restrictions we placed on the Fed to manipulate monetary policy will allow a free economy to function properly. When you combine this with effective and punitive regulation I expect our economy to become the dominate economy in the world.

The Government must set an example for our citizens and we have significantly reduced the size of Government without compromising services which will enable us to operate within our revenues.

It is estimated that this year our tax revenues will increase by four hundred billion over last year and our expenses will be reduced by three hundred billion. The bottom line is revenues will exceed expenses by four hundred billion this year and we can start retiring some of our debt. We will no longer spend more than we have."

The fact is the interview is most likely perceived as boring inasmuch as there are no dissenting opinions or another politician sitting in the wings waiting to tell everyone that what they have just heard is wrong. The Media will have to find new ways to generate viewership.

After the commercial pause Kathy Andrews asked, "Senator Danforth before the break you discussed several of the key actions already taken by this Congress. What else can we expect this year?"

John smiles and says, "Kathy I am glad you reminded me. We are very close to significant health reform which will please everyone.

From what I have seen this plan will result in savings to insurance companies, medical providers, and most importantly savings to the consumer.

Early financial indications suggest that the 2.5 trillion current cost of health care in America will be decreased by six hundred billion with no adverse financial impact on insurance companies or medical providers."

Jim asks, "Senator Danforth it is hard to believe the impact the Restoration Party has had on Congress in the past year. President Howard seems to be supportive of an opposition party. How do you explain this?"

John, as relaxed as if he is talking to his grandson by a fishing pond, says, "Jim this is a new era. Old style politics are dead and our job is to the very best we can for Americans. The President is extremely supportive and his contributions to the success of this Congress have been substantial."

CHAPTER 100

Joe Winston and Bert Braddock have known each other for many years but over the past few months with Bert providing security for Joe they have become friends. Bert and his two associates, Alan and Zack, are diligent, professional, and serious in their efforts to prevent harm from visiting Joe Winston.

Joe keeps a very busy schedule and tries to accept as many invitations as possible. When it is convenient Joe and Bert like to drive and today was one of those days. It is 9:00 pm and Bert is pulling on to I-95 South in Baltimore with Joe in the passenger seat after speaking at the Baltimore Chamber of Commerce annual meeting.

Bert pushes the black Mercedes S.L up to eighty miles per hour and sets the cruise control. They expect to cover the 150 miles to Richmond in a couple of hours. Bert settles into his seat and looks over at Joe and said, "You look a little beat tonight Joe."

Joe smiles, as he glances at Bert, tilts his seat back a little, and said, "Bert this is not my kind of life but I guess I'm going to have to get used to it."

Bert said, "I'll tell you one thing Joe the twelve thousand people who attended the meeting tonight thoroughly enjoyed your comments."

Joe uncomfortably said, "Thanks Bert."

Bert looks down the interstate and checks his rear view mirrors and said, "Joe I don't think you realize how important you are to this country. I don't believe anyone in the world could have accomplished so much in such a short period of time. So when you get a little tired just remember you are waking up millions of Americans."

Joe thought about it for a little while and said, "Bert I really appreciate that, especially coming from you. The truth is you and men like you have done more for this country than I could ever do."

Bert looks at Joe as if he is crazy and said, "Bull shit Joe. I did my little part but you are saving the United States of America. Following is easy; leading is hard."

Joe is always uncomfortable with compliments even from people he respects and decides to change the subject. He said, "I have never really asked you much about your service but I do know that most of your actions were dark. What drew you to your career?"

Bert laughs and said, "Maybe too many comic books and too much hero worship. My Uncle was a SEAL and that's all I ever wanted to be since I was ten years old."

Joe decides to press Bert a little because he is interested and Bert isn't exactly the talkative kind, "You mind telling me about what you liked and didn't like with the SEALS?"

Bert is in a rare mood and he normally conserves words as if he may need them later said, "No I don't mind. I loved the challenge of competing with other talented men to become a SEAL.

When I heard that only 3% of those who tried actually made it I knew I would be one of the top 3%. The tougher it got the tougher I get. I never had the slightest doubt that I would be a SEAL."

Joe said, "What about after?"

Bert checks the mirrors and scans every car near them with his learned skills before saying, "I was Gung Ho and couldn't wait to be in the action. The more difficult the mission the more motivated I became.

The problems started when I began to realize that we were basically being used for political purposes and being controlled by civilians who believe that making a sacrifice for their country means having to make another speech."

Joe laughs and said, "Okay Bert I get it. You will never hear me complain again."

Bert joins Joe and laughs also, "No I didn't mean that Joe. I mean we loved our country and believed that it was our duty to comply with orders. As I said the problem began when the orders appear to be issued by idiots and the results of their ignorance was the death of thousands of patriotic men and women willing to die for their country.

Anyway after I had seen enough I cold cocked a dumb ass senior officer that issued a bad order, against my advice, that resulted in three of my friends being killed. That was the end of my career."

For a few minutes they sat in silence as the powerful automobile moved effortlessly toward Richmond. Finally Bert said, "I will tell you this Joe. God forgive me but I absolutely loved the danger and the planning and execution of a mission.

It is one of the great mysteries in life how a man can be a ruthless unemotional killer one minute and be completely normal the next. Nothing will ever give me the sense of satisfaction I felt as a SEAL."

Joe knows that Bert has probably never talked this much about his military service in his life and simply didn't respond. Instead he decides to change the subject, "Bert do you really feel that I might be in danger?"

Bert looks at Joe with a cold look he might give a low level bureaucrat and said, "Joe what's the matter with you? If you ever lived in my world you would be scared to death. You are in grave danger and you need to be more alert to your surroundings.

You are the man who is the symbol for the Restoration Party and will most likely be our next President. So let's see who might want to harm you. First of all most of the foreign countries we have been subsidizing for decades are not very happy with you. Secondly, you have the Democrats and Republicans and it would be a grave mistake to assume they have nothing but good wishes for you. Thirdly, the Radical Muslims will not be very pleased and will want to strike out at the United States and you are the symbol for our country.

Just think about it Joe. Lastly this country is filled with maniacs who are just flat out nuts. Wake up Joe this is serious and you can't underestimate your importance to our country."

Joe sits for a few minutes and knew that Bert was right, "Maybe so Bert...... maybe so."

CHAPTER 101

It is 3:30 pm in the Volusia National bar and the boys had just finished their round of golf for the day. The ladies are with them on this trip and are spending the day in Orlando shopping.

The day could not be any better. There is barely a cloud in the sky, the winds are calm, and the high for today was a wonderful seventy five degrees. The men order cold beers and are relaxing in the comfortable chairs surrounding the polished mahogany table sitting about ten feet from the bar directly in front of the fifty inch plasma located above the bar.

Robbie said, "Adam and I had you two clowns beat until that lucky little shit chipped in on the 18th." He points at Lee with fake contempt.

Lee, with a satisfied smile on his face, looks hurt and said, "What do you mean lucky? That's where I was aiming."

"Lucky!" said Robbie.

Lee is busy with the scorecard and puts the pencil on the table and announces, "Robbie, you and your poor partner, Adam, who got no help from you today, owe us $42. If you don't mind I would like to be paid before you forget, as usual."

Robbie reaches in his pocket and pulls off a wad of bills and peels off two twenties and two ones. He makes a show of wadding the bills into a small ball and throws them toward Lee with a grin on his face and said, "Here you go you lucky little geek shit!"

Adam and Joe always enjoyed Robbie and Lee jabbing at each other and as they sip on their cold beers Adam slides his money in front of Joe and looks up at the television and said, "Hey, have you guys noticed that the twenty four hour cables stations are really reaching for something to talk about since politicians are no longer trying to destroy each other?"

Robbie said, "Isn't it amazing how many industries thrived on the negative energy generated in the past. When John pushed the Campaign reform measures through the Senate and Howard signed it the email bloggers and advertising sales people in the Media raised holy hell.

They claimed it would cost them tens of billions in lost revenue. Who would have ever thought an industry could make so much money simply by creating controversy?"

Lee interjects, "Well that's just too damn bad. Those blood suckers are worse than the damn partisan politicians."

Joe said quietly, "I have also noticed that here we are a year away from elections and there are no political ads on television. How nice is that?"

There is no question that as a result of their efforts these men have managed to rescue the country from almost certain death. The topic of their significant accomplishments is never something they discuss. In their minds something needed to be done and they did it. No fanfare. No pages in history books. No hero worship from a grateful nation. They simply answered a call to duty.

They are interrupted by the girl's returning. They are carrying several bags each and laughing loudly as they have clearly had a wonderful day shopping. They placed their bags and purses on the bar and pulled up chairs next to the boys. Linda asks, "Joe we are famished. Can we go to Stonewoods tonight?"

Joe said, "Okay. I'll make a reservation for 7:30 and we meet back here at 7:00. I am going to head up and take a shower and figure out where to invest my $42."

CHAPTER 102

CAMP DAVID, MARYLAND
NOVEMBER 7, 2011

President Howard and Ann are relaxing for a few days at Camp David. Since they met the Winston's seven months earlier a friendship had quickly developed and they spoke occasionally on the phone. Ann and Linda had seen each other once more and enjoyed their time together.

President Howard and Joe only had one opportunity to visit since April but it is also clear the men like each other and more importantly the President trusts Joe. As odd as it may seem Joe appears to be the President's friend.

They speak occasionally on the phone and their conversations generally have more to do with their personal lives not political issues.

James and Ann sat by the fire the great room and Ann couldn't be more pleased at the tremendous change in James since January when he was a defeated and beaten man. James is more relaxed and confident now than he has ever been in his life.

The emergence of the Restoration Party, at one time, seemed to be the worst thing that ever happened to him in his life and now it is clearly the best thing that could have happened. James seems to smile more easily and to be at peace with the world.

His metamorphic change is truly astounding and his approval ratings are back over 50%. She glances over at her husband who seems to be looking into the blazing fire but she knew the man and he was far, far away. "James you seem to be dreaming Honey. What are you thinking?"

James turns his head toward the woman he loves and smiles, "I was just thinking how funny life can be. For some reason I am just very contented and extremely happy."

The President stands up and walks over to Ann and leans over and kisses her gently on her forehead and says, "Well as hard as it is to admit I allowed myself to be sold on an ideology that never had a chance. I allowed it and bought into it because I wanted to be the President of the United States."

He walks over to the fire place and pokes the logs a little and then continues, "Ann I owe a lot to John Danforth. I used to think he was the worst politician in the world and now I know he is simply a decent man who loves his country and he was never willing to compromise his principles."

Ann smiles and looks up at her husband, "John is a wonderful human being."

James continues, "Ann when we had that dinner with Joe and Linda I had no idea what to expect. Joe Winston has more talent in his little finger than I have in my entire body but he is the most humble and decent person I have ever had the privilege of knowing.

Joe and John have never criticized me for any thing I may have done wrong in the past. They have only encouraged me and, if you will, forgiven me without saying so. I guess what I was thinking when you asked me the question is that I feel very blessed to be involved with the changes we have made and the difference we are making in our country. Yes. I believe that's it. I am actually proud of myself."

Ann stands up and walks over to the fireplace and put her arms around James and said, I loved the old you but I really love the new you.

CHAPTER 103

Bert Braddock is driving the black Lincoln Navigator to the restaurant with the Winston's and Ravenels while Zack is driving the other Navigator with Lee, Carolyn, and the Fields. They pass Granada and turn right a couple of blocks later into Stonewood's parking lot.

Bert notices there are about fifteen or twenty people congregated out front waiting for tables. He scans them very carefully and it appears as if there is no danger so he put the car in park and walks around to open the doors while carefully observing everyone in the area. The second car follows suit and the four couples walk toward the entrance.

Unfortunately someone recognizes Joe and the crowd starts buzzing and requesting autographs. The group has become unaccustomed to this and they are never offended by the public attention and feel privileged and honored to be of service.

Joe graciously signs several autographs and several people requested pictures of Joe with their spouse to which he submitted. He thanks everyone for their support and the party heads into the restaurant.

As the four couples enter the restaurant's front door they encounter another group of twenty or so patrons who crowded around Joe to shake his hand, pat him on the back, or to get his autograph and more pictures.

Joe and his party are extremely patient and the manager of Stonewood's finally walks over to save them. He said, "Mr. Winston. Right this way please your room is ready."

Bert Braddock is standing nearby with Zack carefully looking at every person in his range of vision and allowing his instincts and training to alert him to any possible danger.

Joe politely says, "Thank you." as they follow the manager to a small private room in the southeast corner of the restaurant.

To the left of the entry area they had just left there is a large bar that is packed to capacity with people celebrating the end of another day and preparing to enjoy their evening.

Sitting on two stools at the bar facing South two men watched the commotion and one of them looked contemptuously at Joe and his party as they mingled with their admirers in the lobby.

When the manager led them away the man who appeared to be angry said to his companion, "There goes the man who is going to destroy this country. He is smooth talking, devious, evil, mother fucking capitalist."

His friend looks at him strangely and said, "Who are you talking about? Joe Winston?"

"Who else would I be talking about?" He snaps.

The angry man is a liberal activist and worked very hard for Howard during his campaign and is convinced that Socialism would best serve our country. His name is Robert Alexander and he is a sociology professor at Bethune Cookman College in Daytona Beach.

His extreme left wing views and hatred of conservatives is unrelenting. He is a man who lives in world of theory and academia that knows little of business and refuses to accept or respect views that are contrary to his.

Robert is a small man with a big mouth and tonight his alcohol intake has far exceeded his capacity. He peers through his dark rimmed glasses that sit low on his nose and taps his glass loudly on the bar gruffly and said, "Bartender bring me another."

His friend Will Edwards is disturbed by this behavior and says, "Robert you need to calm down and relax."

Robert looks at his tall skinny friend and said, "Fuck you Will. I hate that son of a bitch and all that he stands for and I think I'm going to walk over there and tell him."

It is clear to Will that he could not reason with Robert. He is angry and drunk so Will considered his alternatives and said, "Will I have to go." He stands up and pulls a twenty out of his pocket and drops it on the bar and leaves.

Robert ignores his friend and decides to walk down to the private room that contain Winston and confront him. The private room is only about four booths from the Restroom door.

Robert stumbles when he gets off his stool and starts toward the private room. He passes by the Restroom and just before he reaches the entrance to the private room Bert slides out of the last booth, stands up quickly, and blocks the mans way. Bert said, "Sorry sir this is a private party."

Bert surprises Robert and he stammers, "I'm sorry...I am looking for the Restroom."

Bert studies the man carefully and determines he is drunk and politely points and said, "You just missed it. It's right there."

Robert slurs and says, "Thanks."

He goes into the Restroom, which is empty, and looks in the mirror and said to his reflection, "Come on Robert. Think! By God you are a patriot and that man is trying to destroy your country."

The Restroom door flew open and two men who were enjoying themselves walk in and Robert quickly washes and dries his hands and leaves..

Bert notices strangeness in the man's eyes and keeps a close eye on him as the man leaves the Restroom and bolts out of the restaurant.

Two hours later the four couples finish a wonderful meal and had thoroughly enjoyed the evening and are preparing to leave the restaurant. Bert whispers to Joe, "Hold up a few minutes and let me check around outside. There was strange little weirdo here earlier and I just want to make sure he's gone."

Joe said, "Sure Bert."

Bert and Zack walked outside and took a good look around. When they were satisfied the man is gone Bert walks back inside where Joe is surrounded by people once again talking with them as if they are his old friends. Bert gives Joe the all clear sign and goes to pull the car up to the front of Stonewoods.

The Navigators are parked in the back of the lot and Robert saw from his car, parked close to the entrance, that the two men had about one hundred yards to walk. He looks at the Smith and Wesson 357 Magnum revolver in his hand and then he looks up toward the restaurant and sees Joe Winston and his party coming out of the door.

He glances quickly behind him to see where the two men are and saw them getting into their cars. He makes the decision that it is time for him to do what he must. With the weapon in his right hand he opens the door with his left hand and exits the car.

His heart is beating rapidly and he is having difficulty catching his breath but he is not deterred as he conceals the gun behind his back and walks quickly, but unsteadily, toward Joe Winston. When he is within ten yards he stops and raises the pistol to shooting position and yells loudly, "WINSTON."

Everyone turns around toward the sound and sees a man holding a handgun. Several people are frozen in place and scream while others chaotically run in every direction to get away from the gun.

Bert turns the corner and sees the man standing in the road with a gun aimed at Joe's chest and hits the accelerator hard. Joe sees the man with the gun and pushes Linda behind him to protect her.

Everything appears to be happening in slow motion the crowd screaming and scattering for cover, the Navigator bearing down on the man with the gun, Joe protecting Linda, and the man with the gun. The man cocks the hammer and tries to level the gun at Joe's chest and jerks the trigger. Nothing happens. The man quickly looks at the gun and realizes the safety is on. He takes the safety off and aims, as the Navigator is right on him, he squeezes the trigger a split second before the Navigator makes contact. Lee Roth lunges just before he sees the bright orange flame and hears the deafening sound of a gunshot.

The gunman flies a good twenty yards through the air and hits the pavement with a loud thud. Bert jumps out of the vehicle and directs Zack to the gunman and he runs toward the crowd of people that have formed a circle looking down on the ground with horrified looks on their faces and many screaming and crying.

Bert, a man familiar with violence and death, is as panicked as he has ever been in his life rushes toward the circle of people and pushes several people away in an effort to reach the center. As Bert enters the center of the circle he sees Robbie's look of anguish and disbelief as he holds tight to Emily who is crying uncontrollably.

He is afraid to look down because he already fears what he will see. He is surrounded by hysterical people crying and screaming and he hears the sirens approaching as he looks down at and sees Joe Winston.

CHAPTER 103

ORMOND BEACH, FL
NOVEMBER 7, 2010

The Volusia County emergency services responds quickly to the 911 call and within five minutes the area is surrounded by seven police cars with their lights reflecting off every building in a five block radius, two emergency rescue vehicles, and one fire truck are also present to cover every contingency. The sounds of dozens of police radios permeate the area as crowds continue to mill around and tell their stories.

A paramedic checks the shooter and pronounces him dead as the crime scene investigators are snapping pictures of the body and everything in the area that might possibly be evidence.

Crime tape is being placed around the area by three uniformed policemen and the bright lights of the Media illuminates the area where chaos still reigns.

Two patrol cars are in position to escort the large red rescue vehicle to Halifax, which is one of the best trauma units in the country, located near the Daytona Speedway. Outside the rescue vehicle there is a brief heated exchange between the paramedics and a man who enters the rescue truck. The doors slam shut and the life and death race begins.

The early news reports, based on interviews with patrons of the restaurant, reported that Joe Winston had been shot. Within minutes the report is picked up nationally and before the emergency vehicle would arrive at Halifax the entire country would have heard the tragic report.

The paramedics, a man and a woman in their early thirties, work hard to stabilize the victim. As the man sets up the IV and compression bandage the woman calls the emergency room to give a status report, "We have a male victim, mid fifties, with a gunshot entry and exit wound in his left chest cavity. BP 52/28, pulse 44, and respiration is slow but appears stable.

Victim suffered significant blood loss prior to treatment but it now appears under control. Victim's donor bracelet indicates blood type O positive. Our ETA is three minutes."

The reply came in a completely dispassionate voice, "10-4"

The emergency vehicle with two police cars leading the way speeds south down Nova Road toward International Speedway Blvd with a sense of urgency. Sirens are wailing and flashing lights warn of their presence.

The paramedics are using all their skills to keep the victim stabilized. The male paramedic says to no one in particular, "It's a good thing the shooter used a FMJ (full metal Jacket) instead of a hollow point....just might make a difference in this man's life."

Joe Winston's shirt is covered in blood and his pale face is the picture of despair. He looks down at Lee's unconscious body and sees the tubes feeding him vital liquids and the bloody bandage pressed tight on his chest.

He grasps Lee's hand and leans down and in a broken voice, whispers in his friend's ear, "Hold on Lee.....please.... hold on. You are going to be alright ....hold.....on Lee!"

CHAPTER 104

The attempt on Joe Winston's life that almost ended Lee Roth's life inspired a nation that values heroic action. Lee was indeed a hero and his willingness to give his life for his friend and America's new favorite son was a tribute to the goodness of man.

Joe stayed by his friend for weeks until he was out of danger and he has made no public comments until today. A press conference was scheduled for 2:00 pm at The Jefferson hotel in downtown Richmond.

It seemed as if every media organization in the world was present and the nation waited anxiously to hear the words of Joe Winston. Never in the long and historic past of The Jefferson have so many people attempted to gain entrance. It took the combined effort of the Richmond Fire Department, the hotel, and the Restoration Party to avoid a serious problem.

There had been wide spread speculation as to Winston's comments such as he had developed cancer, he would be asking Congress to withdraw all military personnel from the Middle East, he would make prayer in school mandatory, he would suggest stronger sanctions to be placed on N. Korea and Iran, and even one report that suggested he would ask congress to terminate all entitlement programs. The truth was they had no first hand knowledge and absolutely no way of knowing what Joe Winston planned to say.

At precisely 2:00 pm Senator Danforth approached the podium in the grand ballroom and the room fell silent as John said, "I would like to thank everyone for their attendance and their patience today. Three months ago a deranged man attempted to kill Joe Winston and only the brave action of his friend Lee Roth prevented the death of Joe. Lee saw the assailant raise the gun and aim it at the chest of Joe Winston and without hesitation threw himself in the path of the oncoming bullet.

Lee was willing to give his life for his friend and as Lee told me later, Joe Winston is far more important to the world than I am. What courage...What love...What loyalty...Lee was willing to die for his friend and his country.

Lee Roth, Robbie Ravenel, and Adam Fields made a commitment to do whatever was necessary to help Joe restore America to her greatness. I remember vividly, three years ago the media referred to these men as greedy capitalist. Today even the most cynical skeptic would agree that these men personify the word patriot.

We are not here today to reminisce we are here today to hear from Joe Winston."

The Senator turns and extends his arm toward Joe as Joe stands and approaches the podium. Immediately the familiar chant begins, Joe, Joe, Joe, Joe, Joe, as Joe embraces his father in law. Joe smiles warmly and waves to the crowd as many reporters near the podium notice that Joe looks a bit thinner and a little older.

Joe raises his hands as if he is requesting that the crowd allow him to speak and they respectfully calm down and fall silent.

Joe says, "Senator John Danforth is America's real hero. For over thirty years he battled contentious opposition in Washington and never....NEVER....compromised his principles. He labored hard for his country and his constituents and was punished by party leaders because he would not succumb to their demands. He could not be bought! His leadership in the Senate is a testament to the old adage that good triumphs over evil.

John Danforth is the father of the Restoration Party and he recruited me to take an active role in the restoration of America. He told me it was time that I stopped being selfish by avoiding the political process. He gave me a choice to either sit on the sidelines or help win the game. His compelling arguments left me no choice and helped me to realize that ignoring a problem doesn't make it go away. Today Washington works the way John envisioned it should work."

Joe turned and pointed at John and respectfully said, "Thank you John. Thank you for saving our country."

With those words the audience acknowledged John with a five minute standing ovation as Joe walked over to John, embraced him, and whispered in his ear. "Was it worth it?"

John leaned his head back and looked up into Joe's eyes and said, "It damn sure was son."

Joe returned to the podium as the crown calmed down and slowly became silent. He smiles warmly as he says, "I think everyone will agree that Washington is working hard and harmoniously to resolve our issues. I think everyone will agree that economy is rebounding faster than expected. I think everyone will agree that we are entering a new era of hope, opportunity, and freedom.

America is strong once again. We are respected once again and the future for all Americans looks brighter because we will all work together to resolve issues."

He pauses and glances at his notes but not needing them and says, "I am here today to announce that I will return to my private life secure in the knowledge that America is in capable hands. Thank you very much for your support and the kindness you have extended to me and my family. God Bless America!"

With those comments Joe Winston exited stage right. Bert had the car ready and they were almost at the airport before anyone knew he was gone. He boarded a private plane destined for Flagler Beach airport in Florida and would soon be with his friends and family at Volusia National.

As John was leaving a young reporter trying to make his bones yells from a crowd of reporters, "Senator how do you feel about Joe quitting?"

The Senator stops dead in his tracks and looks for the person who asked such a rude and ungracious question. He fixes the young man with his piercing eyes and says, "Son. Joe Winston will go down in history as the greatest leader this country ever had…..and he never served a day in office."

THE END

He believes his business success or failure is insignificant. He believes the degrees he holds or doesn't hold is irrelevant. He believes that his fame or absence thereof is meaningless.

What is important is his ability to entertain, educate, and inspire you.

He is a patriot and a patriarch who is uniquely qualified to offer you plausible reasons that have caused our current situation and practical solutions to return America to her greatness.

LaVergne, TN USA
10 March 2010
175436LV00004B/3/P